Copyright © 2020 by A. E. Murphy

All rights reserved.

No part of this book may be reproduced in any form or by any electronic or mechanical means, including information storage and retrieval systems, without written permission from the author, except for the use of brief quotations in a book review.

HE WAS ALWAYS BEAUTIFUL, BUT HE WAS ALWAYS
VICIOUS
A.E. MURPHY

VICIOUS

A. E. MURPHY

To Kirsty-Anne Still, your cover inspired this book. Without your artistry, Kane Jessop would not exist. Thank you so much, for that and everything else.

8 YEARS OLD

We've been raised to be kind to others, and always smile when using our manners. Because manners without a smile just ain't genuine. I mean... *isn't* genuine. I keep forgetting to talk proper. Mee-maw doesn't like it when I don't talk proper now that I'm becomin' a little lady.

A little lady, which means I ain't been raised to fight. So when the new boy from way over town pushes my brother off his bike and brings his foot back, stretching the hole in the knee of his ripped jeans, I don't know what to do.

I just stand here and watch as he kicks my brother in the ribs three times, making him gasp and choke for air. I don't know why he's doing it. My brother done nothing to this boy and I'd know because I'm my brother's best friend and we are always together. My brother doesn't do anything to anyone, ever.

"Pussy," the boy snarls and spits. His white, bubbly saliva hits my brother's neck as he cries and hugs his ribs.

I stare, wide-eyed, like a rabbit in headlights. Unable to move.

I want to help my brother, my twin, but I can't bring myself to even make a sound.

The boy pushes his long, unruly brown hair out of his face. It's knotted and messy, but it still looks so silky and glossy, and it has strands of gold through it, like a sprinkle of sand on dirt.

"What you lookin' at?" he snarls at me, lifting my brother's bike from the ground and mounting it.

I'm mad, I feel mad like I have never felt. It's burning inside of me. I can feel it twisting a knot in my chest, boiling the acid in my stomach, but I can't do anything about it. Mee-maw will be upset if I tantrum in company. I'm too old and I'm a little lady.

But my brother... he's hurt. I should hurt this boy too.

"My bike," Matthew, my brother rasps.

"Tell your mom to sell her plastic tits and get you another one," the boy retorts, grinning as he twists the rubber handle, making his palm white. Is he pretending to ride a motorbike? I notice his nails and pull a disgusted face. He's a nail biter. Such a nasty habit. Mee-maw hits me on the hand with a stick if I even think about putting my fingers near my mouth.

"I'm telling!" I say, finally able to speak again, but it's weak and high-pitched, making me sound pathetic.

"You tell anyone about me, Imogen Hardy and I'll tell your grandpa you showed me your panties."

My jaw hits the floor and my eyes fill with scorching tears.

He laughs at my reaction and bikes away, pedaling my brother's bike like he has been riding it for years, not seconds. We watch him go down the dirt road, dust kicking up from the back wheel in a cloud of evil behind him.

"How does he know your name, Immy?" my brother asks as I help him up.

"I don't know," I reply, checking his ribs when he lifts his yellow character shirt. There's an ugly purple swelling on his side. "Let's get you home."

"Don't tell Mee-maw."

"She's gonna wonder where your bike got to."

"We'll let her think it was stolen outta the shed."

"But—"

"No, Immy. Don't tell. Okay?"

Frowning, I nod. Too young to understand why my brother won't tell somebody who can do something about Kane and what he did. It seems so unfair.

"It's guy code, we don't tattle and you shouldn't either."

"How are you my age but so much smarter than me?" I ask, pouting. "And braver."

He shakes his head and rubs his side. I can see how much it hurts with every step. "I'm not brave, Immy."

To me he's the bravest boy in the entire world.

26 YEARS OLD

It has been a while since I saw the plumes of dust this dry road is kicking up behind me. I remember being a teen and holding onto the back of cars while on a skateboard and getting mouthfuls of this vile dirt. I broke my leg in two places being that stupid, thinking I was one of the guys, neglecting my family to fight for *his* affections.

The one with the vicious tongue.

The one I used to love to hate... and now I just hate and I don't like it at all. There's nothing good about the hatred I feel for this man. It doesn't bring me pleasure, or pain, or any kind of emotion, not even rage. My default setting for him is hatred and it'll remain that way forever.

I pass the semi-busy looking shops on New Hope Road, while thinking it should be false hope road. Or false hope hole in the fucking ground. This place has the default setting of despair in my heart. What once was my incredible childhood, quickly became the setting for all bad things that ever happened to me.

I see people look my way, a kid points at my car. It's flashy, it was ridiculously expensive, and it wasn't made for these dusty-ass roads. It's going to need a clean before I make it to the end of the street and I only got it cleaned on my way into town this morning. An excuse to delay the inevitable.

My phone starts to ring, it's Webber. I don't answer. I don't want to talk right now; it's better he thinks I'm already there even though I'm not.

I'm late.

I'm never late but I almost didn't come despite the fact I have to. I can't not be here. I need to be here.

I need to say goodbye.

The parking lot is full of vehicles, cars packed side by side on a gravel surface. An ominous shadow from the church and its steeple point to the only remaining space. I don't use it. I park on the grassy verge beside the church, getting as close to it as possible. I'll likely get a ticket if the town's only traffic warden isn't inside saying his goodbyes.

I climb out of my car, pointed heels crunching on the uneven cobblestones that lead up to the church doors which are closed. Looks like I'll have to make an entrance.

9 YEARS OLD

Kane joined our school six months ago and even though all he does is cause trouble; nobody is kicking him out. Grandpa said it's because his daddy gots ties with the district and Kane gets a free pass. I don't know what that means exactly but I don't think it's a good thing.

He's the worst boy I have ever had the displeasure to meet in my entire life. Displeasure is a new word I learned right before Kane stuck a pencil down the back of my dress last period. He's always doing stuff like that.

He pushed me over last week during recess too. I hurt my butt and grazed the palms of my hands. He thought it was funny that my new dress was ripped.

"Show me your panties," he said when I dusted myself off. Why anybody would want to see my yellow and pink polka dot panties is so weird. And also gross. Mee-maw always said never show nobody your privates, especially not boys or men. She said boys gots the devil inside of them and a girl's privates makes that devil hungry.

I don't know why he does these things to me; I don't know what I ever did to him to make him so cruel. He always does it to my brother too but only when he's with me, so now even Matthew doesn't speak to me in school.

"You're so ugly you make my eyes want to roll to a different planet," he hisses in my ear after yanking my braid and pulling my head back so hard I almost tip backwards.

I don't respond, I just scowl at my desk, wishing I was strong enough to hurt him back, to pull his stupid hair and say mean things. Mee-maw says if I ignore him, he'll stop, but it has been six months of ignoring him and he hasn't stopped. He never stops.

"Are you okay?" my closest friend, Poppy-Rose who I've known since kindergarten asks on a whisper when I snap a pencil with both of my hands.

"No."

"He's only doing it because he likes you," she says, repeating what my mee-maw told me when I asked her why he's so mean.

"Then he needs to unlike me," I huff, screwing my work into a ball and scowling at it.

It's a stupid thought that *displeases* me because if he likes me why does he hurt me and my brother? And everyone else too, but he seems to really love hurting me, and the teachers never do anything about it.

The last time I tattled on him he threw my backpack into the school swimming pool and pushed my brother in after it. Luckily my brother can swim, Grandpa taught him last summer. I had to learn to crochet with Mee-maw and I absolutely hated it. I wanted to learn to swim, it's so unfair.

"Are you going to tell Mr. Beecham?" Poppy whispers, leaning in as close as she can.

I shake my head and turn to a clean page.

"You can't let him do that though."

"I know," I growl and shift away. "Leave me alone."

26 YEARS OLD

The door isn't locked when I give it a hard shove while smiling at the upside-down cross still etched into its surface, a reminder of the days I thought I was something tough and fierce. I was nothing but a poser, throwing my weight around everywhere it didn't matter. Something I paid for dearly.

The door groans as it opens into the lobby where three glass double doors line each of the surrounding walls.

I see people look through the glass from their seats, their bodies twisting as they try their darndest to figure out who is here.

Too late to turn back now.

I don't even feel slightly nervous or sorry about interrupting. Truthfully, I don't care at all.

Pushing open the door on the right, my heels click when I step into the packed room full of my prior community.

I spy my mother at the front, weepy eyed with a tissue against her nose, I spy my old neighbors and shop keepers, and the man who delivered the paper to our house everyday until his grandson took over. I see the grandson too.

All the people from my past are sitting in this room.

Somebody fetch this girl a bomb.

I raise my chin as the dead silence is cut through with sharp whispers. Some ask who I am, some ask if it's really me, I hear them say I look different, I hear them insult my tardiness, I hear others defend me because I must be distraught.

When I finally reach the front, I make it a point to sit far away from my mother. I don't acknowledge Father David or even apologize for interrupting. It looks like he's quite far into the service anyway.

He doesn't acknowledge me either, nor does that bitch's closest friend who used to bake the shittiest cookies I ever tried. I broke my tooth on those fucking things when I was around seven. She's sitting to my left, weeping, as my mother keeps leaning forward to try and catch a glimpse of me or make eye contact at the very least over the five people between us.

I probably should have sat at the back but I wanted to make a statement. I wanted them to see me with my head held high.

"Where were we?" Father David calls and the whispers slowly float away.

I listen to him drone on and on about how Jesus calls to the old bitch and how heaven has a new angel and a ton of other phony BS that I just loathe to sit here and listen to.

"Would anybody like to say a few words to honor such a beloved member of our church and community?"

Of course the shit baker to my left stands and click clacks her way to the pedestal.

I try not to vomit as she gives a teary rendition of my grandmother's life with lies and over inflated compliments, and overexaggerated confessions of love and loyalty.

My mom goes next, sobbing like she ever gave a fuck about the old lady to begin with. Two-faced hooker just wants what's in my gran's will.

My fingers twitch as I get restless.

This is BS, I can't do this.

26 YEARS OLD

I stand, cutting my mother off and slide out of the bench as best as I can what with so many legs blocking my way.

"Where are you going, Imogen?" Father David asks softly, pretending to be a kind herder of his sheep. "Stay, your grandmother would want you to say goodbye."

"My grandmother wouldn't want me to say shit," I retort and half the room gasps.

"Hasn't lost her terrible manners I see," somebody hisses but I pay them no mind.

"Let's watch our language in this house of God."

I roll my eyes. "That's exactly why I'm leaving."

"I know it's painful, being back here, being with all of us after all you've been through and lost—"

Before I say something I'll probably never regret but know I shouldn't say, I turn on my heel and head towards the double glass doors.

"Imogen," Father David calls. "Say your goodbyes, it's the only chance you'll ever get."

I stop, rage bubbling under the surface, hands clenching, face burning. "If you're sure."

"I am." His smile is soft and understanding, as though he understands anything when he understands absolutely nothing. "Come. Speak of your love for your grandmother before it's too late."

With a graceful spin I march back towards the front and my mother steps down, unable to look me in the eye. I climb up the few steps and address my adoring fans.

"You asked for this," I say to the man with a sardonic smile and his falls as the error of his ways sinks in through his thick, leathery skin. "What shall I say?" This question is posed more to myself than anyone else.

"Be nice," my mother mouths at me but I give her the bird and a small chorus of outrage fills the silence.

"Look at that." I wave a hand at my mother and address the "adoring" crowd. "Ain't my ma such a chip off the old block. Telling me to be nice. Whatever could you mean, Ma? What good reason could I possibly have to not be nice?"

Father David steps towards me, no longer looking victorious at having turned my decision. "Perhaps we should—"

I raise a hand to cut him off. "I was three when Mom abandoned me to a woman she despised, a woman who abused her as she was growing up... can you imagine it? Being so *messed up* by a person and then handing over your babies to her to also be messed up." I'm not wording this well but I'm angry and emotional and they asked for this.

"Mee-maw," I continue bitterly, "such a bright beacon of hope in the community, right? She raised *everybody's* kids. She made cakes and smiled and hosted events. She was prim and proper and wore perfectly ironed clothing and never showed even an ankle. She taught us all right from wrong such as who to play with, who not to play with, who was trash and who wasn't... and the best thing she ever taught me." My sarcasm is as evident as my ire. "Something she *always* said to me..." I scan the room, looking for no face in particular, relieved when I don't find the face I'll always deny I ever looked for. "If you *don't got* anything nice to say, don't say anything at all. But I never did listen to the old shrew."

There's a collective gasp that only stops me while I relish in it and let it taper out. Father climbs up and reaches for my arm, he must think I'm distraught but I'm not. Truth be told I've never been happier.

"So I'm going to say what I want to say and then I'm going to get the hell out of this fucking town that destroyed me and everyone I ever loved." I look directly at the white coffin behind me and declare, "Mee-maw, you're an old cunt."

More gasps ensue and a spluttering Father. Mothers put their hands over the ears of their children.

"I despised you then, I despise you now and I hope your soul stays locked in your body as maggots and worms feast on you slowly. I hope you feel every single second of the decaying process that helps the earth reclaim you." I look at the room of familiar and unfamiliar faces who stare back at me in horror. "You don't know the real mee-maw. You'll never know the real mee-maw and for that, I envy the fuck out of you all."

Then I drop my shades, hop down from the wooden ledge and stride down the center aisle.

I did it. I said goodbye.

"Chew on soap you old hag," I hiss as I slam the glass door behind me.

9 AND A HALF.

THE HALF IS IMPORTANT.

"Why did you invite him?" I hiss at Poppy when Kane sits on the wall that lines the ice-skating rink.

"I didn't," she hisses back, glaring at Kane who is now surrounded by his friends. "Mom did I think. She's friends with his daddy now."

Everyone is friends with Kane's dad. He builds and sells bikes, or somethin' like that. They own a really big store with like a million motorbikes and about a hundred men always ride through town on these big stupid machines making loads of noise.

People rush outside to watch them, Grandpa said that they protect our town from bad people but Mee-maw says they are the bad people. Mee-maw said people like us don't associate with people like them. I don't know what that means but I'll listen anyway.

She said they're Satan worshippers, but Grandpa said she's just being a busy body. Grandpa always says that about her when she gets a bee in her bonnet, which is often. Especially now she's on the church committee and she's an important person. She's trying to get motorbikes banned from inside town. I don't think she knows that Grandpa is a *bike enthusiast*. I don't know what that means but I

9 AND A HALF.

know he loves the bikes and that's what he calls himself, but it's our secret. I can't tell Mee-maw and I never will.

He lied to Mee-maw about where we were heading just last week to look at a huge bike he called Harley. He said back in the day he rode bikes like this with Kane's granddaddy, but it was a really long time ago and Kane's granddaddy is dead now.

It must be a really long time ago because he's so old and the picture I saw of him on a bike at home he had a black ponytail. I have never seen my grandpa with anything but silver hair.

He left me with the machine to go have a drink with Kane's daddy in the office and that's when I saw Kane and his friends cycling down the road, an entire gang of them. Kane thinks he's like his daddy but he's just a punk kid with the devil in him. I hate him.

I hid behind Harley as they passed and then ran inside so fast to lock myself in the toilet when I knew Kane couldn't see me no more. I stayed there until somebody knocked on the door, because they might need the toilet and because I didn't want to get in trouble, I decided to leave.

When I opened the door Kane stuck his tatty brown boot in. The toe of it was scuffed and pale, his jeans were torn but then all his pants are torn. He tussles and fights too much with his friends.

"Thought you could hide from me, Immy?"

"It's Imogen!" My hands curled into fists by my side as I backed away from him, wondering if he was going to hit me, or pull my hair, or push me over. "Get out."

"Not until you show me your panties." He grinned and pushed his knotty hair from his face. It's too long for a boy. Mee-maw said that Satan himself has long brown hair just like Kane and his daddy. "Bobby-Ray said you show him your panties all the time."

"Bobby-Ray is a liar and God will punish him."

"God ain't real, Immy. Just like Santa."

"Santa is too real!" I yelled, feeling my cheeks heat with that familiar anger that I only ever feel around him.

"No he ain't," he shouted back, grabbing my shoulders and

squeezing with his skinny fingers. It hurt, it stayed sore for two whole days after. "Santa ain't real, the Easter bunny ain't real, your tooth fairy ain't real and your momma is a whore that don't love you!"

"Don't talk about my momma."

"You're a dreamer, kid," he snarled, shaking me so hard my head started pounding. "You're a dreamer and nobody wants you. You're shit. You ain't gonna be shit! You gonna grow up to be a cock sucker just like your momma and nobody gonna love you!"

"KANE JESSUP!" Kane's daddy boomed and Kane's face went from snide to horrified in a second. "WHAT IN GOD'S NAME DO YOU THINK YOU'RE DOING?"

"We were just playing," Kane lied, turning immediately but his daddy already had his hand in his hair. He threw Kane from the room so hard Kane stumbled and collided with my grandpa who glared down at him like he was nothing but trash. He is trash. The stinkiest awfullest trash.

"I'm sorry, Regen, I'll deal with my boy. Y'all know he's been fucked up no thanks to that useless mother of his."

I wanted to know why his momma was useless but I didn't ask. I just moved to my grandpa and hugged his side.

"I didn't do anything," Kane cried, looking furious, and his daddy smacked him around the back of his head.

My grandpa and his daddy looked at each other before we all walked away. Kane gave me a hard stare as his daddy grabbed his collar and I knew I was in for it. I knew I was in for it big.

But I ain't seen him until now. *Haven't*. UGH. I need to speak proper or Mee-maw will make me bite soap.

He looks at me and sneers as Poppy fixes her light up headband that she just got from me for her birthday.

"Let's skate," she orders, holding out her hand to me and we go around and around, giggling and wobbling on the ice.

Kane, surprisingly, leaves me alone for the entire night.

If only the rest of my life could have been the same.

26 YEARS OLD

"A speech fit for a funeral," a familiar voice rasps as I click the button to unlock my car. My entire body burns with remembrance and hatred. He should be thankful I don't have my gun on my person right now. "Show me your panties, Immy."

I don't turn, I don't give him the satisfaction. I have spent too long already staring into those ocean blue eyes, losing myself in them and the array of emotions he often showed. Though only to me. His emotions were only ever mine.

I'll not give him a second more. I *can't* give him a second more.

"It's like that is it?" he asks as I yank open my car door. "Ain't seen you in years and you're just gonna drive away?"

I climb into the driver's seat, twist the key in the ignition and stare ahead as the expensive as shit engine purrs like a kitten. He has ahold of the door and he's staring down at me. I can feel his gaze burning my profile like lasers. I can see his thick, shoulder-length hair framing his face. There's never been a man who suits long hair better than he does.

We remain like this for the longest time, him staring at me, me staring ahead, car humming, door open, his arm resting casually along the top.

Finally he steps back, surprising me.

"Not gonna keep you pinned, babe. You wanna go, you go."

I hate it when a lump rises in my throat, and I hate that he knows exactly what to say to make me want to stay.

With strength I've been gathering my entire life since meeting him, I pull the door closed and peel away, leaving tracks in the grass and earth.

I scream at the top of my lungs when I get far enough and hit the steering wheel with my palm three times until it feels bruised. I let it all out. What I'm letting out I'm not entirely sure. I'm trembling but I'm also numb. I don't feel the pain I'm displaying in my outcry but I keep screaming until my voice is hoarse, I yank on the wheel until I feel it might break, only stopping when my phone rings bringing my senses back to me.

"Did you go?" Webber asks the moment it connects.

"Yep." I pop a piece of gum into my mouth and consider stopping for water.

"How was it?"

"I called her a cunt."

He laughs quietly before finally asking on a serious note, "Did you see him?"

"Yep."

There's a pause. "And?"

"I'd still kill him and everyone in this fucking town if I knew it wouldn't land me in jail."

Webber chuckles, a deep and handsome sound. "That's my girl."

12 YEARS OLD

"Jesus, Matthew... what happened to your eye?" I ask, racing across the kitchen to see to his swollen, weeping face.

"Nothing," he replies, sounding defeated.

"Was it Kane?"

"No."

"You're lying."

"Leave it," he snaps, moving to the freezer and grabbing a bag of frozen peas.

"Dear Lord," Mee-maw gasps, pressing her hand to her chest. "Matthew, what happened to you?"

Matthew doesn't reply, he takes the pills I pass him for the pain and swallows them down with half a glass of water that Mee-maw pours and leaves the room with slumped shoulders.

"That boy..." Mee-maw starts, whipping her cleaning rag against the counter. "How on earth can I take him to church lookin' like that?"

I don't reply because I have nothing nice to say about her question.

"What is he getting himself into, I wonder?" She pats my cheek with a wrinkled hand. "Why can't he be more like you? My good girl, getting straight As, spending her time with good and wholesome people. You know I found a packet of marijuana in his pants last laundry load."

I nod, I did know because she hasn't stopped bringing it up, nor has she stopped using God to shame my brother who is suffering right now.

"May I please be excused?" I ask, hands balling into fists by my sides.

"Of course." Her saccharine sweet tone grates on me.

I walk away, knowing no amount of arguing with her or telling her that she's wrong will actually change her mind.

Instead I stomp up to my room which is across from my brother's and close the door quietly behind me. After diving onto my bed I scream into my pillow and punch it over and over again with my fist. I'm so angry. I'm just angry all the time.

Poppy-Rose thinks it's because of hormones, but I think it's just because my life is so unfair. So unfair.

I pull out my diary and scribble in it so hard I tear through a page.

'Hate it here. Fucking cunt bitch bastards. Hate them. HATE HER! She's mean and cranky and nasty. It's not fair. IT'S NOT FAIR!'

Then I stick it under my mattress, put away my pen and walk across to my brother's room. With a tap on the door I call his name, "Matthew?"

"Not now," he replies sharply.

"Why?"

He doesn't reply so I return to my own room and scowl at the dolls on the shelves by my window. I don't even like dolls. Their porcelain faces and weird eyes freak me out. I used to turn them around but Mee-maw got angry and called me ungrateful, said they're beautiful pieces that I need to learn to appreciate.

How do you appreciate something so ugly?

12 YEARS OLD

My hidey phone vibrates in my desk. I rush to it, panicking that Mee-maw might have heard it, I must have accidentally set it to vibrate instead of silent. It's Poppy's old phone and I connected it to my neighbor's Wi-Fi after taking their password during a cookout they had last summer.

Raising it, I smile at the screen when I see Poppy's name.

Poppy: Momma just bought me this cute makeup pallet, she said I'm old enough to start playing if I want!

Imogen: Your momma is so cool.

Poppy: Why don't you come round? We can do each other's faces to one of those tutorial videos online!

My heart swells with excitement but it's already four. Mee-maw won't let me go out now and she'll wonder how Poppy got in touch with me to begin with.

Imogen: You know Mee-maw isn't gonna let me go anywhere now.

Poppy: I'll get Momma to ask her.

Imogen: REALLY?

I hear the house phone ring minutes later and stuff my cellphone back into its usual hiding spot. I wait anxiously, legs bouncing with anticipation.

Finally, after some laughter and chatter from Mee-maw, she calls my name.

"Yeah?" I call back, descending the stairs.

"Patrice is coming to collect you for dinner."

I try not to look too enthusiastic about it. Mee-maw says ladies should handle themselves with dignity and squealing like a piggy is not dignified at all.

So instead I simply say, "Thank you, Mee-maw."

She beams with pride and opens her arms to me. "You make me so very proud, little girl. I wish your mother had an ounce of the goodness in her that you do." She kisses my head and gives me a gentle push towards the bathroom. "Wash your hands and face, make sure you're presentable. I'll give your shoes a shine."

"Thank you, Mee-maw."

26 YEARS OLD

"Don't you dare! Don't you fucking dare!" I shout at my car when it starts to make a peculiar choking noise. "You're new and you just had a service! You don't get to break on me now! Not here, not now!"

The car splutters and coughs and a shit load of smoke billows from the engine. I pull over immediately and switch off the ignition. Armed with my trusty little fire extinguisher, I move to the glossy black front and lift the hood. Settling it on its metal arm, I waft away the smoke and look at the beast of a machine. I'm not bad with engines, I've tinkered with a few in my time, but I have no idea what is wrong.

I pull out my phone and call my emergency breakdown cover. They arrange for a tow to come and take me to the nearest garage. I almost laugh at the hilarity of it. The closest garage is owned by Kane's father.

I have cash, I'll bribe the tow guy to take me to the next town over. Anywhere is better than here.

Imogen: This stupid motherfucking car has broken down!

I attach a picture of the lingering smoke and exposed engine and send it to Webber. It takes him no time to reply.

Webber: Shit, that's not good. It's a new car.

Imogen: I KNOW! *sobs*

Webber: You don't think he had anything to do with it do you?

I think back to my meeting with *him*, meaning Kane, outside of the church.

Imogen: I wouldn't put it past him.

Webber: If he did, don't worry, you got this. You're strong and so fucking brave. You can handle anything.

Imogen: I completely fucking agree.

I sit in my car and wait, praying that the tow truck isn't from Faceless, the town where I grew up and just cussed out my dead grandmother in front of those absolute assholes I called my community, my neighbors, my friends.

When the tow truck ambles down the road, I'm relieved to see it's an old school friend behind the wheel, somebody I knocked about with back in the day. He also smiles when he sees me, and then laughs when he sees my car.

"Traded in your bike for a fancy ass car that only men with little dicks drive?"

"That's a lot of words in one sentence for you, Ren," I retort and give him a brief hug. "How have you been?"

26 YEARS OLD

"Good, annoyed that you rolled into town without dropping in on the rest of us folk."

Now I almost feel guilty, almost but not quite.

He pushes his black hair back with a meaty arm guiding his hand. "You look great though, Immy. Really good in fact." With a lingering look on my body, he points to the truck. "Get in while I hook your shit car up."

"Eyes on mine dickwad, and I'm not letting you hook anything up until you promise to take me to the garage in Leander."

He lifts a shoulder and smiles apologetically. "No can do, only got enough in the tank to get us back to Faceless Mechanics."

"Then go back to FM, fill up the tank and come back and get me. I'll wait."

"Don't be like that," he pushes, pouting slightly. "Lotta folks around here that will wanna see you. Make their curious hearts feel inferior for a while, show off your fancy pants and your shiny shoes. Let them see how well you're doing."

"Designer gear doesn't mean I'm doing well, Ren."

"Ain't you doing well?"

I smile genuinely. "I'm doing just fine... *out of Faceless*, where I want to fucking stay."

"Potty mouth. Your mee-maw woulda made you chew soap."

"I said worse at her funeral."

His brows jump and his smile stretches. "Now there's a story I like the sound of. Come on. I'll take you the long way round."

"Thought you didn't have enough gas?"

"I got just enough to park under the water tower and show you what you missed all those years ago."

I pull a small can of mace spray out of my bag and point it at him. "I can kick your ass with this, or my fists, you just pick which flavor pain you want."

"Still as feisty as you ever were, don't worry, I ain't touchin' you. Not sure about your *flavors of pain*, but I don't much fancy having my ass kicked by Kane Jessop. Only just got on his good side after rear ending his classic Challenger."

I wince at that. "Surprised you're still alive."

"Naww, he's not like he used to be."

"Don't, Ren," I snap, shaking my head. "Don't."

"Sure." His eyes soften with understanding.

13 YEARS OLD

"Your boobs are so much bigger than mine," Poppy-Rose declares, pushing hers together by pulling her shoulders in. "It's so unfair. I started developing way before you."

"I'm hardly in a bra, Poppy, there's nothing there but pointy nipples. Don't get too envious." I shake my T-shirt clad chest at her where absolutely nothing moves an inch. I'm like a boy.

We both giggle and I fall back dramatically onto her bed where an array of magazines rest with parts cut out of them. We've been creating a dream board of who we want to be when we're older.

I want to be a famous actress and earn loads of money. Poppy wants to marry a wealthy man so she never has to work a day in her life. She decided this after she got a paper run two weeks ago but I took it over after three days because she couldn't do it. She hated it. I don't mind getting up early and doing the work, plus I love the money at the end of the week.

Plus Mee-maw lets me do it thanks to Grandpa stepping in to defend me, telling her that working teaches me good values.

Mee-maw wants me to marry into a wealthy family and raise my future babies. She said there's no greater role in life for a woman than keeping her husband and home happy. I don't want to be anybody's wife.

I look at myself in the mirror after sitting up and flutter my mascara lathered lashes. The black tint really makes the hazel of my eyes pop. It almost makes them look green. I've always wanted green eyes, there's no prettier eye color.

"Let's go to the old bleachers," Poppy whispers, an excited look in her eyes. They're so big and wide, she looks like a cartoon. "Where all the big kids hang out."

"Mee-maw will kill me," I utter.

"She won't know. We'll go for like ten minutes tops. Let's just go see what all the fuss is about."

The thought does excite me. I've always wanted to go there. My brother goes there sometimes. I think that's where he buys his marijuana joints. He still smokes those despite the fact Grandpa gave him the belt the last time he caught him smoking.

"What if Kane's there?" I question, wanting to avoid him at all costs. He's the only person I know who is mean to me. Even now after all these years he still does everything he can to make my life miserable and everybody says it's because he likes me, but I don't see it. I don't want him to like me. He's gross and dirty, and his hair needs a good comb through. His entire family are rotten and I don't want to speak to any of them.

"If he's there, we'll go."

"Okay," I say after a brief moment's deliberation. "Let's go."

She pumps her fist and bites her lip which makes me laugh, then we check ourselves over in the mirror again and head out before her mom can ask us where we're going. It's not lying if we don't have to answer with a lie.

It takes us a while to get there because it's so far out of town and for the first two-thirds of the way, we chat animatedly about how exciting

13 YEARS OLD

this is. For the last third we talk about going home instead but I manage to convince her otherwise.

"We're almost there I think," I whisper as we head towards Buchanan river. I've never been but I know it's around here somewhere.

We hear loud chatter and playful screaming the closer we get and sure enough we find ourselves fifty yards from a large group of teens all screwing around by the massive body of dark water. The sun will set soon, we shouldn't have come here. Already I feel uneasy about it.

"Let's go," I say and Poppy nods, grimacing when somebody falls into the lake and everybody laughs.

We start to run back the way we came, panicking that we might get caught where teenagers are drinking beer and smoking weed. I can smell it in the air even from this far away.

Poppy grabs my hand as I start to run ahead, she's not as fast as me so I pull her behind me.

I stumble on an empty glass bottle and fall to my knees, gasping and panting through the pain. Poppy helps me up and I test putting weight on my leg.

"Are you okay?"

I shake my head. "It really hurts."

She cringes and my eyes follow hers.

"Oh no, my skirt," I say, looking at the tear in the knee and the mud stain. My blood is starting to soak through too. My hearts starts hammering in my throat so hard I don't hear bikes approaching, wheels spinning on the dry grass, chains turning around metal.

"SHOW US YOUR PANTIES, IMOGEN!" Kane yells, and I hit the ground again when his hand at my shoulder shoves me hard.

Three boys bike around us, Kane and his two friends, Ren and Mallick. Mallick is the only black boy in our entire town, I'm not allowed to talk to him but I don't understand why. Still, I keep my eyes down.

When I try to stand again Kane climbs off his bike, dropping it without a care, strides towards me and pushes me over once more.

13 YEARS OLD

"Go on, Immy," Ren jests, grinning from ear to ear. "Show him your panties."

Mallick circles us all on his bike, doing wheelies and popping bubbles with a piece of blue gum in his mouth.

"What is it with you and her panties?" Poppy argues, helping me up again. "Go buy your own."

The boys laugh like she's stupid and I don't get it. Poppy doesn't either.

When I stand, Ren comes forward and grabs a handful of my long grey skirt. "I'll show you her panties," he declares and yanks my skirt so hard the top button pops loose and it slips down my thighs.

I scream and grab at it, tears burning my eyes at the humiliation I feel. Poppy helps me pull it up but we both fall to the ground when Kane tackles Ren and they land in a heap on the floor.

"What the fuck man?" Ren cries, as shocked as we are.

Kane's fist spikes before hitting Ren in the jaw. Why are they fighting? Aren't they friends? I'd never hit Poppy like that. They roll over and Ren gets a hit in too, I see blood. I don't know whose blood. I don't care whose blood, so long as they are hurting each other and not me.

"Come on," Poppy hisses and we run again but I struggle to hold my skirt up. I'm a mess.

We don't talk, we don't try to explain it to each other, we just run and run until we can't anymore.

"Mee-maw is going to kill me," I whisper, looking at the state of myself. "What do I tell her?"

"That you were playing on my bike and fell off?" Poppy suggests. "We can't tell her about Kane because he might tell her where we were. He knows we're not allowed past the grocery store."

I press my lips together. I never tell Mee-maw about Kane anyway because she just tells me it's my fault and I shouldn't look at him and maybe he wouldn't bother me. She says I must be doing something to get his attention but I'm really not.

13 YEARS OLD

We rush home despite the pain radiating through my leg. I mostly hop which hurts my other leg but I can get through it. Pain doesn't bother me. I'd rather feel the pain of my leg than be locked in my bedroom and grounded for two weeks.

Poppy leaves me at the end of her street because we figured if we showed up without her bike my mee-maw would ask how I fell off it if it wasn't with us which would lead to more lying. Truthfully, I'm hoping she's busy so I can sneak up to my room, get rid of my skirt and pretend like I don't know where it is. Maybe she'll think it was stolen from the clothesline in the yard. It wouldn't be the first time that's happened. This will be the first time I've lied about it though. Not that it'll be my first lie, I can't say I'm the most honest person but Mee-maw gets so mad about so many things.

I jump the low fence lining the back yard, she's less likely to be in the kitchen at this time so I slip in through the back door and leave my scuffed shoes by the refrigerator. My breath sounds so loud in my ears as I creep through, sock clad feet on the black and white tiled floor.

"Imogen, is that you?" Mee-maw shouts, sounding cheery and saccharine as per usual.

I run-hop to the bathroom as quickly as my injured leg will carry me and slam the door shut louder than I anticipated. Her feet follow me, I hear them getting closer and I start scrubbing the mud from my hands and arms.

"Imogen?" she calls through the door and raps her knuckles against it.

I can't breathe right, my chest feels tight, like a fist has reached down my throat and is gripping my airway.

"I'm just using the toilet, Mee-maw," I lie, teeth chattering.

There's silence for a moment and then the door opens regardless, revealing the barren toilet and me standing wide-eyed at the sink with suds up to my arms. I grip the soap bar too tightly and it slips out of my hand and lands in the basin.

13 YEARS OLD

"I fell off Poppy's bike," I explain in a rush as her blank, steely gaze takes me in.

"Your skirt," she breathes. "Your brand new, beautiful—" Her hands go to the broken top button and her face becomes red and angry. Her entire body trembles and her voice gets deep and hoarse. "What have you been doing?"

The way she asks me sounds demonic and I gulp audibly.

"N... nothing, Mee-maw. Honest. I f...fell off Poppy's bike and hurt my knee."

She grabs my hair and twists me, revealing my dirt covered back.

"WHAT HAVE YOU BEEN DOING?"

"NOTHING!" I implore. "Honest, Mee-maw. We were just playing!"

"You're lying," she hisses, grabbing my hair so hard my scalp burns making me whimper. "Your skirt is torn, you've mud all over your back. You've been with a boy!"

"What?" I shriek, tears filling my eyes. "No! Mee-maw! No!"

"Don't you lie to me, little girl. I can always tell when you lie! You're as terrible at it as your mother was and still is. Look at the state of you. How will any man respect you now? You're a child and already you're fornicating with Satan." She drags me into the hall, ignoring my begs and pleads for her to let me go. "You're a dirty, dirty girl. You will be punished. You will not be like your mother!"

"NO PLEASE I DIDN'T DO ANYTHING!" I scream as she drags me up the stairs. My mee-maw is old but she is strong. Not that I dare fight her back, she's my mee-maw. "Please, Mee-maw. Please. I didn't do anything."

"You'll not be allowed to venture out with *that girl*. I'll be telling her whore of a mother what she's been teaching you! I knew I shouldn't have let you play with her. Girls without fathers are a menace to society."

She throws me into my bedroom, making me stumble on the rug.

"I don't know what you're talking about," I sob, tears flowing freely now. "Please, Mee-maw. I didn't do anything."

13 YEARS OLD

"Your virginity is your virtue. It is for your *husband*! God has willed it!"

"Mee-maw, noooo," I screech, twisting out of her grasp when she yanks down my skirt. "Please no! Please. I swear, I didn't do anything. I fell over. That's all. We were playing!"

She hits the back of my bare thigh with her hard-bottom slipper and the sting makes me scream.

"STOP CRYING!" she bellows at me, hitting me again, her hand tangled in my hair once more. She whips that slipper through the air and I lift my leg as she brings it down on my other thigh. I take about five hits before I drop to the floor and grip my discarded skirt, holding it against my chest. She stops hitting me and just breathes heavy as though the exertion was too much.

With a whimper she moves to the wall and leans against it.

"How could you shame us like this? We took you in so you wouldn't go into care and this is how you shame your family?"

I hiccup and look at my mee-maw who now looks so sad and frail despite her youth and usual strength.

"I'm sorry, Mee-maw," I whisper because I don't want her to be sad. I don't want her to be hurt by my actions. "Are you okay?"

"My heart," she whispers, clutching her chest. "I can't take the same heartache your mother put me through. I need you to be the good one. I need you to be everything she wasn't. I want you to be a young lady I can be proud of."

"I'll try, Mee-maw," I breathe, wiping my eyes on my arm. "I'll be good."

"You're never to see that girl again. You'll only befriend the people I choose; do you understand?" She levels me with a cold look that I daren't argue with. Though I open my mouth, ready to tell her that I don't want to lose my only real friend, and instead close it and nod.

"Okay, Mee-maw. I promise."

"Good girl." She holds out her hand and I rise and move to her side, limping on my hurt leg, rear and thighs swollen from the beating. I hug her and sob into her side, accepting her comfort and warmth. She kisses my head. "I love you very, very much."

"I love you too, Mee-maw."

26 YEARS OLD

"Found the stray just outta town," Ren calls when he drops down from the truck. "One of our own. Though she'll deny it till she's purple in the face."

Rolling my eyes, I push open the door after spying a coffee machine, one of those fancy vending types, and climb down, taking Ren's hand because my heels aren't fit for this sort of drop.

"Atta girl." He winks at me and catches my eyes when I look around the mess of broken bikes and cars and the few men working on them. "He's probably at your mee-maw's wake."

"I wasn't looking for him," I lie and pull my hand free of his dry grip.

"Damn... is that you, Imogen Hardy?" a man with red hair and freckles calls. I used to go to school with him too but I don't remember his name. "You know Kane almost had us all convinced you were dead or somethin'."

That makes my heart beat a wild thump, sending a jolt of adrenaline through my already tense body.

"Don't leer," Ren snaps. "Get back to work." He dips his head and grins at me. "Coffee?"

"I can get my own."

"You sure? Got some of those fancy pod things in the office if you'd rather one of those. Truth be told don't know when that coffee machine there was last cleaned."

Just great. I can't go another hour without coffee, that's assuming my car takes that long to fix.

"That actually sounds good," I reply quietly and follow him through. He barks at somebody else to drop my car and fill his tank but I don't pay much attention. Instead I try for a Wi-Fi signal. "Can I have the password?"

"Sure, it's written on that yellow paper by the computer screen." He points in the general direction and switches the coffee machine on at the wall.

I make my way over and input the jumbled letters and numbers into my phone. Then I plug my phone into one of the stray cables and let it rest on the desk.

"Make yourself at home," he jests, his smile easy and handsome.

"You've still got that scar I gave you. It's small, but it's there." I motion to his upper lip at the corner where stubble doesn't grow.

"I have." He touches it absentmindedly and his smile gets wider. "I deserved it."

"You did."

We share a light laugh and then I turn my attention to the few photos on the wall behind the computer. I smile at the first one, it's of Kane and his father when Kane was an awkward teen. The next one has my smile fading because I'm in it. I look so happy and carefree, so at ease with my life. I was such a good pretender.

After a moment he hands me my coffee. It's warm and the cup is clean and it tastes delicious.

"I'll get started on your car."

"How long will it take?" I ask.

He grins and rolls his eyes. "I ain't looked at it yet."

"Right, well... I'm going to wander."

"In those shoes?"

26 YEARS OLD

Pressing my lips together, I stand and glower at him. "Go fix my car."

"Yes ma'am." He tips an invisible hat and backs out of the room. Meanwhile I play on my phone, answer emails and messages and search Google for cabs in the area wondering when I became a *ma'am*.

The temptation to go through drawers is almost unbearable. I want to search for any information on Kane and what he's been up to all these years. Well... search for stuff I don't know already.

I don't. I'm not that psychotic.

I do however finish my coffee, stand and decide to go to my car, get my flats and walk until my car is fixed. I can't be here. The room even smells like him. Like leather and car oil and sweet, musky aftershave.

Closing my eyes, I recall every time I got to inhale his scent. It was like a drug to me. He was a drug to me. A dangerous, soul destroying drug. The catalyst of all my worst moments.

With a frustrated growl, I exit the room, yanking on the door and making the open venetian blinds rattle against the square glass window. I move to my car while Ren is poking around in the engine. He looks up so I motion for him to unlock the car using my keys. He does so and goes back to his job while I open the trunk and rummage through my suitcase. I wasn't planning on staying but it's a long ass drive, seventeen hours to be exact. I was going to fly but I couldn't find a flight out on the same day and securing a rental for after I landed would have been too much hassle. So I packed and took a road trip. I love road trips, it's been a while since I went on a road trip.

Now I wish I'd flown.

As I'm pulling on my flat black pumps, a car rolls into the lot behind me and I don't know how I know it's him but I do. I've always been hyperaware of his existence on this plane, especially when he's nearby. I swear I'd know if he died even if he were a million miles away. Though I wouldn't come and cuss him out at his funeral, I would dance on his grave. I absolutely would. Then I'd sit back against his headstone, have a gin and tell him to go fuck his own corpse.

My soul stiffens in my body but I pretend I don't know he's here and I also pretend I don't care.

No, scratch that, I don't care, there is no pretending about that part.

"Kane," Ren calls when a car door closes, he's trying to give me a heads up.

I flip down my sunglasses and slam the trunk closed before turning towards the car that just pulled in and ejected its only person.

I try not to look at him, I try so hard but my strength from earlier has depleted and I can't fight the magnet that is Kane Jessop.

He stands tall, taller than he used to be, muscular, more so than he used to be, his hair is as long as it always was and just as shiny but nowhere near as tangled. I could probably push my fingers through it now and it probably wouldn't even snag.

My heart crawls up my throat, hammering a disoriented beat as it tries to figure out whether we still love him or not, whether we ever loved him or not, whether we even know him anymore or not.

He stuffs his hand into his pocket and licks his lower lip, his ocean blue eyes roam over me, wary and tired.

"Give me your eyes, babe," he whispers and it feels like my world freezes. "You gotta give me your eyes."

My hand itches to rise and push the plastic bridge of my grey tinted glasses until they're resting on my head, but I don't. Instead I raise my chin, stare him down through my shields and retort quietly but firmly, "Stopped giving you things a long time ago, Kane. I'm not about to start again now."

14 YEARS OLD

Matthew laughs loudly at my self-deprecating joke; he hasn't laughed like this in so long. He bumps his arm against mine and holds the bottle out to me.

"Live a little, sis. You only get one shot at this shit."

"Mee-maw will kill me," I grumble, pushing the bottle away.

He sneers and downs the rest of his beer before tossing it far across the vast expanse. "Mee-maw can go fuck herself." I've never heard such *vehemence* in his tone, nor have I ever heard him speak that way about Mee-maw.

Vehemence is a new word I learned this week. I love learning new words, it helps me feel as though I can express everything inside just a little bit more. It also makes Mee-maw happy.

"She's going to moan at you anyway and beat your ass for something else. Might as well be something worthwhile." He holds his fresh beer to me from the box by his side and I bite my lip as I question what to do here. "Come on, sis. Don't be a pussy."

I glower at him. I'm not a pussy.

Snatching the bottle, I take a large gulp and grimace. It's warm but the taste isn't as bad as I thought it might be. The bubbles are weird though, it's not often I drink fizzy drinks.

"You've got to stop letting her treat you like she does. Don't let her hit you."

"Her heart," I argue.

"She's a manipulative old crow. Her heart is fine. Just fucking tell her to piss off."

"Last time you did that, Grandpa punched you in the eye."

"Yeah well he's hardly gonna punch you is he?" he replies with a laugh and clinks his bottle against mine. "Grandpa is so in love and so tired, he doesn't want to see that there's somethin' wrong with the way Mee-maw treats us. But it is wrong. It has always been wrong."

He's right, it is wrong. I hate it, every moment of it. I feel like a caged bird, broken, without a voice, without love.

I drink more of my beer and swing my legs slightly. "Mom called yesterday. Said she wants to take me shopping for my birthday."

Even though my birthday was four months ago.

Matthew shrugs and I watch his throat bob as he gulps his beer down. "Let her. Bout time she gave us something for bein' hers."

"Yeah," I agree softly. "Mee-maw said—"

"Fucking hell, Imogen!" Matthew snarls, hopping down off the wall to throw this beer bottle too. I hear it smash against something hard in the distance. I love that sound, the way glass shatters on impact. It's like the sound I get in my head before I snap and write bad words in my diary. "You're such a coward. Stop it with the *Mee-maw said.*"

"Don't mock my tone."

"Then stop sounding that way!" He glowers at me, his familiar hazel eyes so angry and sad combined. "You need to stand up for yourself! You need to stop letting people manipulate you. You're fierce, you're a bitch. You tell *me* where to shove it all the time, so I know you have it in you. Fight back!"

"Like you did with Kane Jessop?" I comment wryly, recalling their fight last year where my brother got his ass handed to him.

"I might have lost but at least I fucking tried. Kane hasn't bothered me since, not really. You know why? Respect. He respects me now because I fought back."

"So I should go and sucker punch Mee-maw?"

"Hell no."

"Don't say hell."

He rolls his eyes dramatically and continues, "I'm not saying hit her, but you should overpower her at the very least. Rip that slipper from her hand and tell her she ain't never touching you again."

His wisdom is making me feel more powerful than I likely am. So badly I want to tell her to get lost and go suck her ugly God's dick, but I never do. More than anything I want to kick Kane in his, but again I never do.

I drain my beer, feeling a spurt of courage, and throw it as far as my brother threw his. It shatters and I smile at the sound as he laughs and hands me another. This one goes down even easier than the first and I find myself feeling more powerful than I ever have.

"I think I'm drunk," I say and smile sweetly at my favorite person in the whole entire world.

"Good, then I can finally tell you," he declares, handing me one of the last two beers from the box.

"Tell me what?"

"I'm dating Poppy."

"WHAT?" I shriek and he winces. "As in Poppy-Rose?"

He nods with another grin, looking far too proud of himself. "But... it's Poppy. *My* Poppy."

I only just got her back after Mee-maw stopped me seeing her for four months. Four longest months of my life, though we stayed friends in school, outside of school she was hanging around with other people. It made me so jealous.

"You ain't dating her."

I pull a face. "I didn't mean it like that."

"I know, but I'm just telling you what's what. She's mine now, more than yours, you gotta be cool with that."

"Does Mee-maw know?"

He grits his teeth and pulls on my hair making me yelp. "If you ever ask me about Mee-maw again, I'm going to fart on your pillow."

"I'll get pink eye again."

"Exactly."

"You're disgusting."

"Yep." His perfect teeth glint in the setting sun. "Let's stay out late, make them worry."

I chew on the inside of my cheek and consider it, then I consider being grounded for the next month and promptly shake my head.

"Well, you're gonna have to. If she smells that beer on you, you'll be in trouble anyway. May as well enjoy your freedom for a while before she locks you in your room forever."

He has a point.

"Fine. I'll skip curfew." I have *never* skipped curfew before. *Ever*.

With excitement glinting like an evil entity in his eyes, he grabs my hand and tugs me away from our abandoned crate. "Let's go get more booze."

"Why? I'm already drunk."

"Nah, you're not nearly drunk enough."

We go to the lake, or what the cool kids call the patch. The last time I came here was the first time Mee-maw gave me a proper beating with her slipper. Though not because I was here, but because of the state of me when I made it home.

It's heaving with teenagers making out, drinking beer, smoking cigarettes and weed. My brother pulls me along, keeping me close incase my tormenter is here, though hopefully he won't be as he works at Faceless Mechanics now with his daddy and spends most of his free time there.

I wish I had a daddy that wanted to teach me things like that. A daddy who wanted to spend time with me and help me find my way in the world. Sometimes I feel so lost and weak, like the world doesn't want me to progress.

14 YEARS OLD

My brother introduces me to his friends, some of them I have classes with but I don't talk to them. Mee-maw says they aren't church going people so I have to avoid them. They seem nice though. But then so does Mallick the black guy and she told me he was born a sin because of the color of his skin. He's the only one in Kane's group that has never been outright mean to me. He doesn't even laugh when they do mean shit too. I don't know how he can be born a sin, he doesn't seem like a bad person.

I spy him across the small fire that is surrounded by a shallow moat, likely to stop it from accidentally starting a bush fire. Don't they know that fire can jump?

Whatever. I'm not saying shit to anyone about that. I don't want to look uncool.

Mallick spies me too and smiles, he raises his hand and waves and I wave back. It's not the first time we've smiled at each other but this time it feels different.

"Don't let Mee-maw catch you looking at the black kid," Matthew whispers in jest. He's not being racist; he's just making fun of me and my fear of the only parent I've ever known.

I ignore him and blush when I catch Mallick's eyes again. He's really quite good looking and he's always so polite. I don't know why Mee-maw would think bad things about him. Does she even know him? How does the color of your skin define you as a person? If him being black makes him bad, then am I bad because of all the bad stuff other white people have done?

"He's into you," Poppy whispers in my ear, seemingly appearing out of nowhere.

She hugs me around the waist and rests her chin on my shoulder.

"You think?" I question and she nods, her cheek brushing against my ear. The thought that he might like me does send a certain thrill through me

"Yep."

I lean back against her chest and inhale her cherry scent. She loves cherries, especially the body mist her mom always buys for her.

Maybe I can convince my mom to buy me a signature scent. I want somebody to hug me and smell something like vanilla, or peaches. Something pretty and feminine, but soft.

"Are you mad that I didn't tell you about Matthew?" She sounds so concerned. She also won't let me go so I can look at her while I talk to her.

"It's weird," I admit because I'm not sure how I feel about it. I didn't even know they were into each other like that.

"I know but... he's amazing."

I smile softly because I agree with her on that.

"So, we're okay?"

I nod genuinely and hug her arms that hold me tight. "Definitely."

"Thanks, Immy." Then she releases me and looks at the dark sky. "Your mee-maw is gonna kill you."

Matthew passes me another beer and mouths the words, "Fuck it."

"FUCK IT!" I yell and everyone around me cheers. We all raise our drinks and scream the same two words in a loud chorus.

26 YEARS OLD

"Did you do this to my car?" I ask politely, trying to remain calm as I face off with the man I swear I loathe.

"Told you I wasn't gonna pin you," he replies just as politely and pops a piece of gum into his mouth. He offers me one but I shake my head so he stuffs them back into the pocket of his open leather jacket. He wasn't wearing this jacket at the funeral, likely out of respect. It's laughable thinking about *him* being respectful to anyone. "I meant it."

I don't know whether to believe him or not, either way I have no evidence so I nod and continue with my plan.

"Ren," I call, looking at him over my shoulder. "How long?"

"Couple of hours babe, that's if we've got the parts I think we need."

"Prognosis?" Kane asks, chewing his gum as he approaches my exposed vehicle.

They speak in mechanical tongue for a short while and Kane's brows shoot up. I fucking hate how nice looking he is. It doesn't suit him, it never did. Mostly because it suits him too much. He's everything a respectable daddy would tell you to stay away from.

26 YEARS OLD

Kane shoves him out the way and starts tinkering with the engine. I wait a while, wondering if this is us now. Are we both civil adults that can do this mature shit and be near each other without all the excess?

I almost laugh at the thought of that ever being a reality. Kane and I will never be stable. I'll always hate him and he'll always want to hurt me. It's how we fucking roll.

"It's gonna take longer than a couple of hours, babe," Kane calls after a minute. "We definitely don't have what you need for this piece of shit." He kicks the wheel and I know he's doing it to get a rise out of me. "Who's your old man? Only men with little dicks drive cars like this."

"That's what I said," Ren comments, looking proud of himself and they bump fists like the *"good old days"*.

"Trust me, his dick works just fine," I clapback and Kane's gaze darkens and a muscle pulses in his cheek.

Ren looks away, Kane steps towards me, his hands stained with oil, his nails still as short as they ever were.

"What's his name?" Kane demands and I can't tell if he's trying to call my bluff or if he wants to shoot him in his face.

"Webber."

"Even his name is dumb as fuck."

I roll my eyes. "And you're still the same bully you always were."

"And you're still the same flippant bitch." Kane pulls his keys from his pocket; he doesn't bother waiting for a reaction he knows he's not going to get. "I'll drive over to Leander and see if they've got the part we need." He looks me up and down with a new look that I can't decipher. "You coming? I think we've got some shit to talk about."

I laugh humorlessly. "Get in your shit Challenger and go fuck yourself."

"Now, now children, let's not get nasty with each other," Ren says around a genuine laugh. "This ain't high-school. We're all adults here."

"Shut up, Ren," both Kane and I chorus.

I glare at Kane as though it's his fault we both spoke together, but he just winks at me, still chewing that gum in his mouth.

Finally, after staring at me for the longest fucking time, he utters, his tone strong, "You look amazing, Imogen. Seeing you now, can't believe I ever convinced you to suck my dick all those years ago."

I yank my mace from my bag, cover my eyes with my arm and listen as the hiss of the canister is soon covered by his pained roar.

"YOU FUCKING BITCH!" he screams as his buddies fall about laughing.

"I'm so glad I didn't choose that flavor pain," Ren chokes, tossing his friend a bottle of water. Kane scrubs his face with his oily hand while pouring the crystal-clear fluid over his face. It drenches every part of him, making what's visible of his black band T-shirt between the zippers of his leather jacket cling to the muscles of his chest.

"How about now you suck on my dick?" I snap, feeling proud and strong. "And don't ever speak to me again, not like that and not in any kinda way."

"Psychotic cunt," he yells, turning towards the building. "Such a fucking cunt."

Ren winks at me. "You better hope I fix this car before that shit wears off or he's coming for you."

"Thought you said he'd changed? Doesn't look like he's changed at all, Ren." I stuff the mace in my bag and hitch it up my shoulder.

"I said *he's not like that* as a general statement. He'll always be crazy when it comes to you, Immy."

With a snort I walk towards the long road that leads into town. My hands are shaking and I don't think it's because of what I just did. It's all for him. All of it. Only Kane has ever been able to make me tremble.

14 AND A HALF

I took the beating, of course I took the beating. I didn't stand up for myself. I certainly didn't tell Mee-maw that the first boy I ever kissed was a black boy with such gentle hands.

I was drunk and I let him hold my waist as we kissed. It was a bit messy, but I liked it. He was a fast kisser, mind, and when I still think about it, it still makes me grin and squeal into my pillow with happiness.

Matthew was right, if I'm going to get a beating anyway, may as well be for something good.

Matthew hasn't been grounded because they can't keep him in. He didn't get home until noon the next day and our Grandpa tried to give him the belt but Matthew ran before he could catch him.

I wish I could have been that brave. Maybe then I wouldn't be stuck in my room like I am on such a nice day. If only I had the courage to sneak out and go to the lake with my friends.

Poppy messaged me for a little while this morning but she's busy with my brother. They're inseparable and so happy and in love. It's crazy to me. They're so good to each other.

Poppy's mom said that you never forget your first love, but she said it in a way that sounded like they'd never be each other's last love and that makes me sad. If they stay as happy as they are now, but forever, why would they ever break up?

Though I often remind Poppy that she wanted a rich man and my brother is as broke as a hobo.

She doesn't care. She said if it meant being with my brother, she'd get a job. He's looking for one too but in Faceless there's absolutely nothing for kids our age. Leander is a bit bigger but it's too far away and then there's Burnet which is closer but that ain't much different to Faceless.

At least I still have my paper route, though Mee-maw has been taking my money from that, telling me I need to save for a fancy college. Because a fancy college is where I'll find myself a nice man. Maybe he'll rescue me from this hell.

"Imogen!" Mee-maw calls through the door and I hear the key twist in the lock. She pokes her freshly cut head of hair through and smiles at me in that faux, saccharine way that she always does. "Could you be a dear and run to the grocery store? I've run out of eggs and my hip has flared up. And you know I've got that cake to make for—"

"No problem," I interrupt. Desperate to get out of the house and stop listening to her ramble on about things I don't care about.

"Good girl. Come and collect the money on your way out. Dress nicely now."

I pull a face at her back and do what I'm told. I pull on a pink dress that's getting too small in the chest. My breasts are so much bigger than they were last year.

I cringe at the frills on the long sleeves and yank at the armpit where it feels too tight.

I wish I could wear normal clothes, shorts and whatever else. I'm fourteen and a half, my clothes are what a five-year-old would wear.

Sighing, I slip on my socks, some clean panties and head to the bathroom to brush my teeth and wash my face. I've lost weight, I've been bored in my room so I've been watching videos on how to fight and Mee-maw hasn't let me have breakfast or snacks for about a week. It's all part of my punishment for missing curfew. Though dinner I must attend because family dinners are important for a family dynamic and appearances. We often have guests for dinner.

Appearances mean everything to her.

"Mee-maw," I say as I reach the bottom stair. "My clothes are getting too small."

She takes one look at me and hums thoughtfully. "Well that just won't do."

"Do you think this time I can get some jeans, and shirts like what my friends wear?"

"But those dresses and skirts look so good on you." She tugs on the front of said dress and sighs heavily. "I guess we will have to go shopping this week. Do you have something for school tomorrow?"

I lift a shoulder. "I have my gym clothes, they still fit."

"Yes, yes, they will do just fine." She hands me a few dollars and waits for me to slip on my flat shoes. "A dozen eggs, the free-range, not Kenny's barn raised. They don't have quite as nice a taste to them."

"Okay." I head out into the warm air and smile at the blue sky.

Ah sweet freedom.

Mee-maw waves as I go and I give her a slight wave back before running as fast as my legs can carry me. Every step I take I inhale a deep, fresh lungful of air. I wish I'd called Poppy first, I might have been able to meet her for a little while but if Mee-maw finds out she'd tan my behind.

I huff. I wish I could be like Matthew. *I wish.*

"Morning little lady," Martin, the grocery store owner calls when the bell rings as I step inside. It's cool in here, fresh and crisp from the clean store and the overhead air conditioning. "How's your mee-maw doin'? You're looking well. Getting older I see."

He leers at me in a way a man his age has never leered at me before. I don't exactly know what it means but I do know that I don't like it. It makes me feel like bugs are crawling along the top of my skin.

"She's good. She just sent me for some of those free-range eggs you stock. Do you have a dozen?"

"You're in luck, last two cases are right here." He pats the almost empty box at the end of the counter and grins at me, showing two missing teeth from his bottom row. "Is that all you need?"

Nodding, I approach and hand him the money. He rings it through the old till and slides my money and eggs along the counter.

"You know I used to serve your momma back in the day too. You're her spitting image," he comments, giving me the same look as before. "She used to help me in the shop to earn some pocket money for herself. I'm sure we could work out a similar deal, as a favor to your momma and the good old days."

I bite on my lip and consider it. I don't make much doing my paper route because Mee-maw takes all my money. "What would I do?"

"Mop the floors, stock the shelves, things like that." He rubs his jaw, peering down his nose at me with excitement in his eyes. "Washing windows and the likes. Nothing too strenuous. I'll pay you three dollars an hour."

My heart starts hammering in my chest and my happiness grows. "Really?" Mee-maw would let me work; she wouldn't have a choice. I could tell her he's giving me two dollars an hour and pocket the rest. Or even one dollar. Would she believe that? "When can I start?"

"Soon as you like," he replies as I pocket my change and pick up my eggs.

"Tomorrow? I need to tell my mee-maw first."

"Absolutely."

"Thank you, Mr. Martin. I'll be back as soon as school is finished."

"See you then, little lady."

I leave the store with a skip in my step, cradling the carton of eggs along one arm.

I'm on such a happy cloud that I failed to notice Kane, Ren, and Mallick in the vicinity. They're now following me down the long road on their bikes. I keep my head low.

"What the fuck are you wearing?" Ren asks, balancing on his skateboard at a really slow speed as Mallick does wide circles around us on a bike and Kane flanks me on the other side on his. He thinks he's so cool with his leather jacket, and red skulls and fire painted along the black frame of his stupid bike.

"You look like one of those creepy girls from the horror movies. That one in the hotel," Kane puts in and they all laugh.

"It's called The Shining, I think," Ren finishes and Kane nods, his jaw moving as he chews on a piece of gum. His blue eyes flash dangerously when my eyes meet them.

"Whatchu looking at?" he asks, dropping his bike to harass me on foot.

"I need to get back to Mee-maw," I say softly, ducking and trying to sidle past him but he snatches the eggs from my arm and holds them above his head. "Kane. Please."

"Show me your panties and you can have them back."

"Last time I showed you her fuckin' panties and you punched me in the jaw," Ren retorts, laughing as though it's hilarious. "You either wanna see them or you don't."

Kane holds my eyes and steps closer so we're chest to chest. "That wasn't because of that."

"So... I should do it again?"

"Naw," Kane snaps and an evil glint sparks in his eyes. "Apparently she already showed Mallick, didn't she, Mallick?"

Mallick doesn't respond, he just keeps circling as he always does.

Kane gets so close I can feel his minty breath on my lips. "Who the *fuck* said you could kiss my friends?"

"Who told you—?"

"Everyone told me. Everyone has been talking about it. Especially Mallick, right Mallick?"

Mallick doesn't look at me. I thought we were cool. I thought we might have been more than cool.

"RIGHT MALLICK?" Kane yells but his eyes hold mine and he gets so close our foreheads touch.

"I heard him," Ren puts in and Mallick shakes his head. He doesn't want to be here anymore than I do.

"Heard you let him touch your titties."

"I did not," I gasp, folding my arms across my body. "Why do you care anyway?"

Kane shrugs and steps back, grinning evilly as he opens the carton of eggs.

"What are you doing?" I ask nervously, hands clenched and shaking as I hug myself.

"You don't kiss my friends," Kane hisses, narrowing his ugly blue eyes. "You don't kiss anyone." He brings an egg down onto my head with his palm. It cracks and the gooey middle slides down the side of my head and over my ear. It hurt too but I try not to react beyond a wide-eyed, humiliated stare.

"OOOOOOH!" Ren cries and catches the egg Kane tosses his way. He smiles evilly and throws one at my chest, it hits my breast with a hard thud but cracks on the ground at my feet.

"STOP!" I scream when Ren throws his and it hits me on the shoulder. That one doesn't crack either but it really hurts.

I drop to my knees as the assault continues but now they've learned to push their thumbs into the eggs before tossing them so they crack on impact.

I cover my head with my arms, listening to the sound of my breathing until the very last egg is cast. I count every hit, including the ones that missed.

Rage comes pouring out of me as their laughter echoes through my mind.

I lose it. A haze of red-hot lava distorts my vision and with a battle cry worthy of the big screens I grab Ren's discarded skateboard and charge at them. Kane's eyes go wide the second before I hit Ren across the face. Blood sprays through the air in dark red droplets that seem suspended in slow motion and Ren hits the floor with a grunt. I don't stop, I charge at Kane and swing but he blocks it with his arm. He cries out in pain and shoves me and the board away from him.

I keep going. I kick him between his legs so hard his eyes bulge out of his head. He goes down too but I can't control it. Hot, angry tears fall from my eyes as I climb on top of him and smack him and punch him in the face and chest and neck. My hands, arms, fingers, body all ache as I unleash every ounce of my anger onto him.

He fights for control, grabbing my wrists but his arm is limp and useless. He's bleeding on his cheek from my scratches, he has a swelling under his eye but I can't stop.

I want to kill him. I want to stop him from breathing but I run out of energy. I'm completely out of steam.

He rolls me over, grabbing my wrists with one hand and pinning them above my head. I don't fight him I just cry and cry, and sob, and choke.

"I hate you," I say, channeling every single memory I have of the torment he has put me through. "I hate you. I hate you. I wish you would just die."

Kane's eyes roam over my face and for a flicker of a moment I see something other than his usual angry, evil self. I see... something tender.

Still, I push him off me and look at Ren who is bleeding badly from the mouth.

Kane starts laughing maniacally, he rolls onto his back and looks up at the sky as his friend gargles on blood and I pick myself up.

"Bitch broke my arm," Kane declares, still laughing like it's all so hilarious. "Fuck. That hurts."

I start to walk away, and then I start to run, keeping my tear blurred eyes ahead. They don't say anything to me or come after me and I don't stop going until I'm home.

I sob all the way there, chest constricting, heart pounding

painfully, eyes burning, blood in my palms from where my nails have dug through my flesh.

"You took your time," Mee-maw comments when I walk in. She hasn't seen me yet.

I run upstairs, grabbing the key off the hook on my way up and I lock my bedroom door from the inside to delay the telling off and beating I'll get. She has another key, she's organized, but at least I can vent in my diary while she fetches it.

I scribble on the pages, cussword after cussword, capitals and lower case. I press so hard I dig through the paper in some places, leaving gouges in the blank sheet beneath.

"You open this door right now," Mee-maw demands, hammering it with her fist. "Where are my eggs?"

Throwing my diary across the room, I stomp to the door, twist the key and swing it open so hard it bounces off my desk behind it.

"All over my fucking body!" I scream at her, unable to control my temper. "NOW LEAVE ME ALONE!"

I slam the door in her astonished face and mentally prepare myself for the slipper. But instead she walks away and the beating doesn't come. Instead, an hour later she brings me a glass of warm milk and a small slice of the cake she baked. She must have gotten more eggs from somewhere.

We don't talk about what happened and for that I'm relieved. Every time I think about it I cry. If I talk about it, I'll only cry harder.

She does however impart some wisdom on me. Wisdom I'll never forget.

"Unassuming girls don't get hurt."

I wanted to disagree and reply that strong girls don't get hurt. That's why I'm hurt, it has nothing to do with how I look and everything to do with how weak I am. But instead I just cried again and trembled and she stroked my hair with tenderness and love.

26 YEARS OLD

I don't know what made me come here. I never got the urge before but seeing the two-story home that I grew up in, riddled with weeds and dirty shutters hanging from the windows, scratched and flaking paint, the porch swing is broken too, it satisfies me in some deep and disturbed way.

I guess after Mee-maw lost Grandpa and then me, she stopped looking after the place and herself.

I want to spit on the ground but instead I approach the door and open it. It's a mess from the wake. Mom is alone, cleaning up plates and cups, sniffling like she has a right to mourn the mother who abused her as badly as she abused me.

She looks up with familiar, sad eyes and drops the trash bag. When she moves to me, looking for comfort I sidestep out of the way. I'll never forgive her for what she did, or more aptly, *didn't* do.

She looks solemn and defeated and goes back to her cleaning. "It's late. Are you staying? I thought you'd be halfway back to your life of grandeur by now."

"I'm not staying, I'm just waiting for my car to be fixed." I sniff dryly, there's too much dust in here. Mom could have cleaned before she hosted people but she always was a lazy bitch. "You look like shit. You need a better surgeon. He's butchered your face."

"You're such a bitch."

"Gotta be raised with love to know how to display love," I retort, looking at her ballooned cheeks and eyebrows which are uneven from botched Botox. "Was a life of filling yourself with plastic more fulfilling than being a good mother to me and Matthew?"

She starts to wail, dropping to her knees like a class A actress.

"Oh go pop a Xanax," I snap at her, grabbing the bag and making myself useful.

"You're so mean."

I laugh coldly. "It's how I was raised, but then you know that better than anyone."

She picks herself up and we work side by side to get the old cunt's house back to near pristine. It takes another hour and I know my car isn't going to be fixed until tomorrow. I brought it on myself by spraying Kane in the eyes. I'm not sorry. He deserved it.

"Hungry?" Mom asks, pointing her thumb towards the kitchen. "There's so much food left."

I head that way and start tearing through the wrapped containers and dishes. That's the only good thing I remember about my childhood, the food.

We tuck into everything, digging forks and spoons into each dish. Mixing pie with casserole and potatoes, then blending the desserts in our stomachs until we can't eat another bite.

There's a loud knock at the door. I'd know that knock anywhere.

Rolling my eyes I nod towards the entrance hall and demand harshly, "Be a good mother and get rid of him."

"Who?" she questions, eyes round with intrigue.

"Who do you think?"

Her lips form a circle. "Kane? Is that Kane Jessop?"

I nod.

"How can you tell?"

"I just can. Now please go tell him I ain't here."

"Can't," she responds, looking at a spot above my shoulder. She points there with the spoon in her hand and I sigh while turning slowly. Of course he's not just going to stop at the front door.

Standing beyond the kitchen window with red, bloodshot eyes is none other than Kane Jessop. He smirks and lifts his hand, I'm about to flip him the bird when I see the hammer he's about to bring down on the glass.

"OKAY!" I yell, standing and showing him my palm. "I'll talk to you."

He nods, eyes sore but lit with that maniacal excitement that is so him and moves away from the glass squares. I see a glow in the dark as he lights something close to his face with an orange flame.

"That boy is still so psychotic." Mom hisses and I hum my agreement. "He should be in jail."

"Oh believe me," I utter, going into the hallway to slip on my shoes, "he absolutely should."

14 YEARS OLD

Kane came to school today with a black cast on his broken arm, he's been off all week. He wasn't kidding when he said it was broken. How he didn't cry I don't know because that must have really hurt.

Still, I raise my chin and carry onward, ignoring the whispers around me of what happened that day. The rumors about it are insane. According to other kids Kane and Ren saved me from getting my ass beat by muggers. Other rumors are that they tried to rape me. Others are saying I lured them into the bush and jumped them with a bunch of guys.

I can't keep up to be honest and I'm not about to try. Their phony concern and enthusiasm make me nauseous. They're just being nice to me to get the information and I'm admitting nothing.

And to add a cherry to the top of an already awful day, my locker has been vandalized at some point during my first two classes. It's not the first time and I doubt it will be the last.

'*You'll get it.*'

That's what they wrote in red ink, I assume the red is symbolic of blood. I almost roll my eyes at the lack of creativity.

Matthew starts to scrub it off with the sleeve of his shirt but it's dry as desert sand and is not budging.

He looks around, glaring at those who have come to see my reaction. I'm not giving them one.

"Fuck off," he yells, squaring up to all of them like he can take them all on. Though these days I reckon he could. He's been working at a plantation just on the outskirts of town and he's really beefing up.

Meanwhile I started my job at Martin's grocery store. It's not as hard as I thought it would be. He mostly just has me doing everything he said, and Mee-maw is happy with the arrangement because she knows him. Though she asked him to give my money directly to her and my heart sank.

It soon lifted again when he told her he'd be paying me a dollar fifty an hour and at the end of that shift he promised me he'd give me the rest at the end of each week. He knows what's up and I'm so grateful for that.

At lunch the words on my locker are gone and Matthew is sitting at Kane's table at the far end, laughing at something somebody said and I wonder when they all became friends. Kane has a girl called Maisy straddling his lap as she draws on his cast in neon green ink. She's the girl who painted his bike, I think. She's in the year above us, is crazy good at art, and her parents are bikers like Kane's granddaddy was. His daddy isn't so much into it as his granddaddy but he joins the rides sometimes. They call themselves the Renegades and last year they were part of this huge Thanksgiving parade in the city, holding up torches and turkeys. It was actually quite fun to watch.

Mee-maw let me get a lightning bolt on my cheek in yellow glitter. She was so much fun that day but she had indulged in a brandy with her closest friend Margery who is awful at baking but always insists on it. I broke my tooth on her stupid food. Lucky for me it was a baby tooth.

14 YEARS OLD

"You're staring," my friend Katie tells me.

I quickly look away from Kane, hating how the image of him kissing Maisy is now stuck in my mind. He grabbed her so viciously and pulled her mouth to his, tongues tangling, spit swapping. So gross. But then I recall my kiss with Mallick and I get it. I understand why he wants to kiss Maisy like he does. It makes your whole body feel so alive and nice.

My eyes drift back over and Maisy is threading her fingers through his hair, it looks so soft and light to the touch despite the thickness.

"You're staring again," Katie hisses and I look back at the table, this time mentally swearing that I won't glance their way again. "You're so quiet lately."

People keep telling me that. Reminding me daily that a year ago I was this vibrant, excitable girl but now I act as though the life has been sucked right out of me. They're closer to the truth than they realize. It has been sucked out of me.

I guess I'm just starting to wonder what the point in any of this is anymore.

"Mr. Martin," I say, eagerly approaching my boss now it's quiet instore. "I'm done for the day."

Really, I want my wages that he promised me. I've already decided exactly what I'm going to spend them on. New clothes. If I can afford anything which I probably can't. I might be able to save enough eventually.

"You've done such a great job this week," he compliments, brown eyes twinkling with warmth. Yet at the same time they always make me uneasy. Like putting your hand into a hole in the ground not knowing what's hidden in the depths but you know there's probably a snake in there. "You earned *every* penny."

He places his hand on my shoulder and guides me around a tall shelf. His other hand reaches into his pocket and he starts thumbing through notes.

"Of course I have to take into account the damage caused by those boys to my windows on your behalf." My heart sinks because I was worried he'd say that. As soon as Kane got word that I was working here, they spray painted my name and the word "WHORE" beneath it. I was mortified. I didn't cry though, I just got a bucket of soapy water and cleaned it off as best I could. It left a stain that Martin had to deal with. "But you did such a good job of cleaning it off that I'll only charge for the cleaning equipment. So I'm taking three dollars from you. Is that fair?"

I nod, my face falling. I only made seven dollars after the money he gave to Mee-maw. That leaves me with four.

He hands me the four and I force a smile as I stick it in my pocket.

"But," he adds, narrowing his eyes and thumbing through more notes. I wish I had as much money as him. "I know a way for you to earn thirty dollars. How's that?"

I nod eagerly. "Sure. What do you need?"

"Come back here at start up tomorrow, before school. Think you can manage that?"

"Absolutely, sir." I grin and turn on my heel. I turn the corner of the shelves so quickly I don't spot anybody standing there and collide with them so hard they grunt and go back a step. "I am so so—Oh, it's you."

I was sorry until I realized who it was.

Kane shoves me away with his good arm and picks up the bag of potato chips that he dropped on the ground mid-collision. "Is somebody gonna serve me or what?"

"Mr. Martin," I call, and the man appears behind me but my eyes linger on Kane's black T-shirt and faded blue jeans with the rips on the knees. He ruins so many of his pants, but I think he does it on purpose because other boys in school have started doing it. Ripped jeans are in now.

14 YEARS OLD

Kane stares him down despite the fact Martin has over a foot of height on him but the man is oblivious to it.

"Right you are," he says and walks on ahead. "What have you got there Mr. Jessop?"

Kane shoves the chips in his direction as I leave the store.

"Salted are my favorite too."

"Seems we have a few favorites in common," Kane replies, and I wonder when his voice got deeper. It seems more like his father's now than his, and his legs look stronger. Or maybe I'm just noticing him in ways I didn't before. Is that my hormones manipulating me? I can't stand him but I also can't stop looking at him. It's like in my twisted brain the meaner he is to me the more I want him to like me.

I race home with my four dollars and a skip in my step. I have money. My own money.

The next morning, I leave extra early, Mee-maw isn't around and Grandpa doesn't care. I'm fortunate. I worried I might have to lie because if she thinks I'm working she might try and take more money from me.

The grocery store and the rest of town is so quiet and still a bit dark. Did I come too soon?

I approach the glass doors and jolt when Mr. Martin appears like a dark omen from between the dark shelves.

He smiles at me, showing his crooked teeth and unlocks the door. The bell jingles above and I jolt again when he locks it behind me.

I'm jumpy today, I think it's the excitement of having so much money within my reach. I've never had that much money.

Ever.

"This way," Martin calls cheerily and leads me into the staff office where he does all his paperwork and talks on the phone.

"Umm..."

He flicks on the light within and holds the door open for me. I don't know why but something is screaming at me to turn back.

14 YEARS OLD

That niggling feeling I always get when it comes to him is now lighting an inferno in my stomach that is making me extremely nauseous.

"Come on," he urges, grabbing my arm and yanking me inside. He points to a stack of boxes on his desk. "Help me move these to the corner there."

Is that how I'm going to earn the money? By lifting boxes?

I start to move the first one. It's heavier than it looks.

"Here?" I ask, straining as I walk to the far corner of the cramped office.

"Perfect." He brings the next one over and we do this until the desk is clear. "Now, help me move this."

He starts tugging on a filing cabinet, it's metal and heavy but we manage to shift it some.

"Have you got a boyfriend, Imogen?"

I shake my head and follow his next instruction which is to move three more boxes while he starts putting papers into the filing cabinet.

"Pretty girl like you? That's surprising."

"I'm not allowed a boyfriend," I reply, crinkling my nose up.

"Ah, your mee-maw is a nice church going lady. I imagine she's a good influence on you. Though your momma never did listen when she should have."

I lift a shoulder.

"Bad egg that one but looks like she gave life to a good kid. You're a very sweet girl. Very conscientious."

"What does that mean?" I ask, excited at the thought of learning a new word.

"Conscientious?"

I nod once.

"Well it means you think about things, I guess. You're very smart, very dignified."

I make a mental note to look up the word later for a better definition. "It's my new word of the week."

He chuckles quietly and suddenly reaches out to grasp a lock of

14 YEARS OLD

my chestnut brown hair. "It's softer than it looks. I wish my hair was that soft."

I shift to the side and laugh cautiously. "That's silly."

He laughs too and brushes his fingers down the back of my arm. It sends spasms of displeasure coursing through my body. I sidle away again.

"So, no boyfriend... have you ever been kissed?"

My cheeks heat.

"Don't worry, I won't tell your mee-maw. It'll be our little secret."

I look at the clock on the wall and frown. "I should probably go."

"Don't you want your thirty dollars first?"

Biting my lip, I turn to face him and back up a step when I see how close he's standing.

"That's okay," I whisper when his hand curls around my arm and his thumb rubs my skin. "I really should go."

"No, no," he says flippantly and bends, so his face is level with mine. "You're in no rush. School doesn't start for almost an hour."

"I know but—"

He places his finger to my lips. "A hundred dollars."

I tense because I know I've made a grave error. I'm probably not leaving this room until he gets what he wants and I don't think he needs my help around the store.

"I'm okay. But thank you, Mr. Martin."

"I just want to teach you how to kiss," he implores gently, his tone non-threatening but his words have tears filling my eyes. This is a grown man.

"I don't want to learn."

"Two hundred dollars."

The thought disgusts me but that's so much money. Could I kiss him? It's just a peck on the lips right?

"I don't want to kiss you."

"That's okay, we can do other things."

My back hits the wall when he starts to tug on his belt. My eyes go wide. Is this happening?

"Your momma used to let me. I used to give her a hundred dollars every time she put this in her mouth. I'm offering you two hundred."

I feel sick.

I jump at the sound of somebody making a crow noise from within the store. It's loud and screechy and it couldn't have come from anywhere else.

"What in God's name?" Martin hisses and moves to his desk. He pulls out a Glock and quietly loads it when another crow noise has us both looking at each other. This one is closer than the last.

"Did you tell anyone where you'd be?"

I shake my head frantically. Though I really wish I had told somebody, namely my brother.

He opens the door slowly and peers out into the dark store.

I hear footsteps running towards the front of the shop.

"WHO'S THERE?" Martin booms and steps out. He shrieks with pain and falls to the floor with a thud, that's when the sound of a gun popping has me shielding my ringing ears. I scream and drop down into a crouch, wrapping my arms around my head.

Mr. Martin groans and the air fills with a tangy scent as blood starts to pool from beneath him.

"Oh my God," I breathe, unable to comprehend what I'm seeing. What is happening?

"Come on!" Kane yells at me, extending his hand over Mr. Martin's body that's blocking the doorway. "Don't step in the blood."

His eyes are wide and alive, the blue is vibrant with excitement and fear. His long hair is tucked behind his ears but some of it is cutting across his face in a different direction to his parting. I don't know why I'm noticing these things, like the fact he's wearing the same clothing as yesterday, or the fact he's here at all.

"Come on! The cops are coming, that shot would have been heard for fucking miles! MOVE YOUR ASS!" He grabs my bicep with his uninjured arm and yanks me towards him.

I carefully step over the puddle of blood that is growing by the second, and the lifeless man that I'm almost certain was about to hurt me. I knew it too, yet I still came. I had a feeling but I just thought that he's an adult so he wouldn't, but then look at Mee-maw. She's an adult and she hurts me all the time.

"Wait," I utter, pulling back when Kane starts to drag me away.

"We don't have fucking time."

I drop to my knees by the blood and reach carefully into Martin's back pocket. With some yanking, I get the wad of cash free, watching his closed eyes for any sign of life. He's still breathing.

Kane grabs me again as I pocket the money and we run from the store which he unlocks using his sleeve.

We go around the back and duck down an alleyway between homes, then cut through somebody's yard and keep going until we're almost at the school.

He stops me suddenly. Panting as much as I am from the exertion.

"You went there to help him move shit around and then you left for school," Kane says, shaking me to get my attention. When I don't immediately look at him, he pinches my cheeks with his finger and thumb. "Give me your fucking eyes, Imogen. I need to know you hear me."

"I hear you."

"Okay. But only if they come to you. Don't go to them."

I start to look away again, unable to hold the intensity of his gaze but he gives my cheek a gentle pat and presses my body into a brick wall.

"Immy, repeat it."

"If they ask, I left for school and he was... he was fine."

"Exactly."

My brows pull together. "Did you shoot him?"

"What? No!" He pushes a hand through his hair and snags on the knots. "I put a board on the ground with a nail on it. He fucking stood on the nail but I didn't know he had a gun. He shot himself the dumb fuck."

I close my eyes and tears leak from the corners. "Maybe we should just tell somebody."

"Give me your fucking eyes." They ping open and he shoves me hard against the wall. My head aches where it hits it and a gasp chokes me. "How fuckin' stupid are you? Huh?"

"What did I do?"

"You never should have gone there, you seen how he looks at you!"

He's right, I ignored the signs.

"You're so stupid, Imogen. So fucking stupid." With another shove, he steps away and leaves me shaking and reeling. "Go to school. Stupid fucking cunt."

"Don't talk to me like that," I yell, running up behind him and pushing him by the shoulders, he stumbles forward a step before spinning to face me, fury in his bulging eyes.

"Then stop being so fucking dumb and naïve!" He spits at my feet, his blue eyes glowing with rage. "And keep your mouth shut. Don't let me remind you."

Sirens pass us by, and he doesn't even flinch, he just carries on to school like it's no big deal that he just almost killed a man. Or aided in his fate at the very least.

26 YEARS OLD

"Are you fucking insane? What you're going to smash up a dead lady's home to get my attention?"

"Always had to be extreme with you, Immy. You fucking loved it when I went wild for you." He brings the cigar to his lips and pulls it into his mouth before releasing a waterfall of smoke that he sucks through his nostrils. The effect is mesmerizing.

"So... what?" I ask, dazed by him for a moment. "This is you going wild for me?"

He eyes me with a dark gaze as he blows the smoke away from us both. "This is me wanting to talk."

"We've got nothing to say to each other."

"We got everything to say to each other."

I shake my head and wrap my arms around myself. "Say what you want to say then. I'm not promising I'll listen, or even care, but I'll make a good effort to trick you into thinking that I'm doing both."

Looking me up and down, he rolls his tongue over his lip. Why does he do this? Stare me down like he's searching for all of the cracks in my mask while working out how to break them.

"You left," he says simply, ignoring my harsh tone and words. "You fucking upped and left."

"Yep."

"You didn't say goodbye."

"Nope."

His brows pull together. "You didn't say goodbye to nobody."

"Anybody," I correct and he throws his cigar on the ground and pops a piece of gum into his mouth.

"Your fancy ass can't handle the way I talk no more?"

I don't want to admit to him that the way he talks still makes my stomach flutter. "Get to the point, Kane."

"Been a long time since you said my name like that, babe."

"Wish I'd never had to say it to begin with."

He chuckles and rolls his shoulders but then his face returns to how it was. Guess I'm not escaping this "talk" that easy. "You gonna tell me why you left?"

"Because I was done with your loser ass," I retort harshly. "Wanted better than you. Wanted better than this."

"You weren't complaining when you were bouncing on my cock on the back of your bike, in the back of my car, in your mee-maw's bed and every fucking place else you made me put my dick in you."

"I was a dumb kid. I thought you were the best I could get. Worshipped you. Had you on this pedestal because you were the hottest guy in school. That's all it was."

"Yeah?" he asks, his tone bitter, his teeth gritted. "What the fuck changed, Immy?"

"We didn't have shit! I was tired of having nothing." I press my palms against his shoulders and shove. "You gave me nothing but shit."

"That's a fucking lie and you know it!" He pushes me back, just like when we were kids, but not as hard. "We had it all. Might not'a been much, but what we had was everything."

"It's cute that you thought that." With my fingers scraping my hair back, I smirk at him, relishing in the confusion in his gaze, the

26 YEARS OLD

pain hidden in their depths. Even now, after all this time there's pain. "I was playing you, Kane Jessop. That was my plan, right... make you fall for me and leave you high and dry. Revenge for all those years of torment."

"Fuck you. That ain't the truth and we both know it." He charges at me until my back is against the side of the house and his cigar and mint scented breath is fanning across my lips. "What we had was fucking insane but it was our kind of insane. It was real." He presses his forehead to mine, angry, bitter, enraged and barely hanging on. "So *what the fuck changed?*"

I look away.

"Oh no, you don't get to avoid me. Not again." He grips my face with his hand and searches my eyes. "You look at me when we're talking."

"We're done talking."

"No we ain't!"

"Then *I'm* done talking!" I shout.

"NO YOU AIN'T!" he booms so loud the neighbor's dog starts barking.

"Let go of me."

"Naw," he holds me tighter. "Not letting you run from your past anymore. Time to face it, Immy. Time to face me. Why did you leave?"

"Because I couldn't be here anymore." My tone this time is softer, more defeated. "If you're so bothered, why didn't you come for me?"

He punches the wall by my head but I don't flinch. I stopped flinching a long time ago. "I fucking did come for you. I didn't stop looking for you."

"You're lying."

He steps back, eyes flashing with hurt. "Am I? What the fuck do you know about it since you weren't here?"

"I know you didn't find me!" My bitterness at past events is being displayed in a way I don't want it to be.

"I FUCKING TRIED!"

We stare at each other, hurt, hearts heavy, love lost.

"Just go," I beg, wrapping my arms around myself. "Please. Kane. *Just go.*"

"Not until you tell me why."

I sniff and wipe my tears on my arm, ducking out from under him so I can put some distance between us. "I hope you never find out."

Mom knocks on the window, drawing our eyes to her darkened front beyond the glass. She's holding my phone.

"Webber," Kane grunts and spits on the ground. "He the one that got you that fancy car? Those fancy clothes you're wearin'?" He stalks me back towards the house. "How much he pay you to fuck him every night? Wrap those thighs around his hips so he gets his three minutes? How much you worth these days, Imogen?"

I feel something hit my back and my entire body tenses with rage beyond the type of rage I've ever felt.

"Take my whole wallet on your knees with my cock in your mouth."

Turning, I look at the wallet on the hard, cold ground, and then at him with a furrowed brow and a dropped jaw. Is he for real?

"You think being vicious at our age is fun, or sexy? It's not. Clearly one of us has outgrown the other." I kick his wallet at him and pull out mine. "I'll give you everything in my wallet to fix my fucking car so I can go home."

"Thought I was your home, Immy?"

"Once upon a time so did I." I yank open the back door and slam it shut behind me. I'm shaking, I'm devastated, my body is cracking open and spilling out feelings I long since locked away.

He hits it with his fist and screams an elongated, "FUUUUUCK!"

Less than a minute later I hear a bike in the distance and know that it's him driving away.

14 YEARS OLD

I approach Kane, something I've never done before, desperate to speak to him about what I heard this morning. I hug my books to my chest and keep my eyes down.

Ren wags his brows at me, stitches no longer visible at the corner of his mouth from when I hit him. He has almost healed.

"Save me," Ren jests, jumping onto Mallick's back and making them both fall into the lockers behind them.

I shift my bag up my shoulder and stare at Kane's collar. This is the first time we've spoken since that incident a week ago.

"Can we talk?" I ask him.

"You gonna look at me?"

I raise my eyes and huff. "What is it with you and eye contact?"

He doesn't reply, just stares at me with a disinterested and vacant expression.

"*Can we talk?*" I repeat, with attitude this time.

"What's in it for me?" His friends lean closer, all of them interested in whatever this is between us.

I bite my lip and give him an urging look.

14 YEARS OLD

"You gonna show me your panties?" His arrogant grin makes me want to punch him in his stupid fat head.

Shaking my head with disbelief, I go to walk away and I'm surprised when he shifts in order to follow.

"Woooooo!" Ren cheers, laughing loudly when I glare at him. "Kane's getting midday laid!"

"Shut up Ren," both Kane and I chorus and their group around them laughs.

I glower at Kane as though it's his fault we spoke at the same time, but he just grins down at me and pops a piece of gum into his mouth.

Maisy, who wasn't even in this corridor when this began, skips over to us and throws her arms around Kane's neck. She plants her lips on his and steals the gum out of his mouth, all the while keeping one eye on me. That's gross.

I make it obvious that I find her vile.

"What are you guys doing?" she asks him, her tone whiny and annoying.

"Be back," Kane whispers to her, sucking on her lower lip for a moment and I wonder what that feels like. My cheeks heat and I look at everything but them.

"But—"

"Mais, get the hell off my neck," he says firmly and pushes her away. "I go wherever the fuck I want."

She guffaws as though she can't believe he just spoke to her like that. What on earth did she expect? *It's Kane!*

I lead him through a door to the right, not realizing it's a closet and immediately regretting my decision.

"This isn't science class," I mumble, feeling like an idiot for not paying attention to the door numbers. In my defense they all look the exact same. It's confusing.

"This is intimate," Kane comments, laughing lightly.

"I didn't realize it was a—" I blow out a breath of frustration. "It doesn't matter. We *need* to talk."

His eyes narrow into slits and his lips rise at the corners. "I told you, you gotta show me your panties first."

I punch his chest, right in the middle and he goes red faced with a cough. I can tell he so badly wants to react. I got him right in the diaphragm.

"Can you not be serious for one minute?"

"I was being serious," he rasps. "Figure since I saved you from being molested, the least you can do is show me a bit of what I'm missing."

"You're gross. I will *never* show you my panties."

"You really think so?" His tone is hushed and bitter, his eyes glowing in the dim light that comes from the glass pane above the door. It highlights the dust particles in the air making this small space sparkle. "Sounds like a challenge to me."

I go to hit him again to get his attention but he grabs my wrist and holds it tight.

"He's fucking dead, Kane," I hiss, ignoring his pain and kicking an empty metal bucket out of the way. "This isn't time for jokes. What are we gonna do?"

"Relax," he says with a roll of his eyes. He looks better now. The pain must have passed. What a shame. "They're closing the case."

"What?"

"He fucking shot himself. We didn't do anything wrong."

"I know but—"

"Except for you because you stole something from his pocket." He grins evilly. "Didn't know you had it in you to be honest."

I think of the money I hid inside the seam of my schoolbag, underneath all my books, the only way to get to it is through a hole in the inside pocket which I made to stash my phone. It has been burning a hole there for a week. I've been terrified of spending it in case they somehow know I stole it and are tracking it. It's stupid really, but what if it's possible?

"I didn't do anything," I lie and his brow jumps.

"Sure you didn't. I ain't seen nothin'."

14 YEARS OLD

I blow out a breath, feeling a little bit relieved. "Okay. So we're okay?"

"We're okay." He twists a lock of my long chestnut hair around his finger. "Now show me your panties."

"Stop asking me that, you pervert." I shoulder past him and shove open the closet door. It hits Ren who was eavesdropping on the other side and because he screams like a girl, everyone looks our way. *Everyone.*

"I've had better to be honest," Kane calls, fiddling with his jeans like he's only just pulled them up.

I gape at him, horrified, and then look around at my peers.

"I despise you," I tell him, making sure he can hear it in my tone and see it in my eyes. "I *despise* you."

"Man, did she give you a blowjob?" Ren asks quietly as I rush away.

Kane doesn't reply but I know he's enjoying every moment.

I really do despise him and everything about him.

15 YEARS OLD

"OH MY GOD!" I screech, covering my eyes and turning away because Poppy is legitimately straddling my brother and they're both butt naked.

"OH MY GOD!" Poppy shrieks and I hear movement.

"Sis!" Matthew yells as though this is all my fault.

"I didn't do anything!" I cry, feeling around for the door handle but I end up knocking a bottle off the top of his dresser. I must have turned too far.

"It's okay, we're decent," Poppy pants, sounding breathless, which is *so gross* and I hear the bed dip.

I peek through my fingers first and look at my best friend in nothing but my brother's T-shirt who is beside her. "When did you start having sex?"

"Like a month after we started dating," Poppy admits with a shrug. "It's not a big deal. Everyone does it."

My brother, looking smug and icky, with his bare chest and his open pants and his flushed cheeks, winks at me in a brotherly way.

"Mee-maw might have killed you if she caught you."

Matthew shrugs and puts a cigarette between his lips. "I don't care. What are you doing walking into my room anyway?"

"Laundry," I snap, scowling at him. "I thought you were out."

"You didn't hear the bed creaking?" Poppy asks, giggling like it's hilarious.

I motion to the door with a sweep of my arm. "The radio is on."

"She just wanted to see me naked," Poppy jests, lifting the T-shirt to flash me her nude body. She's developed too, much like I have, except my breasts are bigger as they always have been.

"You're such a whorebag," I mumble, looking away.

"And you need to live a little. Buy some hot clothes and put yourself out there. You're wasting your life here."

Matthew nods his agreement. "You're wasting away. You've become Mee-maw and Grandpa's slave. And every night I hear you crying in your sleep."

Wow. I can't believe he just called me out like that.

"Is that why you don't want to do sleepovers anymore?" Poppy asks, looking concerned.

"I have nightmares, I can't help it." I don't tell them why I have nightmares. I don't tell them that every day for the past year I have been terrified that the police are going to knock on my door and take me away for Martin's death, or the money I stole and still haven't spent. I don't tell them that I can't get his lifeless face out of my head and that sometimes I wake up paralyzed with him sitting at the end, staring at me, bleeding from every orifice while he masturbates his disgusting, crooked penis.

"Come on." Poppy stands and looks for her clothes. "Live a little, let's go shopping. I know you've got savings. You've been doing that paper route for over a year."

I shake my head. "Mee-maw takes all the money for that. Puts it in savings."

They both gape at me and Matthew instantly gets angry.

"Why the *fuck*, do you let her do that?"

He stands and starts to dress, cigarette hanging from between his lips. This place is going to stink of smoke and Mee-maw is absolutely going to notice. Not that he cares.

"I've had enough."

"Leave it," I beg, not wanting to cause any trouble for our grandparents. As strict as they are I don't want to hurt them.

"No, Mee-maw is treating you like a slave." Matthew pulls on a clean T-shirt as Poppy also dresses.

"Matthew," I beg. "Don't! Please don't. Because she'll think I've been complaining."

"YOU SHOULD COMPLAIN," he booms, shrugging off Poppy's hand when she places it on his shoulder. "You're so fucking weak, Imogen. You need to stand up for yourself. You need to live!"

"I'm not weak," I yell back, hands balling into fists by my side. "I just—"

"*I just*," he mocks, making his tone high and whiny. "*You just* let everyone treat you badly. You're going to end up committing suicide or shooting up the entire fucking school, Immy. You can't go on like this!"

I've thought a lot about the former though the latter hasn't crossed my mind, I have considered smothering the old cow while she sleeps.

"What do you want me to say?"

"That you'll stick up for yourself," he bellows, gripping his hair with both hands. "Fucking stick up for yourself!"

I want to scream at him. I want to tell him to mind his own business but I can't because he's right but it's all so much easier said than done.

"It's not that simple, Matthew!"

"Fine, if you won't tell your mee-maw how it's gonna be," Poppy interrupts, smiling sadly at me, "then at least stop letting her control every fucking aspect of your life."

"You don't get an opinion when your momma just bought you a car," I state simply and huff. "Fine. I have *some* money saved up."

Poppy's brown eyes sparkle with excitement. "How much?"

"About seven hundred dollars," I answer and chew on the inside of my mouth. "Give or take."

"How—"

"Where—"

They both ask at the same time.

I don't want them to think I'm a total loser but I also don't want to out myself so I lower my voice and reply, "I stole it."

They both gape at me.

"You're lying," Matthew hisses, narrowing his hazel eyes on me.

I shake my head. "I'm not. I stole it from Mr. Martin when he tried to make me have sex with him. I was fourteen. Then he died like a couple of days later so I never spent the money and I never told anyone."

So it's a different version of the truth but it works.

"He did what?" Matthew grits. He's so clearly affected by my confession. "Did he hurt you?"

I shake my head. "He didn't get the chance. I ran."

"Oh my God... that's horrific but also badass." Poppy throws her arms around my neck and squeezes so hard I can't breathe. "Why didn't you tell me?"

"I worried somebody thought I might have had something to do with his death."

"Did you?" Matthew questions, smirking.

I lie again, it's too easy to lie, "No. I didn't hear about it until after school."

They both believe me and both promise to take it to their graves.

I am getting so good at lying. Too good. It's becoming easier to lie than it is to breathe.

26 YEARS OLD

I call the garage, it's only nine in the morning but I need to know what's happening with it. I also need my things because I really want a shower.

"Faceless Mechanics, Emmy speaking, how may I help?" a young sounding woman calls cheerily after answering their local phone.

"Is Ren there?"

"Ren? I think so." There's noise as the phone clatters on the wooden desk. "Yeah, he's working on some fancy-ass black Jag I think it is."

"That would be mine," I say cheerily, and laugh when she starts to splutter an apology. "Can I talk to him? I just need to know where we're at with the fancy-ass black Jag."

"I can do you one better, the boss-man just walked in." Her tone becomes sickeningly sweet when she calls a friendly, "Hiiii Kaaane."

"Morning, Emmy."

I hate the way he says her name. It sounds too much like Immy. I'm the only Immy in this town.

Why am I feeling jealous over a fucking name? There's something wrong with me.

"It's the lady calling about her car."

"Imogen?"

"I didn't get her name."

There's rattling and I consider hanging up but I'm not a complete dick.

"Imogen?" he repeats but louder this time because he has the phone in his possession. "Or have you gotten your mother to call for you?"

"It's me," I respond after a second. I needed a moment to register the fact I'm hearing his voice and how different it sounds. It's so deep and sultry but also gravelly and rough. Everything you want a man's voice to be. "How goes my vehicle?"

"It goes nowhere. I need to source the part we need."

"Fuck."

"We can if you want to."

I bristle. "Don't be a pig."

"You said it."

I roll my eyes. "That's not what I—!" I stop myself when I start to sound hysterical. "Please just fix my motherfucking car."

That latter part of my tone wasn't much of an improvement.

"I'm tryin' Immy. We don't got the parts on hand is all. I'm heading to Leander in twenty to see what they got. If they have it I will have you back on the road in no time. Okay?"

"Okay. Thank you."

"My my, looks like becoming a city slicker got you some manners."

"How do you know I'm a city slicker?"

He laughs loudly. "Apart from your pristine shoes, shit car and the fact you have a boyfriend called Webber?"

"Fair point." I find myself grinning, transporting myself back in time to when we were allowed to make each other laugh.

He clears his throat and his tone changes. "So I'll pick you up in thirty minutes or less."

"Who? Me?"

"Not speaking to anyone else, am I, babe?"

I should fucking hope not. "I'm not going anywhere with you."

"Why not?"

"Because it's a bad idea."

"Because why?"

I laugh nervously. "Because it's you."

"And? Can't an old *friend* take you out for a kickass breakfast?"

My stomach pangs with hunger and I consider it despite all the alarm bells ringing in my head.

His chuckle sends a shiver down my spine. "You're thinkin' about it."

"Kane... we can't."

"Why? Because of Webber?"

"That and because I'm not the girl you knew."

"Seen it, don't believe it. You were the girl I knew when you cussed out your mee-maw in front of the entire congregation. You were the girl I knew when you sprayed me in the eyes with that fucking mace." His voice rolls through me like warm, liquid silk in my veins. "Why won't you tell me why you left, Imogen? The real reason."

"Because it doesn't matter anymore."

"It'll always fuckin' matter!"

I press my lips together and rest my head on my hand. "Why do you need an answer so badly?"

"Closure," he snarls. "I need fucking closure. I deserve it after all that time I spent looking for you."

Did he really? I can hardly believe it. I don't know if it's true at all but would he lie?

"What if the closure doesn't bring closure?"

"What does that mean?" He goes silent and I just know he's drawing his own conclusions. I'm waiting for it, waiting for what his mind conjures. "Did you fuck somebody else? Is that what it was?"

I open and close my mouth, unable to find the words and because of my hesitation to reply, I hear the phone crack. He's squeezing it way too hard.

"Was it somebody I know?"

"I... I don't know what to—"

"*Did you fuck one of my friends, Im?*" he demands, his tone strained and angry. "You better answer me."

"Would you hate me if I did?"

"Yes," he replies, sounding as hoarse as I do. "Who was it? Which friend?"

"It wasn't a friend," I whisper.

His silence drags on for an age, though his hoarse breathing can be heard loud and clear.

"Marshall," I add, feeling my chest crack open and spill me heart right out of it. "I had an affair with Marshall."

I hear him beat the receiver against the desk three times before the line goes flat. Disconnecting the call on my end, I stand and move towards the stairs and just look at them to help take my mind off this pain I feel. I stayed on the sofa last night. Unable to venture up to my old room, my prison, my old life. I don't want to get transported back to that time.

"Why did you tell him that?" Mom asks me, sneaking up behind me with a coffee in her hands. "What's the point in hurting him after all these years?"

"He asked for it, Mom. He wants to know why I left. He wants closure. I'm giving him closure."

She squeezes my shoulder and nods sadly until I push her hand away.

"Oh don't try and love me now you phony ass bitch."

Her hand slaps me across the back of my head making my ears ring, though I'll not give her the benefit of a reaction. "I am still your mother!"

Rolling my eyes, I leave the room before I punch her in the face for hitting me first. I stare into space for a while and reply to the messages on my phone. There aren't many, most of them are from

Webber, some are from my friends in the city, one is from my client.

Around twenty minutes later there's hammering on my door so loud the house shakes.

I freeze because I know it's him and I don't know what he'll do now that he has his *"closure"*.

"I've got it," I say to *that bitch* and move to the door quietly.

He keeps hammering on it until I open it and the moment I do; he shoves it so hard the handle bangs on the wall behind it. I see a sprinkle of plaster hit the wood floor and frown. I just mopped there yesterday.

I'm about to tell him to calm down when he holds my car keys out to me and drops them on the floor between us with a clatter before I can grasp them. He kicks them further into the hall and I watch them go, following the movement with my eyes and head.

I inhale sharply when he tangles his fingers in my hair and rips my head back. His lips slam down over mine so hard my teeth mash against the satin underside. I taste blood and feel bruised as he crushes our mouths together in a punishing kiss.

Releasing my lips but not my hair he hisses, "Fixed your car."

"Meaning you're the one who fucking tampered with it," I argue, I don't know why I'm surprised. "All that about not keeping me pinned was just for show. You knew I'd be coming back."

"Biggest mistake I've ever made, not includin' fuckin' you to begin with."

"Excuse me while I pretend that hurts." My bravado means nothing, he can see I'm feigning strength, and my lip trembles as I realize what this means. "Thank you."

He pulls harder on my hair and pangs of pleasure tingle up and down my spine making me whimper. "Now get in it and get the fuck outta my town."

I fall back when he releases me and watch him through tear filled eyes as he walks away, slipping on shades as he goes and lighting a cigarette when he hits the end of my long driveway.

It's funny, I've been gone for so long, yet it hurts just the same as before.

"Kane," I call, choking on a sob as the reality hits me.

"Fuck you, Immy," he states, giving me his middle finger over his shoulder. But then he turns and raises his hands to the sides. He wants to be finished but he's not. "You know what's worse is I knew. Deep down I knew. And I asked you and you made me feel bad for not trusting you. You were nothing but a lying coward. You still are."

He's right, I was a coward, I still am a coward, but he'll never understand why. Not until he walks a day in my shoes with my memories and the pain I keep locked tight.

"I'm so sorry, Kane."

"Bite me," he replies, shaking his head. "Never want to see you again, Imogen Hardy."

"Didn't I already try to make that happen?" I snarl back, feeling defensive because his words hurt despite the fact I deserve them.

"Then you'll do a great job the second time around."

I watch him go until I can't see him anymore and then I close the door and lean against it, rubbing my chest as though that will take away the painful throbbing of my heart.

"I'll get the gin," Mom utters softly but I shake my head and look for my keys.

"No. I need to leave."

"Don't rush off." She reaches for me but thinks better of it. "Stay. Please."

"You never stayed when I asked," I snap, scooping them up off the floor and swinging them around my finger. "I can't be here. Especially in here. I don't know how you can stand it."

"Imogen." Her tone is pleading but I'm not interested. I stopped being interested a long time ago. That's the funny thing about relationships like this, people only start to care when you finally stop.

Without a goodbye, I leave. I'm not about to hang around. Not again.

15 YEARS OLD

I've never owned a bra before, not like this. Mee-maw gets me those girly vests with the little bow in the middle, but this is unreal. I've never felt so supported and had better looking cleavage.

I laugh with my best friend as we try on outfit after outfit, bra after bra, walking in and out of the changing rooms, looking sweaty and disheveled from the workout. That's one thing they don't show you in movies, how much effort it is to keep getting changed.

I see myself in jeans for the first time, high-waist jeans that hug every inch of my curves, a grey crop top only held up by my boobs and shoulders. I test it out, raising my arms to see if my nipples appear at the bottom but there's a fabric insert that keeps them safe.

"These are so comfy," I say, turning every way, looking at how the dark blue denim really accents my figure. I'm finally getting a figure. Seemed unfair that I got my period before I was hit with a womanly body, but now I have the body I always desired. I don't look like a little girl anymore.

"Buy it," Poppy urges, resting her chin on my shoulder. We look at each other in the mirror and grin. She's so pretty and she's always been there for me even when Mee-maw wouldn't let us play together. She got over that with the influence of our local reverend, thankfully.

"She'll never let me wear it."

"It's your body, it's your choice."

"I know." I inhale for courage and let out the breath, praying it takes away my nerves with it. "I'm going to buy it. I'm going to wear it to the patch tonight, and I'm not going to let Mee-maw hit me."

"YES!" Poppy cries and rips the tags off the clothes before I can stop her. "No use in getting changed to get changed."

"I want to shower," I whine.

"We'll shower at mine, don't worry." She tosses some bras into the fabric basket and all but drags me to the till. "You look amazing."

"I feel amazing." I also feel terrified, nauseous, sick, and guilty, but feeling like my own woman for the first time, trumps all that.

We meet Matthew outside and Poppy immediately takes the joint from his lips and takes a long pull of the peculiar smelling smoke. She offers it to me but I shake my head. "I prefer alcohol. Weed makes me tired."

"When have you tried weed?" Matthew asks, laughing like I'm hilarious.

"I haven't, but you keep smoking it around me and it always knocks me out."

Grinning, he walks us to Poppy's car and opens the trunk. I chew on the inside of my cheek when I see the bottle of vodka, half a bottle of whiskey, some flat looking soda and a crate of beer bottles. "You gonna party as hard as we do tonight?"

Nodding, I pick up the vodka bottle and untwist the cap. "Shall we start right now?"

I take a gulp, choke, spit it on the ground while laughing and then take another gulp before high-fiving my brother. We all pile into Poppy's car and Matthew and I don't stop drinking until we reach her house where we take it in turns to shower, apply makeup, do our hair, and then finally walk to the patch with our alcohol.

15 YEARS OLD

"I love your hair," Poppy tells me for the hundredth time.

"You're only saying that because you tamed it," I reply, hearing myself slur and hating it immediately. It feels weird and I want it to end, but then I also want another drink to make it worse. My hair has always been naturally curly and wild, thick ringlets if it gets too short. The longer it is the less of a twist it has but it's so thick and heavy that I usually just braid it. Today Poppy convinced me to leave it down and she blow-dried it for me after my shower and used some kind of sweet scented oil through the ends.

Also, I found a body spray that smells like salted caramel. I never want to smell like anything else!

Music plays from a huge portable speaker, I sway my hips to it and close my eyes. I'm not one to dance but the alcohol has made me feel as though dancing is a great idea right now.

"FRESH MEAT!" somebody yells, I think it's Ren who must have just arrived. And it is very rare to see Ren without Kane.

Great, just what I need, Kane Jessop.

I open my eyes while wondering why that sounded more like excitement in my head. It was meant to sound like bitter hatred.

"Oh my God," Poppy says and starts laughing hysterically.

"What?" I ask, snatching a beer from my brother.

"They're talking about you! They don't know it's you."

My cheeks heat as I feel Ren approach and Matthew glares at him over my shoulder.

"Who's the new girl?" Ren asks as I turn. "Great ass—oh my God it's Prudence."

"Prudence?" I question, frowning at him as he circles me like a vulture and whistles long and low.

"As in you're a prude but damnnnn... look at this tight body."

Gross.

"Don't be a fucking pervert," Matthew admonishes and squares up to Ren. "That's my sister."

"It was a complimentary observation." He raises his hands in defense and backs up with a huge and playful grin on his face. His black hair is getting long and shaggy. I wonder if he's copying Kane. Nobody can pull off long hair like Kane. "On a less skeevy note, you look beautiful, Immy. You should dress like that more often."

"Where's Kane?" Poppy asks, knowing I'm secretly dying to know. Not because I want to see him but because I need to know if I'm going to.

I need to mentally prepare myself for his insults.

"He's somewhere knocking about." He puts one finger to his nostril and sniffs dramatically.

"He's not on the heavy shit is he?" Matthew asks and I'm still wondering when they became pals. He looks genuinely concerned. "Has he got any Es?"

My eyes go wide as I take in what my brother just asked for.

"It's not a big deal, Immy," Poppy whispers, sliding her hand around the bare skin of my back. "It's all fun and games."

"Until somebody dies."

Poppy lifts a shoulder. "That's not gonna happen. Come on. I need to pee."

I leave them to their drug dealing and follow Poppy around the bonfire.

There's an old abandoned trailer at the very tail end of somebody's property. We all use it for the plumbed in toilet and the owners stopped trying to tell all the local kids no because they all started egging their property. So now they simply leave it open with notes asking us to keep it clean, which the majority of us do. The boys piss outside, usually in the lake or bushes and the girls use the trailer.

I finish my beer and toss it into the pile of glass bottles about twenty yards away. My nose is starting to tingle.

"Do you need to go?" Poppy calls through the wall as I lean against the side of the trailer.

"Nope. I'm not breaking the seal." I don't want to pee all night.

I hear the door to the toilet creak shut and lock and laugh to myself when she turns on the tap so I can't hear her relieving her bladder. I don't know why people get so amused or embarrassed by toilet related sounds. We all have to do it. It's a natural thing.

As I'm contemplating weird things through an alcohol infused haze, A footstep crunches behind me seconds before a large, warm hand slams over my mouth.

I scream against the palm until Kane laughs in my ear like my reaction is hilarious. I was terrified.

"Show me your panties?"

"Get lost, Kane," I snarl, turning and shoving him so hard he goes back half a step. Well don't I feel weak. Half a fucking step. That's it. Because he's a wall of muscle and I hate him for it. "That's not cool. You freaked me out."

He takes me in, eyes lingering on the bare strip of skin at the top of my jeans. Then he strokes my arm from my shoulder to my elbow. "If you want me to stop, you know what you've got to do."

"Show you my panties? You're sick." I push his arm away. "Stop touching me."

"Why? You like it." His grin is arrogant and gross but it also makes me feel warm inside.

"I do not," I lie and we both know it's a lie. I hate Kane Jessop but his touch has my entire body trembling every single time.

With a lingering look he points out, "You're drunk."

"A little bit," I admit, looking at Poppy when she stumbles down the stairs of the trailer and falls onto her knees.

I forget about Kane as I laugh so hard I can't see straight. I bend over and try to tug her up but she almost pulls me down with her.

"Everything hurts," she says around a hoarse laugh. We can't control our hysterics. That was too funny. The little *eep* noise she made, the squeal that sounded like a pig in fear.

I'm genuinely laughing so hard I cannot breathe. I hug my stomach, still reaching for my best friend when two other girls step over her to enter the trailer. They're laughing too.

My brother who appears out of nowhere, scoops her up, lifting her until she's standing and pushes his grinning mouth against hers.

They make out with tongues, still laughing which makes it look gross and messy. And I back up directly into Kane who I had completely forgotten about.

"Hi," I utter turning to face him, still giggling and out of breath. His hands come to my hips to steady me, large and strong and so hot through my jeans. "That's so gross, right?"

I make a noise in my throat when Kane's hand tangles in my hair at the base of my neck and yanks. He towers over me, bending my head back, exposing my throat and forcing my lips to part. With hands splayed against his chest I remain still, like a deer in headlights, like a possum before it plays dead.

His eyes hold mine which must be wide like a startled animal. The blue in his glows in the dark and his lower lip shines from where he just licked it. It gives off a menacing glint, like a weapon in a movie, except this weapon isn't deadly. No, not deadly. This weapon is soul destroying.

"You're hurting me," I lie, still startled but unharmed. In fact my entire body is a live wire right now. I've been plugged into something powerful and I'm tingling all over. I'm glowing from his touch so bright they could probably see me in space.

"No I'm not," he replies on a whisper, still holding my eyes. "Wet your lips," he breathes and I immediately comply, feelings twisting in my stomach as he watches my tongue roll over them before they roll together. He groans, going slightly cross-eyed. "Do it again."

Once more my tongue tastes my lips and then roll together and he backs me up into the trailer side. It's cold against my shoulders through the thin fabric of my shirt. His hand presses against the curve of my spine, against my bare flesh. He holds me in place, just in case I run.

"And again," he orders, watching my face with furrowed brows and a pained expression.

I can feel him against my hip but I pretend I can't. He's rock solid and I can't breathe.

15 YEARS OLD

"Again," he whispers and I hear Poppy and my brother sneak away per Poppy's instruction.

I do it once more and he gets closer.

"Just once more." His voice is so quiet, his eyes so focused, his brows furrowed.

"Why?" I ask quietly, and gasp when his hand slides over my ass, grips it tight and yanks my body tight against his.

He doesn't explain with words, he doesn't tell me that he wants me. He doesn't need to. The way he is handling me says it all. And I'm not about that. I'm not going to be his toy, not anymore.

My hand stings when I slap him, sending his face to the side. Nobody has ever touched me there before.

"Not on your life, Kane Jessop," I hiss in his ear and shove him away from me. "Not if you were the last man on earth."

"OOOOOOH!" Ren and two others cry. "BURRRN!"

Kane tenses and I burn with a raging fire.

"God," I growl as his friends appear from around the side of the trailer. This was all for show, it was all for them. "I fucking despise you, Kane Jessop."

"PRUDENCE SWORE! SHE FUCKING SWORE!" Ren cries dramatically. "My dick is so hard right now."

One of his buddies pushes him onto me but I move out of the way and run after my brother, letting Kane's heated blue gaze burn into my back.

"COME BACK HERE PRUDENCE!" Ren calls dramatically and in jest. "COME BACK AND SWEAR FOR ME AGAIN!"

That was mortifying.

Poppy throws her arms around my neck, forcing me to dance with her in the thick of around thirty other teens. Some I know, some I don't. I drink another beer and shoot another shot. My body moves to the music naturally despite the fact I've never danced like this.

It's freeing. It's crazy. I can't believe I'm here and I'm doing this.

15 YEARS OLD

"YASSSSS QUEEN!" Poppy screams for no apparent reason and everyone raises their fist to the starry night sky.

Best night of my life so far. Minus the Kane part.

And also minus the Maisy part that follows when my brother and Poppy vanish and I need to use the toilet, I brave going alone. Big mistake.

"Look at you trying to fit in," Maisy calls as she follows me away from the crowd with two of her girls. She's dressed to impress that's for sure. She's wearing the shortest skirt I ever saw and a top that ties around her neck leaving her entire back bare. I can see a piercing on her naval. I always wanted one of those. "Update, it didn't work."

I ignore her and continue on, frustrated when she rushes ahead and blocks my way to the trailer toilet.

"Maisy," I say, exasperated. "I'm just trying to enjoy my night."

"And I'm just trying to protect my boyfriend from weird little Mormons like you."

I shake my head gently and try to step around her but she moves directly into my path.

"I seen the way you look at him." She sneers, giving me a distasteful glance up and down like I'm dirt on her shoe and she's wondering how best to remove me.

"I don't look at him." I try again to step around her but again she blocks my path, this time putting us chest to chest. I'm happy to confirm that I have better titties than she does.

Unfortunately in my drunken stupor I fail to see the hand she raises and puts to my throat. I choke dangerously when she shoves me over by my throat only. I land on my back with a painless thud, though it certainly knocks the wind out of me.

"Stay away from Kane," she states around a laugh and they walk away, high fiving each other. They call me names as they walk away like words are supposed to hurt me right now.

I stay like this, winded and tired and drunk, just looking at the sky, wishing I was anywhere else. Well... I definitely don't wish to be at Mee-maws. My stomach churns when I think about going home to

15 YEARS OLD

be beaten, made to do no end of chores, have my money taken and my new clothes tossed in the trash.

No. My drunken brain doesn't want that any more than my sober brain does.

I'd rather die.

Yes. I would genuinely rather die than go back there.

I stand up on wobbly legs and almost fall again. I am way too drunk, yet my brain has never made so much sense. This could all be over in a heartbeat. I could escape this reality. I could escape these people and this abysmal life. I could flee it all. *In death.*

But how? What's the best way? A tall building? I live in the middle of fucking nowhere. There's a cliff but it's miles away. I could get Grandpa's gun and shoot myself. That would be quick and it would probably make a mess in Mee-maw's kitchen. Revenge and freedom all in one package.

But then that would look like a choice. It would look like I meant to do it. That would hurt my brother, Poppy... I don't want them to hurt. It'd be better if it looked like an accident.

I can't swim. *I can't swim.*

There's a dock half a mile down the way, it has a couple of rickety looking rowboats that fishermen use from time to time. I don't know how to row a boat but I'm sure I can learn. It doesn't look too complicated.

My feet move me in that direction and my heart begins to race, especially when the trees and brush put me out of sight of the party. It's so dark here, I can hardly see where I'm going.

This is the best idea I've ever had in my entire life.

I almost feel excited. I wouldn't have to be brave or strong anymore. Maybe I'll be reincarnated and come back in a better home. Maybe I'll just vanish entirely. Anything is better than this. *Anything.*

I pick up the pace, running now, a low branch slices across my cheek and the tears that fall from my eyes sting the shallow wound. I stumble and fall twice but pick myself up quickly. I don't look back. I don't have regrets.

I'm not even scared of this. I'm more scared of life.

The trees clear and I see the boats attached to the jetty. I start to walk, out of breath, and approach the wood that holds the rope keeping the rickety little boats in place. I untie it and wrap it around my arm. The boat rocks side to side, just looking at it is making me nauseous.

My adrenaline spikes, my heart is racing, beating a fast rhythm in my throat. I could actually do this. I could actually get in this boat, let myself float out and just drop in. Hot tears fall and my teeth chatter. I try to convince myself otherwise because my brother will miss me, but really he's all I have and he's never around anymore. I'm a burden to him. He'd be free without me. All I do is disappoint him with how weak I am. He tells me all the time that I'm weak, that I need to be stronger but how can I be stronger than I am?

The mind isn't a bicep. Mine is deteriorating. I'm tired, so tired. Not just of life but of sleep too. Of the nightmares, of the guilt, of the feeling that nobody truly loves me for me. Not even my brother.

I look around and nod. I'm resolute.

This is the best decision for everyone.

"Okay," I whisper and put one foot in the boat. "I can do this."

Fear is such a heady, consuming feeling. It's natural to fear an element you can't conquer. But my fear of living beats it until it's nothing and I sit down and shuffle until my legs are over the wooden edge and my foot is touching the wobbling vessel.

Tears are still soaking my cheeks despite my lack of feeling. That could be the alcohol but really I think I'm just numb to life now.

"What are you doing?" Kane's voice cuts through the silence. It really is quite silent out here. Beautiful too.

I grit my teeth and pull my foot out of the boat. "Why are you here?"

"Followed you," he admits, his voice deep and gruff.

I climb unsteadily to my feet and glower at him. His blue eyes are so vibrant, even in the dark. Maybe Maisy was right, maybe I do look at him in a weird way.

"Why?" I ask, forcing my anger through my tone. "Why must you always, always bother me? I don't do *anything* to you."

He lights a cigarette between his lips and smirks at me as smoke blows from his mouth. "Wanted to see your panties."

"You know what? Fine," I snarl. "You want to see my panties? I'll show you. I'll show you every single fucking inch of me if it means you'll leave me alone!" I yank up my crop top, forgetting that I don't have a bra on underneath and his cigarette falls from his mouth and lands on the moist earth. The warm, balmy air hits my breasts and my nipples immediately tighten.

I drop the top beside his dead cigarette and stand in front of him naked from the waist up.

"More?" I ask, slurring. "Want me to take these off? Want to see my panties?"

He stares at me, dumfounded, eyes wide and on my tits, lips parted and dry.

"I'm not wearing any panties," I whisper and he gulps. His throat bobs with it.

When I pop open the button, uncaring about anything right now, his demeanor changes. He seems to shake himself free of whatever stupor I put him in. With a quick move he scoops up my top and throws it at me. I manage to catch it against my chest.

"Put your shirt back on," he demands, scowling at me.

"You asked to see," I argue, holding it tight like a shield. "You asked. You always asked!"

"To piss you off!" he yells, looking at me as though I'm nothing. "Not because I actually wanted to fucking see you. Christ, Imogen, I'm not that desperate." He picks up his cigarette and throws it in the lake, then he pops another one between his lips and lights it. "But if you're desperate for a bit of me, Immy, I wouldn't mind getting my cock sucked."

I pull my top back on and level him with a glare. "Go on then. Get it out."

He snorts and inhales his cancer stick. "Naw, you'll fuckin' bite it."

"What is there to bite though? Heard you're smaller than my pinky."

"We both know that ain't true."

"Could'a been a candy bar in your pocket," I retort, referring to the trailer. "Didn't feel all that big to me."

"You felt many cocks to know what's big and what's not?" The way he says the word cock has me wanting to see it even more. This started out as a bravado and a bluff but now I think I'm being serious.

What am I doing?

I turn away from him. "Fuck off, Kane. Go back to your party and your girlfriend."

"Jealous?" he asks, sounding arrogant and snide.

God, I hate him.

"I could not give a crap," I reply and walk towards my boat that hasn't drifted too far. Grabbing the rope, I tug it gently back. "Go away."

"What are you doing out here, Immy?" he asks, his tone serious now, unlike before.

"Killing myself." I step into the wobbly vessel and almost fall but after a few seconds I find the courage to move and sit on a narrow plank. I push away from the dock but he steps on the rope I discarded, stopping me from floating away.

"Don't say stupid shit like that," he snaps, thick, perfect brows pulled together. He pushes a hand through his hair and grips it atop his head. "It's not funny."

I untie the rope from the boat and smile genuinely. "I'm not joking."

"Sure you are," he utters, watching me drift further away. "You wouldn't be that much of an idiot."

"Okay." I watch as the lake gets wider around me. My heart isn't beating anywhere near as fast as it was when I was half naked for the first time in front of a boy. But not just any boy, the boy I hate the most. "You don't care though, right? So just walk away. When they find my body in a few days, they'll say it was an accident because I can't swim."

He walks to the edge of the dock and glowers at me. "You're not funny."

"Not tryna be."

"Come back here or I'm going to get your brother."

"Why? You hate me right?" I question, teeth chattering again, eyes swimming with tears again, I don't remember when they stopped for them to restart. "I'm ugly, stupid, disgusting, desperate, hated, just like my momma, unloved. Isn't that alllll the shit you've told me through the years?"

"So what, you're gonna kill yourself because of shit I say?" He looks perplexed, like he doesn't know how to handle the situation and sadly, I'm so fucked up inside that I love it. I love that he's watching me do this. I love that he's doubting me. I love that he'll see my last moments knowing he didn't take me seriously. I want it to hurt him, I want him to feel it.

The power of knowing my decision tonight will haunt him forever only drives my resolve.

"Absolutely." I reach for the oars, unsure on how to hook them on. "Go on, run along and tell people. By the time you get back it'll be too late."

"Imogen, come here," he orders and the tone of his voice has me wanting to row back, just so I can punch him in his dick.

I manage to rig the oars to the rusted metal resting things, and then I start to row... *badly*. I turn in almost a full circle and feel a spike of rage when Kane laughs. He still doesn't believe me and that only makes me want to do it even more. That's how messed up I am. That's how tangled I am inside.

When I feel I'm far enough out and the sparkling black water is glittering beneath me, I pull the oars in and touch the water with my hand. It's freezing but I hardly feel it. I start to wonder if there are predators in here. Will I get bitten before I drown? Will I drown or will I miraculously learn to swim?

I look at the party in the distance and the dwindling fire. Everybody is leaving, it must be late.

"I'm not kidding," he calls.

"Neither am I." I stand up, hips aching as I try to keep balance.

"IMMY!" Kane barks, sounding panicked now. That's unusual. *Thought he didn't care.*

"Yes, Kane?"

"I'm leaving. You can throw your little temper tantrum by yourself."

"Okay," I reply. "See ya."

I pinch my nose and ready myself. I can do this. Drowning isn't painful I don't think. It might make me panic but inevitably it'll bring me peace. I hope so anyway. I've read about it. I've read about all kinds of different ways to die. I find it far more fascinating than I should.

I sway a little, lift one foot over the side of the boat as Kane walks away and my drunken state does the rest. My entire body hits the water and the cold immediately assaults my senses. My eyes sting, my mouth fills with salty fluid and I automatically grasp at the surface. My fingers splay as my feet kick and my entire body aches. I've never been in water like this before. It's hard to move and the fact I'm drunk isn't helping me at all. My body is heavy and the further I sink, the more I panic and the heavier I feel.

My lungs start to constrict painfully, and I start to change my mind. This isn't painless. I'm not slipping away. This is torture. I don't want to die, not like this. I want to run away. I want to see the world and leave this place behind. There's got to be something for me out there. There's got to be more.

And I'm not going to see it.

I'm not going to experience any of it.

I have nobody to blame but myself. I should have waited, I should have thought this through.

I try to scream but swallow water, and the dark murkiness claims me as the moon drifts further away. It is consuming, drowning, there's pressure in my chest which feels like it's crushing me. My stomach feels heavy and my throat is burning. I need to breathe. I need to breathe so badly but I can't keep my eyes open.

So this is what death feels like.

"Fucking breathe, damn it!"

My body retches and water gushes out of my mouth and nose. Rough fingers push away my hair and the world spins around me when I open my eyes, which blur in and out of focus. I sit up slightly, slumping over somebody's sodden thighs.

He hits me on my back, on my chest, everywhere until I can breathe relatively normal again.

I cling to the back of his wet T-shirt as he yanks me up to a more upright position.

I'm about to ask if I'm in hell when he drags me to my numb feet with a hand at my throat and another around my bicep. My legs buckle from the weight of my soaking wet body and I feel his arm shaking, he's tired.

We both fall and he gives up trying to lift me and rolls me onto my back. His finger and thumb pinch my cheeks painfully and he shakes me until I look into his glowing, furious blue eyes.

"WHY WOULD YOU DO THAT?" he yells, baring his teeth, water dripping on my face from his hair and his glistening skin. "Why the fuck would you even try it?"

I smile and then laugh humorlessly. "I told you I was gonna."

"There are so many people in the world who would love your life."

"Trust me, Kane," I bite out, looking him directly in the eyes. "Nobody would love my life."

"You're fucked up." He scans my face as though seeing me for the first time. "You're so fucking mentally deranged. I swear you're so—"

"Fucked up. You just said. Like I don't already know." My smile fades and my bottom lip trembles. "I'm drowning. I'm still drowning. Even though you pulled me outta that water, ain't nothing gonna change. I'm still gonna be drowning and you're not gonna be able to save me next time."

He pushes away from me and stands, trying again to drag me to my feet. "Get your crazy-ass up."

I flop when I right myself, unable to muster the energy to be present in this moment on two feet, but he catches me and starts rubbing my arms with his hands.

"What the fuck do you want from me?" he questions harshly. "You want me to stop asking to see your panties? Is that why you did this?"

"Not everything is about you!" I snarl, trying to push away but my heavy body can't handle the weight. "I guess I'm just crazy."

"Yeah y'are." He hugs me when I start to tremble. A tender move for him. "We need to get warm."

"I need to never go home again," I admit, walking with his arm around my waist. "Ever."

"Home life hard on you?"

"You have no idea," I murmur, wondering why I'm telling him anything at all. He doesn't care.

The fact he doesn't ask just shows he definitely doesn't care.

We walk, both of us gaining strength as we make our way towards town.

My legs are like lead under my body. Every step is pure, heavy agony.

I stop and sit on a wall that edges a front yard, then bury my face in my hands after pulling my thick hair over one shoulder.

"Come on, it's fucking late. I want to go to bed." His tone holds frustration, but I just don't give a damn. "Immy."

"I'm not asking you to stay with me!" I snap, rubbing my temples to alleviate my pounding head.

15 YEARS OLD

"But it's not like I can fucking leave you!" he yells back.

"Why not?" I question, annoyed that he's still here, annoyed that he saved me even though I'm relieved he did. "Why are you always there. Why do you call me names, treat me badly, torment me, hurt me, and then save my fucking life?" With what little strength I have I stand and approach him. "And then tell me to get dressed when I offer you the one thing you've been asking for since we met." I laugh breathily and place my palm against his chest. "You don't want my panties. You don't want me alive. You don't want me dead. Then what do you want?"

"I don't want anything."

"Then go and leave me the fuck alone."

He steps closer. "Don't tell me what to *fucking do*."

Rolling my eyes, I step around him but then stop. My heart is hammering as I remember what I felt in the depth of that water.

"What now?" He's referring to the fact I've stopped.

"I don't want to go home." I'm not kidding either. I really don't want to go home. I can't go back to that prison, that hell.

"Ever? Is it really that bad?"

I hug myself and wet my lips. I'm so thirsty. "Do you have Poppy's number?"

"Nope."

"Oh." I stare at the spaces between the houses, considering sleeping in somebody's shed. That's how much I don't want to go home. "Can I stay at yours?" I loathe to ask but I don't have any other choice. "And then tomorrow I'll go to my mom's. She has a place in San Antonio. It's like three hours away but there are buses…"

"Shit. You're serious," he mumbles.

Nodding, I look deep into his eyes. "It's all I'll ever ask you for. I need to get away. I'm going to die if I stay here." I look back the way I came and consider returning.

"Fine. You can stay with me." He grins after a moment, back to his usual arrogant self. "But you've gotta show me your panties."

I laugh, looking at the ground as I try to hide it from him.

26 YEARS OLD

"As I live and breathe," a familiar, raspy voice calls. I heard him coming because he came on his bike and I can't bring myself to feel bitter about it. "Imogen Hardy."

"Mr. Jessop."

He grins at me, that familiar smile that is so much like his son's.

"Mr. Jessop?" he questions, pretending to be offended. "When did we get all formal, kid?"

I stifle a groan when his wife, Kane's stepmom pulls up behind him on her dark pink bike with matching helmet and leathers. She's still as outlandish as I remember.

"I told you to wait for me!" she snaps with a thick accent.

"My bad, doll."

She strolls right past him and comes at me with her arms outstretched. "As I live and breathe. I heard you were in town."

"I see your accent hasn't reduced none," I comment, returning her hug and mimicking her accent.

"Don't you start now," she playfully admonishes and holds me at arm's length. "My oh my, aren't you just a beauty."

"I could say the same about you."

We share a smile and I hug her again. "It's so good to see you guys."

"You say that like we're the ones who ran away."

I wince. "It wasn't personal."

"We know. But it was somethin'." She moves to West, her husband aka Kane's father and looks between us both. "I bet you're wonderin' why we're here?"

"You'd bet right, not that you're unwelcome."

West steps forward and hands me a small envelope.

"What's this?"

He shrugs. "It's a letter from your mee-maw."

I bristle, ready to tear it in two but he grips my hand that holds the flimsy paper.

"She said you'd likely never come home, but you might come to Kane. Kane wanted nothin' to do with her, so I said out of respect as her dyin' wish, I'd deliver it to you."

I look at the paper burning fiery pain through my skin. "What's in it?"

"I don't know, she said it was real important and to open it when you're ready."

My chin trembles as I consider crying over the old hag one more time. "I don't want it. I don't want anything to do with her."

"What did she do to you?" Felicia tightens her dark blonde ponytail, eyes awash with concern. "I mean... other than what we already know."

"It doesn't matter anymore," I reply on a whisper. "She's dead. Where she belongs. I hope if hell exists, that's where she ends up."

15 YEARS OLD

"Well you can't stay on the couch, my dad will find you and call your mee-maw and then there will be no runnin' away," Kane hisses at me, arguing his very valid point. "He don't bother me in here." He peels off his damp T-shirt and drops it into a hamper by the door.

"Fine, but you're staying on the floor."

His brow jumps. "Like hell I am."

"Shh," I hiss, placing my fingers over his lips.

He bites the tip of the middle one until I pull away. As I'm shaking it to relieve the pain he chuckles and pushes down his jeans. He has mud and grass stuck to his legs from the lake and when I inspect myself, so do I. We're both filthy.

"Will I be able to shower?" I ask even more quietly.

Nodding, he moves to his closet and grabs a large gray towel, then he moves to his drawers and pulls out a T-shirt before slinging it over the top of the towel and holding them out to me.

"You're so neat and tidy," I comment.

He looks at his room as though seeing it with new eyes. "Naw. Felicia does most of it. Bitch treats cleaning like it's crack. She's got issues. Likes everything to match. Fucked up if you ask me."

"Your stepmom, right?"

"Mom," he corrects. "She's been a mom since we met."

My heart cracks and the center oozes through the broken pieces. "That's actually really sweet."

He shrugs, nonplussed and hands me the towel and T-shirt. "Leave the shower runnin' so I can sneak in when you're done."

"You're not going to ask to join me?"

When he gives me a heated look instead of laughing at my joke, I flee the room, padding quietly to the bathroom.

I make it super quick because I'm so tired. Washing my hair with Felicia's shampoos, washing my body with shower gel that smells like peaches. I love peaches. I also brush my teeth with an unopened spare toothbrush and pray they don't notice until long after I've gone. I hide it in the cabinet above the basin ready for me to use again before I sneak out in the morning.

I dress in the T-shirt, wishing I'd asked for some boxer shorts too. It smells so clean and fresh. I love fresh laundry.

With a sigh of complex contentment, I leave the shower running and give my hair a quick brush. Then I exit the bathroom and quietly slip back into Kane's room.

He passes me, bare chest brushing against my arm, and I notice that he's pulled back the bed covers. I search through his drawers, mostly to take up time but also because I need something to wear so I'm not so exposed.

I grab a clean pair of his folded boxer shorts and pull them on, then I slip under the cover, twisting my wet hair above my head, and get as close to the wall as possible.

It's so warm and snug. His mattress is a dream. I don't think it has any of those awful springs in it like mine. It's like laying on foam. Perhaps that's what it is.

Closing my eyes, I listen to the shower running and wonder if he's thinking of me right now.

Is he thinking of my almost naked body like I'm thinking of his?

Pushing that thought away I burrow deeper under the covers.

I tense when I hear him speaking to somebody in the hall and consider hiding under the bed but by the time I think of it, the conversation stops and the door opens. He locks it behind him, and I hear a drawer open then close. The towel hits the floor and I swallow and try hard not to think about it.

After another moment, he scratches somewhere on his body and switches out the light. Then the bed dips beside me and I find I can't breathe.

I expect him to make some lude comment and ask me to show him my panties, but he just groans and rolls onto his front away from me.

My entire body feels tighter than when I woke up on the riverbank and choked up a lung. My lungs still feel sore, as does my throat and body. I can't believe I did that.

"You better not snore," I say on a whisper and the bed shakes with his silent laughter.

"I really fucking hope you do."

I huff and tuck the duvet between my legs. I'm finding it so hard to relax next to him. This is the first time I've slept with a boy. It's crazy. I'm not sure I like it. I don't even like him which makes this all the more uncomfortable.

I toss and turn, fidgeting as I try to find a better position.

I can tell he's getting frustrated with me but I can't stop moving.

"I'll sleep on the floor," I say when he growls for the millionth time.

"Shut up," he hisses and shoves me onto my front. I turn my head so my cheek is pressing against my pillow and make a quiet squealing noise when his body treats mine like a mattress.

He presses his chest against my back and his leg over my thigh. His weight crushes me into the clean scented bed linen and his arm rests over mine, so his hand is resting on my wrist.

"Go to sleep," he demands, angry and definitely annoyed.

I puff out my cheeks, trying not to move though to be honest, I don't want to move. I've never been comfier.

"If you tell anybody about this, I'll come to San Antonio, find you, shave all your hair off and glue it to your back," he warns and my body shakes with laughter I sorely need. He covers my mouth with his hand, yanking my head back with it. My eyes cross because it feels good. I don't know why I like it. It should hurt but instead it makes me want to wriggle against him to see if he feels the same. "Quiet."

I do as I'm told, finally slipping into an easy sleep. Trying not to worry or panic about the future or how much trouble I might get into if I get caught.

Wearing clothes not mine, with a bag full of my savings, and my phone fully charged, sandwiches packed, and a belly not growling with hunger, I climb off the bus and step into San Antonio.

I've never felt like such a dick before. Why did I do this? This is terrifying. I have no idea where to go or if she still even lives here. I have no idea what to say to her.

But first I need to figure out how to get there.

I wander around aimlessly for a while, stopping at a little café on a bustling city street. I ask them if they know the area but they don't speak great English and then they usher me on when I ask their customers too.

My stomach is clenching with nausea. Why oh why did I do this?

I think back to this morning when Felicia caught me sneaking out wearing her clothes that Kane took from her closet. She could have flipped her shit and called my mee-maw but instead she sat me down, made me a killer breakfast and asked me about my night.

Kane wasn't here to save me, he'd already left for work at the garage with his dad. Kane whose chest I woke up on like it was mine to rest on. Kane who had his arms wrapped around me tight. Kane who did what he could to hide his morning boner from me so I wouldn't feel uncomfortable.

"I'm a virgin I didn't do anything," I blurted as she poured coffee.

"I ain't judgin'," she replied, smiling sweetly.

"I just needed somewhere to stay."

"Of course." She handed me a coffee. It was my first ever coffee. It's the vilest thing I've ever tasted. "I'm bettin' your folks don't know where you're at."

"No and please don't tell them. They know I'm safe but—"

When my eyes filled with tears she placed her hand on my wrist. "I ain't a mother, I ain't a role model, I ran away when I was a teen so my daddy wouldn't touch me no more."

Her story had my lips parting.

"I got myself into some heavy shit. It wasn't until I was seventeen and woke up on a strange lady's couch, gums aching from all the coke I'd rubbed on them, head spinning, stomach retching, that I finally turned my life around. She made me breakfast, she gave me coffee, she gave me a shoulder in those moments. A shoulder if I'd gotten it months before, I might not have become addicted, I might not have put myself in dangerous situations." She squeezed my wrist. "I know a lost soul when I see one. And if y'all ever need a place to crash, I ain't gonna turn you away. You hear?"

"You're so nice. My mee-maw would close the door."

She grinned and lifted a shoulder. "Well, she ain't no proper church goin' woman now is she?" She sipped her coffee and levelled me with a comforting look. "Sometimes, breakfast with somebody who cares can be the deciding factor between life or death."

I froze, going wide eyed. "Did Kane tell you?"

"I have no idea what you're talking about," she said in a way that let me know she knew exactly what I was talking about.

Then she rounded the table, kissed my hair like a mother should and gave my shoulder a squeeze.

I want to return the favor; I want to make her feel validated and reassured like I do. "I probably shouldn't tell you, but last night I called you stepmom to Kane."

"Hmm?"

"He corrected me and said you're his mom, not his stepmom."

Her eyes filled with tears immediately, but she smiled through them. "That boy has a big heart. It's just a shame he has louder fists."

Then I went to Poppy's and picked up my stuff, my bag with the money, my phone and my clothes. I messaged her telling her to let everyone know that I'm safe. I imagine they'll all be worried and that makes me want to go back even less. I don't want to see their disappointment in me. I'm such a coward.

I should have stayed longer. I shouldn't have done this. This city is huge and scary. I've never seen so many people in one place before. I'm pushed, shoved, stepped on, sworn at and almost fall onto the road twice.

Why is everybody in such a rush?

I find a traffic cop who is really nice and tells me the directions to get to where I need to be. When I tear up because it's all lefts and rights and streets I don't recognize, he hails me a cab.

It takes me all the way to Dellcrest Forest and stops outside a brownstone building with a broken front door and young men sitting on the steps. I pay the cab fare and hike my bag over my shoulder, hoping I don't get mugged and lose every penny I have.

Litter lines this street like sand lines a beach. I step over broken glass and rush up the stairs as the men cat call and make lude comments. Don't they know how fucking uncomfortable and scary that is?

"Apartment two-A," I whisper to myself and head up the piss stained stairs. It's so gross here.

I use my elbow to push open a door that leads to the few apartments on this floor, and quickly rush to the apartment I need. It's crazy thinking this could be my life now, that I might live here and have to deal with this every day. Would I get used to it?

15 YEARS OLD

I rap on the wood over and over again. "Please open. Please. Please. Please."

My heart is racing, my palms are clammy. I just need to be inside somewhere so I feel safe.

I knock louder, more frantic, until finally I hear my mom yell, "WHO THE FUCK IS IT?"

"It's me... it's Imogen."

"What in the world?" Latches unclick, a chain drops, and the door opens a crack.

My mom's hazel eye peers out into the hall and widens when she sees me.

"Immy, what are you doing here? Is your mee-maw with you cause I ain't done no cleanin'?"

"No, it's just me," I reply, smiling at her. "I just really needed to get away."

"Well then you better come in." She steps back, still peering into the hall as I sidle past and take in her tiny studio apartment.

It's not messy or unclean, but there are dishes in the sink and a pile of laundry that needs dealing with. There's only one bed but I don't mind sharing.

"Does Mom know you're here?" she asks, locking the door and guiding me to the small two-seater table. It has a wilting flower in a little glass jar in the middle.

"No. I ran away," I admit, biting my lip. "I can't take it there anymore."

"Oh it's not that bad."

I look at her incredulously. "Mom it's hell. Can I stay with you? I'll go to school here. I'll get a job. You wouldn't have to provide for me."

"Honey—"

"Please, Mom, please. I can't live there anymore."

"What about your brother? Don't you want to be near him?"

I shrug. "He's never home. He has a girlfriend now."

She nods gently. "Do you want a drink?"

"Can I have a water please?" I sit as she moves to the kitchen and rinses out a glass. "Can I stay? Please?"

"Honey—"

"Stop saying it like that. You're my mom. Why would you have me if you don't want me around?"

Her eyes round with sadness. "That's not it. I do want you around but look where I live! There isn't enough space for me, let alone you too. And it's rough round here. I don't know about the schools either. There was a random shooting on the next block." She hands me my water and continues, "Where you're living now is safe, and cozy, and comforting."

"That's why you stayed?" I snap, feeling bitter that she's not immediately excited to have me around. "Mee-maw is awful, Mom. She beats me, sometimes she starves me, she doesn't let me go anywhere or do anything."

"It's only for a few more years and then you'll be out on your own in the world. There are worst places to live."

Wow, is that really the response that a mother should have when her daughter tells her she's being beaten? Is that normal?

I glower at her. "You're not gonna let me stay, are you?"

"You can stay tonight, but tomorrow you have to go back. There's no space for you here."

Standing, I rub my eyes with the heels of my palms and clench my hands into fists. "You're a shit mom. I wish God never gave me to you!"

"Honey—"

I pick up her vase and throw it across the room. "DON'T CALL ME HONEY!"

"You're being unreasonable." She looks at the broken glass on the floor and the watermark on the crappy beige wall.

I move towards the door, angry and spiteful and delicate.

"I hate you," I hiss at her and stomp out the way I came.

"Imogen," she calls after me but she doesn't follow.

15 YEARS OLD

"YOU STUPID, STUPID GIRL!" Grandpa booms at me, his face red. "Do you have any idea how worried we were?"

"And how much shame you've brought upon us with your actions!" Mee-maw sniffs dramatically and dabs under her eyes with an embroidered hanky. "After the last time you broke curfew, you'd think you'd have learned but clearly you have your mother's poison in your veins."

She looks at my grandpa who nods.

"We called the police, we were worried. We had everyone out looking for you."

"I'm sorry," I whimper. "I'm sorry I wasted everyone's time and upset you and scared you. I'm just so tired of being trapped here in this perfect image. I just want to have fun."

"FUN IS PARTICIPATING IN A BAKESALE NOT DRINKING AND FROLICKING WITH BOYS!" Mee-maw yells so loud her voice sounds demonic. Grandpa starts to undo his belt. "You have humiliated us after all we have done for you and your brother and this is how you treat us?"

"Please try to understand," I beg, backing up against a wall when Grandpa flexes his belt between his hands. "Please... please... PLEASE!" His belt hits the side of my thigh making me scream and drop onto my hands and knees. "I'm sorry. I'm so sorry!"

He hits me again, this time on my back and Mee-maw stands and watches.

"PLEASE STOP!" I arch when he hits me again. God it burns and bruises. I've never felt pain like this. I thought Mee-maw's slipper was bad, but I didn't know the full extent of the kind of pain I could feel.

"WHAT THE FUCK DO YOU THINK YOU'RE DOING?" Matthew's voice is like cool water on lava. He dives at our grandpa and wrestles the belt from his hands. "You're sick! Both of you are fucking sick!"

"How dare you speak to me like that, boy?" Grandpa hisses, angrier than I've ever seen him. They square up to each other as Poppy helps me off the floor, whispering soothing words as I sob uncontrollably. My body hurts so bad. My skin is on fire.

"Swing for me, Grandpa, please give me an excuse to knock your frail ass down. Beating on a girl half your size and for shit you did when you were a teen," Matthew snarls and Grandpa at least has the gall to look slightly ashamed.

Mee-maw clutches her chest and her rosary beads. "Oh my, the heavens sent me such plagued children."

"Did you ever think that you're the problem?" I ask her, hiccupping slightly. "Did you ever stop to think the damage you've caused us all by beating us and treating us the way you have?"

"I have punished you accordingly for your sins. No worse than my mother punished me as a child and I turned out just fine!"

Well that self-proclamation is entirely laughable, if I wasn't so distraught.

"I need to sit down," Grandpa whispers and moves to my bed. He sits on the mattress side and he too clutches his chest.

Is there no end to their mind games?

"You didn't turn out fine," I say to her, clinging to Poppy for support. "You're a controlling, horrible woman."

She looks hurt. "I only want what's best for you."

"I need some water," Grandpa rasps, flexing his left arm.

Matthew loses his rage and moves to the old man's side. "Are you okay?"

"No," Grandpa hisses and everybody goes quiet. For a moment his eyes go glassy as he stares ahead. He lets out a horrifying choke and falls onto his side on the floor.

"Oh my God," Poppy whispers and pulls out her phone. I'm too shocked to move. I thought he was laying it on heavy like Mee-maw does. "I'll call an ambulance."

Mee-maw screams and rushes to her husband's side, shoving

Matthew out of the way. She clasps the old man's hand. "Don't you leave me now, Regen. You hear me? Don't you dare leave me now."

"My chest," he chokes, struggling for breath.

I press my hand against it, crouching beside him. I can feel it racing under my palm. Its rhythm is erratic.

"DON'T YOU TOUCH HIM!" Mee-maw shrieks at me, shoving me so hard I fall onto my sore rear. "You did this! YOU!"

26 YEARS OLD

"You ain't goin' nowhere till we've had us some lunch," Felicia admonishes, and West Jessop tosses me his helmet.

"I've got a really long drive," I utter, feeling bad when her eyes flash with hurt. "But lunch would actually be great right now."

I pull on his helmet and follow him to his bike.

"You know I got you," Mr. Jessop says softly, lifting his leg over his huge Harley and motioning for me to do the same.

"Go on now," Felicia insists and I climb on behind him.

"Where are we going?" I ask though it sounds muffled.

"To eat, like I said."

"And to find out why the hell you ran away all those years ago," West adds and shoots forward before I can climb off and run again.

15 YEARS OLD

Mee-maw hasn't spoken to me since Grandpa died a week ago. Though she held my hand at the funeral today as she wept at his graveside. I shed a few tears too. He was my grandfather after all and I loved him, I still love him.

Matthew hasn't taken it so well, he blames himself, but Mee-maw blames me. Matthew is male, he can do no wrong. I'm starting to see this more and more the older I get.

I'd like to say it's nobody's fault what happened but what if Grandpa dying was God's way of punishing me for trying to take my own life? What if Kane Jessop never should have saved me and death needed to take a payment for his loss of my soul?

The service was beautiful, everybody in town attended. The wake was even more so. There's so much food, so many well-wishers and people who seem to genuinely care.

And of course in my grandpa's honor, bikers that he knew back in the day all rode ahead of the hearse. It was amazing. Kane's father, Mr. Jessop passed me his helmet and offered me the space on the back of his bike. Felicia encouraged me and told Mee-maw I'd be safe as they weren't going even half the speed limit. They were trying to cheer me up and for a short while it worked. I expected her to argue but she nodded and off I went, holding West Jessop's waist. Trying not to let my tears soak the inner foam of his helmet.

Mee-maw and I clean up together side by side in the living room after everyone leaves. Matthew is in the yard, smoking a cigarette and saying goodbye to Poppy. Or so I thought because I watch him through the window climb into Poppy's car and drive away. He doesn't come in to say goodbye and I bet Mee-maw won't say anything to him.

We move into the kitchen and place the clutter on the countertop. There is so much to do but that's good. It'll keep us busy.

"Do you need to sit down, Mee-maw? I can do this," I offer when she stops and looks at the dish in her hand.

She's trembling, she often trembles when she gets mad. I know the signs. I tense, ready for whatever might come my way.

"It was too much strain," Mee-maw utters, sounding so broken and defeated. "It was too much strain, what you did."

"I'm so sorry, Mee-maw," I reply softly. "I didn't mean to cause him any stress."

She stares at me for the longest time before throwing the empty plate in her grasp at me. It hits me in the head, cracking painfully against my temple before smashing on the floor. I feel warm liquid trickle down the side of my face and press my hand to it. Crimson blood highlights the grooves of my palm, making me look yellow and pale in contrast.

It takes a moment for me to register what just happened.

Oh my God. My head throbs angrily with an ear-splitting headache. I blink to rid myself of the dizzy wave that almost knocks me off my feet.

"If you'd just behaved as I raised you," she hisses at me, absolutely no remorse for the damage she just inflicted.

When she raises a cup, ready to throw that at me too, I run, fearful that she might actually kill me this time. I push open the front door and stumble out into the dark.

I don't have my phone, any money, nothing.

"You get back here!" Mee-maw shrieks at me but I keep going, keep running as best I can considering my state of dizziness.

My head isn't too bad thankfully. I go into a local gas stop and use the bathroom to clean myself up. It'll bruise but the gash stopped bleeding on the way here. It is so sore. I wince as I prod it and grit my teeth as I wash the dried blood from my cheek and hair and pull my braid over one shoulder.

What do I do now?

I could walk to Poppy's but it's all the way on the other side of town and she'll be with Matthew who I'm angry with for leaving me today. If he'd stayed, this probably wouldn't have happened. I walk for a long time, letting time pass me by. It gets colder and my arms ache from where I hug myself.

I figure Mee-maw might be asleep and I might be able to sneak in, so I go home to check but I see her through the window, sitting on the sofa with a glass of something in her hand. She's never normally up past ten. She's waiting for me and like hell am I giving her the satisfaction.

There's only one place left other than home.

I stand outside Kane's bedroom window and peer inside. His dad's bike isn't here, nor is Felicia's and I don't think his car is in the garage. The house is dead silent and completely dark.

Biting my lip and knowing I can't keep going for much longer, I push on the window, relieved when it slides open.

I'm mental for doing this but I really don't have any other choice. Frustratingly, it gets stuck halfway, but I can fit. I'm terrified a neighbor will see me and call the cops. Though I wonder how random it is for them to see girls sneaking in and out of Kane Jessop's bedroom window.

I turn over an empty plant pot, stand on it and climb in. Knocking something off his desk. It's a photo of him and his dad I discover when I crouch down to pick it up. I put it back where it was and find the same T-shirt I wore last time hidden in his top drawer. It's black with a picture of the demented teddy from Five Nights at Freddy's.

I peel off my clothes, drop them in the space under his desk so they're out of sight but also not a tripping hazard. Then I pull on the T-shirt but leave my panties and climb into bed.

I might never sleep anywhere else again, this bed is so comfy. It's like lying on a warm, cushy cloud that doesn't get you wet.

Well…

I think what's worse about this entire thing is, I feel safer in the bed of my bully than I do in my own at home. What a fucked-up world I've been planted in.

When Kane gets home sometime later, he curses because seeing me startles him. I feign sleep so he doesn't kick me out, although it's not a complete lie because I am half there. I was asleep when he turned on the light and woke me up.

I'm surprised when he sighs, switches off the light, rids himself of his clothes and climbs into bed behind me. Staying still, I keep my breathing calm and my eyes shut. The bed dips as he gets comfy and I almost squeeze my eyes tight when he shines a light on my face.

He leans over me.

"Imogen?" he whispers and his fingers brush my hair back, lightly touching the sore wound on my head. He seems to stare at it for the longest time before he turns off his torch, presses his chest against my back, his thigh between mine and relaxes.

16 YEARS OLD

"Move over," I hiss, giggling drunkenly when his eyes open, startled and confused.

He groans and moves to the edge of the bed so I can collapse face first onto my side. *My side.* I have a side. After a moment he rolls towards me and prods the back of my shoulder. "Why is this a thing now? You're a fuckin' bitch to me in school, why are you always comin' to my bed?"

"Your mattress is amazing," I reply, sighing with contentment. "Play with my hair."

"Play with your own hair," he argues but his fingers start stroking my scalp and pulling to the ends. A shiver rolls down my spine. "You've been drinking."

"Gin," I answer, closing my eyes and rolling my tongue over my minty tasting lips. "So much gin."

"With Marshall?" he questions, his tone mocking. "You got a thing for him now or somethin'?"

"Yep," I admit and think of a guy I've known since kindergarten but have never actually engaged with. He's gorgeous, on the football team, tall, dark and did I mention drop dead gorgeous? He also goes to church every Sunday so now I make it a point to also go with Meemaw every Sunday looking like a pretty little church going girl in reserved clothing with minimal makeup.

"Why?"

"You've seen him right? He is fine with a capital F." I keep my voice low so his parents don't hear.

"He's not into you. He has a type and you're a train wreck. Too much baggage."

"Fuck you, Kane," I snarl but choose not to let him antagonize me.

He shifts behind me, moving closer, making me hyperaware of his presence in this bed. "It's true. You don't do much of anythin' Prudence. Never seen him with a girl that doesn't put out. We both know you don't put out."

"Don't call me that."

He grins in the dark but then it fades and becomes a glare. "Why the fuck did you throw my gym bag in the pool today?"

"I don't know what you're talking about," I lie and pat his hand when it grips my hair tight and pulls backwards on my head. "Get off me you psycho."

"Shhh," he warns, grabbing my shoulder and rolling me onto my back. He looms over me in the dark scowling down at me.

"Did you know your eyes glow in the dark? But not in a good way, in a creepy way. Like animal eyes at night."

He crosses them for a moment, exasperated. "Do you want me to kick your drunk ass outta my bed?"

"I'd prefer it if you didn't, but also, I'm not going anywhere so deal with it."

"I could drag you out of here and toss you on your ass."

I flutter my lashes at him, feigning innocence. "And I'll tell your daddy that you smashed the front of your car into Mr. Bennet's wall and drove away so you wouldn't have to pay for the damages."

"You're such a bitch."

"You keep saying that like I care."

"Fine," he snaps and my eyes reopen. He looks thoroughly annoyed. "If I can't get you the fuck outta my bed with force, I'll just make you want to leave it."

"Do your worst."

His smug smile is so apparent, even in the dark. I still hate his arrogance. I still hate him. Even though he lets me stay in his bed on the odd occasion I need to crash, he's still an absolute dick to me in school.

He logged into my school account in the library and emailed all my teachers an image of my head supcrimposed onto a nude model's body. Luckily, they figured out I was hacked because Meemaw's well-behaved granddaughter would never do such a thing, and he's just lucky I didn't tattle on him. He'd have been in so much trouble.

So naturally I waited until he had to take in his final paper that counts for a lot of his calculus grade, and I dumped his bag in the swimming pool. It was a handwritten paper that he worked super hard on. So much fun.

Watching him grit his teeth and stand there with clenched fists before uttering my name was the best thing ever. Such sweet revenge.

"You really want my worst?" he asks quietly, and I nod which makes his smile malicious. "I know exactly what to do to get you out of my bed and back into your own."

"If you fart, I'm holding your head under the blanket."

"I'm not gonna fart," he breathes, trailing his fingers up my arm.

It isn't until I feel his breath against my lips that I realize he's about to kiss me. That wasn't what I expected to happen. I tense, ready to push him away but his head diverts, his lips brush over my chin and land on the center of my throat.

A spasm of hot pleasure hits me so hard my blood immediately boils. I inhale sharply. Nobody has ever kissed me there before.

His hair tickles the skin of my shoulders as his lips gently lift. I swallow, surprised by how intense that felt.

"You gonna slap me, Prudence?"

16 YEARS OLD

I shake my head and try to roll over but he pulls me back. "I want to sleep."

"Told you, I'm gonna make you leave," he whispers, eyes excited.

Scowling at him, I sit up and he follows. "If you want me to leave, Kane, all you've got to do is ask."

We stare each other down, my scowl versus his.

"Okay that easy, huh?"

I nod once. "That easy."

"Leave," he commands, and I start to shuffle to the end of the bed.

When my feet hit the floor I stand and look for my clothes.

"You're really goin'?" he asks quietly, still not wanting to wake up his parents. "Just like that. No fight?"

"It's your bed, Kane. I'm not a total dick. You want your space I'm going to give it to you."

"I'm not about to let you leave at this time."

I snort. "I fuckin' came here at this time. What's the difference?"

"Just get back in bed," he snaps, swinging his legs over the side and rubbing his eyes with the heels of his palms. The moonlight shines a blue sheen on the contours of his bare arms and back. He's so toned and lithe. I bet it's from all the work he does at his daddy's garage.

"Not unless you admit that you like it when I sleep with you."

This time he snorts so I start to slip my shoe on. I'm being stubborn and likely stupid but I can't help myself. Winding up Kane Jessop gives my life the kind of spice it didn't have before. Because these days I can honestly say I give as good as I get, if not worse.

I hear his footsteps approach and stifle a yell when he grabs me around the middle and tosses me onto the bed as though I weigh nothing. I bounce once and wince as my brain hits the forefront of my skull.

"Stop being an idiot," he hisses, nodding for me to move up the mattress.

I do so, because I'm too tired to keep up this game, and the moment my head hits the pillow I roll away from him and yawn into my hand.

When he rolls in my direction, just to piss him off even more I hiss, "Don't touch me."

He stops and I feel his glare pierce the back of my head. I just know he's pulling all kinds of faces at me right now. Still, he doesn't argue because that would mean admitting that he likes spooning me, which he often does when I stay. I will never admit that I actually quite like it too.

I still wake up sprawled across his chest at five when his alarm goes off, with his boner under my thigh and his arms holding me tight as they always do. Damn it. I swore to myself before I fell asleep that I wouldn't let this happen again.

He groans, a noise he often makes and presses his hips upwards, something he sometimes does.

I reach over him and hit the alarm on his nightstand and his hand travels down my body, gripping my hip to hold me in place. Something he has never done before.

I freeze when his hard length rubs against my most sensitive, untouched place. It sends a zap of pleasure up my spine and back down again.

He rocks his hips, pushing against me and I become extremely aware of the fact only his boxers and my thin panties separate us. He's still asleep, I can tell by the way he mumbles, but he rolls me onto my back and buries his face in my neck which is another experience entirely.

I grip his solid biceps and hold tight, unsure on whether or not I want him to stop. This feels so weird and so good.

I feel myself get wet between my thighs as he keeps rocking and I bite my lip to stop myself from crying out when his lips touch my neck. His tongue tastes the space his lips tease and a whimper escapes me. I can't hold it back and I know he wakes because his body becomes dry cement.

"Not dreaming," he murmurs.

"Nope," I confirm and he lifts his head.

A deviant smile takes over his handsome features. "Thought you never would, not even if I was the last man alive?"

And just like that I'm not horny anymore. "Get the fuck off me."

He laughs quietly and drops his body onto mine. "Show me your panties, Immy."

"You're such a dick."

Leaning into my ear, he bites the lobe and whispers, "Show me your pussy, Immy."

I don't know why but his words and the way he says them has my sex clenching with need. I hold his eyes when he lifts his head and know that he has sensed the change because his pupils expand larger than they were and his lips part.

"We're both gonna regret this," he utters so quietly I can hardly hear him.

His lips hit mine, desperate and greedy and I return it. Angry that he's made me feel this way. Angry that he's made me feel so much desire for him when I despise him like I do. His teeth lock onto my lower lip as our bodies move together. Our groins meet, his cock against the delicate folds that are swollen and wanting.

I grip his hair, meeting his kiss with equal fervor, trying to show him how fucking mad I am that he's doing this to me.

"God I fucking hate you," I whisper between kissing before his tongue dives into my mouth. Likely to shut me up. It works.

Holy crap.

I buck my hips up, needing more, needing him to hit the right spot but the right spot is too deep inside of me.

He reaches between us, still kissing me furiously and adjusts himself in his boxers but the back of his hand hits my clit and sends a zap of pleasure through me. Even more so than before.

He freezes and looks at me with wide eyes. "Jesus, Immy... you're so wet."

I grab his hair and pull his lips back to mine while fumbling with my panties and trying to push them down.

He does the same with his boxers. Awkwardly getting them low enough to kick them off entirely. Then he grabs the bottom of my shirt and pushes it over my breasts, sucking my nipple into his mouth before I get the chance to protest. Not that I would, but still, I didn't have time.

The feeling sends me wild, it's a mixture of pleasure and pain and the fear that he might bite or suck too hard.

"Do it," I beg when he lines himself up. I feel the head of him part a place that has never been touched before. I wince. This is it. This is happening. It's not something I've obsessed about but there's no going back once we've started. "Do it. Just do it."

"Fuck, Immy..." He looks so pained as he slips out of place but quickly puts himself in the right spot.

This isn't loving, or tender, or gentle.

"I should be kind and tell you I'm not about to be your first but I'm not a nice guy. I'm gonna fuck you, Immy. I'm gonna make you come, and I'm never gonna let you forget it." He covers my mouth with his hand and thrusts forward so fast I feel my virginity tear. I release a pained moan that he swallows as he rocks twice, ensuring that he's in as far as he can get.

He's so big, which I already knew but this is insane. I feel so sore and stretched yet the way he's kissing me and the way his body is on mine, lights a fire deep inside.

"I'm not even sorry," he breathes in my ear, slamming home again. "You're a fucking bitch, Immy." His hand tangles in my hair and exposes my throat which he kisses and bites making me sob with pleasure and pain but I like it. I like every second of it. "You're a bitch and I never want to stop fucking you."

I moan, long and unsteady as he pins my hands above my head and presses our foreheads together.

"Stop making noises like that," he growls, biting my ear. He gets faster, thrusting harder, reaching out and throwing his alarm away when it starts to blare. Our combined sweat glistens on our bodies and the blanket slides away. "Stop making noises like that, you're killing me."

"Shame," I pant, looking him directly in the eyes. "Because I'm not even nearly there yet and if you come before I do I'll never let you live it down."

He stops and stares at me right before a wicked smirk lights up his face. "That sounds like a challenge."

"Whatever makes me orgasm."

"Drop your legs," he commands. "Make them straight."

I do so and he adjusts his position so my legs are closed and his thighs are straddling mine. He's still buried inside of me but now the base of his cock is pressing directly on my pulsing clit.

My lips form an O when he rocks against me and I think I might get there way before he does.

"Challenge accepted," he breathes against my lips and kisses me again.

He rocks just as hard as before but slower now so I really feel every drag and every millimeter of friction against that sensitive bundle of nerves.

I hum, enjoying this way more than I want to let on and he kisses up and down the side of my neck. His hand wanders, exploring my body, massaging me as he thrusts. It feels insane. It's an entire range of feelings all at once.

I spiral so suddenly I don't feel it coming until my inside is literally twisting itself and exploding outwards.

"Oh God, oh God, oh... God," I groan, arching my back and digging my nails into his shoulders as the orgasm I never thought I'd have, attacks every inch of me. I've never felt anything like it.

Chuckling, he spreads my legs, hikes my thigh over his arm and powers into me, fucking me just like he promised. There's no pain at all anymore, just tingling pleasure as my orgasm carries on at a lower level.

I'm covered in sweat and so is he but it doesn't deter either of us from tasting the other's skin. He tastes even better than he looks. I can't get enough. I hold his body tight against mine as I do to him with my mouth what he's been doing to me and feel him unravel. He buries his face in the crook of my neck and grips my ass with his hands between my body and the mattress. Every thrust is a powerful, frantic drive as he swells and spills himself inside of me.

He yells so loud I have to bring his face back to my neck and finally, he thrusts once, then twice, jerks with a gasp, and drops onto me like a dead weight.

"Wow," I whisper, wishing I'd had sex sooner because I have been missing out.

I look at the broken alarm on the ground and squeal at the time.

"Get the fuck off me," I hiss, shoving him to the side.

He laughs, unperturbed, and watches me look for my panties. "You might want to shower first. You're covered in your virgin blood."

I glare at the mess on and around the apex of my thighs and scowl when I see him smirking with so much pride.

"If you tell anybody about this, I will kill you in your sleep," I hiss, pointing directly at him like an angry parent.

His grin stretches into a beaming smile. "Something tells me we won't be doing much sleeping from now on."

At that I laugh sardonically. "If you honestly think I'll be doing this with you again, you're deluded. You were okay but we both know I can do better."

His face darkens. "You're such a bitch."

"You made me that way."

"You'll want more. They always do."

"You're so gross."

He reaches into his nightstand, pulls out a cigarette and moves to the window to light it. "Be quick in the shower, I need to get your scent off my skin."

"Since I'm the one rejecting you, that doesn't hurt at all." I pull a fresh towel out of the closet and look at him over my shoulder. "Thanks for warming me up... you know... for Marshall."

16 YEARS OLD

I see his sneer before I turn and head towards the bathroom where I have the hottest shower of my life.

I managed to return to Mee-maw's before she wakes up, and I get thirty minutes in bed before I have to get ready for school. I have my own clothes now, but I buy them myself and launder them myself. Mee-maw doesn't approve of what I wear but ever since Grandpa's death almost a year ago she leaves me alone when she's not taking out her rage on me. I don't go out of my way to hurt her but I do my own thing now within reason, without getting into any trouble.

She hardly speaks to me at all anymore. It's sad because in between the beatings we had a great relationship but now she just wants to control everything I do. Her lashing out at me is more frequent despite the fact I don't actually do anything wrong. My grades are good, I don't dabble with drugs, I drink very rarely and don't get drunk when I do, I work at Ice-Queen, a new ice-cream parlor in town, I buy my own clothes, snacks, school equipment, and I go to church on Sundays.

What more does she want from me?

Though since I made friends with Marshall she's been a lot nicer to me. She says he's a nice boy from a nice family.

I agree.

He's sweet, funny, so adorable and good-looking and he has this stupid laugh that I love.

We've been hanging out lately, he walks me home from school and last night he met me at the patch for drinks. Not too many, but enough.

And then this morning I fucking had sex with Kane in his bed which I don't exactly regret because it was so good, but I do wish it wasn't with him because he's going to hold it over me forever. Either that or he'll just expect sex all the time now.

The thought makes me tingle down below.

I startle when Marshall meets me at the end of my drive in his truck.

16 YEARS OLD

His daddy owns a vineyard just out of town, so they aren't hard up for cash. It should intimidate me but I never thought about it until now.

"This is surprising," I say, eyes widening as I approach.

He winks at me, all tall with large shoulders slightly slumped forward due to his height. Another thing I adore about him, he has no arrogance whatsoever, so he doesn't have a swagger kind of walk, like Kane for example. He's popular without taking advantage and he's gorgeous without arrogance. "I wanted to surprise you so I'm glad it had that effect."

Laughing, I take his hand and climb into the passenger side.

I am so sore between my thighs. God, I ache. When I sit down I wince but he thankfully doesn't notice.

"Wait!" Mee-maw calls, rushing after us in her slippers and gown which is tied tightly over a neck to ankle nightgown.

"Everything okay, Mrs. Hardy?" Marshall asks and she hands him a bag.

"I made you both some lunch."

I look between the two of them, wondering when they conspired behind my back, but Marshall looks as perplexed as I do.

"Your momma gave me a call, said you might drop by this mornin'," she explains and smiles at me in a way she hasn't in so long. "Both of you have a good day at school."

Marshall walks around the car after thanking her, climbs in and places the bag between us.

"Throw it away, I think it's poisoned," I jest and he grins a toothy slightly lopsided smile.

"Mee-maw makes the best food in this county, I ain't tossin' nothin'."

"That she does," I agree, looking into the bag. "You know she's done this so we have to eat lunch together."

His smile broadens. "Well I'm glad she thought ahead. That's if you don't mind me joinin' you, Imogen Hardy?"

I lift a shoulder, feeling giddy. "Not at all."

26 YEARS OLD

I hold the pink coffee cup in my hands and turn it slowly. Felicia has been looking to me to answer her question for some time but I don't know how. What would I even say? How do I explain any of it? They wouldn't understand. They'd hate me.

"I don't know what you want me to say." I sip my coffee and hold her gaze. "What is it you think you know?"

"We don't know shit, kid," West admits. "You were in the wind. Completely fucking gone. The only reason we knew you were alive is because your mee-maw kept sayin' it but the Sherriff's office confirmed it. Never seen Kane so relieved when he got that call"

"Until they said you didn't want to speak to him and to stop lookin'." Felicia's tone is devasted and I feel it right there with her. "He still didn't stop though."

"Sure didn't," West utters, staring me down with a curious expression.

"We just don't understand," Felicia whispers, looking hurt. "We were all so worried about you."

West looks at me intently, his eyes imploring me to be honest with him. "Did my son do something to hurt you?"

I open and close my mouth.

"Did he?" Felicia asks. "You can tell us. We know you guys had a *different* sort of relationship."

She can say that again.

"Unhealthy," West puts in, frowning. "Abusive, perhaps."

"What Kane and I had is in the past."

"Does he know that?" West snaps, looking frustrated. He slams his hand down on the table. "Because he waited for you, he looked for you, he called the cops *every day* to find you. So if he wasn't abusive and you guys were okay, then why?"

Fuck. Kane wasn't lying. I had thought he'd moved on. But I knew he wasn't lying when he said that to me. This confirmation just makes everything harder to accept.

"Because she was fucking Marshall," Kane announces as he walks into the room. *Speak of the devil and he shall appear.* He leans against the archway that separates the kitchen from the dining room. "Ain't that right, Imogen?"

His blue eyes blaze with the same fury he exhibited earlier and all eyes, including his, pierce through me.

"And instead of telling me about it, she ran."

My heart hammers in my throat and my eyes burn as West and Felicia look at me with the utmost betrayal.

"Is that true?" Felicia whispers.

"You let all of us think the worst because you wanted to be with another guy?" West looks as though he can't believe it.

I look at my cup and then stand. "I should go."

"This time stay gone," Kane orders, looking as bitter as he sounds. My heart shatters as he looks at me as he did earlier, in a way he never has or did. I mean I thought he hated me when we were kids, but that was nothing compared to how much he loathes me now.

"She was just a kid guys," Felicia defends. "Come on."

I don't wait to hear what they say, it's right that they stay mad at me. It's better this way. I have a life to get back to.

16 YEARS OLD

Kane has been staring at me ever since I sat down alone with Marshall, much to the envy of almost every girl here. Sitting with Marshall I mean. I don't have a fucking clue why Kane is staring at me like he is. Though both could strike me with the envy of their admirers, they both have plenty between them.

And over the course of the next few days as Marshall and I get closer it's more of the same. Which is frustrating because I don't want Kane staring at me and I don't want to have to compete for anyone's affections.

The weekend passes and Marshall and I have our first date, officially. We go to dinner, he pays despite me offering, and then he walks me home and kisses me at the door, soft and sweet.

"You're so beautiful, Immy," he whispers, cupping my cheek.

I was on cloud nine all night, so much so that I couldn't wipe the smile off my face. Especially now when he seeks me out just before lunch break and kisses me in front of the entire cafeteria. Staking his claim.

Kane, who is sitting with Ren and Mallick by the trophy display, glowers at me like I did something wrong, even worse than he did last week. Truth be told since we had sex I've actively avoided him. He tried to talk to me yesterday, asked me how I was, I replied with a brief, "*fine,*" and went on my way. It was weird, he never asks me if I'm okay. Usually he just asks me to show him my panties, but I guess he's bored of that now I've actually shown him not only my panties but what lies beneath.

Now he has to know that I'm okay, especially now I have Marshall's tongue down my throat. The guy can kiss. It doesn't quite zing me the way Kane's did that night but I had consumed alcohol so that could be why. I try not to overthink it.

"I have to get to football practice," Marshall whispers, pulling away with swollen lips and flushed cheeks.

"Have fun," I reply, grabbing his shirt at the collar and pulling him back in for another kiss.

He grins and licks his lips as he backs away. And I lean against the wall watching him go.

"That was so hot," Poppy says, also watching Marshall go. "So hot."

"Right?" Selma, a newer friend of ours agrees, wagging her brows at me. "You joining us for lunch?"

"Absolutely."

"It's about time," Poppy jests, bumping her shoulder with my own. "I hardly ever fucking see you anymore."

"That's your fault," I scoff, and point at my brother who is talking to Mallick. "You always leave us behind for that loser."

"She's right," Selma singsongs and links her arm through mine.

"Screw you both, I dedicate more time to you bitches than you deserve," Poppy retorts, swanning ahead with a sway to her hips. "Besides, I can't help it that he can't keep his hands off me."

"Ewwww."

"So hot," Selma sighs and looks in Kane's direction. "I want what you both have."

16 YEARS OLD

"It's bliss, Selma. Pure bliss. I don't know how I'll ever go on if Matthew ever leaves me."

Wrapping an arm around her waist I put in, "He won't leave you. He feels the exact same."

"Does he tell you that?"

"All the time."

She looks at Matthew but her smile fades. "Kane Jessop is coming our way."

Selma's eyes light up and she smooths her hair. I roll mine his way but don't get chance to utter anything as he grabs my arm and demands, "A word?"

"I have a few of those for you," I reply, smirking.

"Not playing, Imogen."

I go cross-eyed at the girls who are interested in this exchange way more than they ever have been. "I'll be back. Prince of the dickheads wants my attention."

He starts dragging me away from them by the bicep, which kind of hurts but not much.

"Slow down," I snap as we go, ignoring the curious gazes of our peers. Everybody watches Kane Jessop all the time, but he's a volatile enigma. He's an ass to almost everyone and that only makes them want him more.

He yanks me around a corner, down an emptier hall. There's work being done to the few rooms at the end so the rest of the rooms in this area aren't being used due to noise. Though there's no noise right at this moment which is good. I have a feeling I'm about to get a headache.

He tests the first door on the right but it's locked. The second door isn't. He pokes his head inside and yanks me in after him. The room is dark, lit only by the sunlight through the closed blue roller blinds on the window. It's a science lab, nothing special. All the equipment has been put away leaving empty desks with little gas taps on them.

He slams his hand down on the door beside my head after

backing me into it and then pinches my cheeks with his other hand and forces me to look at him.

"Give me your fucking eyes."

"Give me a reason as to why you dragged me in here."

His brows pull together. "You're kidding, right?"

"No. Why would I kid about that?" He's so confusing.

He's also looking at me like I've grown a third head. "We fucked, I took your virginity, you don't think we should have a conversation about that before you jump another man?"

"What's there to converse about?" I snap, raising my chin defiantly. "We had sex, jeez, it's not a big deal. I enjoyed it, thank you. Is that what you wanted to hear?"

With his blazing eyes on mine he moves his hand from my chin to my hair. "What are you gonna do the next time you can't go home? Crawl into his bed?"

My mouth closes because I hadn't thought that far ahead.

"Reckon you can do that? Come to my bed and then go see him the next day? Do you think I could keep that a secret?"

"Kane," I utter, pleadingly now. "I really like him; you know I do."

"SO WHAT THE FUCK WAS I?" he booms, shouting directly in my face.

"Don't yell at me!" I shove his chest so hard he goes back two steps. "I didn't realize this was complicated."

"Yeah, well, it is complicated!"

"Why?"

"Because seeing you kiss him is making me so fucking angry, I can't see straight." Grabbing my hair and ripping my head back, he looks at my lips like they disgust him. "I gotta get the taste of him outta your mouth." His words are spoken more to himself and I have no idea what he's about to do.

Like a rabbit in headlights, I stare at him, frozen in time. At first I think he's going to kiss me but then his knee hits the back of mine and

16 YEARS OLD

I go down with a gasp. My shins hit the floor and I gape up at him, confused and shocked.

I don't register what he's doing until I feel his swollen, rock hard cock against my lips.

"What are you--?" I don't get to finish my sentence because he pushes his way in until the head of him is resting on my tongue and he's groaning long and low. He doesn't taste bad but I am livid.

I bite down, closing my teeth around his thick, jaw aching girth.

He grabs my hair and glares down at me. "Don't be a dick, Immy." Then he smirks while he pushes further into my throat making me squeak, and demands, "Suck it."

I want to tell him to fuck off, I want to bite, but my tongue rolls against the underside of him and he chokes on a moan that has my entire body lighting on fire. There's something so erotic about the noises he makes. I've laid awake at night touching myself, thinking of him and his noises. He starts rocking against me, guiding himself along my tongue and lips, whispering curse words as I make him wild.

Groaning, he grips my head with two hands and holds me in place, fucking my face now so hard I gag a couple of times. Yet even though I should hate it, I'm so wet, so needy, so turned on by this. My nose hurts, and my throat constricts when he pushes so hard his cock goes further than it should and my nose gets crushed against his body. He smells so good, so arousing and heady. So fresh and clean.

I hum, getting into this now as I get used to it, hollowing my cheeks as I suck. Smiling when he chokes on my name kind of like I'm choking on his dick right now.

"Fuck, Immy," he rasps, and when I look up his eyes are on my face. He plays with my hair, pulling it up to the top of my head with both hands. That feels nice too. "You're so fucking hot. I hate you but I fucking love looking at you with my dick in your mouth."

I bite down making him laugh and then he jerks, losing himself but before I have to swallow any, he pulls out, grabs my hair, yanks my head back and spills himself all over my face and my parted lips and tongue. I squeeze my eyes shut as he yells out his release, his voice husky and deep and desperate. His hot seed doesn't stop coming, there's so much of it. Thankfully, it doesn't taste as bad as I expected but I'm not sure I'd like a mouthful of it. His hand pumps his length with a violent kind of fervor, making his body jerk and his breath catch.

At last, he stops, releases my hair and zips himself up without waiting a second.

"Kiss him now," he states, that smug smile back in place. "Tell me what he thinks of your new flavor."

I stay here on my knees, stupefied for a moment as he turns back to the door and yanks it open. "Hey wai—" The door closes behind him and I can't chase him because I'm covered in his come. Like some porn star hooker, in a science class, while I'm dating another guy.

What the hell is wrong with me?

After cleaning myself up, not an easy task even with a sink nearby, I catch up with Poppy and Selma in the cafeteria who immediately notice a change in me.

"What happened?" Poppy asks and I start laughing so hysterically I can't breathe. I don't know what to tell them and accepting the situation is just too much for my brain to handle.

They look at me like I'm crazy. I drink my drink and chuckle around the straw.

"Seriously," Selma urges. "What happened?"

"Nothing. He's just a massive, huge, dick."

Their confusion increases but they don't question me further, especially when I catch Kane sitting across the room and he tips his bottle of water at me like it's a tumbler of whiskey. He rolls his tongue around the rim and motions to his phone, meaning I need to look at mine.

I do and I clasp it so hard against my chest and so quickly that I almost drop it.

16 YEARS OLD

Kane: If you want your pussy ate, come to mine tonight.

I meet his eyes as he casually chews on his bottom lip, blue orbs hungry and alight with amusement and excitement.

Oh shit. What have we started?

He leaves the cafeteria with Ren, giving me a great view of his ass, and I pick at my food until Marshall approaches about thirty minutes later, looking confused. He nods for me to follow and I do so.

"What is going ooooon?" Poppy begs on a hiss, looking at me like I'm the answer to all the good gossip, which I guess to her, I am.

"Everything okay?" I ask Marshall when he pulls me to a quiet part of the hall beyond the cafeteria.

Why do I keep getting guided and dragged to secondary locations today?

"Why did Kane just approach me with his thugs and tell me I'm not dating you no more?" His eyes are angry, but he also looks concerned. "Is he giving you trouble? I thought your feud was a thing of the past?"

My feud with Kane has never been a secret, nor has it ever been a thing of the past. Though we don't get at each other like we used to, we still despise each other. Or at least... I think we do.

I shift on the spot, uncomfortable and unable to meet his eyes.

"It's probably best we don't see each other anymore," I admit, hating Kane, hating this. He's going to tell him what we did, what I did, and Marshall deserves better than that.

"I'm not scared of him."

"I know," I reply, hiking my bag up my shoulder. "But—it's just not gonna work between us."

"Did you tell him to break up with me?" His eyes darken, the brown in them turning black. "Because I don't like these games, Immy. Thought you were different."

"I'm not playing a game. I just don't want you in the middle of our mess."

16 YEARS OLD

"What she means to say is," Ren blurts, appearing out of nowhere and slinging his arm around my shoulder.

Kane grabs him by the hair and throws him away, then he looks at me.

"Mine later, right?" he asks, smiling at me with infuriating smugness. "Finish what we started in science class."

Marshall looks at me, ignoring Kane entirely, "What is he talking about?"

"Don't," I beg Kane.

"He's talkin' about her mouth on his dick, minutes after you kissed her." Ren starts laughing like this is hilarious and my eyes fill with tears.

"Thought we'd save you the embarrassment. She ain't worth dating." Kane winks at me. "She's a whore, just like her momma."

My fist hits him in the mouth before I even register what I'm doing and his head snaps back. Blood covers his teeth and trickles out the corner of his lips. I felt the crunch just as badly as he did. My hand is throbbing, but it was worth it.

I turn away from them all, enraged, wanting to get a gun and just shoot him in the face.

"Oh come on, Immy," Kane calls after me and spits his blood onto the floor. "I was just playin'!"

"So she didn't suck your dick?" Marshall asks him, sounding confused and I'm just done with men altogether.

Everyone watches me as I all but run away, but nobody says shit about what Kane just said. Nobody calls me a whore or insults my useless bitch of a momma. Everyone just watches.

"Immy," Kane yells, chasing after me. Which is surprising, but not enough to make me stop. I leave the school which will probably get me into serious shit and head directly across the road towards the patch because it's not like I can go home at this time of day. Mee-maw would flip her shit and she doesn't use a meager slipper anymore to beat me with. "Immy, come on. I was just fucking with you both. I've called you worse."

I turn on him so sharply he almost walks into me. "Why? Why can't you just leave me alone?"

"Leave you alone?" He looks at me incredulously. "You're the one that comes to me! It's my bed you sleep in."

"BECAUSE YOU MADE ME FEEL SAFE!" I scream at him, hitting his chest so hard my hand stings. "And it's messed up, because you're awful."

"I'm awful?" he yells back shoving me in return. "I'm the awful one?"

"YES!"

"You're the one who fucked me and ditched me seconds later... for another fucking guy I should mention. But I'm awful?"

His words make me falter. "It wasn't like that."

"Fuck you. That's exactly what it was like and we both know it."

"I didn't realize sex with you was so sentimental." I almost laugh at the ridiculousness of it. This is Kane fucking Jessop. He's the biggest player in this school.

"You don't realize a lot of shit."

"Then enlighten me."

"Okay, here's one you never saw, the fact I stayed in that fucking store all night to save your stupid ass and you never thanked me for that. All you did was panic over the fact you thought you killed somebody. You didn't ask me how I was doin' and I was the one who actually fuckin' played a hand in his death." His voice is quiet but firm, an angry hiss through bared teeth. Blue eyes project his ire. "It's all about Immy, Immy, Immy. As always."

"You're always horrid to me, how am I supposed to know any of this?" I ask, thinking back to that day and thinking that I took note of the fact he was wearing the same clothes as the day before. I also think back to the fact I never fucking asked him if he was okay. "We never had this conversation! And I tried talking to you."

"Like fuck you did. You told me how you felt, begged me for reassurance and fucked off."

Is he right? Could he be right? I wrack my brain trying to think of that moment. "Did you really stay there to save me?"

"Knew you wouldn't listen to me," he admits, shrugging nonchalant like it's not a big deal when in fact it's a huge fucking deal. "Heard him make you that offer, seen him lookin' at you before the way a man looks at a woman he wants, not a kid. Doesn't take a genius to figure out what game he was playin'. So I stayed, just to be sure, and I was right."

I can hardly believe what I'm hearing.

"You saved me."

"Twice," he points out, smirking now, his anger gone. "And you still spoke to me like I was shit on your shoe."

"That's not true. We were both bad to each other."

He smiles, a terrifying sight but also one so handsome and alluring.

"Naw... I was worse." He steps closer to me. "I don't know what it is about you that makes me so fucking crazy, but I think I figured it out the other mornin'."

"You mean when we—"

"Fucked? Yeah."

"And what conclusion did you draw?"

Grinning, he grabs my hair and yanks me so close the entire front of my body collides with his. "That you're mine, Imogen Hardy, and I'll stick a nail through the foot of any man that tries to touch you."

I inhale sharply when he shakes my head just enough to get my eyes off his nose and on his.

"You fuckin' look at me when I'm talkin' to you!"

"I am looking at you!" I growl, gripping the front of his shirt. "And you don't just get to tell me I'm yours."

"I do."

"You don't!"

"Babe... I fuckin' do."

He kisses me in the way only he kisses me, despite the split on his lip that I caused. He tastes sweet, like apple juice with a tangy hint of blood that doesn't bother me in the slightest. His tongue devours my mouth and he groans like it's life's elixir. My hands thread through his hair and I go up onto my tiptoes to put us at a more equal height.

But then I pull away because people are watching, more aptly, Poppy, my brother, and Ren. Ren who has his phone out and a huge grin on his face.

"Delete it or I smash it," Kane snarls at his friend who quickly does as he's told while still laughing.

"Are you screwing with my head right now?" Poppy screeches, looking at me like I've just pooped out a boulder of kittens. "When the fuck did you guys start liking each other?"

Kane and I look at each other. My brow rises and I say with a shrug, "Never."

He adds on a quiet voice, "Shall we skip and dick at my place?"

I nod, not wanting to go back after everything that just happened. Despite the fact he's the one who caused it.

"The school will call Mee-maw," Matthew interrupts, his tone playful.

I give him my middle finger as Kane wraps his arm around my shoulders. "Do I give a fuck?"

"My little girl is growing up," Poppy sniffs dramatically. "But let me just tell you that we *will* be discussing this later! You massive whore."

"Don't call her a fucking whore," Kane barks over his shoulder.

"You literally just called her a whore back there," Ren announces, laughing again because he just finds everything so funny.

"Are you forgettin' the panty incident?" Kane asks, Ren, releasing me so he can walk backwards.

"That's fucked up, man. What's alright for you isn't for me. We're meant to be brothers."

Kane grins at me, ignores Ren, and tucks me under his arm again. "I got you."

"Bit late for that, Kane. You started this shit."

"I'm not sorry," he admits and I blink at him. "Led you to my bed, didn't it?"

"Thought you didn't like me there."

"Like you there now I can touch you."

I giggle, unable to stop myself from emitting such a girly noise. "You're such a dick."

"And you're a bitch."

"Yeah," I agree, tilting my head back so he can kiss my lips. He makes it a gentle one. "You sore where I hit you?"

"If I'd known you swung a fist like a man, I wouldn't have been so close when I insulted your deadbeat mother."

I glare at him and move as far away as he allows before he yanks me back and walks me backwards with his hands gripping my biceps.

"I'm not mad you insulted my deadbeat momma; I'm mad you compared me to her. I ain't like her. Not at all."

His answering smile is infuriating.

"You know I still don't like you, right?"

"Not asking for you to like me, Immy. I don't think we'll ever be friends. But you let me put my dick in you from time to time I'm thinkin' we can make each other happy in other ways."

Why do I get turned on when he talks to me like that?

"You know Marshall is probably going to tell everyone about what you said."

"When I claim you in front of the school, ain't nobody gonna talk about you."

I groan with exasperation. "Dude you are so arrogant."

"Am I wrong?"

"No but be a little humble sometimes!"

"Am I wrong?"

"I just said no!"

"Then what's your deal?"

I blink twice to calm myself and leave it. There's no arguing with him, *ever*. I know this all too well.

16 AND A HALF

THE HALF IS STILL IMPORTANT

I grab his hair, holding him against me, forcing his face into the sensitive parting of my thighs. My head goes back as electric like tingles assault my body as his tongue and fingers get me to where I so desperately need to be.

Suddenly, he stops and lifts his head, his lips swollen, pink, and wet with me. "You don't want me to pass out before you come, you gotta let me breathe a little."

"Oh shut the fuck up whining," I retort, pushing him back against me, ignoring his chuckle and smile. He loves it when I'm bossy with him. "Oh my God..." His tongue does this flicky thing over my clit that sends me wild and his fingers hook inside.

I grip his hair tighter, clamp my thighs around his head and come, crying out so loud I wouldn't be surprised if somebody on the next street called the cops. My orgasm is destructive, it burns right where he's touching but also everywhere he's not.

I flop, a limp heap of glistening limbs and he climbs up my body, inserting himself into me as he goes.

"We good?" he asks, scanning my face with those gorgeous eyes of his.

"We're good," I answer, rolling him over and taking control.

I push up and down, losing myself in a way I would have been too ashamed to lose myself three months ago when this started between us. My hips rocks, my breasts bounce and my breath comes out in ragged pants.

"You took your pill right?" he asks through gritted teeth. He always checks which I'm glad of because I don't want to forget and do something stupid like get pregnant. Felicia thankfully helped me procure said contraception so that Mee-maw wouldn't find out. Kane pays for it despite me saying it's fine. He said, "You're the one taking the fucking thing so I don't knock you up, the least I can do is pay for it."

Kane Jessop, for all his faults, is a considerate guy.

"Of course. First thing I took this morning."

"Good." He grabs my hips and starts driving up into me from below. The sounds of his skin slapping against mine is so erotic and his moans only adds to that. I feel him swell and usually that feeling always gets me off. This time is no different. He comes, burying himself deep inside while he fills me with his seed, and I follow straight after, placing his hands on my breasts to make it last a bit longer. "You've got such great tits, Immy."

"Why thank you," I reply, smiling down at him as he rolls them with his hands. He always seems to get lost in a private moment when it comes to my breasts, always seems to just lose himself as though they have hypnotized him. But then I'm the same when it comes to his penis.

I climb off him after a moment, glaring at him over my shoulder when he smacks my bare ass way too hard. I don't give him the satisfaction of reacting, I just grab a towel and make my way to the shower where he joins me because, *as he says*, "Any moment where you're naked and my hands ain't on you, is a moment wasted."

That's when I realized Kane knows all the right shit to say to stay in my panties for as long as he needs.

I of course encourage his good behavior with the occasional BJ here and there, usually in places people should not be giving BJs. Like last week was in the staffroom at my workplace. I put butterscotch syrup all over his dick and licked it off. I thought he was going to have a heart attack. Now, whenever we have ice-cream or hear the ice-cream truck that rides through town, he gives me this look that sends a tingle to my belly.

I head home, because it's Saturday afternoon and Mee-maw is making a dinner for Matthew and me. Poppy is joining us too. Mee-maw has been in foul spirits lately, so this is a surprise. She's so good to everyone else but when it comes to me and Matthew she often reminds us that Satan has our souls now and if we don't repent soon it will be too late.

Kane follows in his red challenger, a car that catches just as much attention as he does. And to say he catches attention would be an understatement.

"You can never wait for me can you?" he asks, winding down the window and trailing alongside me.

"You always make me late." I yank open the door and climb in, grinning at him. "Thanks for the ride."

"You only need ask."

"Yeah right, like I'll ever ask you for anything."

"Why not?" He looks mildly offended. "You ask me to eat your pussy all the time."

"One." I tick off a finger with another finger. "That's totally different and two, asking you for anything would mean admitting I need you for stuff other than orgasms."

"And that's a problem because..." His words trail off and he turns to look at me, fully facing me now.

"Because I don't need you. I'm an independent woman."

He throws his head back and laughs like I'm hilarious. I don't see what's so funny.

I scowl at him, pursing my lips petulantly.

"Oh come on, babe..." I love it when he calls me babe, but I'll never admit it. "Let go of this feminist society shit. You can rely on your boyfriend and still be, *a strong and independent woman.*" His voice becomes a mocking tone at the end and I hate him.

"Don't make fun of me."

"I'll always make fun of you," he answers proudly with a grin that's entirely too handsome.

I push his long hair back behind his ear and lean over the seat to kiss him.

"Do you still hate me like you used to?" I ask against his lips.

"Naw." He deepens the kiss, pulling me closer awkwardly. "We're cool, Immy."

"That why you called yourself my boyfriend? Thought you didn't like labels." I narrow my eyes suspiciously. "It was legit you who said, *let's just keep fucking and forget about the rest.*"

"One." He copies me by ticking off his finger with another finger. "I don't sound like how you just made me sound, my voice is much more manly and sexy. Two. I stand by it. Labels are trash. They mean shit."

I frown. "So you're not my boyfriend?"

He opens and closes his mouth, then yawns loudly and puts his hands back on the steering wheel. "If you want to call me that to make yourself feel better, I'll be your boyfriend."

"Don't sound so dejected."

"Dejected? New word of the week?"

I nod. "I'm learning so many."

"Your brain is getting too big, Immy, don't let it start oozing out your ears or you'll leave for a college too far for me to fuck you in." He restarts the engine and clicks his neck.

My heart flutters. "Is that your way of saying you want me to stay?"

"Don't be a dick." He pulls out into the road, checking his wing mirror just in case. "I ain't your keeper, you can go anywhere you fuckin' want. But all I'm sayin' is. You want this dick, you gotta stick around. I ain't leaving my dad to chase pussy."

"To chase pussy," I repeat, this time I'm offended. "That's all I am to you? Pussy?"

"Hell don't ask me that." His hands tense on the steering wheel. "We're not about that heavy, we're all about the hot."

"So you're saying if a girl comes along that you like better than me, you're going to leave me for her?"

"I've seen every girl in this town, Immy. Ain't a girl here I like better."

I punch his arm. "THAT WASN'T AN ANSWER."

"Fucking hell, you don't gotta yell. I'm right here." I grab his hair and pull, ripping his head to the side, forcing him to pull over again. "What the fuck, Immy? Come on."

"I am never speaking to you again, Kane Jessop," I snarl at him, kicking open the door and slamming it behind me.

"Watch the fucking car!"

"Fuck your car," I call, giving him the middle finger over my shoulder as I walk away. "And fuck you too."

"You walk away from me babe, I ain't comin' back! I ain't chasin' you!"

I'm too mad to care. I deserve better from some guy who is using me as a pussy on hold until the line connects for his new bitch. "Kane Jessop, you're the worst boy there is. Don't chase me. See if I care. I'll have you replaced by tonight and we both know it."

"Like hell you will! Nobody in this town is dumb enough to touch what's mine. Nobody."

"I am not yours!"

"Like hell you ain't!" He rushes after me, grabbing me around the middle, trying to lift me but I start pulling his hair again and slapping his chest. My feet drop to the ground and I keep hold of his hair. "You psychotic bitch. Let me go!"

Somehow he twists my wrists, forcing me to release his hair.

"Fuckin' come here to give you a ride to your mee-maw's and this is how you treat me?"

"I fucking came to your house to give you a nice mornin' only to find out I'm just your time filler until the next best thing comes by!" I shove his chest. "You're such a dick."

"That's not what I said."

"You implied it!"

"I don't know what you want from me!"

"Tell her you love her!" somebody yells from across the street.

"I don't fuckin' love her for me to tell her that," Kane barks back and even though I don't love him either, his admission stings. I bring my knee up into his dick before he realizes what I'm doing and stroll away.

"Get it girl!" the same person from before yells and I continue on my own sassy and merry way.

"Such a bitch," Kane rasps, cupping himself between the legs and groaning.

"It's not like I did it hard, pussy," I reply, only feeling a little bit guilty about it.

He doesn't come after me and for some reason, I'm really annoyed about that.

"You're late," Matthew hisses when I enter the house, rosy cheeked and out of breath.

"I got into a fight with Kane."

"Oh no." He looks mildly concerned. "What happened?"

"They're always fighting," Poppy puts in. "It's like foreplay to them."

I put my finger to my lips, getting her to shush because Mee-maw has ears like an animal and she doesn't need confirmation that I'm no longer a virgin.

"Mee-maw?" I call, kicking off my shoes and quickly braiding my wild hair. "Sorry I'm late."

"Are you?" Mee-maw asks, entering the kitchen and narrowing her eyes on me. "Where have you been?"

"I was with a friend." I move to the sink to wash my hands, a mealtime rule, and then help her dish up the dinner. Poppy and

Matthew take it through to the dining room which is set up to the nines.

"There are seven plates here," I hiss at Poppy who shrugs.

"Oh, yes, I invited the Joneses," Mee-maw explains and I suddenly don't feel so hot.

"You mean Mr. and Mrs. Jones?" Poppy questions.

"That's right. And Marshall. He has been away at football camp and returned two days ago. I thought I'd treat him to a nice meal. Lord knows that boy likes my food. Best way to a man's heart is through his stomach, ladies. Learn a lesson here." She hums as she sets the table and I look at Poppy who cringes.

Marshall and I haven't really spoken since that entire thing and Kane hates him purely because he kissed me. This is going to create issues. So many issues.

"We just won't tell him," Poppy suggests, meaning Kane, and I like that idea until Matthew puts in, "Marshall ain't keeping his mouth shut."

With a heavy sigh I mentally assess the situation. It would be so much easier to lie but there's a massive chance I'll get caught out which will cause even more issues. I'm good at lying but I can't speak for other people. "I'm not lyin' to him, there's no use. Besides, Marshall probably won't even speak to me. I really embarrassed him."

Poppy nods. "Yeah, he's not used to rejection."

I sigh heavily. "This is going to be hell." But then I think back to our earlier conversation that I got mad at to begin with. "Actually fuck, Kane Jessop. I'm done with him. I don't care what he thinks."

Marshall is surprisingly pleasant during our dinner and his parents even more so. They force us to sit opposite each other and I realize that they're still trying to get us to match. That's why they invited Poppy, to keep Matthew occupied so Marshall and I can talk.

Marshall looks uncomfortable though and I don't blame him. Mee-maw is asking him so many questions, some of them invasive like, "did you meet any girls at camp?"

Marshall answers them all like a champ and pulls a face when she's not looking which of course I laugh at.

His parents ask me questions too and unfortunately, his nosy mother asks me something I really don't want to be asked, "So... you and the Jessop boy."

Everyone at this table becomes harder than the fucking table itself. And not in the sexy way. In the... oh shit way.

"Rumor has it you dated for a while? Perhaps you're still dating?"

Those nosy good for nothing church dwelling trolls. Keeping calm, I school my features so they don't see my surprise.

I consider lying but it's not as though Kane and I have kept our thing a huge secret, he can't keep his hands off me and vice versa so instead I opt for the truth, knowing Mee-maw will probably beat me later.

"We were, but it didn't work out."

Mee-maw's eyes find me and through gritted teeth she lies, "My granddaughter realized what a terrible influence he would be. But we all have to experience the bad people in order to truly learn who the pure ones are."

She did that so effortlessly, turned what I would be judged for into something else. She's so manipulative.

"Of course," Mrs. Jones agrees. "I'm sorry it didn't work out for you."

"Thanks. It wasn't serious." Saying the words out loud physically hurts me. I feel like I'm betraying him in some way, despite the fact he doesn't love me or care about me beyond what I can do to him in the bedroom.

Later, after dinner, Marshall and I sit on the porch swing out back, overlooking Mee-maw's ill-maintained garden. Since Grandpa died she just doesn't have it in her. He was the gardener. She prefers the housework indoors.

I've told her to pay somebody because Lord knows Matthew isn't going to help and I already do enough house chores. Whether or not she will is another matter entirely.

"They're trying to set us up again," Marshall says, breaking the silence. It was so awkward. I'm glad he's gotten right to the point of it all. "I know you're not into me like that."

"That's not true," I blurt, feeling bad. "I was so into you."

"But you were into Kane more?"

I lift a shoulder. "Things with Kane have and always will be complicated."

"Would'a been pretty simple with me."

Laughing gently I look at where Poppy and Matthew are whispering amongst themselves. They're everybody's teen dream relationship. They're so in love while also being best friends. It's so sweet it gives me toothache.

"Do you love him?"

"Kane?" I question and laugh nervously. "No. I can't stand him."

He looks confused but then his eyes light up with innocent excitement.

"Then date me again, appease my parents." His words come as a plea and I can't tell if he's joking or not. "Appease your mee-maw."

"After everything that happened?"

"Look, it's not about sex or anything," his cheeks go pink in the dark, I see the color. "I really like you. You're not like the other girls in school."

Something is off about this. It's almost too easy. "Is this to get back at Kane? To prove that you're a big man or something?"

"No." He scratches the peach fuzz on his jaw. He's almost a man but not quite, it's still attractive though even if compared to Kane he's practically a preschooler. Not his fault that Kane started puberty before he was born. He could probably grow a full beard if he wanted to. "This is purely because I like you, my parents like you, and because I need them off my back."

"Right."

"I like hanging out with you."

"We haven't hung out for three months," I point out and he looks at the sky. I was right when I guessed that something is off about this. It's weird and random and I can tell he has a motive. "What's wrong? What is it?"

"Nothing," he snaps, annoyed now. "Forget I asked."

"Hey," I soothe, placing my hand on his thigh. "I'm more trouble than I'm worth. You've gotta find somebody else."

"Sure." He doesn't look as though he believes me.

"Friends though?"

He smiles for real now. "Sure. I'm sorry I stopped talking to you after what happened."

"I deserved it. I wasn't good to you. And that's why I know there's a reason you're asking me to date you and I don't think it's got anything to do with the fact you like me."

Laughing, he looks back through the window and whispers, "Maybe one day I'll be able to tell you."

"When you can trust me, you mean?"

"Exactly."

"Well..." I hop off the swing and turn to face him. "If you need a cover for what you actually wanna be doing, I'm your girl."

"Thanks, Immy."

"No problem Marshall."

"*No problem, Marshall,*" Kane mimics, making his tone high-pitched and whiny. He has just rounded the house, likely having jumped the gate. "This is interesting."

"Oh fuck off, hillbilly," I snap at the guy I've been secretly having sex with. Although dinner tonight proved that my love life ain't so secret. "Go get your hair cut."

"You like my hair when it touches the insides of your thighs," he argues and looks Marshall up and down. "Fuck off, poser."

"Kane, he's a guest. You fuck off."

Kane's eyes darken and my brother grabs his shoulder before he can approach. "Why don't we go hang out? I've got a doobie in my pocket that's just dying to be lit."

"Naw, I've got some unfinished business to take care of with your sister." Shrugging my brother off, he keeps going and stops with his forehead against mine. Our eyes connect, his are blue and fierce. Mine are hazel and defiant. His mouth moves as he chews on a wad of gum.

"Why are you in my personal space?"

"Why are you pretending you're bothered?"

I scoff and try to look at Marshall but Kane nudges his head against my own. "Eyes on me, babe. You better tell me right now; did you invite this prick?"

"Don't call him a prick."

"Mee-maw invited him, his parents are inside," Poppy explains, frowning at us both. "And if she catches you out here, Kane Jessop, she's gonna take it out on Imogen."

"That's what he's countin' on," I say with a roll of my eyes. He wants Mee-maw to catch me so she beats me and I run straight to his bed. "Kane back up. I'm not in the mood."

"Not in the mood?"

I shove his chest and step around him. Looking at Poppy, I say, "I'm going inside. Call me when he's gone."

Kane snags my braid and pulls me back a step.

"This is how it's gonna be?"

"Yes, I don't want to be your toy anymore," I admit, turning and yanking on my braid until he releases it. "I'm done."

"Done?" He spits his gum into a distant plant pot and wets his lips. "So just like that you get to decide it?"

"I don't want to be your time filler!" I hiss, exasperated now.

"You ain't my time filler."

"Then what the fuck am I?"

"You're..." he hesitates as he tries to think of a word. "Mine."

"That's not an answer."

"It's the only fucking answer I have you argumentative bitch."

"Don't call my sister a bitch," Matthew snaps and I send him a grateful smile.

I shrug and catch Kane's eyes without blinking. "And it's a shit answer. So, go about your evenin' and I'll go about mine."

"Tell me what you want from me," Kane growls, grabbing my bicep and pulling me around the building. "I swear you just wanna fight, right? That's it. You want dick and then fire? Because I'm not feelin' these games, Immy."

"Fuck you, Kane, you love the games. You play them more than I do."

I watch him light a cigarette but I take it from his lips, snap it and throw it on the ground.

"You know how much I hate those."

"Yeah, well, I'm stressed."

Pointing towards the road I demand, "Yeah, well, go be stressed somewhere else and smoke your death sticks for comfort *alone*."

"You want me to quit? Say the word, Immy and I'll quit." He tosses his packet on the ground. "You want me to get down on my knees and eat your pussy, just say the word and I'll do it." He gets down on his knees and looks up at me. "You want me to worship every inch of your body, I'll do it."

"I want you to figure out what you want from me."

"No, you want me to figure out what you want from *me*," he corrects and I find myself stammering to form words that make sense. "I know what I want without the labels. I wanna keep on going with you."

"But you don't care if I leave."

"Wouldn't be here on my knees if I didn't fuckin' care, Imogen." With that he stands and cages me in. "Now tell me, what the fuck do you want from me so I can do it and make you stop being such a fuckin' bitch."

"Stop calling me a bitch for a start. Stop insulting me at all."

"Hell naw. That's our thing. I say it but I don't mean it and you know it."

He has a point. I fight a smile and his eyes go to my lips. I know he's seen it.

"What do you really want?"

"A date," I blurt and regret it immediately when his brows hit his hairline.

"A... date?"

"Yep, I wanna be wined and dined, and then dined on."

"Fuckin' don't want much," he grumbles but I can see his smile. "And that'll chill you the fuck out?"

I place my palm against his chest. "I want you to want to date me. I don't want you to do it because I said so."

"I've never done that before. I just smile and bone. It's how I am." He pinches my chin softly and drags his thumb over it. "But I can think of worse people to eat with. We can do that."

"Seriously?"

"Why do you look so pissed again?"

"Because you're an idiot."

He growls and pushes his hair back. "You're impossible. Fuckin' impossible."

"I'm tryna be!"

Walking away, I'm forced to stop when he snags me around the waist and buries his face in my neck. "Come on, Immy. Show me your panties and let's forget about this shit."

I'm ashamed to admit that I am tempted.

"Guys, Mee-maw is coming," Poppy hisses, poking her head around the corner.

"I should let her catch me so she tries to beat your ass and you end up in my bed tonight," Kane whispers in my ear and kisses my jaw. "But, swear it, don't care if she's becomin' an old lady, she keeps sending you with bruises I will shove her on her ass."

"Even you're not that vicious," I reply through the side of my mouth which he kisses.

"I'll be waiting for you at lights out, down the road in my car. Don't disappoint me, Immy." He pushes his hard cock against my rear as his hand holds me across my stomach, keeping me against him. "All this yellin' has made my dick hard. Need you to fix it."

"Or you'll find somebody else to?" I retort.

He kisses me again and slips around the front of the house. I bend low and scoop up a candy bar wrapper that has blown into the garden just as Mee-maw joins me.

"That's a good girl, keepin' our home clean." She rubs my arm and follows me to the trashcan. "Marshall is going to pick you up for school in the morning."

"Okay, Mee-maw." I don't argue, there's no point.

"There's my good girl."

Good girl? What am I? A dog?

We all head inside, Marshall included and when they leave not half an hour later and Mee-maw faces me, I'm already ready to run.

"Kane Jessop?" she shrieks and I roll my eyes. I knew it was coming. "You've been dating Kane Jessop?"

"Yes." I raise my hand. "Don't you dare throw anything at me!"

"Why won't you do as you're told? Why won't you learn?"

I shrug. "I guess I must be stupid!"

"Stupid, no. Tempted by demons, yes. The Jessop family are not a nice family! This is such an embarrassment."

"Grandpa used to go see Mr. Jessop all the time!"

"He's the only mechanic in this town," she seethes, and raises her hands to her hair to neaten her white bun. "He didn't have much of a choice."

"Not true, he used to take me with him and we'd sit on the bikes."

Sorry for ratting you out Grandpa.

"Don't you bad mouth your grandpa when he isn't here to defend himself!" She steps towards me and I step back. "You are not to see that boy ever again, you hear me?"

"I'll see whoever I want," I reply and that was absolutely the wrong thing to stay, still, I don't stop. "I'm a good kid, Mee-maw. I get good grades. I go to church. I help around the house. I work. I don't do drugs or get into trouble. What does it matter who I date?"

"Who you date and spend your time with is everything. It's the view of yourself that you give to your neighbors." Her voice is so deep.

"I don't care what people think of me!"

"Well you should!" She smooths down her apron. "You're just like your momma, she never listened either!"

"What about Matthew? Huh? He does what he wants when he wants. You don't even moan at him about chores! How is that fair?"

"Matthew is a boy. Boys have a different purpose in this life. He needs to rid his body of his demons so when he finds a nice woman to settle down with, he can repent his sins and be a stable family man!"

"You sound insane! Because I have a vagina I'm meant to be perfect my entire life? Well I'm not perfect, Mee-maw. I'll never be perfect. I don't want to be perfect!"

"I will not raise two harlot daughters! It was shameful enough with the one. By God it took me a long time to win back the trust of my community. And then she just had to get pregnant with you two at sixteen." She whips a hand through the air and shrieks, "*SIXTEEN!*"

"You were seventeen when you had mom."

Her hands ball into fists by her sides, stretching out the few wrinkles and making her knuckles white. We all do that when we're angry. It's a Hardy thing. "I was married and to a good man! Your mother was sixteen and hadn't finished school! Your daddy didn't want nothin' to do with his bastard children."

My deadbeat dad doesn't even live in town anymore, he and his family moved not long after the scandal that was him knocking up my mom. He never came back for me no matter how often I fantasized about it as a kid.

"That's not my fault."

"No, you're right, it's not, but the least you can do in return for me taking you in, is *behave* and hang with pleasant and wholesome people. I only *just* tolerate Poppy. But I *will not* tolerate Kane Jessop. No, I will not." She points up the stairs. "Go to your room. You're grounded until further notice."

"For dating Kane Jessop?"

"YES!" she shrieks, losing her cool again.

Grumbling under my breath I stomp up the stairs and slam the door behind me, knowing how much she hates it.

Imogen: Marshall's parents outed us to Mee-maw and now I'm grounded!

Kane: Sneak out. What's the big deal?

Imogen: I'm not deliberately disobeying her, Kane.

Kane: So what, you're just not gonna see me no more?

Imogen: I didn't say that… I'm just saying I'm going to let her cool off. I'm not trying to be a bitch to her. I only run when she hits me. You know this.

Kane: You put up with way too much, Immy.

Imogen: What choice do I have? Just gotta keep saving for college and get my ass out of here the moment I graduate.

Kane: Sounds dope.

Imogen: Don't sound too enthusiastic, Kane.

Kane: Ain't nothin to be enthusiastic about, Imogen Hardy. If you fucking leave me I'll have to move onto a basic bitch. I don't want a basic bitch.

Imogen: There's a compliment in there somewhere and maybe an admission that you like like me.

Kane: Don't be racing ahead there. I'm just saying if I'm gonna be stuck here with my dad, I want to be stuck here with you.

Imogen: We should text more often. You're much nicer and easier to understand.

Kane: See, I didn't think that was nice.

Imogen: In comparison to your usual. It was nice.

Kane: Fair point.
  Kane: So are you sneaking out or what? I need to get my dick wet.

Imogen: Give me an hour.

Kane: Babe I'll give you whatever the fuck you want if you swallow my junk again.

Imogen: No. So gross. You can put it on my tits.

Kane: That's good too.

Imogen: ;-)

26 YEARS OLD

"Wait!" Felicia calls, rushing after me, her blonde hair getting tangled in her lips. She spits it out, making me smile despite my sadness and links her arm through mine. "Don't run. Not again."

"You gonna keep questioning me?"

She shakes her head. "Only about everything I've missed."

"Promise?"

"Of course. I'm not mad with you for shit you did as a kid. We all make mistakes. I want to know what made you the gorgeous woman you are today."

"Me too." Kane's voice has my bottom lip quivering. "Shit, Immy... I'm fucking mad but... don't leave without telling me what I've missed."

"Can we do that?" I ask him, not releasing Felicia's arm. "Can we talk without fighting?"

"Worth a shot," he puts in, tucking his fingertips into the pockets of his jeans. The breeze picks up his hair and throws a few tendrils across his face. They cover one of his eyes as he looks down at me, hatred swims there but it's not as prominent as it was.

"Okay. Good because I want to know about you guys too."

He nods but doesn't smile. It must be hard for him after my admission. Though it's saying something if he still feels hurt by it after all this time. It wasn't supposed to be this way.

"Did you go to college?" Felicia asks and I confirm with a dip of my head. "Did you graduate?"

I shake my head. "Nope. Dropped out."

Kane snorts so I shoot him a dirty look.

"So what do you do?" He sounds mocking and arrogant making me want to spray his face again. I feel Felicia guide me back inside and just decide to go with it. West's smile at my reappearance is tight but I know he's hurting for his son who obviously did some hurting of his own all them years ago. Trust me when I say their pain was nothing compared to mine.

"Tattoos, Kane," I respond with a proud grin as his ocean blue eyes darken. "I do tattoos."

"Are you good?" Felicia asks as Kane assesses me in a new light, through narrowed slits and a slightly raised chin.

"I won Best Tattoo Artist of the year in Minnesota six months ago."

"Impressive," Felicia breathes, widening her eyes. "Can you do me one? I'll pay you! I been lookin' to get somethin' on the back of my left shoulder."

"Sure, just hit me up."

Kane keeps on assessing me. He's looking for any lie I might tell. He always was good at calling me on my shit. He's getting sloppy though.

West is the one who asks, "Is that where you're living now?"

I reply with a nod and say, "In St Paul, Minneapolis. It's so nice."

"You don't need to tell us your full fuckin' address, ain't nobody chasing after you," Kane snaps, thinking I've got some kind of hidden agenda.

"Kane," Felicia hisses. "You promised."

I take his attitude with a pinch of salt as I always did.

"What have you been doing with yourself?" I ask him to take the subject off me.

"Workin' with my dad, took over the garage so he could spend time with Felicia," Kane responds flatly.

"No wife? No... kids?" I try so hard to smile genuinely but I just can't. I hate it. Even after all this time.

"Nope. Fuck that." He smirks at me. "I treat a few to my bed sometimes but I ain't never settlin' down again."

I laugh hysterically for a moment. "You thought we were *settled?*"

"We were fuckin' happy."

"Sure, you psychotic fuckwit!"

"Says you, fuckin' banshee. Soundin' like a dyin' cat every time you opened your mouth." He makes his tone high and mocking. "*Kane Jessop. You're such a dick Kane Jessop. Give me your di—*"

"Don't need to hear this," West barks, shoving his son back. "Y'all are both fucked up. Royally. Thought you mighta been abusin' her but now I see you're both as bad as each other."

"She started it," Kane retorts, glowering at me. So much for doing this without arguing.

"I'm leaving, this is pointless." I stand but Kane puts his foot on the bar of my stool, trapping my legs between the island and his body.

"Before you've had the chance to tell us your story?"

I huff and glare at my ex like a petulant child. "I don't have an interesting story to tell."

"Lie," he calls, staring into my eyes. "You're lying, Imogen Hardy."

Well... he called it that time.

17... IT'S MY BIRTHDAY

"You are lyin' to me, Imogen Hardy." Kane hooks me around the back of my neck and our lips smash together. It's painful but then his kisses always are. They never just *are*. They always have to be something. Painful, teasing, sweet, soft, funny, stupid, bliss, heaven. I've never kissed Kane Jessop and said, his kiss was okay. They're always more than okay and his arrogant ass knows it.

"I'm not lyin'." I'm breathless and needy and looking deep into his eyes as our bodies press flush together.

"You are so lyin'."

"Kane, when I said don't get me a birthday gift, I meant it."

I didn't mean it. I want flowers and candy, and shit along those lines. Instead he got me nothing. Though he did tie a ribbon around his erect cock this morning before telling me, "Happy birthday, babe. Now make a wish and blow my brains out."

I sat on his face instead. That was fun.

"Come on, we'll go buy you somethin'." Kane leads me to his challenger just as his daddy pulls into the compound with a shiny looking black Harley. It's the same one my grandpa used to touch

17... IT'S MY BIRTHDAY

fondly but could never ride because its engine had been stripped. It was more there for show than function.

West climbs off the bike and yanks off his helmet sending his shoulder length hair in all directions. He shakes out the tangles and pushes it back with a large hand before tossing the helmet at Kane who places it on the metal table by the challenger. He's been tweaking his engine; I don't know what he's been doing to it but it sounds even better than before.

"Rides like a dream, not too heavy either." West clears his throat and winks at me. "Happy birthday, kid, come by later, Felicia cooked you up a cake."

"I'll be sure to. Thanks Mr. Jessop."

He slaps the bike keys against his son's chest as he passes and Kane spins them around his finger.

"I fixed it," Kane says, moving to the bike and motioning for me to sit on it. I often sit on this exact bike while he works on his car or someone else's. It's always here but it never moves.

He looks so proud of himself. "Took me two months but I fixed it."

"You are amazing."

"That's the only nice thing you've ever said to me," he states with a grin.

"That's a lie."

"Naw. We both know it ain't."

"Isn't," I correct and he glares at me.

"Are those sirens I hear?" he jests, smacking me on the ass and squeezing, his favorite thing to do. "Did someone call the grammar police?"

Laughing I smack him back and also squeeze his incredible derriere. "Can you take me for a ride?"

"Depends what kinda ride, darlin'," he answers, still spinning the keys. I fucking love when he calls me darlin'. Especially in his husky, gruff, gravel on concrete voice. I need Jesus to help me repent from my nasty ass thoughts about Kane Jessop.

17... IT'S MY BIRTHDAY

"On this," I motion to my favorite vehicle in the whole damn world.

"Naw. It's not mine." He kicks a leg over the back of it and kisses my ear.

"Your daddy won't mind." I'm practically begging, desperate to feel this baby purr between my thighs. West and Kane have been giving me lessons over the past few months. It was hella scary to begin with but it has been so much fun.

"Not my daddy's either."

"Someone bought it?" I almost want to cry. This was my bike. It has been since I was little. This was my grandpa's bike. I might even steal it. But then where would I keep it?

"Nope," Kane plugs in the key and wraps his arms around my waist. "I fixed it for you."

I tense, body cement, brain not working, eyes glistening. "No you fucking did not."

"Sure did. She's yours."

"Seriously?" I squeak, trying to turn to look at him but his body at my back holds me in place. "You're lyin'."

"Why would I lie?" He gives me a tender squeeze. "Are you cryin', Imogen Hardy?"

"No," I fib, wiping my tears on my wrist as I look at the speed dial and the new rubber handles.

"Don't get sentimental on me now."

"I'm not. I still hate you."

"Good," he whispers, chuckling as he bites my ear. "Let's go pick you out some leathers that aren't Felicia's hand-me-downs."

"Leathers too?" I relax back against Kane's chest. "You're spoiling me."

"Too scared not to. Don't wanna black eye *again* for underperformin' my duties as your boyfriend."

Twisting, I glower at him. "I have never given you a black eye."

His brow raises, it's all he needs to do to remind me of the time

17... IT'S MY BIRTHDAY

we were playing basketball and I accidentally elbowed him right on the cheekbone. He had a shiner for about three days.

"That was *not* my fault. Your head got in the way of my arm."

"Victim blamer."

Laughing, I twist even more so I can kiss him and then sigh with contentment. A sweet moment of calm passes between us before my heart thuds, reminding me I still live with the female equivalent of a powerless Hitler. "Mee-maw is never gonna let me on this."

"Mee-maw won't ever know." He licks my ear now, making me shiver. "Show me your panties, Immy."

"I'll show you anything you want."

There's a water tower just outside of town that doesn't get used anymore. We head there with a backpack full of food on Kane's back who is holding onto my waist, his black and yellow helmet on his head, his protective leathers zipped to his chin.

Mine flap open a little, I like to feel the breeze on my throat.

I slow to a stop in the middle of the nowhere lane, surrounded by overgrown yellow grass and a few sparse trees.

Kane climbs off first before helping me down.

"I still feel bad that all I got you was a pair of Vans for your birthday," I grumble, it has been eating at me ever since I got given the bike and the ridiculously expensive leathers that were from his dad and Felicia as well as Kane. I chose silver and blue. I look bad ass. Kind of like an astronaut.

"I really like those sneakers," he argues and I know he does because he wears them a lot.

I kiss his jaw which he shaved this morning just for me I bet. Then I pull the bag off his back, almost yanking him down with it.

"You know what, Kane Jessop?" I help him shake out the picnic blanket and stomp down the long grass to make a space for us both.

"What?" he asks, looking at the blanket and checking the grass for any nearby snakes or nasty bugs.

"This is just... really nice and sweet."

17... IT'S MY BIRTHDAY

He puts his fingers down his throat and pretends to gag, laughing when I jump on his back and wrestle him to the ground. We roll over, our feet getting lost in the grass but our heads on the cushioned plaid blanket. It's so soft and it smells so good.

As he peppers kisses across my cheeks and nose, I giggle beneath him and smile at him when he stops.

"I saw you with Mandy Fucknugget yesterday."

"Pretty sure that's *not* her name," he replies, grinning down at me. He loves it when I get jealous. And boy do I get jealous.

"You're not elaborating."

He bites so hard on my bottom lip I squeeze my eyes shut until he lets it ping free. "Stop looking at me like that. I didn't touch her. We were just talking. Like you talk to Ren, or Marshall." The way he says Marshall shows his displeasure for my newer friend.

"Marshall has got nothing on you," I whisper and his eyes soften in the way his eyes only soften for me and nobody else. "We're just friends."

"Uh-huh." Dipping his head, he sucks on my neck below my ear as I hook my ankles around his thighs. "It better stay that way."

"If I didn't know any better I'd think you were worried about losing me."

"It's America, it ain't that big, I'd find you if I lost you."

I laugh and push his head away when he goes in for my neck again. I'm so ticklish there and he knows it. It can be my most sensitive zone or my most torturous one. It all depends on the approach. Like now he's forcing his way there which has set off my tickle receptors, *totally a thing*.

"Move," I demand, still giggling. "I'm hungry."

"Me too," he mumbles against the swell of my breast, having unzipped my jacket.

He goes down, getting lower and lower as I equal parts laugh and moan, but then he stops at my naval and asks the question he always asks, "Pill?"

17... IT'S MY BIRTHDAY

"Oops." I whisper. "We're good, so long as I take it at some point today."

He grins up at me and lifts my top so he can kiss and lick my bare skin.

I hum happily and pull on his hair. "How long have we been dating now?"

"Like six months maybe?" he replies, still kissing me. "Why?"

I lean up on my arms and grab his hair to get his attention. "Do you think you might love me?"

He blinks, stupefied and sits up onto his parted knees.

I quickly add, "Not yet. I just mean like... do you think it might happen? I don't know much about it but I figure when you spend as much time with somebody as we have, isn't love the next thing?"

"I don't know dick about love." He reaches for the bag and drops it beside me. "I don't wanna talk about something I don't know dick about."

Huffing, I cross my legs and tip out the contents of the bag between us. I don't make a big deal out of his dismissal because truth be told I don't know how to answer that question either, and to say he has made me the happiest bitch alive would be the biggest understatement in anyone's lifetime. Plus I don't want to fight on my birthday.

"Do you think you might love me?" he asks, surprising me as I unwrap the PB and J sandwiches that Felicia made. Kane is the fussiest eater ever. As he said, *"If it ain't meat or it ain't a sandwich, I ain't interested."* Sure he's not entirely serious but I once tried to make him Mee-maws special kale and cheese pasta. He almost vomited. I told him, "I *"ain't"* ever gonna *make your hillbilly, fried chicken lovin' ass good food again."*

He annoyingly replied, *"You just keep talkin' in that accent babe and I'll only ever eat you again."*

Did I mention how much I love it when he calls me babe?

"I don't know dick about love," I answer, repeating his words from before.

17... IT'S MY BIRTHDAY

"You love me." His arrogance is so fucking irritating. He's always so sure of himself, yet he's never sure about me. Or that's how it seems.

"You think?"

"Yeah." He stuffs a sandwich in his mouth.

I take a small bite of mine like the young lady I am and stare at him. He looks so much more like a man now than he did a couple of months ago. The muscles in his arms are stronger, probably from all the extra hours working on my bike. *My bike.* I can't believe I have a Harley. Grandpa would be so jealous.

"Why do you think that?"

"Because no girl I know would put up with my shit like you do," he admits, smiling softly at me. "Not even for my amazing dick skills."

"What shit?" I ask, genuinely curious. "You mean because we fight sometimes?"

"Yeah, sometimes I goad you just because I like to see you mad at me."

I glower at him. "That's not funny, Kane."

"It is."

"It isn't."

"Babe... it is."

I shove my sandwich into his laughing fly trap of a mouth and smirk when he gags. "Too far?"

"You're such a bitch." His words are muffled by the slop in his mouth.

"Takes one to know one."

He rolls his eyes but holds his smile, still chewing the sandwich half in his mouth.

"Reckon we can get away with fucking on the bike out here?" I ask making him choke on the remaining food in his mouth. Laughing, I pat him on the back and hand him a soda. He chugs it down without pause and wipes his chin when a droplet trickles down from his lip. When he twists the cap back on I wrap my arms around his neck and kiss him again.

17... IT'S MY BIRTHDAY

"I wish we'd spent more time doing this and less time fightin'," I whisper thoughtfully and straddle his lap.

"Naw. All my best memories involve pissing you off."

Giggling, I push my hands through his soft hair and kiss him again. "I ain't never leavin' you, Kane Jessop."

Gripping my ass, he pulls our groins together. "I ain't never gonna let you, Imogen Hardy." Then because he's a prick he adds, "Now take your pill so I can dick you on your new bike."

If only those double negative promises didn't come true.

On my birthday, Mee-maw cooks me a special dinner every year without fail. So Kane drops me off on the corner of my street and I take a brisk walk down. I really hope word of me riding around on my new bike never reaches my mee-maw.

Matthew greets me at the door and hugs me. "Happy birthday, sissy."

"Happy birthday, broey."

We share a smile and I rush upstairs to grab his gift after kicking my shoes off.

He does the same and we exchange presents in the hall. I got him two tickets to go and see his favorite band, Ellipses, who are touring America and are performing in Houston in a few weeks. I sorted it with Poppy behind his back. She's going too.

He curses with excitement and beams at me like he never has. "How the fuck did you get these?"

"Stayed up until two in the morning and checked out at record speed," I reply, slightly laughing. He spins me around but we fall into the wall.

"Now I feel bad because my gift is shit," he admits, scratching the back of his head.

I open my envelope and tip out the contents. I read it aloud and my cheeks flame. "A two-hour slot at a tattoo parlor?"

"He's really good, Immy, he's the one who did the eagle on my back."

17... IT'S MY BIRTHDAY

I must admit that eagle has so much detail it looks like a photograph. "I don't know if I want to get a tattoo."

"I know, but it's the final stage of your teen rebellion before you head out to college." He punches my shoulder playfully. "Cross it off your bucket list, I know it's on there."

"Have you been reading my diary?"

"No, I just know it's on there because I know you." His eyes soften. "Do you hate it?"

"No!" I blurt, hugging him again. "Not at all. I'm just thinking of what tattoo I'm going to get."

"That's my girl," he replies happily and pats my cheek. "Come on."

2 WEEKS LATER, STILL 17

"Does it hurt?" I ask as Kane winces slightly. The soft buzzing sounds as the man with tattoos from his chin to his fingertips works the pen across the skin of Kane's left underarm.

I'm not allowed to see what he's getting, he said he wants it to be a surprise. So I'm sitting across the room, playing on my phone, chewing a piece of gum in my mouth, occasionally looking up to gauge his reaction.

"It doesn't feel fuckin' good," Kane replies, his tone harsh which makes me giggle.

"You're a pussy."

"Fuck you. Wait until your turn and you'll be crying."

"When is my turn? You've been at this for nearly three hours."

"It's gotta be perfect," the tattooist replies, dipping the pen into a tiny bottle of ink.

"Can I see it when it's done?" I ask and Kane shakes his head.

"Not until you do yours."

I look at the tattooist. "Will mine take three hours?"

"Naw," he replies, grinning at the arm he's marking. "Maybe an hour, tops."

2 WEEKS LATER, STILL 17

"Good."

Kane is done not too long later. They wrap his arm and the tattooist, whose name is Stan, cleans up his workstation and rolls up the picture he was drawing from before stuffing it into the bin.

The chair and desk are completely sterile and clean by the time I'm sitting there.

"The image you gave me, you drew it right?" Stan asks and I nod. He whistles long and high. "That's some good art. I tweaked it a little, perfected the edges..." When he shows me the new size and shape of my soon-to-be tattoo I clap a little. It's a padlock, intricate and rustic, with a broken lock that shatters and becomes tiny little birds flying away.

"It's perfect."

"You sure?"

I nod and lie sideways when he reclines the bed.

I hike up my skirt and Kane wags his brows, having pulled the chair closer so he can hold my hand if needed. Truth be told, I'm shaking a bit. I'm nervous of what the pain might be like. I had a look online and found so many different responses varying from, searing burn, to light pinching, to the feeling of a million needles penetrating your flesh over and over again.

Still, I don't want to be a massive pussy like Kane so I school my features and confirm the placing of the tattoo after he traces it onto my skin with faded black ink.

It's on my upper right thigh, meaning this guy has an epic view of my ass.

"Show me your panties, Immy," Kane jests, popping a cigarette between his lips.

"No smoking in here while I'm working," Stan says firmly.

"Naw, I quit for my girl here. I just like the feel of it."

"It made my hair stink," I add, winking at Kane who rolls his eyes. "Don't look at me like that, you love my hair."

"This ain't a conversation I wanna be a part of no more," Stan jests and the buzzing starts. "You ready?"

2 WEEKS LATER, STILL 17

"Yep."

The needle hits my skin, the sharp feeling makes me jolt a little but not so much that he goes wrong. It's not that bad, it feels weird and hot, but it's not terrible. In fact after a couple of minutes I close my eyes, bite my lip, and relax with it.

"Are you enjoyin' this?" Kane asks, making me open my eyes.

"It's quite relaxing," I respond with a soft smile. "It's not painful, not really."

"High pain threshold," Stan comments. "Guessing you felt a lot of pain in your years."

Kane's eyes darken because we both know it's the truth.

"Nothing major, Grandma likes to hit me with belts and shit when she thinks I'm going against Jesus."

Stan chuckles. "Better not let her see your tattoo then."

Kane brings my hand to his lips. "Just eleven more months and I'll get you the fuck outta there."

Smiling I say confidently, "You love me."

He rolls his eyes but he doesn't deny it. Not like he used to. Does this mean he does? Will he ever say it? I'm not saying it first.

26 YEARS OLD

"Aren't people who do tattoos usually covered in them?" West asks, skeptical despite the fact I'm being honest. Well, about that part at least. I can't say I'm being honest about anything else.

"Yes," I reply, pushing my hair back and leaning back as they all assess me. "What? You want me to get naked? I'm not covered, I have meaningful pieces here and there. Some I did myself, others Lonny did."

"Lonny?" Felicia asks and I blanche. I realize my error but there's no taking it back. I suppose it doesn't matter anyway, like Kane said, ain't nobody coming looking for little ole me.

"A genius with a tattoo machine."

"And Marshall, what is he up to?" Kane asks, sounding bitter but curious. "Givin' you a grand life in a big city?"

"Why ask about shit you don't wanna hear about?" Felicia admonishes, throwing him a look.

"He's umm... he went into plumbing." I bite on my lip and look away from Kane's deepening scowl.

"Fuckin' plumbing," Kane utters, shaking his head. "You got a picket fence?"

"No, I live in the city, not suburbs."

We stare each other down and I wonder why I thought this was a good idea. I look at my phone.

"I really should go."

"Back to Marshall? Why didn't he come with you, Immy?" Kane asks as I stare at his collar bone. "Why didn't he take you to your meemaw's funeral and cheer you on while you set her memory on fire?"

"He's busy workin'," I snap, shoving at his chest but he grabs both of my wrists, yanks me to my feet and pins me between his body and the counter.

"Son," West warns.

"Give us a sec, yeah Pa?"

"I think—" Felicia tries but Kane snarls, "I said give us a fuckin' sec. We got shit to discuss."

"We don't got anythin' to discuss," I argue, fighting for my freedom, though weakly I'll admit.

"Kane," West barks.

"Pa, give me a fuckin' minute," he shouts at his daddy who presses his lips together and looks between the two of us.

"Fine, but you gotta let her go, kid."

"Let her go once because you told me to, Pa. Not lettin' her go again without knowin' why she chose that preppy son of a bitch over me."

Well... shit.

Felicia snorts. "The Jessop men are too prideful. Put him out of his misery, Imogen. Tell him what he needs to hear."

"Guys," I beg, wishing they'd stay because even after all this time, being alone with Kane Jessop is doing things to me I don't want to admit.

"Fuckin' hated you for what you did to me," he admits, gripping the counter either side of my body. "Leavin' like that, not even giving me a chance to talk."

I look away but he grips my chin, too hard but not too hard that it hurts. His shining eyes are so angry.

26 YEARS OLD

"You gonna leave again without telling me what the fuck I did?"

"Kane it's been years."

"Yeah and I never stopped looking for you Immy," he admits, gritting his teeth.

My lips part and my heart knits back together, only slightly, but I feel it. "Because of pride? Because you don't know why I left?"

"Yeah, bit of both, lotta the first, hella lot of the last."

I don't know what compels me, whether it's being in his presence, or his scent, or his admission of sadness. Being this close to him has my head swimming with thoughts, desires, needs. My heart is racing behind my breasts which are tight and throbbing as they brush up against his chest. I kiss him, I touch my lips to his but he startles and pulls back without even a second of hesitation.

He rears back, eyes blazing with fury. "The fuck? You tell me you're bedding another man, fucking left me for another man, and think I want to touch that?"

Truth be told I just humiliated myself and I don't know what to say. So I lift a shoulder and bite on my lip again.

"Fuck..." He looks at me incredulously. "You're a bitch, Immy. I used to say that in a nice way, but I don't mean it in a nice way anymore." He paces away from me and growls to himself, "Fuckin' leaves me for another man and puts her lips on mine. Fucking bitch. What the fuck?"

"I'm sorry."

"For which part?"

"All of it."

"If you're so sorry, tell me what I did that was so bad you disappeared."

I hitch my bag up my shoulder and search through them for my keys. "You didn't do anything, Kane. I fell in love. I fell in love so fucking hard. I just wanted to spare you the pain of knowing what I did."

He stares at me, brows pulling together. "Is it because of what happened after homecoming?"

I shake my head and see his irritation increase.

"Is it because I wouldn't leave town?"

"I couldn't stay here."

"I know, but I couldn't leave."

"I know," I breathe and curse myself for letting my tears fall down my cheeks. "You made me so crazy happy, Kane Jessop." His spine stiffens but he doesn't say a word. He just listens as I talk. "So crazy happy. But—"

"Marshall made you happier?"

Nodding, unable to verbalize any of it, I grasp my keys and nod to the door. "I'm going to go. I'm really sorry for coming back here."

"I'm not. Least now I can put you to rest as the bitch everybody told me you were."

"Stop calling me a bitch, Kane Jessop," I snap, unable to hear his hatred for me. "You don't know what the fuck I've been through."

"And whose fault is that?"

Yours, I think but don't say. *For not finding me the first time I went missing.*

17 YEARS OLD

"Can y'all stop kissing?" Ren snaps but he's also laughing. "Do you even have any lips left? Damn. Fuckin' stop for one minute."

"Shut up, Ren," Kane growls against my mouth and presses me tighter into the lockers making them rattle.

"I'm tryna talk to y'all."

"We ain't listenin'," I say but it's muffled because of the kissing that is annoying Ren.

"Break it up you two," my brother barks, grabbing Kane by the back of his collar and yanking him away from me.

Kane retaliates by shoving him and I sigh when they start scrapping in the middle of the hall. It's not a real fight but it sure is stupid.

"Watch his arm! It's healing," I shout at my brother, stepping between him and a laughing Kane. I bring up Kane's arm to my lips and kiss the fresh ink. It's still a bit dry but in a couple of days it'll be smooth and as stunning as he is.

I gently trace the outline of the initial of my name, inset in a crown that's so fucking beautiful and detailed. He says he might not know dick about love, but he does know he'll worship me like his queen until the day he dies. I sucked his dick for that one too. Kane

Jessop might be vicious, but he has a big heart. When it comes to me anyway.

Kane nudges my forehead with his nose but tenses when he sees Marshall heading our way. Ren steps in front of me, blocking me from his view like some grand protector.

Laughing, I pull away from Kane and shove Ren to the side.

"Not today," Ren tells Marshall like he has any right to control me.

"Immy, can I borrow you?" Marshall asks politely and I open my mouth, ready to agree and tag along.

"You can fuck off," Kane snarls at him, yanking me back into his chest with a flesh covered band of pure titanium. "She don't got time for you today Martian."

"Don't be a dick," I snap at the man who is holding me tight. He lets me go and glares at me. "You don't fuckin' own me, Kane Jessop. Remember that."

Marshall gives me a wink and Kane steps forward towards him.

"Are you serious right now?" I shove him back again. "Marshall's my friend."

"So you and him keep remindin' me," Kane argues, shoving a cigarette between his lips.

"I just need to talk to her, Jessop," Marshall snaps, looking irritated. No love is lost between these guys. They can't stand each other. Most of that is because Kane is a prick to him for no reason other than he thinks Marshall wants in my pants. If he does he's never shown it. We just hang out to appease our parents. They like us together and it keeps them off our backs. I thought Kane would understand because it means I get more time with him but he's always like this. It sure is frustrating.

"Maybe if y'all were more accepting, he'd hang out with us," I say, pinching Kane's cheek and his hand snakes around my body to grip my ass so tight it hurts. He kisses me, shoving his tongue deep into my mouth as though guarding his territory down there. It's sort of funny but I don't let him know that I secretly love how possessive he is just as much as I hate it.

"Fucked her this mornin', Martian. Didn't get time to shower after. Lettin' you know that I'm all up in her pussy just in case you tryna be all up in there too."

I rear back, horrified that he just outed us like that in front of the entire hall. I slap Kane around the face, not hard, but enough to make his head whip to the side.

Ren laughs as though it's hilarious but I don't find any of this funny. That was disgusting, not to mention insulting.

"Too fucking far," I snap at him, being serious now. I'm actually shaking I'm so mad. He doesn't trust me at all and that was such a vile thing to say.

"Come on, babe. I was just kiddin'," he calls after me when I stomp away, flipping my hair over my shoulder as I go.

"That was seriously gross, Kane," Poppy snaps, following me and Marshall.

"Do we need words?" my brother asks my boyfriend, shoving him back for real this time.

I hear Kane and Ren laugh when I flip him the bird as I look away, so I don't have to see his smirk or uncaring attitude.

I'll show him, he wants to play that game and treat me that way... I can be a dick too.

"He's so fucked up, Immy. What do you see in him?" Marshall asks, frowning down at me when we make it outside where it's quieter. "He has no respect for you at all."

"You're breaking my rule," I remind him and he sighs. We don't talk about Kane because I don't want to fall out. I might be pissed at Kane right now but no way in hell am I letting anybody else trash talk him.

Marshall pretends to zip his lips closed even though he's unhappy about it. We have rules, there are things I know about him that I'm not allowed to judge, and he's not allowed to judge me for who I hang with. If either of us break the rule, we have to do a forfeit.

He wraps his arm around my neck playfully and winks down at me. Because he's so tall and I'm not.

"What do you need to talk to me about anyway?" I ask, ducking under his arm and putting some distance between us.

"Homecoming," he admits sheepishly and Poppy gasps a sharp inhale. I forgot she followed us for a moment. "I really need you to be my date to homecoming."

"But... you're quarterback and that's a huge statement," Poppy puts in like I don't know that already.

"I've got this. I'll catch you later, Pops," I say to my best friend of forever years.

"Scuse me?" she replies, looking affronted.

"I need to talk to Marshall in private."

"But..." She looks so confused. I get it. Everybody is by our friendship.

"I'll explain everything later," I lie because both Marshall and I know I absolutely won't.

She stops as we go on ahead and I know she's pissed off but this isn't for me to say. Though she quickly catches us up. "Fuck that, I'm in this. She can't go with you, Marshall."

"She can, Kane ain't goin'." He levels me with a look. "He has no plans on askin' you. I know because he told everyone in the locker room what a waste of time it is."

I pout because it's true. Kane won't come with me no matter how much I beg. There's no access unless you're wearing a suit and have a ticket and he is not wearing a suit at all. He said, "Babe... no." And even when I begged he just wouldn't relent. I've never hated him more than I did in that moment. Except maybe now after what he said back there.

"Yeah," I agree sadly, pouting at Poppy. "I could go with Marshall; our parents will be expecting it anyway. Makes sense. Kane's not going and you're goin' with my brother."

Marshall grins, looking excited and relieved. "I'll even pay for the limo."

17 YEARS OLD

Poppy's eyes light up. "And we can double date?"

"Absolutely," I say, feeling evil because I know Kane will hate this but if he isn't going to take me then I'll find my own way.

"Marshall, you got yourself a date," Poppy says on my behalf which has me cackling with laughter. She wasn't hard to talk around. Just offer her something shiny and fun and she's good to go.

Marshall grabs my shoulders and beams at me. "Thanks, Immy."

"What are friends for?"

Marshall walks away backwards, still smiling, and joins his friends who were lingering nearby. They high-five which makes me roll my eyes because now everybody is going to think I'm dating Kane *and* Marshall. Which isn't the case at all but it's what we need people to think. Kane hates it, but if he wants me to not be grounded, Meemaw has to believe I'm dating Marshall, so the rest of town has to believe it too.

"Kane is not gonna like this," Poppy singsongs, a high lilt in my ear.

I shrug and we share a wicked grin. "He snoozes he loses."

"Yeah, I was sad when he said he wouldn't go. But it's not his scene. He hasn't been to any of the dances."

"I thought he'd make an exception for me." I lift a shoulder and look sadly towards where we left Kane and Ren to talk about this. My brother appears out of nowhere, hooking his arm around Poppy's neck and kissing her deeply which of course makes me gag. "I mean, he got my initial tattooed on his arm, you'd think something as small as a couple of hours dancing wouldn't be a big deal."

"Kane Jessop doesn't do school cheer, you knew this when you got with him," Poppy needlessly points out. I glower back at the school where Kane is exiting with Ren, laughing at something hilarious by the looks of it.

"Just umm... don't say shit to Kane about this," I utter, eyes still on him until his find mine. I sneer at him and look away. "I want him to hear it from everyone else."

17 YEARS OLD

"Damn, Immy, you're mean as fuck." She rubs her hands together and smiles evilly. "I like it."

"Like what?" Selma asks, sliding to a stop beside us with her skateboard tucked under her arm. I miss skating. I used to do it a lot when I was fifteen until I broke my leg being an idiot. Mee-maw was actually really nice to me for those six weeks that I couldn't walk. "What do we like?"

"Get it around the school," Poppy orders, still grinning evilly. "Marshall just asked Imogen to homecoming and Immy said yes."

Selma's jaw hits the floor. "Kane will be pissed."

"He'll be too busy wonderin' why the fuck I'm not talking to him," I reply with a shrug.

"You're not talkin' to him?" she asks, eyes wide. "Why? What happened?"

"He basically called her a cheater in front of the entire school, and also insulted her hygiene." Poppy throws a gumball into the air and catches it with her tongue.

"What a dick."

"Right?"

"But..." There's a pause. "What if he gets with another girl?" Selma questions and it's a good fucking question.

I reply through a dangerous grin, "Then I hope he still has health insurance."

"Or life insurance," Poppy adds on a mumble, making me laugh my ass off.

"Babe," Kane calls, getting closer.

I flip my hair and saunter away, linking my arm through Selma's and ignoring him completely.

He can't say shit like that and embarrass me like that. It's not right. He needs to be taught a lesson.

"Let's go dress shopping," Poppy suggests and it's the best thing I've heard all day.

An hour later I text Marshall what color he needs to coordinate

17 YEARS OLD

with and he sends me a screenshot of the limousine his mom is booking. It's so exciting!

Kane: Are you really pissed at me? I thought you were just fucking with me.

I don't reply. I've never not replied before. I want to make him sweat a little. That's if he even cares. When I climb into bed after listening to my mee-maw go on animatedly about how happy she is and blah blah, another text comes through.

Kane: You comin? Bed's cold.

I ignore that too.
 It's petulant and stupid but I'm loving every second.

Kane: Come on, babe. You know I was just fuckin' with you.

I'm not replying until he says he's sorry and means it and promises that he won't do that shit again. He's can be a real ass sometimes and he knows it. But it's not okay. I haven't done anything to make him not trust me. I spend all my free time with him when I'm not with friends. He always gets such a bee in his bonnet over Marshall despite the fact Marshall has repeatedly told Kane we are just friends. Kane doesn't believe it. It's frustrating. But for him to insinuate that I'd have sex with somebody else at all, let alone after we've already had sex, it's just fucked up.

I wake up in the morning to ten missed calls and three texts. Two texts are from Kane and the third is from Poppy. All the calls are him. This brings me some small amount of satisfaction. I shouldn't play these games but... what's wrong with making him sweat a little?

Kane: Come on, Immy. Why you being such a bitch? I've done worse and you've still fucked me after.

Kane: Screw you then.

He's frustrated. He wants me to react which is what I'd normally do. I'm not reacting this time. Especially not now he's blamed me by calling me a bitch.

Poppy: How y'all holding up? Kane at your door yet?

Imogen: Not yet. He still hasn't apologized. He did call me a bitch though.

Poppy: He'll be there with an attitude before you know it.

Imogen: I'm counting on it.

Poppy: LOL. Me too, can't wait.

I kiss Mee-maw's cheek on my way out and thank her for the lunch she has made for me. She's been really chilled out lately which is nice. We've been getting on a lot better than we usually do and she seems to have made a few new friends. One is a born again Christian and by God does he go on about his love for Jesus Christ.

He's a member of some kind of Jesus fan club called the Righteous Voices and he comes to visit Mee-maw every Tuesday and Thursday without fail. He seems to keep her calm and grounded. She's been less shrill and bitter since he intervened and for that I'm grateful.

Mee-maw needs more genuine people in her life. All her friends are so fake and fair-weather. But then, Mee-maw is no different. She'd drop you for the slightest indiscretion.

"Have a good day, sweet pea," she utters, using my nickname from when I was a little girl.

"Thanks, Mee-maw. You too!"

I race down the driveway to the road, hitching my bag up my shoulder and smiling when I see Marshall's car pull up at the end. My hair, which I got Mee-maw to trim last night, bounces behind me, tickling the skin of my back. My t-shirt has a deep V at the back and is tight all around really showing off my cleavage. I want to really make Kane suffer today while I blank him.

I don't want to break up with him, but he needs to know I will if he keeps treating me like he has.

The thought is painful, in fact thinking of him moving on with anybody else enrages me, but I can handle pain. I can't handle this anger I feel at him treating me like that.

I dive into the passenger seat, grin at him, tweak the radio and listen as he talks shit about his coach. Marshall has buffed out these past few months. He's grown a couple of inches too. I stare at his profile, smiling gently as he rages about school and how unfair his teammates are being. I wonder if I'm the only person he vents to.

He's so damn popular and has plenty of people around him, but how many of them know the real him like I do?

"What?" Marshall asks, glancing at me out of the corner of his eye.

"You're my best friend, Marshall Jones and outside of Kane, the handsomest boy I ever met."

His cheeks pink and his hands tighten on the steering wheel. "Now I know you want somethin' since you're sweet talkin' me."

Laughing, I rest my head back and keep on smiling. "Nope. Just wanted you to know that I love you and I'm sorry my boyfriend is such a dick to you. He's missin' out."

"You reckon?"

"Absolutely."

He places his hand on my thigh and squeezes for a brief moment before letting me go. "You're my best friend too, Imogen Hardy. Who'd have thought we'd be here where we're at now?"

"Right? I was just thinking the same thing."

"But I promise you, my future partner treats you the way your boyfriend treats me, they ain't nobody I wanna be with."

I roll my eyes. "Low key insulting my king. You know that's against the rules."

He chuckles and puts his foot down. "How long until you speak to him again?"

"Duh, when he says sorry."

"And if he doesn't?"

I blanche because I hadn't thought that far ahead.

"Immy?" Marshall prompts.

"He will."

"You don't sound so sure."

I lift a shoulder. "He will."

"And if he doesn't."

"Then me and him have got nothing more to talk about."

Pain lances through my chest so powerful I press my hand against my heart to make sure it's still beating. It is, though barely. Would it ever beat again if I left him?

"You love him."

"I do," I confirm, scowling now. "That bastard trapped me."

"Not sure you can blame this one on him, Imogen. Way I see it is he's tried hella hard to make you hate him since you were little."

Smiling again, I acknowledge that he has a point by sticking my wet finger in his ear.

"Gross."

I wipe it on his jeans, laughing evilly the entire time.

When we pull into the school grounds, sure enough Kane Jessop is waiting for me. His shoulder length hair is loose today and his blue eyes are glowing with a scowl. His hands are tucked into his front pockets making his biceps bulge and tighten below the short sleeves of his T-shirt.

Oh he's mad.

He stares me down as I climb out of Marshall's vehicle. I don't even look at him. I raise my chin and all but skip to Poppy and my brother who seem to be having some kind of argument that they don't want any of us to hear.

They stop as I approach and Poppy gives me a tight-lipped smile. My brother stomps away, throwing his hands up in the air as he goes.

"What just happened?" I question, looking at my friend with concern in my gaze. It's unlike them to argue, they just don't fight. So whatever it is must be bad.

"We're disagreeing on college."

"Right," I utter because I totally understand that.

I look back at Kane and my brows pull together. He's talking to a girl called Della. She's sweet and pretty and tall with legs for days. She's also a cheerleader and I just know she wants in Kane's pants though she's never made a move to my knowledge.

I act like it doesn't bother me while listening to Poppy rant about how she thinks Austin is the better choice whereas my brother wants to go to Dallas. They both want to stay in state though so I don't know what the big deal is.

"Just go to different colleges?" I suggest and she looks insulted. "I don't know what I'm going to do. I really want to go to Dallas but Austin is closer to Kane."

"The feminist in me is telling you not to decide your fate based on a guy but what a hypocrite that would make me."

I laugh a little but it's sad. "I hate all these grown up decisions. We're hardly into our senior year and just every day is stress filled with another decision to make that could potentially derail our future."

She hums her agreement and scowls ahead, looking so frustrated. I wrap my arm around her waist and smile at her my biggest smile.

"He's gonna love you no matter where you both go."

"He said he doesn't want a long-distance relationship."

I get that, but... it's Matthew and Poppy. They are relationship goals.

Speaking of relationship goals, Kane Jessop's arms suddenly wrap around my waist. I quirk a brow at Poppy as he hugs me from behind as though everything is normal.

"You chilled the fuck out now?" he asks, nuzzling the back of my neck.

Poppy glares at him. "Are you dimwitted, Kane? Because you sure ain't smart when it comes to women."

"Stay out of this, don't fuckin' need two bitches gangin' up on me."

I stomp on his foot, not too hard but enough to make him hiss from the pain and release me.

"So I guess that's a no then?" Kane shouts as I walk away. "Not playin' this game Immy."

I keep going, smiling smugly as he follows. I can see his reflection in the entrance doors of the school as we approach. Poppy smirks at me, sharing my wicked thoughts and excitement.

It's inside when he grabs my arm and yanks me to the side, shoving me so hard against the lockers the metal rattles so loudly that everyone looks our way. He gives my arm a shake and dips his head, forcing me to look into his eyes. "You got beef with me, we talk about it."

I sigh and try to duck under his arm but he brings me back again.

"Give me your fuckin' eyes, Imogen Hardy. I ain't playin'." He cups my face tenderly with his hand. "Now you're gonna have to tell me what I did so I can fix it."

"You know what you did," I snap, scowling now.

"Is this about what I said to Martian?"

My eyes narrow and my hands ball into fists. "Don't call him that."

"You're defendin' him now?"

"Absolutely. He's my friend."

"He more than that?" Kane questions as the bell rings overhead. People stop watching and start moving. They're used to our fights by now, but this one is actually real. Especially now he just went and thoroughly pissed me off.

"You seriously think I'd do that?" I gape at him, shaking my head slightly. "You're an ass, Kane Jessop."

"And you're not answerin' me." His tone is a growl and he cages me in, still scanning my eyes like the answers might be there. "You havin' your cake and eating it as well?"

"I'm not dignifying that question with a fucking answer." This time I successfully escape, though only for a moment.

"Immy," he snaps but there's a vulnerability to his tone that has me stopping in my tracks and twisting back to face him. He lets me go, allowing me the space to turn to face him because I know he's not going to let me walk away. "Be real with me."

My lips part. He's worried, genuinely. I can see it swimming in his guarded eyes and my heart gives a little flip.

"You're crazy if you think I'd ever cheat on you, Kane Jessop." I approach him and place my hand on his heart. It's beating wildly and I wonder if all those extra thuds are just for me. "You're the only guy I want and need. But yesterday was fucked up. The things you said. And then the constant paranoia. You always talk to girls and I don't say shit. Yet you constantly seem to think I'm some kinda whore." I throw my hands up and let them drop. "Like I ever have the time."

"You smile at him," he blurts when I start to walk away again.

"He makes me happy," I reply and his features sink to a depth I have never seen. "He's just a friend, Kane. A good one. Dig deep and maybe he could be yours too."

"No way am I hangin' with that fucking tool."

I laugh humorlessly and walk away again. "You're the only one acting like a tool here, Kane."

The hall is empty, I'm late for class. I'm going to get a bad mark and Mee-maw will probably be called. Fucking Kane.

"Babe," he tries, his tone softer now. I love it when it gets soft.

"You gotta straighten your shit out, Kane. I'm not sticking around if this is how you're always gonna be. It's fun, but not always and at the moment, *it's not always* is a lot more than the other."

"I don't want to be his friend."

"You don't have to be. But you do have to respect him because he's mine."

He growls and chases me again, this time when he snags me, I let him. He backs me up into the wall and kisses the curve of my neck.

"He's got money, Immy. He's got cash and a fuckin' lot of it."

"So?"

"He's probably going to Dallas like you."

"I haven't decided yet."

"Still." His soft blue eyes search my face and his lips twitch with a gentle but defeated smile. "I'm stayin' here for my dad and for me. I don't want to leave."

"Then stay, I'm not asking you to follow."

"But what if he follows you where I can't?"

"Then you should be grateful I've got a friend who will look after me wherever I go."

His hold tightens as his body becomes cement.

"I want you to stay," he finally says and I've been waiting weeks to hear it. I never thought he'd say it. Never thought he wanted it. And now I'm posed with it I don't know what to do. "Don't know dick about love, Imogen Hardy."

"So you've said."

"But I sure do know that I love you."

My breath catches in my throat where a lump is swelling, making my eyes burn with unshed tears. He's never said it. Didn't think he ever would. And now he has I've never felt such deep happiness.

"Don't want you to leave. Couldn't stand it. So, go to Austin college, we can commute."

"You love me?" I whisper, smiling now.

"Yeah." He says this so simply, so easily. "You love me back?"

I nod, letting tears slide out of the corners of my eyes and down my soft cheeks. "Yeah."

"Then what's left to figure out?" His calloused thumbs catch the droplets and spread them across my cheekbones.

"Everything," I reply even quieter than before and he presses his lips to mine.

I kiss him hard and deep and forever. I don't want it to stop but a teacher rounds the corner and starts shouting at us. I race away without looking back because I might start crying again.

Kane Jessop definitely doesn't hate me anymore.

Well... at least until lunch when he finally hears about me going to homecoming with Marshall. The entire school is talking about it. I sort of regret not bringing it up with him.

"Not happening," Kane states. It's the only thing he says when he approaches, eyes blazing with fury. I know exactly what he's talking about.

"You gonna take me?"

"Fuck no. But we can go to the movies or some shit. I'll take you out to dinner."

"As tempting as that is, I'm going to homecoming, I'm going with Poppy, Marshall and my brother. If you want to join us, you can. If you want to help me get ready or take me to dinner before, you can." I kiss his cheek and smile sweetly. "The invitation is there."

"Are you purposely trying to piss me off?"

"No. I'm going to homecoming with my best friends. Are you purposely trying to be a dick?"

He presses his lips together and pushes a hand through his hair. "Fine. I'll go riding with a few people. You go to your stupid dance. We'll meet up after."

"And you're not gonna give me shit about it?"

"Nope," he grits and I can see him trying. "Not gonna be a dick because I gotta get used to this shit. If you're living in Austin and you're in a co-ed dorm, I need to be able to chill about you and other guys or I might not get any sleep."

"Damn, Kane," I push my hands into his back pockets and grip his rear which is undeniably so tight. "You really are tryin'."

"Shut up," he commands and kisses me deep. Reminding people that I'm still his.

"Tell me again that you love me."

"Shut up," he repeats, smiling at me.

Laughing, I slide my hands up his back and rub his shoulders and neck.

"We'll talk about Austin college later," he whispers in my ear and pulls back with swollen lips and flushed, stubbled cheeks. "And everything else."

"We're good?"

"We're good."

I am the luckiest girl in the entire world.

17 YEARS OLD

HOMECOMING

"Noooo," I utter, rubbing my lower stomach.

"What's wrong?" Poppy asks as she threads a shiny hoop earring through her ear.

"I'm getting my period."

"Damn, that sucks. You got tampons in your purse?"

"Duh. But I really wanted to fuck Kane in this dress later."

She grins at my reflection wickedly. "Does it ever feel weird to you, being in a sexual relationship with somebody?"

"What do you mean?"

"Like do you ever feel too grown up for your own good?"

I nod softly. "I guess. I think about it sometimes and it blows my mind. But then again, Kane blows my mind."

"Yeah from what you've said he *really* blows your mind. I wish Matthew would give me head as often as Kane gives you head."

"Ew."

She raises her hands, brown eyes twinkling with mischief. "I'm just saying. The honeymoon period is over for us." Sadness sweeps away her happiness. "I think he might break up with me."

"No. He loves you. He'd lose his mind without you."

She wets her glossy lips and twists her hands in front of her. "He's been texting Micha Riley behind my back. He doesn't know I know."

My heart sinks and clatters into my stomach. Would my brother do that to her?

"She asked him how big his dick was and he replied, *why? Do you want to sit on it?*"

"Oh my God," I whisper, feeling emotional on her behalf. "Have you talked to him about it?"

"No," she admits and smiles sadly. "I'm terrified of the answer and how far they took it."

"Surely he didn't—"

"I don't know. They were at a party together last Friday and rumor has it they were quite close for the last couple of hours."

I feel nauseous. "He wouldn't cheat on you."

"You sure?"

I don't say I am because truthfully I'm not. If he really texted Micha what she says he did, the evidence is against him. Maybe I don't know my brother as well as I thought I did.

"If anything had happened, Micha wouldn't keep quiet about it."

"You're right," she agrees. "That's how I found out about the texts."

"Did you see them on his phone or hers?"

"His," she answers. "And he deleted the conversation the next morning while I was in the shower."

"Oh my God."

"I asked him if there's anything he wanted to tell me and he was adamant there isn't. I'm just waitin' for him to tell the truth or not."

"What are you going to do if he cheated?"

"I don't know." Tears fill her eyes. "It might kill me."

I move to my friend and hug her. She accepts it but pulls back with a new smile on her face.

"Let's enjoy ourselves," she says with genuine enthusiasm. "I don't want to ruin the night."

"You couldn't ruin it if you tried."

If Matthew hurts her like that I will kill him myself.

She puts on such a brilliant mask that at some points even fools me. She seems genuinely happy until she thinks all eyes are off her and then her face falls and her worries claim her gorgeous smile. Still, I don't probe her because I know it's not what she wants or needs. What she needs is a great night with her best friend, her boyfriend who loves her, and a pretty dress to help make her feel special.

Mee-maw takes pictures of Marshall and I, who looks so good in a tailor-made suit and shiny shoes. His baby blue tie matches my dress and the corsage on my wrist. His parents join in, all of them making a huge deal out of this which is mortifying.

"They're planning our wedding already," Marshall whispers in my ear, making me snort unattractively.

"So sweet," Mrs. Jones comments, loving the interaction between her son and me.

Thank fuck when it's over.

We all pile into the limousine and pass around a bottle of gin that Marshall stashed after stealing it from his mom. It tastes like oranges, so yum. Though I don't indulge too much because I want to be sober for Kane later. I don't know what it is about going on long rides, but he's always worked up afterwards. Some of the best sex we have ever had come after his bike rides. But I get it, feeling so powerful, that beast vibrating between your thighs. It's the second-best highlight of my life riding my bike around when I can. I can't wait to take it to college with me.

Thinking of Kane has me missing him. I'm still annoyed that he couldn't come with me to homecoming. Especially after our win yesterday. Everybody is going, even Ren. I don't know what his deal is.

Matthew and Poppy act every bit as in love as they usually act. But now I'm wondering how much of that is an act and I'm also panicking because I don't want that to be me and Kane. I never want us to cheat on each other or hurt each other and then pretend like we're happy when we're not. I just always want to be happy with him.

Imogen: **If I tell you I miss you will you laugh at me and call me an idiot?**

Kane: **Probably.**
    Kane: **Your stupid party over yet?**

Imogen: **We haven't even arrived. We're still in the limo.**

Kane: **Of course Martian can afford to get you a fuckin limo.**

Imogen: **I don't need a limo, Kane. I just need you.**

Kane: **You better mean that.**

Imogen: **I miss you.**

Kane: **Soft bitch.**

I laugh quietly and bite my lip.

Imogen: **STFU, you miss me too.**

Kane: **Yeah.**

Marshall rolls his eyes at my Cheshire cat smile and I look at Poppy. "Kane loves me."
    "Duh."

"He said it."

"No way?"

I nod, still clutching my phone to my chest.

"Y'all are whacked. Who wants love when you can fuck anything you want?" Marshall comments.

Stupidly my brother laughs, holds up his hand to high-five Marshall and declares an enthusiastic, "Right?"

"Well if that's how you really feel I guess we don't have shit to say to each other anymore." Poppy snarls, her mood souring in less than half a second and I don't blame her.

"Come on, Pops," Matthew tries but she's bitter now and I know there'll be no shaking her out of it. "I was just kiddin'."

"Was you kiddin' when you fucked Micha?"

He blanches and his jaw drops. "That's not... it was..."

The atmosphere in the limo stills, there's a pause, a big one, that doesn't last long but its significance is oppressive.

Oh my God no.

"YOU FUCKED HER?" Poppy screeches and starts hitting him with her clutch. "Oh my God. Pull over. I'm going to be sick."

"Matthew what the fuck?" I ask but he looks horrified. He just outed himself in his panic and didn't even mean to.

"It was just—a mistake."

"A mistake?" Poppy asks, hitting his arm again. "Fuck you Matthew!"

"Guys, calm down," Marshall pleads and hits his hand against the divider. It rolls down and the driver's eyes find us in the mirror. "Pull over."

"We're almost at the school," he comments and Marshall nods, looking out the window. Sure enough we're about to pull onto school grounds.

"How could you?" I snap at my brother who at least looks ashamed.

Poppy sobs quietly, hitting my brother with her bag whenever he tries to touch her.

17 YEARS OLD

"It was a mistake, Pops. I didn't mean to."

"You lied to my face." Her mascara is down her cheeks, she's not going to the party. Not at all. I know her. This night ended and it hasn't even started yet. "I asked you!"

"I didn't want to lose you," he whispers as she downs two large gulps of the gin. I feel her pain and the need to numb it.

"No drinking in the car," the driver warns. "Christ, you're all underage."

Marshall ignores him as Poppy takes another swig and passes the bottle to me. I screw the cap back on and hand it to Marshall who looks at me with concern. I shrug my shoulders and shift closer to him as the scene plays out between them and the car rolls to a stop.

"We've just been together for so long. Neither of us have been with other people. I just..." Matthew explains sadly.

"Maybe this is a conversation you should have in private," Marshall suggests.

"I don't ever want to talk about this." Poppy sounds so drained and defeated.

But I get it. This is so out of the blue. If their relationship out of every relationship in the world can't remain strong and faithful, the rest of us have no hopes at all.

"Not in private. Not ever." She goes to open the door but Matthew yanks her back.

"Poppy, I made a mistake." Matthew's tortured whisper has my eyes filling with tears. He's sorry, but he's too late. Poppy won't forgive him for this.

"So did I," she spits back at him, glowering at him.

This time I grab her. "Fix your face," I say, raising my chin. "Don't let them see. Don't give Micha the satisfaction."

"Micha?" she scoffs a laugh. "I'm going to KICK HER FUCKING ASS!"

"Oh shit," Marshall whispers and I wince when she opens the door and clambers out, shutting it hard on Matthews hand. He cries out, cursing and half screaming and by this point I'm just done.

I want to check on him, I want to ask him if he's okay but I'm so mad I feel like he deserves the pain. He grits his teeth and climbs out, barking at me to stay out of his business and relationship when I call him a fucking idiot. Marshall yanks me back and tells the driver to go around the block. He doesn't want to go into the school while they're fighting and I'm torn between wanting to follow them and wanting to pretend this isn't happening.

"Please," Marshall begs. "Let them deal. Be her support tomorrow."

I nod and chew on my lip as my fingers tap against my thigh. This is so bad. Our entire group is about to implode. Or explode. And it's going to bring everyone around us down with it.

"Are you okay?" Marshall asks and I rest my temple on his shoulder. "That was intense."

"My brother is such an ass."

"He done fucked up. Poppy is a great girl."

I nod my agreement. "Micha is gonna get it."

He chuckles a little though it falls flat.

"What would you do if Kane cheated on you?"

I bite on my lip again, my new comfort.

"Immy?"

"I'd never speak to him again," I admit with a sad smile that definitely doesn't move anything but my lips.

"Seriously? You wouldn't even question him?" He doesn't look as though he believes me.

"I'd walk away and never look back."

"Take me with you, yeah?"

Smiling for real now I grin up at him. "Absolutely."

26 YEARS OLD

A week ago I put my past to rest. But I also didn't. Because I ran away from it again only to be faced with it at every turn even worse than I was the first time. Everything triggers a memory. Everything brings me new pain.

It's as though everything is so fresh and raw, even more than it was the first time because now I know how much pain I caused him but fuck if it isn't better than the alternative. It's better that he hates me for something so simple than to hate me for the truth.

"Babe, you gotta give a little. You're fucking miserable," Marshall utters sadly, his lips a flat line. "I can't stand to see you this way."

"I'm fine," I lie, my default voice in play.

"Fuck you."

"You're gettin' a potty mouth Marshall Jones."

Grinning, he approaches and yanks sharply on my hair. "I spend too much time with you."

When his kind eyes find mine, eyes that know the truth about everything, eyes that hold as many secrets as mine, I collapse into his arms and we both fall to the ground as I sob.

He doesn't talk, he just holds me as I cry and strokes my hair.

It's not until I can no longer bear the pain of crying so hard that I finally stop and feel drowsy as he cradles me to his chest.

"You never should have gone back there, Imogen."

"Yeah," I agree because I wish I hadn't. I was healing, I was doing good, I was feeling good. Now I'm not. Now I don't know how I feel at all. It's all just hazy under a heavy layer of intense pain.

"You still love me though, right?" I ask, feeling particularly vulnerable right now.

"No," he lies making me laugh. "Can't stand you." His lips touch my hair as he rocks us both and I start sobbing again, holding him so tight I must be hurting him. He won't complain. He never does.

17 YEARS OLD

The night was a trial. It wasn't fun at all. Poppy ripped out half of Micah's hair, beat her face pretty badly, and ended up getting arrested. My brother passed out in the limo after taking something to numb *his* pain. Like he doesn't deserve to feel it.

Marshall helped me carry him inside and dump him in his bed much to Mee-maw's displeasure. But she didn't fucking say boo to Matthew about any of it, not that he's sober enough to understand. He's off his face on something strong enough to wipe him out so heavy I panic for a while that he might be dead.

Marshall and I are now standing outside as Poppy's mom sends me a million angry texts asking me why I didn't stop her daughter and how Poppy has ruined her future or whatever. I feel so bad. I should have followed but I thought she and Matthew would talk first. I didn't know she'd walk straight into the school and kick the living daylights out of Micha. She has never hit anybody in her life. I didn't know she knew how.

I let her down and that grief weighs heavy on me. I made the wrong choice and I'm worried she might never forgive me.

Marshall takes my phone off me, turns it off and shoves it in my pocket.

"No good is gonna come from you reading those messages," he insists and he's right. I didn't do anything wrong, not really. We have a rule, we don't get involved in each other's fights because it makes it too awkward when we all make up again. I was respecting their wishes no matter how badly I wanted to be in the middle batting for my best friend. "Come here."

With a sigh I step into his open arms and press my cheek against his chest. He wraps his big arms around me and rests his chin atop my head.

"It's all goin' to be okay, you'll see. You'll sleep and tomorrow you'll all figure this shit out."

"I hope you're right," I utter, holding him tighter. "I'm sorry I was such a shit date."

"Are you kiddin'? This was the wildest night of my life and I've had my share of wild nights. This one time I had Alanna and Casey in my parent's bed while my daddy was in his office."

Laughing, I lean back and peer up at his face. "I heard the rumors about you guys. I can't believe it's true. So gross."

"Definitely gross. Had to eat two pussies in one night. Can hardly handle one."

"Damn. Then I'm definitely never screwing you, Marshall. It's my favorite pastime getting ate like that."

He narrows his eyes and pushes his hand between us. "Stop it. You're making me hard."

Laughing, I slap his chest and pull away. Then I burst into tears, overwhelmed by everything that just happened and the thought of my best friend in jail when she's never even had a detention. I must look like a psycho.

He holds the back of my head as we rock together, his way of soothing me, but it abruptly ends with a thudding sound and my body jerking with Marshall's until he inevitably flies away from me.

I only have to take one horrified, wide-eyed look to realize what just happened. Kane has full force punched Marshall in the mouth and Marshall has hit the porch rail, almost going over it.

They start to fight, *for real*, fists flying, arms grabbing. He tackles Kane to the ground and hits him so hard in the face I feel it in my own.

"STOP!" I yell, grabbing Kane when he rolls them over and returns the hit but twice over.

I jump on his back and hold him around the neck.

"Please," I beg, yanking hard.

He turns, shoves me off him so hard I fall onto my ass.

"Shit, Immy, I'm sorry," he immediately says but Marshall takes this moment of distraction to hit him in the stomach, winding him. He rasps and doubles over but Marshall doesn't keep hitting Kane despite the fact he likely deserves it.

"If you're my friend," Marshall snarls at me, wiping blood from his mouth as he clambers to his feet. "Just for that you'll get fucking rid of him."

"Marsh," I whisper, tears filling my eyes.

"Fuck you, Martian. She don't need you."

Marshall looks at me with a glare so heavy I feel it in my bones. "You're losing me for him. Hope you know that. Would cherish you, every fuckin' moment. But not while he's so hungry for my blood." He spits at Kane's knees, his eye and lip so swollen he won't be able to move much of his face tomorrow.

Kane clambers to his feet still holding his stomach.

"Marshall," I plead.

"Not doin' it, Immy. It's me or him. Be fuckin' smart."

I'm just too tired for this shit tonight.

I look at Kane, fresh tears streaking down my face. "You're ruining my life, Kane Jessop."

His face twists with a look of horror and maybe I'm being harsh but I turn towards the house, push open the door and slam it behind me. The lock clicks as Mee-maw sets about dealing with that and I skulk to my brother's room, check that he's breathing, before heading to mine and collapsing on the bed.

"Are you seeing that Kane boy while you're seeing poor Marshall?" Mee-maw asks through the wood of my door.

"Go away," I utter, hoping she can hear me but knowing she can't. My voice is weaker than my willpower and my soul.

"You answer me right now!" The side of her fist hammers on the door.

I stomp towards it, making every step count. I feel like a juggernaut, rage building with my momentum. Swinging the door open, I level her with a look, hoping she knows I'm not in the mood and I ain't gonna take a beating. I don't have another bed to run to tonight.

"You want an answer, Mee-maw? You wanna know if I'm seeing Kane and Marshall?" My lips twist with a sneer as I unleash my anger on her as she often has done to me over the years. "I'm fucking them both Mee-maw. I'm a whore just like my momma. I fucked Kane last night, I fucked Marshall in his limo and they both just found out about each other and caused a massive scene on your front porch." She looks at me, shaking with rage similar to my own. "You happy with that answer? You raised two whores, Mee-maw. You're a shit parent, a shit mother, a shit grandmother, and when I turn eighteen I'm fuckin' out of here so fast I'll laugh when your head spins and you will *never* see me again!"

Part of me feels guilt when her harsh eyes fill with tears, but that guilt is short lived when she grabs my throat and starts hitting me with the walking cane in her hand. I welcome each blow like an old friend, falling to the floor as blinding pain hits my arm and side. Then she stalks to my nightstand, grabs my phone and throws it at the wall. Mee-maw might be a mee-maw but she ain't old and senile yet and she's got strength and speed my fucked-up body can't compete with tonight.

My phone shatters and I just laugh hysterically, rolling on my back as pain radiates through my body.

"You are done, girl. I will fix you. I have to fix you!" she rattles on as I laugh and hold my aching body. "I'm not going through this again. No I am not."

She locks the window and then walks to the door and I don't even try to crawl to freedom. I just curl into a painful ball and listen to what's left of my sanity lock itself in the hall with my grandmother.

26 YEARS OLD

"It's insane how one moment in your life can change everything." His voice is like a rush of water in my dying, scorched mind.

When I woke up mid-afternoon after a tumultuous night's sleep, I never expected my day to take this sort of turn.

Kane Jessop is standing on my doormat, his hand pressing against the flat wood that is my door so I can't slam it in his face. As in my doormat just outside of my apartment where I live.

"Chicago, Illinois," he comments, a piece of gum rolling around his mouth. I always found the way he chewed gum so attractive, the way his perfectly shaped lips move and his cheeks hollow slightly. "Didn't you say Minneapolis? St Paul to be exact? A well-rehearsed fuckin' lie I bet."

My mouth opens and closes. I'm so dumbfounded I don't know how to react. "What?"

"What?" He laughs humorlessly, his blue eyes dangerous with madness. "All you can say is what?"

"I'm sorry, I'm completely fuckin' caught off guard here Kane. It's been three weeks since I left, I never expected to see you again."

"Yeah, me neither, but here I am."

"Why?"

"Why?" he asks incredulously. "Because you fuckin' ran again, didn't even give me time to cool down. And then..." He steps inside, backing me up into my apartment. He grabs my elbow, eyes blazing, heart hammering so loudly I can hear it battling my own for decibel dominance. "And then I find out, straight from the mouth of your *boyfriend*..."

I wet my lips, holding his eyes, petrified because this isn't happening, or it is happening. I don't know. Am I having a nightmare?

He is seething, his words are low and clipped. "That you didn't leave me for him at all because guess what, Immy, HE'S FUCKING GAY AND HE ALWAYS FUCKING HAS BEEN!"

My heart sinks into my stomach, crawls out my ass and hops on the nearest shuttle to outer space. "He told you."

"Yeah he fucking told me. Said you came home a mess, said we got things to deal with, said he feels bad for betraying you but he's worried you might do somethin' stupid like try to kill yourself again."

It's bad because I had thought about it, it had crossed my mind. Death just seems so much simpler than *this*. But I wouldn't, not again. I'm not that far gone in my mind, not anymore.

"What does it matter, Kane?"

"What does your life matter?" he asks, wrapping my hair around his hand. "Is that what you're asking?"

"Let me go."

"No." He yanks me closer, putting us chest to chest and my nipples tighten immediately. I'm only wearing a satin shift that stops before my knees and a matching nightgown. I wasn't expecting company today and I'm not at work until tomorrow. "Marshall seems to think you've got something to tell me. And if it's not that you left me for another man then I'm wrackin' my brain trying to figure it out." He stares me down. "Did you just stop lovin' me? Because of how I was and what I did?"

26 YEARS OLD

I don't answer, I just stare at him dumbfounded, feeling betrayed by Marshall and overwhelmed by Kane's presence.

"Don't ask me," I finally whisper. "Don't make me tell you."

"Tell me what?" He shakes me slightly and holds me tighter. "Tell me *what*?"

I pull away, slipping out of his hold and I think he senses my need for a moment because he gives me it, he lets me out of his grasp despite the fact he could so easily pull me back. "You've travelled a long way, Kane. Do you want a coffee?"

"Would love a coffee," he bites out, his impatience clear.

"Good, there's a Starbucks just down the road, make yourself comfortable there."

Growling a sound of frustration he pounces on me, wrapping his arms around me from behind. "Told you I wouldn't pin you, I fuckin' lied."

"Yeah I got that when you tampered with my car."

He chuckles, a genuine sound in this moment of absolute madness and sorrow.

We stay like this, suspended for a moment, me tense in his warm arms that still make me feel safe despite everything.

When he realizes I'm not going to talk, he begins, "Never moved on, Immy."

I inhale sharply and shut my eyes.

"Fucked a lot, but never found that connection with anyone else. I'm man enough to admit that shit to you, man enough to tell you everything you need to hear. But you gotta be strong enough to give me the truth, babe. You loved me. You ain't moved on either. Marshall told me you exist, you don't live. But the girl I remember fuckin' lived, she didn't just exist."

My lip shakes as new waves of pain take me over.

"If I tell you, I can't take it back. You have to hold it forever. It'll stay with you. It'll haunt you." My words are whispered, my jaw is trembling, my teeth chattering, my body aching.

"I can take it."

26 YEARS OLD

"I don't think I can handle hurting you," I admit.

"You fuckin' destroyed me already, Immy." Concerned eyes search my face. "What can be worse than this?" Realization dawns and his eyes widen. "Did you have an abortion? That what this is?"

I laugh coldly. "Oh, Kane... I fuckin' wish it was that. I really fuckin' wish it was that."

"Then what, Immy? I'm stumped."

"Let me make you that coffee first."

He lets me go again and follows me into the kitchen. "You need time to sort your head out?"

"Never thought I'd have to tell you. Need more than time to sort my head out." I look at him, eyes filling with tears. Then, finally I admit out loud all the shit I should have admitted out loud so many years ago, "I didn't come back because I wanted to spare you this. You have to understand that, I didn't leave you because I didn't love you."

"I'm startin' to get that, but Immy, we were partners. Anythin' you were feelin', I should'a been feeling right there with you." His words cut me deeper than any of his others. His accent is heavier than usual, it always got this way when he was riled up or emotional which wasn't often. Well, the latter wasn't often, the former was quite often. "Why the fuck did you leave, Immy? Just tell me."

"I didn't leave, Kane," I reply, placing my hands on the small breakfast bar and splaying my fingers. My chipped nail polish is a gentle reminder that I need to get my shit together. I didn't survive what I survived to fucking succumb to the agony of this moment.

"You did."

"No I didn't," I respond firmly and look into his eyes. "I didn't leave." With a deep inhale, I finally admit, feeling a weight lift and a new one settle, "I was taken."

His brows pull together. "What?"

His confusion is exactly as I expected.

"Mee-maw found out I was pregnant."

His body stiffens, I expected that too.

26 YEARS OLD

"So she sent me away, some place I couldn't get away from."

"But—" He looks at me dumbfounded and with no small amount of disbelief. "You were pregnant?"

"Yeah. I was pregnant."

17 YEARS OLD

My brother is a mess. Poppy won't take him back and I don't blame her. He's become slightly psychotic, stalking her, trying to force her to kiss him because in his drug-delusional brain he thinks if she kisses him she'll remember she loves him.

There's no getting through to him. He hardly has any lucid moments these days. What's worse is Mee-maw is taking it all out on me which isn't fair. Because he can't physically feel shit there's no use beating him, so instead she belittles and berates me at every turn then acts nice as pie come dinner time.

I can't wait to get the hell out of here.

"Matthew?" I call into his dark bedroom and find his silhouette by the window before my eyes adjust. "Are you okay?"

"Get the fuck out!" he yells and a shoe hits the wall by my head.

I startle and quickly close the door, trying not to burn the image of him in nothing but his boxers, a cigarette hanging from his mouth and a spiteful look on his face. He has never in my life looked at me the way he started looking at me when Poppy rejected him.

He blames me, he thinks I helped Poppy turn against him which I didn't. I only supported her decision to leave him because he fucking ruined her, I didn't actively make it happen. If she'd chosen to forgive him I'd have called her an idiot but I'd have supported that too. He doesn't get to blame what he did on anybody else. It's unfair.

I return to my room and smile at the sight of Kane sitting on my bed, looking through my journal of all things. A smile lights up his face at something I've written, I should be pissed that he's looking through it but I have no thoughts in my head that I don't share with Kane already.

Things have been different between us since his fight with Marshall. I probably should have been stronger and turned him away but everything is so messed up right now I just don't have the strength to fight with him. He hasn't apologized but then again he never does. We just haven't spoken about it. He showed up a few days later with a shake and a brownie from my favorite place.

He only said, "Sorry I ain't been in touch, gotta get my shit together." And that was it. That was enough. For now anyway. I've got bigger things to worry about than Kane and his anger issues. We haven't had sex though and I think he's feeling that. I just haven't been feeling it recently. I'm too stressed, too tired, too worried about the future.

Mee-maw isn't here so I sneaked him in and I'm glad of it. He's so handsome and with each passing week he just gets even more handsome. His beard is growing just enough to make him look way more man than teenage boy. His voice is deeper now too, gruffer than it ever was. People say you can't tell changes like that in a person you're around every day but I'm so hyperaware of Kane Jessop that I notice everything.

Sensing my sadness, he shuffles up my bed after slamming my journal closed, and opens his arm for me to lay beside him and rest my head on his chest. He kisses my hair and tickles my arm making me relax deeper into him.

"Love you enough to fill the gap he's leavin'," he whispers against my hair and my heart breaks and mends in totally different ways. "He'll snap out of it and get his life together."

17 YEARS OLD

"Will he?"

"Promise you he will, you'll see."

I kiss his throat and place my forehead against the shiny mark my Chapstick made. "Love you too, Kane."

"Then let's get the fuck outta here."

"And go where?"

He starts to sit up, forcing me to move with him. "Fuck it, who cares? Let's go for a ride until we run out of gas."

Giggling gently, I stand and hop on his back when he offers me another kind of ride. I cling to him like a monkey, laughing and squealing when he carries me down the stairs like I weigh nothing. The asshole sways a bit too, making me panic but he rights us and carries me out of the house and all the way to his Challenger.

"I forgot my shoes," I whisper when he drops me by the sexy vehicle and the dry road feels rough under my feet. He races back to get them which makes me laugh harder and we make out for a while before driving into the night with the music playing full blast.

Wouldn't it be magical if this was the end of our story, like in so many books, and maybe we'd fast forward to thirty years from now, watching our kids get married or some mushy loved up tale like that. But in real life there are no epilogues, only pain. So much pain.

I grip the basin and heave. I can't breathe through it; I can't do anything but choke on the violent wave of vomit that is tearing its way out of my body.

I've been feeling sick a lot lately but not like this. This is hell and it hasn't stopped for three days. I keep telling everyone and myself that it's a bug but it's not. I just know it.

"You're pregnant," my brother says while leaning against the door jamb. He's looking a lot better today which is a relief. Since he threw that shoe at me a week ago we haven't hardly looked at each other.

17 YEARS OLD

"Don't take a genius to work it out. You been sick until after noon every day."

All I can do is vomit harder. I don't want to be pregnant. Kane and I are making plans to move in together in Austin while I go to college. We're figuring everything out and a baby just doesn't fit into that plan. I don't know how to look after a baby. I don't think I've ever even held a baby.

"Don't tell anyone," I beg, taking the wet face cloth he hands to me.

"Duh." He frowns at me, looking every bit the concerned brother I remember him to be. "You okay?"

"No." I lean back against the bath.

"You gotta try and rein it in, if I figured it out, Mee-maw will and then you'll be up shit creek without a paddle. She'll probably dose your food with an abortion pill or somethin', ain't no way another of her kids is getting knocked up to a lowlife."

"Kane is not a lowlife."

"I know that, but she don't, she hates him." He has a point, a strong one. "You gonna tell him?"

I shake my head, panicking deep down that he might leave me, or hate me, or take my choice away completely. "Not until I know what to do."

"Shit thing that, keeping a baby from its daddy."

I glower at him. "Fuck off Matthew, we don't even know that's what it is yet. I need to do a test first."

"Good luck gettin' one of those from the pharmacy without tongues wagging."

He makes another great point. I chew on my lip and climb shakily to my feet. He watches as I brush my teeth and spray the small bathroom to get rid of the vomit smell.

"Are we friends again now?" I ask him, not making eye contact because I don't think I can handle what I see there.

He walks away, letting me know he hasn't forgiven me for the shit I didn't even do. I let him go because there's no use fighting with him right now. His mind is made and that's his problem, not mine. The front door to the house slams less than a minute later and I finish getting ready for church.

I really hope he doesn't say anything to anyone.

"You ready?" Mee-maw calls up the stairs.

"Coming," I return and race down towards her.

For all my mee-maw's faults she is a beautiful woman just like my momma, it's just a shame they both have sour-ass-souls. I smile at her standing at the bottom of the stairs, bending slightly to slip on her Sunday heels. I stuff my feet into a pair of black flats and follow her out of the house, taking her arm when she offers it to me.

We drive while listening to Christian music, as is Mee-maw's usual. I bop my head, it's a good tune, not what I enjoy these days but it's still decent enough all the same.

I remember back when me and Poppy were young, we used to pretend we were the most famous Christian Country Rock singers in the world. We'd get dressed up and write our own terrible music about loving Jesus and the Almighty.

I smile fondly at the memory of it.

Imogen: Thinking of you. <3

Poppy: Miss you. I need to see you soon. <3

Imogen: It has been forever. How are you holding up?

Poppy: Better. I've got a date tonight with Bradley Tatum.

Imogen: Damn girl, he fine!

Poppy: Right?

Imogen: You nervous?

Poppy: Don't think I'm ready to move on. I don't want to get hurt again.

Imogen: I bet it's so hard but not every guy is like my brother. And I'm always here for you. Remember that.

It's so hard to admit that my brother is a bad guy because to me he has always been somebody I admired and letting the reality sink in just hurts so bad.

Poppy: I know. How is he?

Imogen: He'll get his shit straight, don't worry about him.

Poppy: I'll always worry about him.

Imogen: Love sucks.

I don't tell her that my love with Kane might have produced a baby because she doesn't need my shit weighing her down and until I know for sure, I'm not telling anybody. No use getting Kane pissed at me until I know definitely that I fucked up with my pill.

I'm not the most responsible. I kept forgetting. I should have gotten something a bit more permanent but it's hard getting birth control without Mee-maw finding out. There isn't a Planned Parenthood around here. Now I really wish I'd made the three-hour journey.

Kane: Church done yet?

Imogen: Not yet. Miss me?

Kane: My dick is so hard. Don't know why. Don't care why. Need you to deal with it.

Imogen: You sure know how to woo a girl.

Can I have sex while pregnant? Is that possible? My heart is hammering in my chest at the possibility that I might be knocked up. This sucks so hard. I never thought it would happen, I'm so naïve.

Before, not having sex with Kane was more about control and because I didn't want to reward him for his bad behavior. But now it's all about my own safety and the safety of the unborn in my stomach. I don't know if it's there but I'm not taking any chances.

"Put your phone away," Mee-maw snaps. "Is it so hard for you to spend quality time with me without looking at that screen?"

I don't answer because that question feels like entrapment and the honest answer will probably get me beaten.

26 YEARS OLD

"Okay, let me wrap my head around this." He legitimately grips his head and stares at me, his incredible lips flat, his tempting eyes wary. "You didn't leave me by choice, you were kidnapped?" Then he laughs like I'm hilarious. "So why didn't anybody but me report you missin'? Why did nobody ask for you? Why didn't your mee-maw do anything?"

I open my mouth to answer all his questions but he raises his hand.

"All you do is lie. How can I believe a word you say?"

This time I lift a shoulder. "Clearly you've made up your mind, Kane." I brush past him, feeling irritated and bitter that he could laugh at my pain and act as though I'm not being honest when I am. Or at least I'm trying to be. "I'm going to get dressed."

He doesn't follow for a moment but when I reach my bedroom his chest hits my back and his hand snakes around my waist.

"What's your name now?" he asks softly. "What does everybody call you?"

"Still Immy, but my surname is Messer."

"And why did you change your name?"

"I was tryna get to that part Kane but you're not interested in listening."

He holds me so tight I can't breathe. "Fuck you. I'm just not interested in listening to more of your lies."

"That's fine."

"You said you were pregnant but didn't have an abortion." He squeezes me again. "So must mean you had the kid, so where is it? Why the fuck wouldn't you tell me?"

"I was gettin' to that too."

He pulls away and mutters a curse. "Naw… I'm gonna need more than just your words, Imogen. I need proof."

"Proof?"

"Pictures, birth certificates, something. You're telling me I got a kid, I need evidence before I let myself feel it here." He hits his chest with his fist.

"This evidence enough?" I ask, pulling up my nightdress to my waist, showing him my lace-clad pussy and the scar only a couple of inches above it. It's a silver and pink blur now, resting below stripes that wrinkle my otherwise tight skin. Evidence that I was pregnant once and it changed my body.

"I don't know dick about love," he reads, his expression intense but vacant, from the tattoo directly above the scar. It sits at the left side in pretty scrawl. "But I know that I love you."

His eyes find mine and mine fill with tears. I register the look of horror on his face as we share this revealing moment. Our souls collide and burn together, forever changing with the intensity of just our gazes locking. Finally he is learning the truth. "Where's my kid, Immy?"

"I told you this would haunt you Kane. There's no going back."

"Where's my kid?" His tone is dark and desperate and his breath is faster now, more agitated.

"I don't know." I close my eyes and tears spill down my cheeks. "I don't know."

"HOW CAN YOU NOT KNOW?"

"SHE WAS TAKEN FROM ME!"

He places his hand against the wall for support. "You're gonna need to start from the beginning."

"I did try," I snap, wiping my eyes on the back of my wrist.

"I know." He rubs his face with his hands, looking ready to vomit. He's trying to stay calm but I can see his pain and turmoil. "I'm listenin' now. I'm listenin' and I ain't talkin' unless I have to. There are so many gaps that I need filling but I'm gonna try and be respectful. But if you give me bullshit or you give me an answer I don't like or believe, I'm fucking done with you Immy. You hear me?"

My body is trembling as I approach the sofa and sit on it. He moves to the window and looks out at the scenery, likely unable to look at me.

"Matthew knew I was pregnant. He was the only one who knew..."

17 YEARS OLD

"Oh dear Lord, save me from this child."

"Fuck off, Mee-maw," Matthew snarls and I hear Officer Barny reading him his rites. What the fuck is going on?

I leap out of bed, tired and dazed and skid into the hall, almost tumbling down the stairs. "What happened?"

My brother has been pinned to the ground with his hands at the base of his spine. His eyes are bloodshot and swollen, his nose is bleeding. He looks awful. He definitely looks high.

"Please Officer Barny, be as discreet as you can."

"Of course," the officer tips his hat and smiles sadly at me. "I'm sorry y'all had to see this."

"What's going on?" I ask, moving to Mee-maw's side as my brother thrashes on the ground like a possessed man.

"What do you think?" she replies bitterly. "He's been poisoning his veins and soul!"

"He assaulted two people tonight, that's all I can say on the matter," Officer Barny whistles and another backs up the police car to as close to the house as possible.

"Please tell me Poppy is okay," I whisper, looking at my brother.

"You know about it?" Barny asks.

I shake my head. "Poppy is his ex, he hasn't gotten over her. She had her first date with Brandon tonight." I sneer at my brother, unable to see past this monster that has taken over him. "What did you do to them? Why couldn't you just leave her alone?"

"Shut up," he retorts, spit flying from his mouth. "You don't know shit about anything!"

"They're both in hospital, I'm sure they'd appreciate a friend visiting tomorrow when they've been treated."

That must mean they're okay for the most part but it hasn't exactly stopped my stomach churning with worry.

I turn to the side and vomit, it bubbles up and unleashes before I can stop it. Mee-maw coos and rubs my back. Acting every bit the doting grandmother.

"It's hard on her, he's her twin," I hear her explain. "His behavior has really gotten to her."

I can't speak around the powerful force of bile coming from my mouth. Snot and saliva stream from my nose and mouth. I hate this.

"I'm so sorry we had to do this on your property ma'am."

"Not at all, Barny. I can only apologize for failing to be a good parent to him. He's always had a demon inside of him this one has."

"Yeah, well perfect fucking Imogen has a baby in her!" Matthew hisses as he is shoved through the doorway. "So apologize for being a shit parent to both of us. I might do drugs but at least I use a fucking condom."

My heart shatters and for a moment the pain of his betrayal outweighs the nausea I feel for just long enough for me to gape at him.

"That's not true," I whisper, horrified.

"He's high on Lord knows what, Mrs. Hardy," Barny explains, still dragging my brother away.

Mee-maw seems too shocked to talk.

"I'm guessin' you ain't gonna bail the boy out?" Barny questions.

"Absolutely not until he has learned a lesson."

"Rehab. I think at this point he needs it."

I leave them to their conversation and get to work cleaning up the small amount of vomit I let loose on the wooden floor. It's making me want to vomit again.

"IT BETTER NOT BE TRUE!" Mee-maw shrieks after returning and when she knows they are out of earshot. "I cannot cope with this. I cannot cope. *I cannot!*"

"I'm not pregnant, Mee-maw. He's just tryna hurt you."

She stares at me, gauging my honesty. I'm the worst liar in the world.

"Don't do this to me child, not again. I can't cope with this again. I don't want to be raisin' no more babies and I can't let it go into care because what kind of Christian woman would that make me?"

"I'm not pregnant!"

She nods but doesn't look convinced. "Your Grandpa will be turnin' in his grave at all this hassle."

"Mee-maw," I insist, placing my hand on her arm. "He's just saying things to get you to stress."

"Yes, I hope so." She looks ready to break and I don't blame her.

"Shall I make you some tea?"

Shaking her head she places her hand on the console table by the door for support. "I need to lie down for a while."

"Okay, Mee-maw. I'm going to call Poppy. I need to know that she's okay."

She nods again. "Thank you for cleanin' up your own mess." She looks so dazed as she moves away from me, every step is slow and calculated.

"Of course." I try for a smile but it's shaky. "What's going to happen to Matthew now?"

"I'm going to get him the help he needs." She wets her lips and looks away. "And Lord knows he needs it. Why me, Jesus? Why?" Her eyes follow me into the kitchen and she watches me clean out the rag and bucket I used before making herself a drink. "Please don't be pregnant. I don't want to raise no more babies."

"Mee-maw, I'm not pregnant and even if I was, I wouldn't be no deadbeat momma like mine. I'm responsible."

"Responsibility starts with safe sex, or not having sex at all!"

She has a point. "I'm not pregnant Mee-maw."

"You better hope not."

I'm already hoping not. I'm hoping not so hard that it's all I can think about.

"Shout for me if you need me," I utter and get the hell away from her.

I try calling Poppy and her mom but I get no answer as is expected. To say I'm worried is a massive understatement. When neither of them answers on the third try, I call the only other person I want to speak to in this moment.

"Kane," I say immediately when he answers the phone.

"What's wrong?" He sounds so sleepy and adorable.

"My brother has been arrested, apparently he put Poppy and her date in the hospital." I sniff unattractively. "I'm freaking out."

"Shit, that doesn't sound good."

"Nope. He's in serious trouble."

"Need me to bail him out?"

"No, let him stay in there and rot for a night."

He sighs heavily. "Hate to say it but that's probably the right call. Is Poppy okay?"

"I don't know. Cops wouldn't tell us anything."

"Want me to go check?"

"Would you?"

"Yeah. Not sure they'll let me know anything but I'll do what I can."

Relief sinks through the heaviness of my chest. "Love you, Kane."

"Love you too." He doesn't say it often but he does say it when it matters, like now when he knows I need to hear it. I hear the twang of his belt as he gets dressed. "I'll call you soon as I hear anything."

Thankfully Poppy is fine, Bradley fared a lot worse. He has a broken

17 YEARS OLD

femur from where my psychotic brother stamped on his leg after sucker punching him onto his ass. Poppy took a kick to the ribs when she tried to protect Bradley but it was when she got hurt that my brother stopped. I'm just relieved he cared enough about her to stop. These days he doesn't seem to care about anybody but himself. He's acting like he's the only one in pain. The violence sounds all too familiar. It reminds me of the first time I met Kane. God I hated him then.

My brother, in his hysterical and high state of mind came home, not realizing just how dire the situation was. He was so high he couldn't even remember doing half of it apparently.

Poppy and Bradley are both pressing charges which means my brother, now home, is looking for a lawyer and is probably going to jail for assault and battery. I haven't stopped crying about it and neither has he. For the most part he's apologetic but he's high again and it's only two in the afternoon. I think he might be addicted. He's so gaunt and twitchy.

"Do you want to go for a ride to the water tower?" I ask him, wanting to get him alone so I can at the very least try and talk some sense into him.

Chewing on the inside of his cheek, he nods and immediately grabs his jacket which was slung over the back of his chair.

We head out, making the long walk to Kane's where I keep my bike. For the most part we don't talk, he texts on his phone and smokes three cigarettes which is an insane amount for any journey. I don my gear and give him a spare helmet. I know West won't mind it.

"Let me drive," my brother demands but I pull my keys away.

"Not while you're under the influence."

Grumbling, he waits for me to climb on and slides on behind me. He pinches my bicep and laughs hysterically. "Don't know how you turn this thing with your chicken arms."

"Fuck you," I reply, my voice muffled through the visor. "My biceps are like stone. I could lift you above my head."

A complete lie. I'm strong but not that strong.

17 YEARS OLD

The engine purrs and my brother spreads out his arms when we pick up speed. I go faster and faster, overtaking cars on the long and dusty road. For a moment in time I feel like everything is normal again and my brother is normal. But then we pull over and he stumbles off my bike, pulls a baggy of pills out of his pocket and pops one on his tongue.

"Want one?" he asks, chewing the thing in his mouth.

I cringe and look away. "You really need that? Can't we just enjoy the moment without the high?"

"Need it," he mutters, kicking at the long grass. "Need a lot of shit to help me get through the day."

"You need to deal with life without those. You're hurting yourself."

"Did you come out here just to tell me off?"

I look away, unable to witness the change in his body and the way he talks now. My brother is no longer a man but a waif and it's terrifying to see. "We could run away," I suggest like I used to. Because once upon a time my twin was my best friend and we faced the world together. "We could get the fuck out of here, go to Austin, get a place together. Go to college…"

"I'm going to fucking jail!"

"That's if they find you."

At that he laughs and shoves the baggy back into his pocket. "You'd do that for me?"

"Yes." I don't even hesitate with my reply and I mean it with my whole heart. I love Matthew, he's my brother and I just want him to get better.

"I'd do it for you too but running away ain't gonna solve this. I fucked up."

"You're still fucking up." I point to his pocket where the bag of pills resides.

"They're antacids."

"Yeah and I'm aunt stupid," I remark sarcastically making him

17 YEARS OLD

laugh again. We settle, heavy and full of remorse for entirely different things. "I'm so sorry you're not coping Matthew."

"I'm sorry I ratted you out to Mee-maw."

"Yeah, that was fucked up."

"I'll steal you a pregnancy test to make it up to you."

Like when we were kids we head towards the main street, giggling amongst ourselves. Matthew heads into the pharmacy and I follow behind. I talk to the lady behind the counter about heartburn while Matthew peruses the sexual health section. Antacids were the first thing that came to mind after our conversation.

Unfortunately the lady is a talker and I don't leave until five minutes after Matthew and to say I'm desperate to know what my current condition is would be an understatement.

He pats his jacket to let me know it's in his pocket and we head to a burger joint on the corner. I hand him ten dollars to get us something to eat and I scarper into the restroom with the test in hand.

I don't know how to use it. It looks easy on TV but I'm scared I'll do it wrong. My heart is hammering in my chest and I don't feel good at all. I don't know why I wasted money on getting food because I doubt I'll be able to eat after this.

I pee on the end of the stick after removing the cap and stuff it into my pocket. It says four minutes and I don't have that kind of time, so I wash my hands and discard the box after burning the results section to memory. Plus means baby, minus means none. Simple and easy.

If only this situation was simple and easy.

"How'd it go?" Matthew asks when I approach the table and pluck a fry out of the little basket. It tastes salty but also bland. Kind of like my mood.

"I don't know, I have to wait a few minutes."

He pushes my burger towards me as I chew on another fry. "Eat. You need to take care of your body."

At his words I laugh, it's genuine but also cruel and then sad because I'm watching him ruin his and there's nothing I can do.

I reach across the table and squeeze the hand of my twin.

"I love you," I say to him. "Whatever happens."

"I love you too."

At that I smile and peek at the test in my pocket and a whoosh of air leaves my body.

"What is it?" he asks as my face stretches with a blinding smile that aches my cheeks and jaw.

"I'm not pregnant."

"You sure?"

I nod and show him the stick, using a menu to shield it from the prying eyes of others. "No plus sign. I'm not pregnant. I must just have a bug."

"There's a lot going around right now."

I take a big bite of my burger and wipe away the grease that rolls down my chin. I've never felt so relieved in my entire life. I'm not pregnant and I don't have to worry about a thing.

To celebrate, I of course surprise Kane at work and throw myself at his grease covered body. I mash my lips to his, shove my tongue into his mouth and grab his hair so he can't move.

His coworker wolf-whistles and cheers us on, which is gross because he's like forty, but I suppose it's what they do at work. It's all good fun.

"Well hello to you too," Kane whispers when I pull back breathlessly and stare into his eyes. "Didn't think I'd see you until later."

I kiss him again, unable to help myself, crushing my lips so painfully against his.

"I'm sorry I said that you're ruining my life, Kane Jessop."

He frowns, confused.

"You're the only thing I have these days that brings me any kind of happy feelin'," I admit, still clinging to him.

His eyes, his smile, his body soften all for me and he looks at me in that expressive way that he *only* looks at me.

"I just wanted to say that," I breathe and pull away. "I'll let you finish working."

I start to drift from him when he slides his hand down my arm and snags me back by my hand at the very last second. This time he kisses me. He doesn't say shit, he just kisses me and watches me walk away with a twinkle in his eyes that mirrors my own.

Matthew, who waited in the lobby of the service station sees me mount my bike and joins me. He's chewing something in his mouth. I don't ask what it is as we pull away, but I wish I had.

I really wish I had. Not that he'd have given me any kind of real answer.

It's as we're driving down the long and dusty dirt road that he starts to have a seizure. It's when his weight brings down mine that we crash into the back of a parked truck and tumble into a dry ditch.

I hurt, my body aches, but I'm okay.

I'm okay, that is, until I see the rolling eyes of my brother and foam coming from his mouth.

I scream, long and loud, a hoarse, panicked cry tearing through my throat as I crawl towards him.

"HELP!" I shriek, fumbling for my phone with trembling hands. "SOMEBODY HELP ME!"

26 YEARS OLD

"That day with my brother was the scariest day of my life... or so I thought," I whisper, wiping away tears. "I mean, shit just couldn't get worse."

"Why didn't he care that you didn't come back?" Kane asks. "He didn't say a thing."

"Right?" I sniff and wipe my nose on a piece of tissue, then I toss it and wash my hands while listening to the hum of the coffee machine. "I wouldn't have left him there."

I try to pour his coffee but my hand shakes so violently I have to put the jug down. Kane steps behind me and wraps an arm around my waist.

"I hated you," I whisper. "I still do."

"Why?" he asks, sounding bitter and hurt. "I tried."

"I know that now but then, you were on this superhero pedestal. I was just waiting and waiting for you to save the day." I let my head drop forward. "Every single day my stomach got bigger and bigger and I just kept praying and *praying* that you'd bust your way in and take me away on your bike and we'd all live happily ever after."

He holds me tighter and presses his forehead against the back of my hair. "I tried. I didn't stop trying. Your mee-maw got an injunction out on me. They said you didn't want to see me. Said you hated me. I didn't believe it, I knew you wouldn't have left on your own but after a while they all started to convince me it was true." His voice cracks and he slowly turns me in his arms. "Eventually I believed I wasn't good enough and you and Marshall were living happily ever after." His fist comes down on the counter behind me. "I never should have stopped."

"I don't blame you. I mean, *I did*, and part of me is still resentful of the life we could have had but never got." I clear my throat and calm myself. "But I know deep down that you never would have known where I was and even if you figured it out there was no way of saving me."

"Where were you?"

"Do you remember Mee-maw's friend, that Jesus lovin' weirdo that you used to make fun of?"

He thinks on it for a moment. "That fucked up cult lovin' freak? The righteous somethin' right?"

"The Righteous Voices."

His eyes glaze over with memory and horror. "They took you?"

"They ran a fucking concentration camp for troubled kids and teens. Full of kids thought to be gay, kids on drugs, pregnant girls." I shudder at the memory. "After the accident, turns out I didn't give the test enough time and I was reading the wrong window on it. I was pregnant. They tested my blood for narcotics to see if I was high while driving. That came back clear but they found protein or something and that's when I found out I was pregnant."

"Fuck, Immy."

"Yeah. My mee-maw had me and my brother shipped off the same night. I remember everything Father Righteous said to her... I could hear him through the wall, she was talking about how she's a terrible parent and how could God forgive her and he was all..." I make my voice deep and put on his accent, an accent I'll never forget. "God gave them to you, Mrs. Hardy, because he knew you would have the strength to send them to us for correction. Their behavior is not a reflection on your parenting, it is because they were born to an unwed mother and her poison is in their veins, tempting the devil to taste their flesh and souls." I laugh harshly. "He was clinically insane."

"Sounds it."

"Mee-maw was so grateful and he was all thank the Lord for putting you in my path." I grit my teeth. "He was a rapist, he was an abuser. The stuff he did... to them..."

"To Marshall?"

I nod and my lower lip trembles. "He had to be stopped."

"What happened?" His eyes become cautious and guarded.

"What had to happen."

18 YEARS OLD

I started getting contractions last night, I've been trying to hide them but they're too intense now. I'm terrified of what's going to happen to me and my baby if I have her here. Not a single girl who was pregnant and has come back since having their baby, has come back with their baby.

A girl I know called Clary had hers last week. She hasn't spoken since. She's just laid on her bed crying and crying. She's a shell of the person she was. Not that she was much of a person to begin with. This place has us all brainwashed. Even me in some ways, I'm losing the person I was. I feel myself spiraling deeper into a depression that's getting harder to climb out of.

Everybody is in love with Jesus Christ. Everybody believes they did wrong and have to get the Lord to forgive them. But they believe that first they must gain the favor of Father Righteous. That's what he makes us call him. And they will try to gain his favor in *any* way possible.

He thinks he's superior and everybody eats up his shit like it doesn't stink. My brother too who was released from here a few months ago, who I thought for sure would save me, left with a new outlook on life. He wouldn't talk to me in the end because those who don't bow to Father Righteous, are to be treated like the plague.

Marshall and I are in that category. Despite the fact we're the eldest here, we are treated like lepers and we aren't allowed to speak to each other.

That's why I'm sneaking into his room now, hiding from the Saviors, which is just a fancy name for guards. They prowl the land like they own it. Watching our every move.

"Marsh!" I hiss urgently, pushing open the door. "Marshall please."

He stirs in his bed, which is all he has in this room. A white bed, in a white box, by a white set of drawers that hold our white clothing. "Immy? You're gonna get me caned."

"The baby's coming," I whisper, tears streaming down my face. "They're gonna take her."

He sits bolt upright, a frown marring his features. "What?"

"She's coming," I groan, gritting my teeth and bending over as blinding pain clenches my uterus, trying to force this baby out of my body. "We need to go. We need to get out of here."

"While you're like this?"

"Please," I beg as he comes to my side. "They'll take her. I'll die. I won't survive this."

"You've held on to yourself for this long, Immy."

"No I haven't. I'm losing my mind." I grip his arm and groan. "Help me."

"I don't know how," he admits sadly.

This isn't the first time we've spoken about escaping. But every other kid who has tried has been brought back by the police and then beaten. The methods they use to get into your head is insane. They use electric shock therapy, intense exercise, isolation, basically low-grade torture techniques that fuck with your head. I've never been made to do the harder stuff because of my pregnancy.

I think back to my first nights here, the desperation I felt. The screaming I did. The kicking and fighting. They had to sedate me so often. I wouldn't rest without a fight and at first my brother was the same, but then withdrawal kicked in and they managed to take over.

The door bursts open and Marshall is forced to let me go.

I try to run, I try to get away but I can't. I feel the prick at my neck and my body becomes weightless. Just as they always do. They drug you and make you lucid and calm. But you're not really calm it's just your body that won't work.

I've tried staying calm for months because I'm terrified of what the drugs are doing to the innocent life inside of me. It's all about my baby now and not me. I can handle whatever they throw my way but she can't. She is only as strong as my blood and flesh that feed and protect her.

"Her water just broke," Savior Sally, who likely fucking dosed me says and I vaguely feel the wetness between my thighs.

"GET OFF HER!" Marshall roars as I'm lifted.

This is it.

Nothing has prepared me for this moment. Nothing.

"Meconium in the waters," is uttered by somebody. I don't know what that means. "Baby is in distress."

I definitely know what that means. Is she okay? Did I hurt her by holding on for so long? Is this God's way of punishing me for not telling them I was in labor?

Even though I knew it was coming I expected it to be different. I didn't expect them to keep me sedated. I didn't expect to only get to hear the sound of her cry. I didn't expect to miss out on the entire fucking birth of my daughter.

They literally ripped her from my womb and sewed me back up. They didn't even let me hold her or see her or say goodbye. What kind of monster doesn't even let a mother say goodbye?

They said it's less painful this way. They're wrong. I'd rather have the pain of her face and her tiny fingers in my memory forever than not know a thing about her at all.

I always knew I'd return to my room hollow and empty, both my body and heart, but I thought I'd have at least gotten to see her face. They didn't even tell me if she was a boy or a girl.

I don't know anything about her.

The only memory I have is the sound of her cry.

I can't move. I'm in so much pain.

Pain they say is a gift from God, like the gift of my daughter to a family who will love and cherish her and raise her as their own.

They didn't even let me say goodbye.

They have won. They have broken me.

My stomach aches with the loss of her kicks and rolls. I'd lie in bed every night and talk to her for hours on end. Sometimes out loud. Sometimes in my head. Apart from my brief run ins with Marshall, those moments at night with her were my only saving grace. How will I survive this now?

Mee-maw comes to visit a few days later. I haven't moved. I haven't eaten. They will force feed me soon, they've done it before when I staged a silent protest at being here. I probably shouldn't have starved my body but it was the only power I had left. I thought they'd send me home but the more I acted out, the tighter a lock and key they put on me.

At most I get up to pee but I'm in a lot of pain, yet they still force me to get up and join them in the gardens where families come to visit their victims. The pain is unbearable, but it's still not enough pain to stop me from punching the old cow in the face. I've never been violent with her. I've never raised a hand back. But I fly at her so fast and with such fury the look of fear in her eyes before I connect is the most satisfying moment of my entire life.

It's her fault my baby is gone. It's her fault I'm trapped here.

My rage overcomes my pain and senses and I don't stop. I've never felt so strong despite being so weak.

"Oh my," Mee-maw cries, acting the victim. Her hand rests on

18 YEARS OLD

her chest and fresh tears roll down her face. Her cheek is swelling, I hit her hard.

"As you can see, she still needs work," Father Righteous insists as I'm dragged away. "Sedate her. Feed her." He apologizes to those around us and calls me troubled.

He's too influential. As I scream that they took my baby he tells them I'm not fit to be a mother. That I'm a raging psychopath and he'll be sure to keep their kids safe from me. That I'm possessed. They lap it up but they know that I'm not. They are the psychopaths. They know what goes on here, they know what they're putting their kids through for the sake of "social standing".

I'm a psychopath. I'm not possessed. I've lost my child and I'm steadily losing my will to live.

I stopped praying for Kane to save me so long ago, but still in this moment a flicker of hope presses on my already tight chest. My eyes, as they often used to, scan the grounds for any sign of him. My ears listen for the roar of his Challenger. My skin prickles desperately for the feel of his touch.

My heart yearns for our child.

There's no emptier feeling than defeat. It's as though any strength I had left is gone.

"She will see reason," Father Righteous says, likely to Mee-maw.

"She's been here almost nine months. The devil inside her is too strong." Mee-maw is speaking like I'm not here.

"The devil is never too strong for God. And where else has a deeper presence of God than here at the Righteous Voices?" A loud chorus of Amen sounds from the crowd around as I start to drop and finally sink into slumber. The drugs take over and I decide that from now on I will keep on lashing out just so they can keep sedating me.

Nobody is going to save me now so I might as well get high. I have no power here. No standing.

Father Righteous is a trusted member of every community in the state. His compassion and love and his ability to turn a child back to the light of God is revered. He has the ability to destroy lives. He's already destroyed mine.

26 YEARS OLD

"I was back to where I was that night of the lake, but even worse than before because I had nobody. I was the leper of the group. Marshall was playing it safe, pretending to be saved so he could leave and send help for me. His parents were already desperate for his return so we knew it wouldn't be long, but I couldn't stand the thought of that hell without him."

"Jesus, Immy I feel fuckin' sick," Kane admits and he looks pale as he strides across the room and puts distance between us. "I don't want to believe you. I can't grasp that this might be fuckin' real." He turns, his eyes sharp. "You didn't kill yourself. I'm glad but... why?"

"I wanted to. I've never felt so done with life. I would have given anything to just fall asleep and not wake up but I couldn't. I needed to know she was safe and loved and I just needed to see her one time."

"Did you?"

I wet my lips and hold my mug. I'm sitting now, on a barstool, looking at him through dead eyes. "Nope."

His brows furrow. "Not once?"

"I'm still alive aren't I?"

"You're gonna fuckin' stay alive."

I don't reply, I just stare at him. Waiting for something, I don't know what, but I know I don't want to be in this moment. "I've never stopped thinking about her, Kane. Her cry echoes through my mind every time I close my eyes. I shouldn't have even heard it really, I was under, but it called to me so deep it woke me up for just long enough for me to hear it."

"Then we'll go back there, we'll demand he tell us—"

"He's dead, Kane," I breathe, choking on my words. "He's dead. And he's the only person who knew where she was."

"He's dead?"

"Yeah. Dead. Somebody stabbed him, severed his spine, watched him bleed out."

He gapes at me, hearing the tone in my voice that I'm not even trying to hide. "Immy…"

"I don't regret it," I admit, my voice even softer now.

"Fuck… Immy." His eyes widen. He's concerned, horrified, just as I knew he would be. "Does Marshall know?"

I nod. "Marshall helped me set the place on fire."

He rips a hand through his hair. "I don't know whether to believe you or not. I feel like you're not being truthful."

In some ways he's right, but not all.

"Google it. It wasn't exactly a well-kept secret. The press had a field day when they learned of the horrors of the Righteous Voices and their fucking cult. So many victims came forward." I laugh and shake my head. "So many. All it took was for me to stand up and tell mine first. Under an alias though to keep me safe. He had more followers than enemies."

"They never caught you? They don't know you killed him?"

I shake my head again. "They know. I confessed, but it was considered self-defense."

"Self-defense." He bites out the whispered words like he's preparing himself for the answer.

"He didn't touch me while I was pregnant. He had that much

respect at least." I close my eyes, to block out the image maybe, it doesn't work. It's even more prominent than before. "I wasn't pregnant anymore. And you know how hot I was. He'd wanted me the moment he stepped into Mee-maw's kitchen and saw me sitting on the breakfast bar. I remember his eyes going up my skirt. So I played him, I played on that."

Kane's hands ball into fists. "He hurt you?"

"Naw." I smirk evilly. "He didn't get the chance. I knew what was coming. I let it happen. The moment his guard was down I stabbed him in the back." My smirk fades. "I didn't feel a thing. Because they *did* break me, just not in the way they wanted. They broke my mind. I had a psychotic break."

"For real?"

"Yeah. I was numb. Couldn't feel a thing. Had to go into a federal rehab facility so they could prepare me to testify against the entire institution and its staff. Had to speak as a witness for other kids there but needed to be sane while I did."

"I heard about some of this but..." He looks so disbelieving and I don't blame him. It's hard to swallow and I'm making him fucking chew it first.

"They put me into witness protection to protect me from the powerful parents who put their kids there and didn't want the world to know what happened. See most of them were brainwashed, but some of them, like me, made it out with something left."

"Your brother was different when he came back. But we all thought it was rehab." He's breathing heavy, his nostrils are flaring. "He kept saying you were happy and to leave you be. I wouldn't leave him alone. And then he got sent down anyway."

My brother's actions that night with Poppy and Bradley cost him his entire future. Bradley's more so than my brother's. Bradley got an infection in his shattered femur and ended up losing half his leg. They threw the book at my brother who with his new morale self, pleaded guilty and apologized.

"I know. I found out after I was in my right mind. Marshall

checked in on him. He's not brainwashed anymore, but he is high again apparently."

"Still in prison?"

I shake my head. "I don't think so. I don't know. I don't care."

"Understandable."

"He left me there. He knew what was happening and he agreed with it. He left me there."

Kane starts pacing. "Are you sure he was the only one who knew?"

"Matthew?"

"No, the fucker who got what he deserved. What he earned. Are you sure he was the only one who knew about our kid's whereabouts?"

"Webber looked into it for me and I haven't stopped. He was the agent who saved me from myself. He paid a private detective too with his own dime. The trail was deader than the fucker I severed."

Kane scratches the stubble of his jaw. "Fuck. I don't know what to do with this. Any of this."

"I told you that you didn't want to know."

He doesn't agree, instead he asks, "That why you stayed away?"

I lift a shoulder. "That and because you became the catalyst for all of my fucking problems. You're in every bad memory I have Kane."

He rears back like I've slapped him and silence falls over us both. We stare at each other, his vibrant and alive eyes holding the dead in mine. "Fuck you, Immy. That was uncalled for."

"Yeah well, I'm vicious now Kane, just like you were once upon a time."

"I'm seein it, don't fuckin' like it. Don't know what to say to make this hurt less."

"For who, you or me? Because trust me, I don't feel a thing."

He blows a breath out of his nose. "About me? Or about all of this?"

"About everything."

26 YEARS OLD

"You must feel somethin', you're still chasing after our kid."

"I just need to see her. I just need to know she's safe and loved." It's become an obsession. I'm almost scared of what will happen when I do find her. I put out a kidnapped child report, but without a photo to go on or even a date, finding her will be impossible. All of the records were destroyed in that fire we stupidly set but he didn't keep adoption files there anyway. I know because I looked.

"So you've said." His eyes are set with determination. "I'll find her Immy."

"You didn't fucking find me."

He throws his cup against the wall, it shatters and I don't even flinch.

"This is a rental," I say flatly and I know I'm being cruel but it's all I know how to be anymore.

"I need a breather." Walking away, he slams the door behind him and I listen to his heavy booted feet get more and more distant.

I don't know if he'll come back. I'm almost hoping he won't. But then seeing him is sparking just a little piece of the old me that I once knew. The old me that he helped me create.

I clean the mess he made, carefully wiping away coffee and scraping up fragments. It's therapeutic and helps me gather my thoughts. Cleaning isn't my most favorite thing to do but thankfully I don't despise it.

My phone vibrates, it's Marshall. Why am I not surprised?

Marshall: How is it going?

Immy: You're asking me how your betrayal is going?

Marshall: Yes. Exactly.

Immy: I hate you.

Marshall: We've been through too much together; you could never hate me.

Immy: Shut up.

Marshall: So it's going well then?

Immy: Kane needed a breather.

Marshall: I bet. Were you nice to him?

Immy: No.

Marshall: Can you try and be nice to him?

Immy: I just talked about it. You know how I get when I talk about it. Or when you try and talk about it.

Marshall: Poor Kane.
    Marshall: But seriously, Immy. He's in this now too. Cut him some slack.

Immy: You do realize that you have just selfishly burdened him with years of maddening pain and unanswered questions?

Marshall: He deserved to know.

Immy: Deserved to know what? A kid he's never going to meet?

Marshall doesn't reply and I stuff my phone into my pocket. Then I check the time and pull out my laptop.

26 YEARS OLD

Like I do every day, I send an email to Webber and ask him for updates. My daughter is now considered to be a cold case. *A cold case.* She could be dead for all I know. And that's the worst part. Not knowing.

The door swings open around half an hour later and Kane strolls in like he owns the place. He starts looking around like he has a right but for the most part he completely ignores me.

I watch as he goes into my room and listen to him yank open my drawers. I don't ask, I just give him his breather. He's figuring something out and I'm not about to interfere with that.

When the final drawer slams shut he returns and yanks open the cupboards beneath my flatscreen.

"You've got nothin'," he snarls like that's supposed to mean something to me.

I give him an incredulous look. "Huh?"

"Nothin'," he repeats, raising his hands. "You have got nothin'."

"Still not following."

"No pictures."

"Nothin worth photographing."

"No trinkets and Immy you used to fucking love trinkets. Had to drag you out of every shop we ever went by to stop you from buying a stupid fridge magnet or a postcard. Or those stupid fucking bean bag baby stuffed animals."

I feel my jaw tick but I keep silent. He's right but it's not a memory I want to cherish.

"You fuckin' said I was in every bad memory."

"I said that," I confirm, turning in my seat and pulling my knees up to my chest. My ankles cross as I hug my legs and watch him move around my space.

"But I bet your fuckin' ass I was in every good one."

He's got me there. I look away, I don't need to feed his ego by admitting that.

"I'm not to blame for what happened to you. I looked, Immy."

"I know."

"NO YOU FUCKIN' DON'T!" he booms, grabbing my arms and dragging me to my feet. "I stopped going to school. I put up fliers. I called radio stations and put in reports. I used to make my daddy's Renegade's fuckin' take fliers with them. There were fliers beggin' for you to call me all across the state. Not one call. I knew somethin' wasn't right so I didn't stop looking for you."

"You want me to thank you?"

"I want you to know that you didn't save me from pain and questions. My life has been nothing but pain and questions because of you..."

I blanche. "Is Marshall feeding you my texts through a fucking wire?"

"Naw, to my *fucking* phone." He tosses said phone on the couch. "Don't know why I ever loved you Imogen Hardy. Still don't know why I ever loved you. But I did. You didn't deserve it. You don't deserve it. I didn't deserve you. We were two fucked up kids that never should have been anythin' to each other."

"So why are you doing this to us both? I gave you an out. I gave you a reason." I'm so eternally confused. "If you don't know why you loved me then why the fuck are you here?"

"Because I needed answers and now I got my answers I've gotta deal. Somewhere out there we got a kid. I've got a kid." His face gets in mine, his eyes are wild and angry. "AND YOU FUCKING KEPT HER FROM ME!"

"Are you insane?" I shout and shove him back. "I didn't fucking keep her from you!"

"You should have come back the minute you were free."

"I was fucked up. I wasn't sane."

"Free of your brain then! I don't know but you should have reached out when you were well."

"I'M STILL NOT FUCKING WELL, KANE!" I shove him again. It's all too familiar. "I'll never be well. I'm damaged. I'm poisonous. I'm unlovable. I'm vicious."

"Yeah, well so am I and you still loved me anyway."

"I killed a man in cold blood and I don't regret it."

"So did I," he whispers.

"That's not the same."

"Isn't it? Let you steal his money. Left him there. Didn't call for help. Didn't even fuckin' care. You still sat on my dick years later and I never wanted to change a thing about that moment."

I bite my lip. "I don't know what the point in any of this is."

"The point is, whether we wanted it or not we were in this life together. You left me, not on purpose at first but then on purpose and fuck you for that. Got a kid out there I could have helped you find."

"She's in the wind. There's no possible way."

"So you say but you didn't give me the option to find that out for myself."

"You want me to say I'm sorry?"

"Yeah," he responds and for a moment I see how haunted his eyes are. He's not doing a good job of hiding it. "I do. I want you to say it, I want you to feel it and I want to fucking see it."

"I'm sorry I didn't tell you about the baby that was stolen from me."

"From *us*," he corrects. "Unless it's not mine."

I almost laugh at that weak attempt to goad me. He doesn't stop me as I sit back on the couch. "When are you leavin', Kane?"

"Right now, just came back to say goodbye and wish you luck in getting your shit together." He tugs on the lapel of his leather jacket and digs into his pocket for a mint. "You're an incredible tattoo artist, Immy. You're a shit fuckin' person."

"Ouch," I respond, my tone deadpan. "Thanks for the burn. Let me rub myself down with some aloe."

Angry, he shoves me backwards onto the couch, forcing me to uncurl, and grips my face, forcing me to look at him.

"You said you hated me." He squeezes harder. It doesn't hurt but it isn't pleasant. "You ain't got nothin' to hate me for."

"Cept maybe your shit grammar."

His eyes narrow. "Table's are turning Imogen Hardy. Because now for the first time since we met. I hate you. For real. I fucking hate you. Wish I'd never met you. Because you're in all my bad memories too. Now you're in the worst." He bites on my lower lip, like he wants to make me bleed but can't quite bring himself to do it. I hold his fiery gaze but don't flinch, despite the pain, and after a moment my lip pings free and he stands and rights himself. "Unless you find my kid, don't contact me. We're back to how we were before we ever fucked except this time I mean it and this time I don't want to stick my dick in you."

"You're a liar and a shit one. You're a worse liar than me." I follow him, round him, and press my hand hard against his chest.

"Move out of my way."

"You don't hate me. You wish you did. That look in your eyes isn't hate, it's pity. You hate that you pity me. I get it. I've got nothin'. I'm nothing like the girl I used to be. The girl you loved. The girl you thought you'd find here today." I press even harder and focus on the feel of his heart beneath my palm, it makes me think of the time I held his heart in my hand when the world was an easier place. Even though the world was a hard place, it was still so much easier than this. "So no, you don't hate me. You're running because you know I'm *not* gonna make it through this and it fucking hurt you too much the first time." I grab his dick through his jeans and his nostrils flare. "And don't lie and say you don't want to stick your dick in me. You've been hard since I walked into that fucking church back in Faceless. It's why you got here so fast after Marshall said I'm still pining after you." My fingers wrap around his girth, he's even bigger than before. Evidence that a man's dick doesn't stop growing at seventeen. "There isn't anything left for you here but this. You want who I was, you ain't getting her. She doesn't exist. But you want a taste? I fuck harder now than I ever did back then. All you've gotta do is ask."

He gets closer, so close his breath on my lips makes my mouth water. He smells of mint and cigars. "Funnily enough, after all you've told me. I'm not in the mood."

"Funnily enough," I whisper, reaching up on my tiptoes. "After all I've told you, it's the only thing that'll get that shit out of my mind." I lick his lower lip, the tip of my tongue against the satin feel. "Don't let me down here, Kane. Fuck me like you want to hurt me."

"I do wanna hurt you," he hisses, tangling his hand in my hair and doing just that.

"I know. Do it."

I beg him with my eyes, knowing if I'm ever going to feel anything again it'll be with him. I watch as his determination cracks and morphs into something new, right before our lips meet and this time both of us are willing.

His kiss is painful but it's refreshing and it's everything I've always wanted. My memories of our past light up in my head as his flavors explode my senses.

I hum, gripping his neck as he turns us by my hips and slams me so hard against the wall I feel it crack. It knocks the wind right out of me and straight into him but he doesn't let up. He grabs my breast so hard I flinch but then he lets up and rolls it gently under his firm grasp. His other hand yanks up my gown and pulls on my thong, snapping it on one side so it slides down my leg.

With a tug my head comes back and my lips part as he bites and tastes me neck. His every move is strong and unrestrained. He's angry, so fucking angry and he's taking it all out on me.

Spiraling tingles of pleasure curl down my throat from every space he sucks and bites. I whimper, desperate and needy sounding sobs of absolute divinity.

He bends low for a split second, lifts me higher, keeping me pinned against the wall and I don't even get time to register the feel of his cock against me before he has impaled me on it.

I cry out, a growling gasp that I can't control. His cock, so big and thick and hot stretches me to my limits. It burns despite how wet I am.

With a moan of his own his body traps mine against the wall before he begins, giving me only half a second to get used to him before he savagely thrusts in and out, getting deeper and deeper with each stroke. It hurts just like he promised, and it feels so good all at the same time. I moan, it's loud, I can't control it. This raging inferno that has claimed us both is fueled by the gasoline of our hate and love. Both emotions exist in us somewhere and combined they create something so beautiful and vicious.

"Your pussy is even better than I remembered," he hisses in my ear, gritting his teeth with each jarring thrust. "I fucking hate you for that."

"Can hardly feel your cock," I lie, panting as sweat beads on my neck.

I shriek when he drops me and forces me onto the floor. My back hits the carpet and I wonder if a bruise will form along my shoulders.

Kane Jessop isn't being nice to my body right now and yet I've never loved sex more than I do in this moment.

He pins my wrists with a large hand as his body slides between my thighs and his cock takes its rightful place seated in my pussy like king of the fucking dicks. Never had a better one than this. Never has it felt better than this.

I'm losing my mind, I can't breathe, I can't think, I can't see.

"You're a fucking bitch, Immy," he whispers right as I'm about to come. "Never should have saved you that night."

"Probably," I reply, taking everything he's giving me.

"Shoulda' let you die."

"Wish you had."

He goes harder, grinding against my swollen clit and I feel it building, an orgasm so powerful I might lose every hair on my body. It'll be the first orgasm I've had since before this all happened. Not for lack of trying.

His groans get louder and more frequent and his hips jerk erratically. I know he's coming; I can feel him throbbing. It feels incredible. I missed this. I missed his noises and his movements.

"Fuck," he hisses. "Not yet, not yet. Fucking. FUCK!"

His hips piston wildly, pushing me along the carpet, making the

26 YEARS OLD

skin above my ass burn. Then he drops, effectively collapsing on top of me as my orgasm ebbs away and my tingling body returns to normal. Well shit. That's disappointing.

"Just give me a sec to catch my breath." His heaving chest against mine makes it hard for me to breathe. When he starts to rock again, still hard, I shove his shoulder.

"Get off me."

He immediately stops and rests on his arm so he can look down at me, bewildered. "The fuck?"

"Get off."

He complies, pulling out and leaning back onto his knees. I scramble to pull my gown down. "You didn't come."

"Lost it."

"Then give me chance to build it up again. You know I always do."

"I'm not in the mood," I admit, hugging myself as I move to the bedroom.

He laughs coldly. "This because of what I said? You lose it because of that?"

I roll my eyes, hiding not only my hurt but everything else. "Nope."

"You know I didn't mean it. You just piss me off is all."

"I don't care, Kane. Go back to Faceless." I slam the bedroom door closed behind me and start stripping out of my clothing. It hits the floor with a gentle thud mimicking the almost vacant beat of my heart.

It's not until I'm under the hot spray of the shower that I let myself cry. The water hides the tears but it doesn't drown out the sound of my sobs.

I told myself I'd be strong, but how can I be strong when I'm nothing but a cracked shell with a hollow center?

The shower door opens and closes and Kane steps in fully naked. His body presses against my back and he holds me so tight I can hardly breathe.

"We'll find her, Immy."

"We won't."

"We will." He kisses the curve of my shoulder. "We'll find you too."

I bite my lip and sniffle like a child. "I still love you Kane. I can feel it there, it's deep, it's buried under a lot of heavy shit but it's there. Couldn't hurt you. I thought it'd be easier this way. I thought you'd move on and forget all about me." It's not a lie either. "I thought you'd get married, have kids... didn't think I'd ever have to explain this shit to you."

"I know." He kisses my neck this time after pulling my hair to one side. "You don't gotta say it again. You don't gotta say shit to me again, Imogen. No more explainin'." He caresses my stomach, gently gliding his fingers over my scar. "Just healing now. Gonna fix you. Gonna fix us both."

"You really think we'll find her?"

"Absolutely. Not a doubt in my mind."

For the first time since she was taken, there's not a doubt in mine either.

"You've gotta hold still," I hiss as he slides his hand up my thigh.

The buzzing machine in my hand rolls over his skin, leaving beads of ink and blood. He told me to tattoo him, who was I to say no? Though there's not much of his skin left that isn't branded already, I get the space over his heart and I'm using it wisely.

"Naw, you won't fuck up." He's so cocky, still the same as he was way back then. It makes me smile, not like I used to, but the smile is real. "You're the prettiest girl I ever saw, Imogen Hardy."

"Stop," I growl playfully, and dip the needle into the ink. Then I look at the tattoo on his inner wrist. It's my tattoo, one that tells the world Kane is mine and always will be. I guess his love for me is as permanent as the ink imbedded in his skin. Even after all this time.

He tenses as the bell above the door beeps.

"Hi honey, I'm home," Marshall announces, his shoes clicking on the sterile ground. "Kane Jessop as I live and breathe."

"Marshall Jones," Kane replies, making me stop what I'm doing so he can stand and shake Marshall's hand.

Marshall eyes Kane's bare chest with no small amount of appraisal.

"Is my Immy working her inky magic?" Marshall asks and Kane, who is chewing on a wad of gum nods and reclaims his seat.

"She's better than she says," he admits, looking down at the piece I've already spent two hours on.

Which is saying something because I can get kind of braggy.

"Agreed." Marshall winks at me. "So y'all are both back in each other's lives?"

"Yeah," I answer and Marshall's face gets all smug.

"So, I made the right call."

"Should'a made that call a lot sooner," Kane puts in but there's no vehemence. He's simply stating a fact he believes. "How have you been, Martian?"

"Never disliked that name, Jessop." Marshall straddles a chair backwards. "But I've been good. As have you. I can tell. Size of those biceps." He whistles low and long which has me rolling my eyes. "Still lifting tires at your daddy's garage?"

Kane nods and smiles softly at me. "Course. Where else would I be?"

"Your ambition is admirable," Marshall jokes, his sarcasm evident in his tone.

Kane flips him off and motions for me to start again. "Fuck you. I'm earning more doing what I do than most people." He's probably right about that. No shame in being a mechanic, and a good one. Heard he sprays cars and does all the pretty shit to them as well now which isn't an easy trade. "What are you doing these days?"

This might be the first time he has ever asked Marshall. Back in school Kane hated him purely because he saw him as a threat.

"Lotta bullshit."

"Right?"

"Adult life fucking sucks man." Marshall says this with such a comical tone.

"Spoken like a true stoner," I put in and we share a smile.

"So how did y'all get from what you were, to you lettin' her tattoo your left tit?"

Kane's eyes do a narrow smiling thing that they do and his lips twitch at the ends. "Decided to stop being mad over shit we can't change."

"Decided it's better if we work together."

"You gonna go hunting again?" Marshall asks and I nod.

"Hunting?" Kane asks, wetting his lips as he looks between us both.

"That's what we call it when she goes looking for, Flipper."

"Flipper?"

I shrug sadly. "That's what we used to call her. She was a mover. Never stopped wriggling."

"Looked alien as fuck," Marshall admits with a shudder and we share another smile but then I concentrate on my art and keep moving the inky needle across Kane's chest. "She used to stick out her elbow or somethin' and it'd look pointy like when a shark's fin breeches the water surface."

I remember those days and the discomfort, but I never complained. I would have stayed pregnant forever if it meant keeping her safe with me.

"I didn't get any of that."

"I thought you would with somebody else."

He brushes my hair off my face and tucks it behind my ear making me smile again, softly this time. I don't smile enough but he never expected me to. I've never been a particularly expressive person and Kane was always happy to just be with me regardless.

Once he told me I didn't need to smile to be beautiful. That I should only smile when I meant it.

He wanted everything to be real between us and I fucked that up and yet here he is, backing my corner, helping me figure shit out.

"Why are you here anyway?" I ask Marshall, still looking at the ink. I don't lose focus, not even for a second.

So far I have the outline done and a small fraction of the shading. It's going to eventually be his Challenger. A car he still has. It'll look like a photograph when I'm done.

"Just checking you're still breathing."

"He means you," I utter to Kane who chuckles. Then without looking up I add, "Lock the door on your way out, Marsh."

"Damn, it's like that is it?" Marshall isn't offended in the slightest, he's just being a drama llama. "That hurts real deep."

With a cutting look his way, I raise a brow and nod to the door.

Laughing he backs away with his hands raised. "I'm gone."

"Get gone quicker."

I put the machine down for a moment and flex my hand, that is until Kane grabs my hips and pulls me onto his lap. He forces me to straddle him without much coaxing and smirks up at me.

"This isn't sanitary," I admonish. "I'm going to have to clean you again, and change my gloves..."

I'm still not sure how we went from shower to tattoo.

He dried me, I dried him, we shared a laugh like when we were kids and for a moment I saw the boy I fell in love with. Though older, the Kane Jessop I remember still smiles at me like the mischievous man-boy I knew. He's still in there, I don't even have to dig deep to find him. It brings me hope that maybe I'm still here too. Maybe Kane Jessop is wishful thinking, or maybe he sees the girl I used to be brimming below the surface of her hurt.

He leaned down to kiss me, softer this time but I pulled away. I don't even know why. I wanted to kiss him desperately. But every time he kisses me, I just remember what I lost.

That's when we got talking instead as we dressed, and he said he wanted the challenger on his chest and could I fit him in. I was desperate to escape my apartment and now here we are.

He's hard beneath me and the feel of it pressing against my parted thighs, covered only by the stiff denim of my tight jeans and the lace thong, is making me tingle through my entire body.

The plastic of my apron crackles as he rips it away and my hands go to his waist.

His muscles are so hard beneath my touch, which I can't say is soft. Months of hard labor at that fucking cult, plus a lifetime of drawing since have made my fingers harder in places. On both hands, not just one. Though he doesn't seem to mind.

"You haven't aged a bit, Immy," he compliments, gripping my waist and bucking his hips up to meet mine.

"You've only gotten better," I appraise and trace the contours of his abs. He's a God. His body has been chiseled by the angels. There's no other way to describe this masterpiece. "I didn't really kill him."

His guarded eyes find mine. "What?"

"It's a story I tell myself to make it all better. I've done nothing but tell lies my entire life, I don't know how to stop."

"You didn't sever his spine with a knife?"

I shake my head, feeling ashamed. "No. I wish I did. I wish I could have hurt him like that."

"So what did happen?"

"I pushed him, he fell, hit his head and had a seizure that put him into a coma."

His hands squeeze. "Can you stop lying to me now?"

I nod. "I'll try."

"No trying, just... stop lyin'. Okay? I don't have time for it and neither do you."

"I thought you'd walk away."

"You want me to?"

I don't know how to answer that. So instead I sigh and choose honesty, picking the first thing that comes to mind. "I don't want to hurt again."

"I ain't gonna hurt you."

"I know," I whisper, chewing on my lip. "You never did."

"Fresh start, Immy. No more fucking around." He sits up, mindful of his tattoo, and holds me tight against him as I push my hands through his hair. "I'm gonna stay here with you, tomorrow we're gonna see this Webber guy and then we're gonna find our kid." He gives me a reassuring squeeze. "Okay?"

I nod. "Okay."

"You're going to be Immy again. You're going to come back to Faceless and be with the people who love you."

"Like who?"

"Like me, like Poppy, like my folks."

"Poppy," I say softly. "How is she?"

"She's good, she's seeing this guy from out of town. Seems to be a decent man."

I frown. "You talk to her often?"

"Not really, but she pops in when she gets time, to check on me, to see if I've heard about you."

"She didn't come see me when I returned."

"She wasn't in Faceless. She told me to tell you to call her." His thumbs massage deep circles into my skin. "Said she's pissed you haven't been in touch." When I look away he moves his head to follow my line of sight. "She looked for you too, you know. Until your brother returned. She asked him where you were and that's when we heard you left with Marshall. Nobody questioned it because he wasn't reported missing either." He sighs heavily. "It's so fucked up. If you'd told me back then that he was gay... I'd have—"

"No use looking back."

"You do, to keep hating on me every fuckin' chance you get. Don't know why."

I feel guilty, I deserve to feel guilty. "My brother said you were seeing someone else. Said you told him to tell me you never wanted to see me again."

"And you believed him?"

"Yeah," I whisper, my guilt winding deeper. "As much as I wanted you to move on and have a family, it hurt knowing you had."

The room is now filling with our mutual pain. We both share a thought but he verbalizes it.

"Let's stop talking about it."

"Okay."

He presses his lips to mine for a lingering moment that's entirely too brief.

"Finish my tattoo," he breathes against my mouth.

"Okay."

A FEW HOURS LATER...

He loves it. *Adores* it. Can't stop looking at it despite the fact I told him not to uncover it. He's a fucking nightmare for anybody wanting to keep shit sterile.

"One day I want a man to look at me the way you look at that tattoo," I jest, feeling less uptight now we've been together for quite a while.

Kane has made himself at home with his suitcase at the foot of my bed. He knew he'd be coming and staying. He's either very presumptuous or very optimistic. Either way, when he dives onto my couch in plaid pajama bottoms, the bandage covering his chest, he opens his arm to me, and I stare at him for the longest time. The length of his body from head to toe, the thickness of his thighs and biceps, the incredible shape of his toned stomach, the scar on his jaw where he cut himself shaving, the way he's pulled his hair up into a messy knot that suits him so perfectly.

"You just gonna stand there?" He's amused, not offended. His arm is still open.

Eventually I can't seem to tell myself a good reason why I

A FEW HOURS LATER...

shouldn't cuddle up to Kane on my sofa, so I do just that. I climb over the arm of the couch, crawl towards him and rest my head on his ribs, far from his incredible new piece of ink. He smells smoky and sweet, a new scent. He must have put some kind of antiperspirant on despite the fact he's clean and fresh already.

My fingertips tickle his side, making his skin break out in goosebumps.

"Feel seventeen again?" I ask softly because it's all I can think about.

"Fuck, I feel everything again, Immy."

I kiss his side, purely to feel his soft skin against my lips and he nuzzles my hair.

I lift my head raising my mouth to receive his and gently we meet. For a while we stay like this, kissing softly, until it gets more heated and our breathing gets more desperate. For a moment there I thought we were going to do soft and gentle but it has become a frenzy of him trying to pull my underwear down my thighs.

He flips us over so I'm on my back and kisses his way down my body. I tug on his hair, stopping when he reaches my stomach and tries to slide my gown up.

"For all my bravado earlier, I don't really want you up close and personal with my stomach."

His incredible blue eyes glitter in the dark. "Why?"

"It looks like the inside of a crisp packet."

At that he laughs until he sees I'm being serious. "You're worried the part of you that gave life to our kid isn't pretty enough for me?"

"It's not my best asset, Kane."

"It fuckin' is." He rips up my gown anyway and kisses below each of my breasts.

When he rests his forehead against my sternum and whispers something, I close my eyes. Unable to watch this moment that was once upon a time stolen from both of us. Flipper never got to hear her daddy's voice.

"Kane," I mutter sadly and grab his hair again.

A FEW HOURS LATER...

"I feel sick," he admits. "Knowing she's out there, not knowing if she's happy or sad, or if the people who took her would'a taught her shit like we would have." He sits up, seeming to have lost the mood. "Would have taught her to drive already, she'd have her own quad, would'a stuck her name in sparkly shit on her helmet."

"Kane," I repeat, even quieter this time. I rub my hand over his shoulder. "Try not the think about it, it's maddening."

"We might'a been young, Immy, but I'd have done the right thing. Wouldn't have treated her like my momma treated me or yours treated you."

"I know."

He inhales long and slow through his nose and I can see his emotions in his eyes like a storm on the horizon. He's processing but it's hurting him.

"Come here," I breathe, grabbing his long hair and yanking. He doesn't move so I tug harder. "I said come here."

Finally, he drifts my way, leaning his body just close enough for me to place my lips on his.

"Let's do something fun," I say, straddling his lap and massaging his scalp with my fingers. I have missed how soft his hair is. He conditions now, I can tell. It's incredibly sexy.

"Like what?" he asks, his eyes guarded now and tired.

"Let's go for a ride."

"Where?"

"Fuck it, who cares? Let's just go until we run out of gas."

He laughs once and grins at me. "Don't have my car, flew here remember?"

"I've got mine."

"Yours is a piece of shit."

My jaw drops. "Fuck you. She's amazing."

"She isn't a she, she identifies as a tin can or some shit."

I throw my head back and laugh for real. It feels good. "You're a mean boy, Kane Jessop."

"And you have shit taste in cars."

A FEW HOURS LATER…

"I have great taste in men though."

His smile is so cocky and arrogant and so entirely handsome it hurts my eyes. "Yeah you do."

WEBBER'S OFFICE

"These are all the files I have on that case." Webber drops the folder onto his desk and looks between us both. "You can't take these out of here. We have to keep the identity of the other families involved under wraps."

"That's fine," Kane utters as he pores over the first two pages and winces. "This is fucked up."

"Immy got the kinder side of Righteous Hill."

"Righteous Hill?" Kane questions, looking up from the files.

"That's what it was called," I reply, cringing. "They didn't have a very creative board meeting before deciding what to name the place that was going to ruin the lives of hundreds of young people."

Webber hums his agreement. "Still gives me chills the kind of things that went on there."

Kane licks his thumb and turns a page. "So they sold the babies?"

Webber nods. "Yep. Only managed to locate around fifty percent of them."

"And there were ninety-something babies born right?" I ask, trying to recall the specific number.

"Ninety-seven in total that we managed to get confirmed. There's

WEBBER'S OFFICE

likely more but without the victims and witnesses we can't know for sure."

"How much was our daughter sold for?" Kane asks through gritted teeth.

Webber looks at me for reassurance. He's an agent but Kane intimidates him. Unsurprising. Kane is a force to be reckoned with. Webber is an old man now, he's in his early sixties and it's starting to show. But he's damn good at what he does. Not to mention he is so compassionate. He's the only person that could get through to me in the beginning. He brought me back to the light when there was no light in my darkness to be found.

When I was in the federal institution, he visited almost every day or as often as he could. He brought me magazines and clothes and dinners his wife made. Without him I might never have found enough of my mind to reach freedom.

"They seem to have had a points system for babies based on their skin color, ethnicity, cuteness, for example. But they often had buyers waiting for the baby to be born who were willing to take it no matter the looks. An illegal practice and a lot of the parents who purchased babies are in prison."

A flare of hope lights up in Kane's eyes.

"They don't know anything. It was all anonymous and well-planned. Any footprints left behind, were erased and well." Webber douses his hope but he looks sorry for it. "You can't contact these families. Do you understand? Some are innocent. Some genuinely believed they were dealing with a legitimate adoption agency and assumed the fee they were paying was to the mother of the child. An illegal activity in itself but not one punishable by law when all other circumstances are taken into account. People desperate for a family will do desperate things."

"So she could be out there with loving parents somewhere," I say to Kane because it is the only comfort I find in times like this.

He keeps looking at the pages.

"Some kids weren't so lucky," he growls. "This one was located when she was four. Sex trafficking."

Webber nods. "Those are the ones we struggle to find the most. There's no paper trail at all."

My heart stops beating as it always does when I think of *that* scenario for our child.

"Oh my God," Kane breathes, his hands balling into fists. "How likely is it that she's one of those."

"Most of the kids that we located were with loving families."

"How likely?" Kane demands of Webber who looks uncomfortable for a moment, and of course distressed.

"I'd say a twenty percent chance."

Kane brings his fist down on the table and glowers at me. "If she's in the hands of a trafficker and you didn't pull me in to help you find her, we're done. We should have made this nationwide. We should have gone to every newspaper."

"You can't," Webber barks. "As frustrating as it is, the children involved are already at risk because of what happened to Righteous Hill and its supporters. They might kill the children so there's no evidence of their existence if they panic and think we could be onto them. Or sell them on, or leave the country, or worse. We have tried to keep this as low key as possible. I understand your frustration Mr. Jessop, but this isn't just about *your* kid. We have forty kids in the wind that need our help and just one word to the press could fuck up the rest of their lives."

"What kind of life do they have if they're with a fucking pedophile?" Kane yells, standing now.

"Stop!" I shout back, standing and placing my hand on his chest, not the tattooed side.

His heavy breathing makes his chest rise and fall visibly. I keep my hand on it until he forces it away with a powerful shift of his upper body.

"There should be something in the media," Kane snarls. "Any-

WEBBER'S OFFICE

thing. Such as... if you were adopted between the dates of X and X, please contact Detective Dipshit of Chicago."

Webber's eyes narrow. "I have done everything in my power to find your child."

"Except notify her fucking father."

"I couldn't legally do that."

Kane laughs coldly and directs his anger my way. "I feel fucking sick. Tryna to forgive you for this, Immy, running out of reasons to justify your choices."

"Justify her choices?" Webber hisses, his dad side coming out in my defense. I sink into my seat, suddenly feeling like piggy in the middle. "You have no idea the mental torment she endured in that hell hole, *boy*. You have no idea the solitary burden she has taken by keeping this to herself. You have no idea the mental torment she has put herself through to find this child." He places his hands on his desk and his glare gets harsher. "You wouldn't have been able to do shit. You still can't do shit. Because unfortunately your daughter's sale was processed by Father Righteous himself which means it would have been a very high price and an anonymous buyer. Kept tightly under wraps. Not a single person working in that hell hole knew what happened to that baby. I questioned them all. Not just me but my colleagues too. They had no reason to lie about this baby and not the others."

"What about babies registered at around that time?" Kane asks, sounding just as frustrated as before. "There has to be somewhere we can start?"

"Do you know how many babies were registered at around that time? In the same county let alone the same state. Chances are she was sold out of state and there's no way to prove that they didn't have the kid themselves... you can't just go around asking for DNA tests without a judge's order and he'd need evidence."

"Or she," I needlessly put in because I don't know what to say.

Kane looks ready to throw the desk out of the window.

Just when I think he's about to blow, due to the reddening of his face and the tightening of his fists, he storms past me and snarls, "I need a breather."

Webber and I both watch him go and keep watching through the glass panel on the door long after he has slammed it shut behind him.

"He seems like a decent guy," Webber says with no ounce or anything but honesty in his voice. "Reckon he'll look after you."

"I reckon."

We don't smile, neither of us are smilers, but we do look back at the files on his desk and I swiftly add, "Thank you for all the work you did for me over the years."

He rolls his eyes; he doesn't take compliments very well. Neither of us do.

I flick through the pages of the huge folder and scan each document that I've already scanned a hundred times. He lets me look at it whenever I get in the mood. He says you can never read an unsolved case too many times, there's always something to be seen that has been missed.

I've read it that many times I know all the names of all the kids that have been found already. I know the temporary stand in names for all those who haven't been found. Flipper included.

The door opens behind me with a rattle and Kane takes his place by my side.

"We good?" I ask him softly.

He grabs my head and pulls my forehead to his lips. "Yeah, babe. We're good. Let's find our kid."

"See?" Webber states, looking directly at me and I know he's referring to his proclamation on Kane being a good guy.

Webber lets us take the folder into the adjoining room where Kane and I spend four hours non-stop discussing each case and page. He reads them thoroughly and I watch him exhaust himself with all the new information. I recognize his posture and his expression to match my own. I look and feel that way every time I look at it too. It's all too familiar.

"He really has put shit together," Kane comments.

WEBBER'S OFFICE

"Not just him, there's an entire team dedicated to these kids. Flipper included."

"Flipper," he utters, stopping and placing his hand over my stomach. "Fuck. We should'a been more careful, Immy."

"I took my pill."

"You were always forgettin'."

He's right. "You knew that and you still kept putting it in me without a rubber."

"I didn't say *you* should'a been more careful, I said, *we*," he responds with a wry smile and I silently decide that yes he did actually refer to us both and not just me. "Bet you're not on anything now either, let me fuck you on that carpet ungloved."

"It's not like we stopped to discuss it."

"We should. We always did as teens."

I almost laugh because for all the discussions we had about being safe, we rarely were.

I roll my eyes. "Well, don't worry your pretty hair off. I get the injection every three months."

His eyes darken and his mood follows their depth. "How fuckin' often you getting dicked in order for you to need the injection every three months?"

"Never you mind," I reply with not small amount of attitude.

"Ungloved or gloved?"

"Kane I've literally slept with maybe two people since you, both were desperate drunken mistakes and yes I used a condom." I shove him away from me, stand and stretch. "I get the injection because it stops my periods. I like not having periods."

"Your periods used to make you a bitch." He stands too and yanks me into his hard body.

"That's so true I can't even begin to find it in me to deny it."

He chuckles, though it's tense and the weight of the situation shows in his smile.

"How many girls you bedded then, Mr. Judgy?" I think back to when he said he only lets girls have his dick but not his heart, though not in that exact way of wording, but absolutely the same meaning. "If we're travellin' that path I deserve to know how many times you've caught crabs from some low-brow bar in Austin."

"You been watchin' me, darlin'?" he jests, grinning with his perfect teeth and devilish eyes.

"Kane Jessop, you answer me now before I assume the worst."

"Had an on and off fling with a woman for a coupla years, nothin' serious. Maybe three before her. Been busy. Don't disrespect women, don't do the dive and ditch. If I'm gonna fuck a girl, unless she's shit in bed, I'm gonna fuck her again."

I feel my entire body become a frosty block of cement.

"Didn't date nobody though, only ever dated you."

"Yeah and you complained."

"That's not fuckin' true."

I narrow my eyes. "You wouldn't even take me to homecoming!"

"Biggest mistake of my life." His admission has me blinking with surprise. "Trust me. Ain't a night that went by that I didn't regret not dancing with you while you looked so fuckin' pretty in that dress. Did I ever tell you that?"

I shake my head, thinking back to that night and the nights that followed. We weren't right after that.

He voices almost my exact words. "I fucked up. Things weren't right. I should'a been a man and let my girl have a good night without the drama I created."

"That was the night I said that thing I said about you ruining my life, I've never been able to forget it. We never really spoke about that."

He sighs and holds me tighter. "Thought it was that night that pushed you away. You stopped fuckin' me, stopped talkin' to me like you did before. Once upon a time I'd tinker with your bike and listen to you go on non-stop for hours, but then that night happened, and I couldn't even get you to tell me what you ate for breakfast. Didn't bring it up because I was worried about what you was gonna tell me." Laughing gently but bitterly he goes on, "Thought for sure you were fucking around with Marshall behind my back. Both of you were moping around after he left you that night. Thought you were heartbroken."

"I was, you ruined my friendship and put me in a position where I had to choose you over him when he was innocent. I shouldn't have chosen you but I loved you too much, couldn't stand the thought of losin' you."

"Maybe if I hadn't been so shit to you, you might'a come to me when you thought you were pregnant."

"I was just scared you'd get mad and think I did it on purpose."

He frowns, looking down at me with a stern expression. "That the only reason?"

I consider lying but I promised him I wouldn't do that anymore. "I wasn't sure if I wanted a baby. Needed to figure that out before I came to you with it. Thought if I made a decision on my own it wouldn't matter what you told me you wanted."

"That's fair," he utters, wetting his lips when he looks down at mine. "Whatever the fuck happened, we're gonna get through this together, yeah?"

"Reckon we can handle it?"

"So long as I keep takin' my breathers and you keep suckin' my dick."

I laugh, though there's sadness to it, there's also genuine happiness that I haven't allowed myself to feel in so long. "You're an idiot, Kane Jessop."

"And I still ain't seen a girl prettier than you, Imogen Hardy."

"You mean it?" I ask breathlessly as I go up onto my tiptoes.

Grinning, he presses his lips to mine and slides his tongue into my mouth without waiting a moment. I hum, happy to be in his arms, happy to feel something other than despair and longing. Dreamt of being right here with him so many times, and now I have it I'm not sure how to handle it.

"Let's spend another hour mulling this shit over."

"Take as long as you need." I kiss his jaw and guide him back to his seat and when he sits I rub his shoulders. He's incredibly tense. Understandably so.

"Before I forget," he says and digs into the inner pocket of his jacket. "You left this at my dad's."

It's the letter from Mee-maw. I immediately scowl at it, feeling no small amount of hatred for the dead cow.

"Burn it."

"You should read it; you'll always wonder what it said if you don't."

"Fuck off, Yoda," I comment, snatching the envelope from his hand. I tear the letter into two, then four, then eight, and I keep going until it's nothing but uneven strips which I then sprinkle into the trash. "Trust me. There's nothing she's got to say that I want to hear."

"Babe."

"If I have to read her apology, it might send me into an early grave. She doesn't deserve the chance to ask for my forgiveness. I will *never* forgive her and I don't want to be guilted into it."

"Fair enough." He pats his thigh. "Sit with me."

Tense and agitated, I do just that, perching myself on his leg and resting my arm along his shoulders. "Do you think it's weird that we're just so comfortable around each other like we were back when we were kids?"

"Naw." He pops a piece of gum into his mouth and I take the one he offers.

Naw is all he says on that question and I have to laugh because it's just so Kane Jessop.

BACK HOME

THE NEXT DAY

I wake in Kane's arms despite the fact he took the couch. I asked him to, said I needed time to adjust, but then I woke up and couldn't sleep. As though sensing it, he knocked on my door and stood in the doorway, eyes locked with mine in the darkness.

"I'm comin' in," he whispered.

"Okay," I whispered back and shuffled up the bed to make space for him.

"Don't go too far," he warned and when the bed dipped under his weight, I found myself against him. I love that he wants me as close to him as I want him to me, despite the fact that I also don't want him too close because it's going to be harder making him move in the end. "Webber said we can go back tomorrow."

"He did."

"We'll do that, but first you gotta call Poppy."

"Okay."

Kane calls her the moment we finish breakfast that he made me eat. Can't remember the last time I ate breakfast.

"You gotta work today?" Kane asks as the dial tone sounds through the kitchen space.

I nod. "Got a client in for a six-hour sitting."

Kane whistles long and low. "That's gonna smart."

"Guy's tough as nails."

"So am I," he puts in needlessly which makes me grin.

"That goes without saying."

We share an affectionate look.

"I'll go back and look through the files while you work," he murmurs right as Poppy answers with a friendly, "Kane Jessop, to what do I owe the pleasure?"

"Poppy-Rose," Kane replies. "How have you been, darlin'?"

My jealousy instantly rears its ugly and nostalgic head. He knows I don't like it when he calls other people under fifty darlin'. Not even Poppy-Rose. But by the flash of his eyes I just know he did that on purpose.

"Got someone here who wants to talk to you," Kane puts in, his tone gruff and amused.

"Oh my God... is she there?" Her tone is all but a shriek. "You're pulling my dick, right? You're winding me up?"

"I'm here." I chew on my lip and stare at Kane's phone resting on the countertop.

"Are you kidding me?" I can hear the emotion in her voice. "I THOUGHT YOU WERE DEAD!"

And now she's pissed, maybe even hysterical. Rightfully so. Just hearing her voice has me feeling every kind of emotion.

"I know. I'm sorry."

"Sorry? You were like my sister my entire life and then you just fucking vanished!"

"It's a long story." Kane, for support, wraps his arms around me from behind. I quickly add before she can question me further, "How are you? What have you been up to?"

She pauses, I know she wants to get madder, but she doesn't. I hear her exhale right before she answers, "So much actually. How much time do you have?"

"Not enough. I have to be at work in forty minutes."

"Well then, I guess for now I can tell you I'm happy, I'm safe, I have the love of a great guy. We just got engaged and now I'm settled in my career we umm... yeah. Things are moving at a steady pace. You?"

"Not much to tell, bit of a loner, I have my own tattoo shop."

"Wait that's yours?" Kane asks, quirking a brow. "You never mentioned that."

"Didn't need to. Bought it with the money I got from the state after my... after the thing."

He nods, looking solemn. "You got deep roots here then."

"It's just a building, Kane."

He doesn't look like he believes me but truth be told I'm not attached to much in this life, especially not a building. Bought it because I wanted to be my own boss, kept getting fired by my old ones.

"That's awesome, Immy. You do tattoos? You always were good at drawing." Poppy sounds so happy, genuinely so.

I smile at the phone, wishing it would morph into my old friend. "It was hell without you."

"I should hope so," she jests, and Kane picks up the phone.

"She'll call you back," Kane promises.

"She better." She laughs lightly and I recall how badly I have missed that sound. "See you later guys."

"Bye," I murmur.

The line dies when Kane hangs up and stuffs his phone into his back pocket.

"You good?" he asks tenderly, turning me in his arms. I don't need to confirm, he brushes my hair back, cups my cheek and presses his forehead to mine. "You're good. Ain't gonna let anybody chew you out. Don't worry, *darlin'*."

"Except you, right?"

"Yeah, but you can take it from me and know that I'll still fuckin' feel the same way about you at the end."

I press my cheek to his chest. "Do you think I'm weak?"

"I think you're the strongest girl I ever saw, Imogen Hardy."

"Pretty sure that's you," I retort, smiling and then squealing when he squeezes my ass so hard it hurts.

"Go to work, I'll meet you there when I'm done."

"Okay."

I pull away but he yanks me back and crushes his lips against mine. I love it when he does that.

As he said he would, he spends the whole day poring over those files. When he returns to me later with a bag of food, I can see how physically and mentally drained he is. This is what I didn't want for him. It's breaking my heart, a heart I was sure could never be hurt again.

He doesn't do much talking, just walks me home and sets about making dinner.

Who'd have thought that vicious unruly boy always getting into trouble would know how to make the meanest spaghetti bolognese I ever did taste? Who'd have thought the boy I once knew would become the incredible man I'm looking at right now?

God, he deserved to move on and find love with a woman less damaged than me, but all I see when he looks at me with that handsome and crooked smile, is total adoration. Kane Jessop never stopped loving me anymore than I stopped loving him. Even our mutual hatred couldn't destroy our bond. A bond that shouldn't exist. A bond that makes no sense.

We were always destined for terrible things, I just never could have imagined it would be this.

"What you thinkin'?" I ask as he moves around my kitchen looking for a bottle opener so we can have a beer to wash down our dinner.

He pops the lids off and tosses both into the trash. I take the beer he offers, and swallow a long pull with lip smacking satisfaction.

"Not thinking of nothin'," he responds, rubbing his face with his hands before leaning over his plate and twisting some spaghetti around his fork. "I'm all *thinked* out."

I know that feeling well too.

"What are *you* thinking?"

"About you," I honestly state and fill my mouth with food.

"What about me?"

"About us, I guess. It's all a little confusing."

"What's confusing about it?"

I motion between the both of us with the bottom of my bottle and take a smaller gulp this time. "We're just acting like no time has passed."

"Yeah, and?" His blue eyes scan my face. Does he really not feel any confusion about our relationship at this point.

"And I just don't know what this is or what you want it to be."

"It is what it is, don't want it to be nothin' beyond what it is."

I laugh, confused and conflicted. "That's not an answer."

"It's the only answer I've got right now." He stuffs more food in his mouth and winks. "Stop thinkin' just eat, drink, try to chill. We need a shut off point or it's gonna tear us apart."

I puff out my cheeks and place my fork on my almost finished plate. "Never been able to just chill. Can't remember a night where I had any peace."

"That why you won't let me fuck you again?"

I stiffen and I know it's visible because his lips twitch into a smirk.

"Yeah, that's how your body gets when I touch you."

I narrow my eyes. "That's not true."

"It is. But it's okay." He licks clean his lips and winks at me. "I'm hoping the beer will soften you up."

My jaw drops and I almost laugh. "I guess I'm just a bit tense."

"Yeah no shit."

"Kane," I admonish, and he smiles again, for real this time, not just a smirk.

"You'll definitely soften up when I eat you later."

My eyes widen and I almost choke on my beer.

His grin is mischievous and boyish. "Remember when you used to get pissed at me, all I'd have to do is drop to my knees and worship your pussy. You'd still be pissed but you were too polite to leave or throw me out after I made you come." His teeth trap his lip and then it pings free. *Fuck*. "I always made you come. Always. Never failed. Fuckin' loved it. Loved conquering your body like that."

His words have me pressing my thighs together. "Stop."

"Even better was you'd completely forget you were pissed and why you were pissed."

My eyes become slits and he chuckles like it's funny when it absolutely isn't.

"Even my daddy called you firecracker when you weren't listenin', said I needed a girl like you to keep me in a good place." He finishes his beer and his smile fades. "He was right. I was a shit after you vanished. Didn't do good things to people. Joined the Renegades for a while and caused all kinds of trouble, hurt some people."

"But you looked so put together when I came."

"I turned my life around, stopped hurting my dad and focused on my work. Took a few courses in Austin."

"I'm proud of you for that. Wish you could'a found better than me."

"You make it sound like there is better than you. You're forgettin' all the shit we did together, all the fun we had." He stacks my plate on top of his.

"Not forgetting any of it, trust me. I cherish every moment. It's just painful."

"It doesn't have to be."

I sigh a heavy breath and stand. "What's the plan now? Where do we go from here?"

"We find our kid."

"That's not gonna happen overnight."

"I know."

I frown. "So you're what, going to stay here until we find her? Your daddy needs you."

"My kid needs me. My daddy will be fine without me. Unless you want to follow me back to Faceless? Set up shop there? I'm assuming the only reason you stayed here is because of Webber?"

I nod. "That and I needed out."

"Does it fall under Illinois jurisdiction? Where was Righteous Hill?"

"Texas, east of Wichita Falls. So it's not Illinois jurisdiction anymore but Webber keeps in touch with their offices for updates. Calls weekly. I call too."

He nods softly. "Y'all have really put the work in then."

I move around the table and slide onto his lap. "I'm sorry it's not helping much."

"Me too. But it just means we need a new angle."

I don't reply, I just detangle his hair with my fingers and pull it back from his face. "Can you ever forgive me for what I've done to you?"

"Immy, you got every part of me. Ain't nothin' to forgive. You just gotta forgive yourself." He yanks my hair and pulls my face to his, kissing me deeper than he ever has.

"Stop!" I squeak playfully, trying to pull away. "I taste like spaghetti."

"The best made spaghetti in this part of the U.S. of A."

We laugh together and go back to kissing. I don't even remember the spaghetti when he pushes his chair back and stands, holding me by my thighs. His hands are so large and warm. My arms on his shoulders tighten to distribute my weight, even though he makes me feel entirely weightless.

He walks blindly to my bedroom, lowering me when we reach the bed.

We stare at each other, chests rising and falling, until he bends and grasps the hem of my chiffon top and pulls it upwards until I'm standing in front of him, braless and with pointed nipples reacting to the cold and my arousal. I gently loosen his belt and push his pants down. When I grasp him he pulls my hand away.

"Not a chance, fuckin' embarrassing how little time it takes me to come with you, Immy. You touch it, I'm going to blow before I get to put it in."

Laughing, I stop when my back hits the bed and he drops to his knees, wraps his hands around my hips and drags me to the side. All my breath hits my lungs with a sharp inhale the moment his mouth closes over my jeans, right where my clit is. He soon yanks them down my thighs and pulls just one leg free. I'm bare to him now, exposed and he doesn't give me a second to think about it.

It has been so long since I let a guy go down on me. In fact I'm pretty sure he's the only guy I have ever let go down on me.

My lips part and my back arches when he parts me with his strong tongue. The feeling is out of this world. I want to clamp my thighs shut to stop the burning tingles that are taking over all my other senses.

He's even better than he was when we were younger, or maybe that's just because I haven't been touched in so long.

I moan and hum, losing all my inhibitions the more my pleasure builds. What is it about both ends of the pleasure and pain spectrum that just make us completely lose ourselves?

My head goes back, I bite my lip, my hands go to his hair and just like that I'm seventeen again, not letting him stop until I'm done. He laughs against me and I lose it. For the first time in years I'm blinded by my orgasm's power as it rips through my body.

I groan so loudly I vaguely hear my neighbor banging on the wall but I don't care about that either. The old bitch is a religious tyrant like my mee-maw was. Just for her banging I'm going to scream louder than I ever have but to be completely honest, that's not just to piss her off, but because that's how amazing I feel.

Kane wastes no time grabbing my hips, pulling me further off the bed and slamming home. We both groan at the contact and this time I don't let my mood, or my fears and insecurities ruin the moment. I hold his eyes, sit up and hold his body, and rock with him. He lifts me, turns and sits on the bed, letting me go at my own pace until his need for more has him pulling my hips at a speed and strength I can't manage alone.

Gritting his teeth, he buries his face in my neck and his grunts get louder. I love the noises he makes, it used to always be about how loud and out of control I could make him. Nothing has changed. Every noise he makes sets off flutters in my stomach and makes my skin prickle with warmth.

He rolls us, pulling out of my body so he can lay me on the mattress and power into me like I know he wants. I feel him swelling despite his control over his body. It feels amazing. I clench down, holding him tight. My hips roll up when he stops, trying again to grasp what little control he has left.

He looks down at me, warning me with his eyes to behave. Of course I don't, I never did.

I rock again, locking my ankles under his ass so he can't pull away and the look on his face as he loses to the pleasure I know my body is granting him is so intense and so fucking sexy I'll never be able to forget it.

I ride the wave with him, feeling it, feeling another climax roll through me. Different to the last but no less powerful.

He drops, his body trembling as I trail my fingers up and down his spine. Lips touch my breast and he rolls us onto our sides, waits for me to get comfortable and then holds me in strong arms.

"This is all gonna work out," he whispers against my hair.

I smile because I think I actually believe him.

FACELESS – TEXAS

ONE WEEK LATER

For legal reasons I had to return to my hometown to listen to the reading of my mee-maw's will. Apparently, I'm on it, so is my mother and brother who also must return. I really don't want to. Not because I don't want to be here, but because I hate my brother and I hate my mother. Also, because I don't want to be here.

"Yeah, we're just rolling in now." Kane is on the phone to his daddy, relaxing during the final stretch of a very long journey that I'm so glad we took together.

If there's one thing I've learned about being in the car for over seventeen hours with Kane Jessop, it's that he makes me laugh at all the right moments, keeps me occupied at all the right moments, and our silences are comfortable and never awkward.

We stopped after the first eight and stayed in a motel on the roadside, had amazing sex, burgers from a local dive and then this morning we had a killer breakfast and for the most part I'm feeling happy even knowing I'm about to walk into this mess of a situation.

"So that's why he wasn't there?" Kane asks his daddy and grips my thigh. "Well I'll be sure to pass on that message but I know she ain't gonna be happy to receive it." He says his goodbyes and puts a cigar between his lips, he doesn't smoke around me if at all, but he likes to have something to help him curb the habit.

"What?" I ask, worried now.

"According to my daddy, Matthew wasn't at your mee-maw's funeral because he didn't think you'd show and he had nothing nice to say to the bitch, dead or alive. Not because he was in prison or anythin' like that."

My hands clench on the steering wheel as we drive down the dusty road that is far too familiar. "Don't care. He's got nothing to say to me that I want or need to hear."

"I agree."

"Feel free to knock him around a little when he tries."

Kane chuckles and tries to stretch out his long legs. "Duly noted."

I think of what my brother might want to say to me but anything my mind conjures just has me flying into a blind range. Mentally of course. I'm not taking my eyes off the road, especially not in a place where kids play and animals wander.

"If he tries to apologize..." I seethe and Kane squeezes my thigh that little bit harder.

He doesn't say anything because what's to say? My brother fucking betrayed me. But then he didn't betray his drugs. He snapped out of his funk to start getting high again but not to save his pregnant sister.

Webber empathizes with him on the rare occasion he gets brought into conversation. He says a lot of the other kids who went through the brainwashing are still suffering today after years of therapy.

Another reason I had to go into the witness protection program for a few years was to protect me from his minions who would have loved to have gutted me for betraying him. To betray Father Righteous was to betray God. A lot of them have seen sense since, I just hope none of them ever try to contact me.

Hopefully by now that type of threat has blown over.

We head straight to a diner by Ice-Queen where I used to work. Kane used to love nailing me with puns when I worked there. Any way he could insert an insult about my apparent frostiness he would and Ren would howl with laughter every single time.

I'm nervous, even though I saw his parents a few weeks ago and I've been texting Felicia, I'm super not okay with this. We both decided not to tell them about our kid until we knew more. Kane is finally starting to understand why I kept it from him. The truth of the matter hurts too much. It's too draining on the soul.

Kane is already frustrated that he hasn't made any progress with the case. I think he was secretly hoping he'd spot something we didn't and crack the case wide open. I know this because I've been secretly hoping that for years. Every time I opened those files I told myself that today would be the day I finally figured this out. It was never to be.

Kane stretches tall, showing me a hint of his abdomen which is tight with muscles and decorated with incredible tattoos. The one I did of his challenger is further up and still quite sore but otherwise it is healing just fine.

This heat is not helping. I'm sweating bullets and so is he. It was nicer in my Jag with the air-con blasting out a frosty breeze.

"You're here!" Poppy screams, racing from the diner with her arms wide open.

I catch her before we both hit the gravelly deck and apart from a slight maturing of her face, she looks exactly the same. She still smells the same too.

"I can't believe it's you," she whispers and I share that very sentiment.

And just like that, when West, Felicia, Ren, and Poppy's mother Patrice all greet us too, it's like no time has gone by at all.

Soon the diner is full of old schoolfriends desperate to catch a glimpse of me. I don't remember ever being this popular back in the day though being with Kane sure brought me some infamy in school.

I just can't believe all these people are here.

"Why did you do this?" I ask Kane, feeling overwhelmed and emotional.

"Just reminding you that you haven't been forgotten," he whispers in my ear and kisses my temple. "Lot of bad memories in Faceless. But there are some fucking good ones too. This room is full of them."

He's right and slowly I allow myself to open up to receive the joy they're putting out. I guess I just let how shit life was at times overshadow how amazing it was too.

We push tables together and drink shakes, coffee, soda, whatever we want. We all catch up and I find myself getting emotional hearing about everybody's lives. Selma has a kid! A little girl who is five. She wants me to meet her but I typically tend to stay away from children, they're a trigger for me. A lot of things are a trigger for me.

Ren failed to mention that he got married and divorced all in the same year.

Poppy doesn't live in Faceless anymore.

Patrice is now manager like she always wanted.

They all have achieved so much in the time I've been gone and it's lovely to see and experience. But it's also emotionally draining. Even though they don't blame me outright for leaving, they also don't understand and eventually we are going to have to have that conversation, but not tonight. It can wait until after my mee-maw's reading.

Seeing Matthew for the first time since Righteous Hill is another trigger. I discover this when he walks through the door of the lawyer's office, utters my name with eyes swimming with tears like he has a right to feel sad and I swing a chair at his head.

Absolutely one of my finer moments. Especially when it hits his arm and he hits the wall. I mean my brother is all muscle now, because apparently betraying me and his niece, and getting sober after years inside has been good for him.

I fly at him, unable to stop myself. I claw at him, bite him, kick, punch and hit him over and over again. I lose my shit on an epic scale and even Kane struggles to hold me back.

My mother sobs like the drama bitch she is. The lawyer just begs us to watch his statue of a naked woman sitting with a donkey. I almost pick it up and beat my brother with that too. I could probably kill him right now and only regret it a little but eventually I simmer down and Kane drags me away as I scream profanities at my brother.

My throat is sore, my fists are sore, I broke a nail and my hair is no longer as neat as it was.

"That went well," Kane comments when we reach the hall and my hysterical crying become hysterical laughter.

We head out for an hour for a long walk to chill me out and the nostalgia hits me like a ton of bricks. I forgot how everyone knows everyone, so I'm stopped constantly, and people are so nice. Most say sorry for my loss and only one person brings up my loving eulogy to my grandmother at her funeral.

I expected worse.

We return and head inside. My temper has regulated itself now so I don't feel like I might kill my brother again. Though the visible damage on Matthew sure makes me feel a little better about being in the same room as him. He has a black eye, a bruise on his jaw and scratches down his neck.

He didn't even try to defend himself because he knew he deserved it.

"I'm sorry," he mouths when I sneer at him as the lawyer drones on and on about something but no amount of apologies can fix what he has done to me. I'll never forgive him but I've said everything I needed to say.

"For Matthew Gabriel Hardy," the lawyer continues though I wasn't listening, "I leave what my husband asked me to leave to him and not a penny more, the amount of five-thousand dollars." He's reading from a handwritten sheet of paper. "For Mary Hardy, my daughter, I leave my belongings and jewelry, there is a detailed itinerary in Mr. Procter's care."

Mom gapes. She's clearly disappointed there's no money. Not even in Mee-maw's jewelry. She didn't buy expensive things.

"She's joking right?"

Mr. Procter continues, "For my granddaughter Imogen Mary Hardy, I leave my home and the remainder of my savings, the land upon which my home was built and my bible in the hopes that one day she may find it in her heart to forgive me and perhaps build her family in the one place I tried my hardest to build ours."

"That old bitch just had to," I hiss, shaking my head, feeling my eyes burn.

Does she really think I'll raise a kid in that house? Is she insane?

"This isn't fair," Mom breathes.

"You were as absent as fucking snow in these here parts," Matthew snaps at her. "Only person who ever spent any time with Mee-maw was Imogen. Makes sense she'd leave it all to her."

"So I trust you won't be disputing the will?" Mr. Procter asks.

"I won't be," Matthew responds, glancing my way.

"I'll be homeless!" Mom shrieks sounding panicked.

"And I grew up motherless," I reply, feeling a certain amount of power in this situation. "Ain't life a bitch?"

Mom gapes at me. "You're a cruel girl, Imogen."

"Calm down, Ma, Immy didn't say you couldn't live in the house." Matthew rolls his eyes but I'm bristling over his name for me.

"Don't call me Immy. That name is reserved for people who give a shit about me."

Matthew looks down at his shoes and doesn't respond.

"Well, this should be quite simple then." Mr. Procter looks like he wants to be out of this situation *now*. I don't blame him. "I just need you all to sign a few things and I'll move it along."

"I thought you'd turn down the money," Kane whispers as we leave a few minutes after listening to the entirety of the will and the itinerary. It was boring as hell. We bailed the second Mr. Procter stood, mostly because I didn't want to have to deal with Mom and I especially don't want to have to deal with Matthew.

"There's gotta be two hundred grand in savings if you count the house value," I reply with a smirk. "If we want to get serious about finding our kid, we need to up our game and for that we need money. The old bitch can pay for it."

"Right." Kane's eyes light up. "That's a good point, Immy."

"I have good ideas sometimes. My little girly brain can think things."

He nudges me with his elbow. "You good?"

"I'm good."

"Imogen," Matthew calls as we reach the car. "Please wait."

"I will stab you, not even kidding," I reply daringly and yank open the car door.

Kane blocks my body, protecting me from seeing him and so he's at a better angle to catch me if I fly at him again.

"Imogen please," Matthew begs. "I'm sorry. I'm so fucking sorry."

I laugh once and climb into the car. "Better move *brother* or I'll run your ass over." I'm not even kidding. I wish I could express my level of hatred for the boy who was once my everything, but it's too intense for meagre words.

His hazel eyes shine with emotion. "I know I don't deserve it. But I miss you. And I'm sorry."

"You're the reason our kid is gone, sorry ain't a word to make up for that," Kane puts in and Matthew looks devastated. "Only reason I'm not beating your ass is because I don't need to be in jail when my girl needs me by her side. But you step foot near us again, I'll end you. Won't even think twice about it."

Matthew's lips part and he remains frozen for the longest moment. Then he takes another step towards us, tries to speak, stops himself, turns and walks away. My heart breaks because even though he deserves everything he gets; I still love the boy I once knew, and I don't ever want to hurt him.

"Immy," Matthew mouths, looking as heartbroken as I felt when he left that prison and left me behind. I correct myself mentally because there's no way he could be as heartbroken as I was back then.

Kane puts the car in reverse and backs out of the space. I don't speak as he drives us to the main road, I just stare out of the window while trying to gather myself.

"The old bitch left me everything," I utter, letting it sink in.

I had no idea she'd do that, none at all.

We pull up the long driveway of an unfamiliar home just a few blocks from Faceless Mechanics. I know the area but I don't know anybody who lives here. It's a nice house, has a garage and the driveway could fit a couple of cars. It has two floors and nets in all the windows.

It seems to be well maintained, could use a fresh coat of paint though. This is why I like having an apartment. I don't have to worry about maintenance.

"This is yours?" I question as he pulls the car to a stop halfway down the drive.

"Sure is. Bought it two years ago."

I grin mischievously. "You lived with your parents until two years ago?"

"Fuck yeah, wish I still did, got meals, got everything cleaned after me, didn't have to pay a bill."

"Ugh, I'm ashamed to admit you have a point. Adulting sucks."

We both climb from the car and he tosses me a set of keys. "Give yourself the tour, I've just got to deal with somethin'."

"What?"

"Just somethin'," he replies cryptically.

"Oookay," I drag the word out and move to the house, sticking the key in the lock the second I reach the door and twist.

Kane has style, I discover as I wander around from room to room. It's a bit of a bachelor pad but it's nicely decorated. Especially the living room which is such a man cave but the lazy-boy looks delightful.

The fridge is empty, I assume Felicia probably did that for him. I heard him ask her to go round and just make sure nothing died inside.

His bedroom is amazing though the spare room is empty. I sit on his incredible mattress and wonder if it's the same type he had back in school but bigger. It sure feels the same.

I help myself to a hot shower, taking my time to steam away the filth that is lingering after that meeting. I lather up my hair, soap down my body, and just hold myself under the heat until I wrinkle and prune.

"Babe?" Kane calls and when I look up he's standing there with a towel open for me. "You've been in there a really long time."

I switch off the water, ring out my hair and slide open the shower door. He immediately wraps me in the fluffy white towel and touches his tongue to the tip of my nose.

"Any cleaner and you'll have no skin left," he comments, holding me even tighter. "Feel better?"

I nod. "I'm starving, we need to get groceries."

"Thought I'd take you to dinner tonight."

I laugh lightly and peer up at him with my hands on his chest. "Like a date?"

"Yep."

"Is Kane Jessop asking little ole me on a date?"

"What's wrong with wantin' to take the prettiest girl I ever saw for a good night on the town?"

Grinning, I cup his face and kiss him softly. "Did you bring my luggage inside?"

"Yep."

"Then I guess I'll get dressed then."

He grins, making his eyes squint at the edges and his lips part slightly showing his perfect teeth. Kane Jessop is the handsomest man in the world.

I thread my fingers through his hair, detangling the tresses that feel like satin against my skin. He closes his eyes, hiding those incredible blues from my view.

STUPID O'CLOCK

Hammering sounds on the door and it isn't even two-thirty in the morning. I sit bolt upright but Kane is already diving out of bed, grumbling under his breath, and yanking on a clean pair of boxers. I do the same, grabbing a pair of his boxers and a T-shirt but he's already downstairs.

"The fuck?" I hear him snarl. "It's the middle of the fucking night."

"Yeah well I can't sleep for worryin'." That's my mom's voice.

I make my way downstairs and peer at the botox infested woman standing on Kane's doorstep.

"Are you fucking kidding me?" I question, frowning at her. "Is this a joke?"

"I just need to know what's going on with my life now." She peers at me with eyes slightly unfocused from alcohol I presume. "Are you throwin' me out?"

"Throwin' you out? You've got your own apartment haven't you?"

"Not anymore, I moved in with your mee-maw to take care of her while she was sick."

At that I laugh. "You're a fuckin' liar. You stayed and ate her food but the nurses were the ones who took care of her."

"I did my bit."

"You didn't do your bit for nobody." I lean around Kane who is glowering at the woman who failed me my entire life. "Fuck off Kane's porch, Ma, before I throw you off it."

"I'm still your momma!"

I laugh again. "You're deluded. Only momma I had was Mee-maw and she was shit too."

"Look, I just need to know what I'm doin'."

I roll my eyes. "And you couldn't have asked tomorrow?" Kane grabs my arm when he sees me going to take a step. "You know what the bad thing is? You come here quicker than a bullet when you're worried about money, but when I called you crying that Mee-maw was beating me, I didn't see you for weeks and even then you pretended I never called you."

"I know I wasn't the best mother growing up."

"Stop actin' like you were a mother at all," I yell, feeling my anger rise. I turn to Kane. "Close the door in this bitch's face."

She gasps, a hoarse and disgusted sound. "Don't you--!"

The door slams shut. "What a shit ending to an incredible night. Can you believe her?" I stomp my way upstairs with Kane hot on my heels. "Comin' here at this time to ask about money. Thinks she was any kind of mother." It's almost laughable.

"She'll be back," Kane points out and I know he's right. "She'll probably contest the will too."

"I doubt it. She knows she won't win. Too many witnesses in this town that would love to speak up against the bitch."

He sighs heavily and then yawns. When I climb into bed, he clears his throat, pulling my eyes his way. "Get naked."

"I can't be bothered to m—" With a strong yank, he pulls his boxers down my thighs and tosses them on the floor behind him. "Well okay then."

"Sit up, arms up."

I like it when he's bossy.

With a grin, I do as I'm told, and he yanks his T-shirt off me too. Then he climbs in beside me naked as the day he was born. Just like the past week and just like when we were teens, he rolls onto my back, traps my thigh under his and soon after his breathing evens out. I thought I'd have trouble sleeping what with all the "excitement", but I fall to sleep faster than a baby on a tit.

APPROXIMATELY 3 DAYS LATER

I have to leave today. It's been an amazing few days catching up with old friends and walking around town. The patch is still used as a teenage convivial lot. But for all the joy I've had, I don't see myself moving back here. It's just too painful and I know Kane wants to come back eventually so I'm wondering now where we go from here.

I have clients in tomorrow and a life to get back to. A shit life but a life none-the-less.

My mother, and I use that word in the biological sense, has been working together with Felicia to get Mee-maw's belongings sorted. I don't want to step foot in that house again and I'm grateful that I have somebody I can rely on to oversee that shit.

I told my mom I'm putting it on the market and that I already have a realtor coming to take pictures. Of course, she sobbed and begged me to let her have it. Fat chance. That house is going to a family with no ties to it. I'm hoping the love of a good and happy family can erase the hatred that festers in that place.

I'm both surprised and unsurprised when Mom shows up at Kane's again while I'm dragging my luggage towards the open trunk of my car. Kane is coming too, a box in his arms, to keep me company on the drive back and also because Webber would like to talk to us both about some new possible leads. I told Kane not to get his hopes up, if Webber had anything solid, he'd have told us over the phone.

"What do you want?" I ask her as Kane nudges me to the side and shoves a box right to the back of the empty space.

"I have a proposition for you," Mom declares, raising her chin.

We both stop loading the car and turn to face her.

"You're kidding?" I say around a laugh. "What could you possibly have that I could even want from you?"

"For the house, I'll tell you what I know about your kid."

My spine straightens faster than a flash of lightning can cut through the sky. "Excuse me?"

"You heard me. I know how you can find out where she is."

My heart starts pounding in my ears as I stare at the woman who looks just like me but has no fucking soul. "You know where my child is?"

"Not exactly, but I know how you can find her."

"Her?" Kane demands, stepping forward. "She's a girl?"

"Yes," Mom answers bravely. "But if you want to know where she is, you've got to give me the house."

My palms start sweating as a familiar red haze comes down over my eyes. "You evil, manipulative bitch."

"I'm just looking after my own skin."

I glower at her, hands balling into fists, anger leveling at boiling point. "Mom, my daughter's whereabouts is still an open case. If I call Agent Webber right now, he will arrest your skanky ass for lying to him all those years ago."

"I didn't know how to find her years ago!" she argues, stepping back when I step forward. "I only just found out."

"She's lying," Kane snaps but I'm not so sure and neither is he by the cautious tone to his voice.

"Look, if we get it in writing and you give me the house I will tell you what I know." Mom raises her hands when I take another step

APPROXIMATELY 3 DAYS LATER

towards her. Kane grabs the back of my shirt, stopping me in my tracks.

"You don't need beating up your momma on your conscience," he says and Mom looks relieved. That is until he adds, "I'll call Felicia."

Her face drops even faster than my spine stiffened when she first made her announcement.

He pulls out his phone, and her shock becomes worry.

"You know the worst part about this, Mom, I was going to give you twenty thousand dollars to get back on your feet and hopefully die of an infection from more botched surgery."

Her face falls even more.

"But now you ain't getting shit." Kane loosens his hold enough for me to stride towards the woman who gave me life. "Not a single penny of mine will ever be yours. That is your granddaughter. You failed me my entire life, and now you're failing her. Expect a call from Webber." I raise my phone and show her the call that has been connected for the past two minutes of this mess. "He's been listenin' and you just got your own ass busted."

"I won't tell him shit."

"Oh you will," Kane states simply. "You'll tell us everything before he even gets here. Felicia and my daddy are on their way. How well do you think they'll take it when they found out you knew about your daughter and their grandbaby being kidnapped and separated? Think you'll ever be safe in the state of Texas again? Think you'll ever be safe in the country again?"

"We don't need to get violent," Mom utters, looking panicked as her blackmail blows up in her face. She starts to back away, looking quite frankly, terrified.

"You ain't leavin' my property until we get the answers we want." Kane strides towards the Frankenstein looking bitch and grabs her by the arm.

She starts to scream and claws at his hand but he picks her up and tosses her into the trunk of the car like she weighs nothing. I raise

APPROXIMATELY 3 DAYS LATER

a brow when he slams it shut and she starts sobbing and shrieking even louder than before.

"Was that really necessary?" I question, lips twitching.

"Nope." He pops a piece of gum into his mouth and offers one to me, then he pulls his ass up onto the trunk and makes me stand between his parted thighs. "You ready to talk yet?" He knocks on the trunk. "You gonna tell us what we want to know?"

"FUCK YOU!" she screams, and the car starts shaking as she goes wild.

We both cringe and Kane dips his head at an elderly couple passing with their little dog. They mind their business but I wonder if that will last.

"Last chance, Mom." She cusses me out some more so I block her out and lean into Kane to whisper, "Is Felicia really on her way?"

"Yeah." He kisses my lips, catching me by surprise. "I'm not risking her runnin' and taking what could be the last thread of information on our kid with her."

He's right. I'm not risking it either.

"Twenty K is fine," Mom calls. "I'll be good with twenty K. Not gonna reach and be greedy. If you was already gonna part with it, what difference does it make?"

Kane closes his eyes, his frustration and anger evident.

We listen to her for a short while longer until the sound of bike engines can be heard in the distance. Kane kisses me again, hops down from the top of the trunk and sighs even heavier than before.

"They're going to go fuckin nuclear on our asses."

"Probably," I agree with a cringe.

"Not gonna let them chew you out but probably won't be able to stop them from chewing me out," he goes on and I laugh despite the severity of the situation.

His parents pull in on separate bikes and the second Felicia's helmet is off, her eyes fly to the trunk of the car where my mom's screaming just got louder.

I love that when Kane told his family it's an emergency, get your

APPROXIMATELY 3 DAYS LATER

asses here, they got their asses here. Once upon a time I had that with my brother, and Poppy, and then Kane. I miss having that.

"Somebody wanna tell us why there's a screaming woman in your car?" West asks, putting a cigarette between his lips and lighting it with a silver lighter that has Felicia's name on it.

Felicia adds, her eyes twinkling with humor, "Who is it?"

"My incubator," I reply and she howls with laughter.

"Now how did your human incubator end up in the trunk of your car?"

Kane takes a cigarette from his daddy but I snap it and throw it down the drive before he can light it. His daddy snorts, almost forgetting the situation we're all in.

Kane doesn't say shit, he just accepts that his smoke is gone and doesn't try to replace it.

"We need to get her inside before the cops come knocking," Kane states and he and his daddy move to the car. "We'll explain everything then."

"Whatever," West lilts, sounding as amused as Felicia. "Better be one heck of a reason, putting us all at risk of goin' to jail like this."

"Hey, we only made a citizen's arrest," I defend. "She was trespassin' on our property."

"Not sure they'll see it that way seein' as she's your momma," West jests and on the count of three, he opens the boot and they grab my flailing mother and carry her to the house. Felicia and I survey the area to be sure there are no witnesses.

"What's going on, Immy?" Felicia asks and I nod for her to follow.

There's no screaming when we get inside and I quickly learn that's because Kane and his daddy have tied my mother bitch to a chair and have slapped a piece of tape over her mouth. The industrial kind. That's going to tear her lips off. Damn.

"Okay so somebody needs to start talkin'," Felicia demands and Kane folds his arms across his chest. "This is seriously crazy."

"Oh we know," Kane murmurs and all eyes fly to him. "I'm gonna cut to the quick, save the full length of the story because we're runnin' short on time what with all the noise she made."

"We promise to fill you in on all the details after we have what we need from her."

"Right, well, shall I make coffee or somethin'?" Felicia asks, looking confused.

"Naw, but y'all should probably take a seat."

They both remain standing and I find this whole scene so bizarre. My mom is making muffled noises beyond her mask, tears in her angry hazel eyes, and I don't actually care at all. I will do anything to find my kid, she needs to learn that and fast.

"Me and Immy have a kid," Kane states, his tone firm and confident. To say West and Felicia's jaws drop would be an understatement. "She would'a just turned eight."

"WHAT?" West booms, looking at me accusingly.

"No, dad," Kane warns. "It ain't like that."

"Then what's it like?" Felicia, forever the soothing voice of reason asks while calming her husband with a hand on his chest.

"I didn't leave on my own accord," I explain, biting my lip and sneering at my mother again. "Mee-maw found out I was pregnant after that accident I had with my junky brother, and she immediately sent me away to Righteous Hill to save her from scandal, and also so people wouldn't expect her to take on my kid if I became a deadbeat momma like this whore."

Mom makes a noise of protest but then falls silent when I kick the leg of her chair. Pain radiates through my foot but it was worth it to see her panic and think I might tip her backwards.

"They kept me there against my will, forcibly removed my baby via a messy caesarian section and didn't wake me up until long after she was gone. I never got to see her, never got to hold her, and until now the only person who knew of her whereabouts is dead. They sold her, but we don't know who to. The trail is dry."

Kane nods and continues, "I only found out when I went to

APPROXIMATELY 3 DAYS LATER

Chicago. I've been speaking to the agent in charge of the case but the trail is as dead as this bitch will be if she doesn't talk."

"She said if I gave her my mee-maw's house she'd give me the information I need to find my kid."

"Our kid," Kane corrects and I smile at him sadly.

"And why the fuck didn't anybody tell us we have a kidnapped grandbaby out there?" West booms, face turning red.

"Don't raise your voice," Kane warns, yanking me into his side. "It's complex and difficult and it needs more time talking about than a few seconds. Okay?"

West looks devastated but he nods, and then he rips the tape from my mother's mouth and holds up his hand. "So you know where my grandbaby is?"

My mom shakes her head. "Don't do this. It ain't fair. I just need a little somethin' to get me by."

"Ain't one for hittin' women," West snarls, "Don't wanna start now."

"Sweety," Felicia whispers and pulls West's face her way. "Let me."

"Don't want you hurtin' your wrist again."

That's sweet... fucked up, but sweet.

"I ain't gonna hit her. Hitting her won't do shit she's got too many balloons in her face." She reaches into West's pocket while speaking, her tone as sweet as sugar. "I've got something more persuasive in mind." She flicks open the lighter and holds the flame to my momma's face. "Stop your wailin', I ain't gonna burn your skin, just your hair. It won't hurt none but I imagine you'll look uglier than you do now and somethin' tells me, looking at your fucked up face, that you wouldn't do well lookin' ugly."

"Uglier," I correct, and Mom's face becomes a glare.

To prove she's not making empty threats, Felicia grabs a lock of my mother's chestnut brown and the room fills with the horrific scent of burning hair.

"Whoosh," Felicia says around a cackle as she pats the flames out.

APPROXIMATELY 3 DAYS LATER

My mother stops wailing the second the fire goes out. "You use too much product. I almost took your entire mop out."

"Please stop," Mom begs.

"You know how to make this stop," Kane puts in, wafting the smoke away from his face. "Dad crack a window."

"I'll do it," I say and cringe when Felicia lights Mom's hair on fire again.

"OKAY!" Mom sobs. "I'll tell you what I know."

"I'll know if you're lyin'." West leans into her face. "Not fuckin' around, Mary. You tell us everything you know."

Mom nods and more tears stream from her eyes, leaving trails of black mascara. She always uses the clumpiest eye shit I've ever seen. "Your mee-maw knew where she was taken."

"That better not be all you have."

"It's not!" She insists, sobbing again. "She used to get a call every month with updates."

"She was being updated on my kid?" I hiss, wishing Mee-maw was alive so I could punch her in the mouth. "How long have you known?"

"Not long," she replies and screams when Felicia moves the flame to the end of her hair again. "I SWEAR! I found a letter for you in the bible she left for you. It explains everything."

My heart starts hammering in my chest. Could the information on my kid have been in that letter I destroyed? I didn't even consider it because Mee-maw insisted she didn't know where my kid was and Webber said she wasn't lying.

"Does it say where she is or who she spoke to?"

Mom shakes her head, showing just how messed up her hair now is on one side. "It doesn't say anything other than how you should leave her alone, she's with a good family, and going into her life now would only mess it up."

I rip a hand through my hair and feel ready to hyperventilate. "Phone records. We can call every fucking number."

Mom nods. "I can help."

APPROXIMATELY 3 DAYS LATER

"No, you're gonna stay away from my family you rank ass bitch," Felicia hisses. "Or I'm comin' for you and I'll set the rest of your shit hair on fire."

We call Webber and give him the new information, but his reply doesn't exactly bring us hope.

"We had your grandmother's phone listened in on for months afterwards. Years, even. We never heard any calls that might contain updates. She was a suspect on the list for trafficking those babies, but we didn't find a scrap of evidence against her. You know this. Woman like her, love of the community, friends with Father Righteous... the perfect suspect. We didn't find shit."

I didn't stay on the phone for much longer, I instead went to the old bitch's house, found the letter and read it through three times.

I don't know if it's a duplicate of the one she asked Mr. Jessop to give to me when she died, but I do know it's full of bullshit I don't want to read. Apologies and excuses as to why she did what she did. An admission that she was going to bring me home but they said I was mentally unstable and wouldn't permit my release until they knew I was stable. More like until they knew I was brainwashed.

And finally, an admission that the baby grew up to be a stunning little girl with the love of a good family and she knows this due to monthly updates. She doesn't say what kind of updates or who keeps her updated her. She does however tell me to leave the girl alone, interfering now could mess with her life and that hits me way too hard.

I growl with frustration and throw the letter across the room. Then I pace in her flowery as fuck bedroom until my legs ache.

Kane continues tearing the place apart looking for some kind of clue. There's nothing. If Mee-maw was getting these updates in person, there's absolutely no fucking way we will be able to track them down. It could be *anyone* she knew. It could be the barista at the local café. *Anyone!*

APPROXIMATELY 3 DAYS LATER

She didn't have a computer because she couldn't work them. She didn't have any other form of communication to my knowledge.

I scream and throw her stupid bible at the wall.

"Hey," Kane soothes, rubbing my arms.

"Don't," I plead and move away. "Not now. I don't want you to touch me right now."

"I know it's frustrating."

"This is the closest I have ever come to a real clue and it's another dead end. Mee-maw knew where she was and she lied, Kane. She fucking lied."

The silhouette of a person standing in the doorway has me reaching for the bible ready to throw it again, this time at my brother's head.

"Just spoke to Mom," Matthew declares, looking anxiously between Kane and me. His eyes then go to my twitching hand. "She told me what happened."

"Fuck off," I utter, too tired, too drained to deal with him.

Matthew raises his hands, a display of defense. "I don't know if it's helpful at all..."

"Oh my God," I whisper, rubbing my temples.

He carries on. "Mee-maw used to visit the library a couple of times a month, something she never did before."

"One," I snap and check off a finger with another finger, "Why should I care? And two... how do you know that?"

"Poppy mentioned it once." He wets his lips. "She worked there for a while when attending college. She said her manager helped Mee-maw set up an email account. She was asking me if Mee-maw had been in touch with me. I didn't think anything of it but now it makes sense."

"Oh my God," I whisper and my hope returns. I look at Kane with wide eyes. "Is it still open?"

"I'd say so," he replies and grabs my arm. "Just gotta convince Mr. Delaware to give us her details if he has them."

I've never moved so fast in my entire life, but one detail has me

APPROXIMATELY 3 DAYS LATER

doubling back. "You kept in touch with Poppy and you never once told her about what was happening to me?"

"I wasn't in my right mind," Matthew murmurs. "I thought I was doin' the right thing."

I don't have time to fight with him about this.

"Fuck you for that." I turn towards the front door and follow Kane straight to the car, calling Webber on the way. "She has an email account."

"You're joking?"

"Nope. Webber... I think this is it. I think we might have finally found her." My tears return and I can't stop them.

"Kane with you?"

"Yes."

"Good. I'll be there as soon as I can."

I inhale and exhale and take the tissue that Kane offers.

"Babe, you gotta chill, don't get your hopes up."

Nodding, because he's right, I try to relax but that's always easier said than done.

"You might not need to come, Webber. It's a small town, they will probably log in without much prompting."

"I need to be there," he replies, sounding emotional. "This could crack the case wide open and even if it doesn't, I gotta be there to stop you from going after whoever is on the other side of those emails. You've got to remember that if your kid is in a happy and loving home, you showing up on her doorstep will only make her family hostile."

"They kidnapped her! They shouldn't get to keep her."

"I know," he soothes, "but we have got to do this the right way. We have to investigate this the proper way. You've trusted me for this long, keep the faith."

Kane squeezes my thigh.

"I trust you, Webber, but if this takes too long and she's at risk in any way, I'm not gonna stop."

"Understood. I'm booking my flight right now. Wait for me."

APPROXIMATELY 3 DAYS LATER

The line goes dead and for the first time in forever, I feel fully alive.

We head into the library, not just Kane and I but Felicia and West too. Matthew didn't follow, lucky for him because I still want to kill him.

"Mr. Delaware," I demand loudly across the deserted library.

"Yes?" He pokes his head around the open doorway behind the counter. "Oh, it's you! I heard you was back in town. How are you?"

"Fine," I respond automatically but I don't bother asking for his welfare in return. "My grandmother used to come in here every so often right?"

"Of course, she was a proud and loving member of our community. Visited a lot of places that woman did."

Kane places his hand on the mahogany wood countertop. "You helped her set up an email account."

"Sure did." He looks so proud of himself until he sees our serious expressions. "Why?" Mr. Delaware now looks wary, true to his name.

"Because we need access to it."

"That's some kinda data protection I think. Not sure I can legally give you that."

I smile but it's not friendly. "I don't give a crap about data protection. That's my mee-maw and what's hers is mine. Now please... tell me her details."

"Even if I do," he goes on, picking up a large journal and flicking through it. He pushes his glasses up his nose and peers at one page before another. "She never used it to my knowledge. I doubt you'll find anything."

"So what's the problem?" West snaps and Mr. Delaware, though a big guy himself, gulps and flicks through the journal faster.

"No problem, I'll help y'all."

I tap my fingers on the surface and look around the empty space. Nobody is in here but then it does close early on a Wednesday and it's almost at that time.

APPROXIMATELY 3 DAYS LATER

"Let's see here," he says and walks around the desk. I watch as he boots up an ancient computer, uses his own log in and opens email. He types in her details at a snail's pace and we all wait with bated breath to see if there's anything there.

My breath catches in my throat.

They're all there. Every single one, month after month for the past eight years.

Delaware moves so I can scroll through them faster. Every update has my heart clenching but it's the first one that has me dying inside.

"Oh my God," I breathe and look at the email, in response to Mee-maw who sent one first asking for information on *my* child. It's very impersonal and informal. Is she speaking with an official or an adopted relative? It doesn't say which makes this more confusing. "She never left Texas."

She was in Paducah, a small town in Cottle County after being abandoned at four months old. Who the fuck did she live with for those four months before she was abandoned?

Did nobody notice that their family members had a kid one day and not the next?

I forward every email to Webber as I read and we all crowd around the screen.

Felicia searches on her phone and sure enough there's an article, just a small one, in Paducah News about a baby abandoned at the church. She was unharmed and well-dressed, but nobody ever came forward for her.

"That would have been when Righteous Hill was burned to the fucking ground," I say, jaw trembling. I don't clarify that it was me who burned it. Kane knows for the most part. I didn't know how else to get the authorities there to crack that place wide open. "Webber said it might happen and said that would be best-case scenario because any kids reported abandoned at that time were DNA matched to potential parents. But she was abandoned in a town too small to make the mainstream media." I wipe away my tears on my wrist. "She could have been with me this entire time!"

APPROXIMATELY 3 DAYS LATER

"This isn't your fault," Kane promises.

"How did Mee-maw know? How did she know this was my kid? How?"

"There's a picture," Felicia says so softly I almost don't hear her. "She's so beautiful."

I rip the phone from her hand and stare at the grainy news article photo. A sob gets stuck in my throat as I finally get to lay my eyes on the being that has always carried the biggest part of me. The photo quality is shockingly bad but I can tell she's smiling. She has the biggest cheeks, just like I did when I was a baby. This gives me hope that she was loved, and they abandoned her because they were scared of going to prison and not because they didn't want her.

How could anybody not want her?

"Mee-maw has been in touch with whoever this is for years." I can't handle this truth. "Why did she get to know all of this and I didn't? How did she know?"

Kane stares ferociously at the screen as he continues forwarding the emails. It's not until he gets to one dated two years ago that he stops. It's the last email. "What do we do now? We know what city she is likely in; it won't be hard to find her adoptive parents."

"Where is she?" West asks, leaning closer so he can see. "Austin? She's been on our fucking doorstep this entire time?"

"I need a minute," I say, pushing my seat back and walking away. I feel like my insides are twisting and turning. I want to vomit but I also want to collapse. This is too much.

"We found her," Kane whispers, coming up behind me. "We found her. It's over. She'll be with us soon."

"No she won't," I breathe, soaking my wrist with more tears.

"She will."

"No she won't!" I yell, turning on him so fast my head keeps spinning for long after I've stopped. "She won't, because she was probably legally adopted by a family who likely loves her and it won't be in her best interests to be taken from them. Mee-maw was right, Webber was right. That child will never be anything more than our biological fucking daughter and we won't be allowed even a fraction of her."

"That's not true," Kane argues, and Felicia opens her mouth, probably to agree.

"I'm not tearing her from the only family she has ever known to come and live with the likes of me." I hug myself, feeling defeated and devastated. "Those emails tell me one thing, she's happy. Why would I want to destroy that? Why would you?"

"Because she's my daughter that I never got to know."

"That's probably for the best."

"Hey," West barks. "You're upset, no need to start gettin' nasty. Not with each other."

"I can't deal with this," I admit, turning away again. "I just... I need to go for a walk."

"She's kinda right though," I hear Felicia mutter as I walk towards the exit. "Can you imagine being that kid in this situation?"

I don't wait to hear their answers, I shove open the heavy wooden door and step into the ridiculously hot summer air.

Immy: We found her Marshall. We fucking found her.

Marshall: Fuck me... you're kidding right?

Immy: Nope. She lives in Austin as far as we can tell and she's good at building shit just like her daddy. The updates we read on her are vague... it's too complicated to put into text. Now we've just got to wait for Webber to make his move. My heart is fucking breaking here.

Marshall: Why? This is great news!

APPROXIMATELY 3 DAYS LATER

Immy: Because I'm about to lose her all over again and we all know it.

Marshall: No you ain't. Have hope. You got this far. Fate wouldn't be this cruel to you now.

Immy: Wouldn't it?

Marshall: Do you need me to call or do you need your space right now?

Immy: Space.

Marshall: I'll call in an hour.

"Immy," Kane calls after me. "Immy, stop. I ain't chasin' you. Fuckin' tired of chasin' you. Spent too much of my life chasin' you."

"Then stop!"

"Naw, cause the past eight years have proven you ain't gonna chase me back!" He grabs my arm and spins me to face him. "Eight years and you still haven't grown for shit. You need to be strong now. You need to get your shit together."

"I'm trying!"

People look our way and it reminds me all too much of my teen years. Maybe he's right.

"Try fuckin' harder because I need you right now too." His angry, sad, pleading eyes come to mine. "I ain't got it in me to be strong enough for the both of us. Not right now. Need you to meet me half way."

My heart shatters as I look into the eyes of a desperate father looking for all the same answers as me. He's right. I'm being a brat.

I wrap my arms around his waist. "I don't want to have to make the choice, Kane. I don't want to have to give her up on purpose."

"Maybe we won't have to." His blue eyes shine with emotion that

APPROXIMATELY 3 DAYS LATER

he only ever shows me. "Keep it together, okay? We just gotta wait. That's all. We just gotta be patient."

"Yeah," I agree and he holds me so tight around the waist my feet dangle above ground. "Ain't nobody loved a boy as much as I love you, Kane Jessop."

"Damn straight." He crushes his lips to mine and follows it with his tongue.

I hum against him, letting my tears soak his cheeks, letting his strength hold me together as mine does the same for him.

"I got savings, I got a house, you got a business and money from your mee-maw. We can get hitched, we can make this work and make them see we are fit to be her parents. It doesn't have to go the way you said. She's young, she'll adapt. I moved in with my daddy age eight after a lifetime of shit from my mom, I adapted, ended up happier." He kisses me again, this time it's brief. "We don't know her circumstances so don't you dare be a pussy and throw in the towel."

I growl with frustration. "I fucking hate it when you're right."

He laughs and I smile at the sound.

"I don't know why you still want me, Kane Jessop. I'm a mess."

"Naw, you're just a little crispy around the edges is all. We'll shed that layer and get to the tender parts. You'll see. Shit, the way you've been this past week I'd say we're halfway there."

This time it's me who laughs. I've never been compared to fried chicken before. "You reckon?"

"I reckon." He tips my head back and smiles at my lips. "Come on, I want to show you somethin'."

"Will it make me feel less sick?"

"I hope so."

West and Felicia appear in my peripheral.

"Y'all ready to talk now?" Felicia asks gently. "We need the full story."

West hums his agreement while standing there with his arms folded and his eyes guarded.

APPROXIMATELY 3 DAYS LATER

"Later guys, give us an hour or two. The truth ain't goin' nowhere," Kane replies, tucking me under his arm.

"How about I cook us all a dinner, you join us at five and we eat together and talk then?" Felicia suggests and I have to admit it's a good idea.

"I'll pick up a crate of beer."

"I'll bring gin," I add as Kane steers me away.

"See you at five," the father of my almost found child calls and leads me to the car. He kisses my temple, a sweet gesture, and takes my keys so he can drive.

He kept my bike. After all these years, Kane Jessop kept my bike in his garage. Not only did he keep it, but he also fixed it and kept it tuned and ran it around every month or so.

Mounting it now brings back so many amazing memories. This bike gave me the kind of freedom I never got to taste as a child. It was the ultimate rebellion. Well, that is until I got pregnant.

I can't contain my smile as I relive the feel of the beast purring between my thighs. Kane sits behind me, he was never a damsel in distress type where he needed to be the one to drive. He held onto me as I rode through town. He gave me that power and he kicked the shit out of anyone who mocked him for it.

Remembering how empowered Kane Jessop always made me feel, just further drills in the fact that this once very vicious and nasty boy would be such an incredible dad to a little girl we never got to raise.

He never once told me he's a man so he should do XYZ. Not once. He only ever told me I could do anything I fucking wanted. Including riding on a Harley too big for me that I didn't even have a proper license for. He had that much faith in my abilities.

I climb off the bike, feeling emotionally overloaded, and then I climb back on but this time I'm facing him. I kiss him, deep and desperate, powerful and damaged. I cling to his shoulders and lose myself in his flavor, wishing I went back all those years ago and lived

APPROXIMATELY 3 DAYS LATER

through this hell with him by my side. Wishing I hadn't carried this pain alone.

"Promise me you're not going to do something stupid if this doesn't go the way we want," Kane whispers, leaning back and I know exactly what he's saying. "Only just got you back. If you fuckin' die now... I'm followin' you. You feel me?"

Nodding, I kiss him again and push his jacket off his arms. "I promise."

His enthusiasm for touching me increases at my words and he lifts us both off the mounted bike and starts to strip.

Laughing tearfully, I remove my clothes right there with him, marveling at his incredible body that is covered in such amazing tattoos that highlight the grooves of his muscles and strength.

"I ain't never leaving you again, Kane Jessop," I promise when he straddles the bike and pulls me onto his lap. I rock against his length which is hot and trapped between us, soaking the length of him in my juices until he's slick enough to slide inside and bring such incredible pleasure to us both. I moan, a genuine sound as a result of so many fucking tingles that him being inside of me brings.

"I'm not," he corrects in jest, poking fun of me picking up his accent and the way he talks.

"Did somebody call the grammar police? Do I hear sirens?"

Laughing, he bites my lip and with his hands on my hips, he guides my rhythm while his thick, rough thumb rolls over my clit. It's incredible.

I bounce a little, moving up and down, clenching the walls of my sex around him. We both get lost in it, grunting and groaning as our pleasure rises and our movements get more frantic. We seek to get more of the good stuff, terrified if we stop for even a second we'll lose this torturous wave of euphoria.

I grip him tight and choke as my orgasm which started in my womb, invades my entire body and rewrites my brain. He follows, holding my hips still as he pulses and throbs inside of me, desperate

APPROXIMATELY 3 DAYS LATER

to seat himself in as deep as he can conquer. Problem is he's huge, and as deep as he wants is just a bit too deep for me to handle.

With a smack to his shoulder, I adjust my position and bite his ear. "Let me go you giant."

"Nope," he rebuts with a mischievous smile.

"I need to shower. So do you."

He chuckles and allows me my freedom, then follows me into the house, smacking my bare ass full force which makes me shriek in pain and run for dear life so he can't do it again.

2 WEEKS LATER

I can't take it anymore. I've waited a lifetime... my kid's lifetime... to finally meet her. I haven't been allowed to see photographs; I haven't been allowed to hear her voice. Because a judge has ruled that she needs a DNA test to prove we are the parents. Webber is supervising it, so he gets to meet her before we do and it just feels so unfair.

I'm not waiting anymore. Kane is trying to keep me grounded but I can't do this.

Which is why at noon I mount my bike. I am not going to approach her. I just want to see her. I just want to look at her.

I *need* to look at her. I mean how many schools are there in Austin anyway?

Google tells me there are a lot of schools in Austin. Google tells me there are a lot of schools everywhere. Will I know her if I see her? What if I don't drive to the right one?

"Where do you think you're going?" Kane asks, doing the belt of his jeans that are hanging low on his hips. "Sneaking off during my nap."

"I wasn't sneaking, I just wanted to go for a ride."

He raises a thick brow and smirks at me while leaning against the

2 WEEKS LATER

door jam. His arm muscles bulge with strength when he folds them across his chest. "You can't lie to me."

I huff and yank off my helmet. "I was just gonna ride, Kane. Leave it."

"You're defensive."

"Yeah because suddenly I need your permission to go for a ride."

He chuckles like I'm hilarious which I absolutely am not. Then he sobers and his look is one of understanding. "We've gotta wait, Babe. We've gotta do this the right way."

I open my mouth to argue but then my phone rings at the exact same time the doorbell goes.

I scramble for my phone and Kane takes my bike keys before heading to the door.

"Webber," I say, keeping my tone firm.

"Your man there with you?" His tone sounds entirely too upbeat.

I inwardly chant, *please be good news, please be good news*.

"Just a sec," I rush out of the garage and into the house, shrugging off my jacket and dropping the heavy clothing on the wood floor behind me. "KANE!"

"Poppy's here," Kane calls back and I hear the door close.

"It's Webber. He has news."

Kane appears in the kitchen where I stop, faster than I've ever seen him move.

I put it on loudspeaker as Poppy enters behind him, looking curiously at my phone on the countertop. I look at my phone and add so Webber understands, "Our closest friend Poppy is here but you're free to talk."

"Hi there folks. Sorry it has taken me so long to get back to you. I can only go as fast as I can get the information."

"It's cool, lay it on us," Kane insists, his mind is on the edge, I can see it in his eyes.

"We got the confirmation," Webber states clearly and my heart starts thudding against my ribcage.

Poppy pulls herself up onto the other counter, hands ringing in

2 WEEKS LATER

front of her. She's been as invested in this since we told her around ten days ago. Kane said I needed a friend in my corner and he was right. She has been every bit the rock we knew she would be. I wish I'd confided in her all those years ago but I guess in my warped, fucked up brain I made a lot of mistakes I'd do again now.

"She's yours, guys. Her DNA matches ninety-nine-point-eight percent."

I'm trembling. This is the news I've been needing to hear.

"So, can we meet her? Have her adoptive parents been notified?"

Kane wraps his arm around my waist and Poppy grins at us both, her own excitement evident.

Webber clears his throat. "Well about that."

"More waiting," I grumble.

"There was always gonna be a waiting period but... I have good news and bad news."

Kane tenses. "Just let us have it, no need for a buildup."

"She was adopted, as we first suspected, and moved to Austin as we already knew. But..."

"But?" I prompt, wondering why he's pausing and making me suffer.

"She was given up to the state when she was five," he continues sadly. "Apparently she was an unruly child—"

"Are you fucking kidding me?" Kane snarls and I calm him with a hand on his chest as my own smile fades.

"Truthfully, looking at the records, her adoptive parents got pregnant. I think that had a lot to do with their decision."

It's like they thought she was a fucking dog or something. Not that a dog deserves that fate, but it's exactly what people do, they get pregnant and get rid of their adopted dog.

"And they were allowed to keep their baby after abandoning a child they swore to love and protect?" Poppy snaps also agitated now.

"The system is fucked, but then we already knew that," Webber says with a heavy sigh. "Anyway, that's the bad news. The good news is... for you guys... she's in an all-girls' home in Austin,

2 WEEKS LATER

Crestview. She's been there since she was six and she seems to be happy there."

"You've met her?" I question and he hesitates again.

"I met her with a court-appointed social worker. She's an incredibly bright kid but she has some serious abandonment issues according to her main carer who is a brilliant and loving woman called Stacey Deegan."

"Oh my God," I choke, and this time Kane tries to comfort me. "Does that mean I'm not allowed to see her?"

"On the contrary, it means you've got every chance to get her back."

You could hear a pin drop, the air turns still and suddenly I feel faint.

"It wouldn't be as easy as showing up and taking her home, we'd need to assess your accommodation, figure out a support group, you'd need parenting classes to help you deal with and understand her issues." He sounds so happy but also cautious. "But, this all means in a couple of months, maybe more maybe less, you could have your daughter back."

"Oh my God," I sob, turning into Kane's body and hugging him as I try to hold myself together by holding onto him.

"You're sure?" Kane questions.

"Absolutely," Webber replies.

"Then tell us everything we need to do and we'll do it."

"I'll send you an email with all the details of her social worker, he's waiting for your call, all the things I know the state will want to see in order to deem you fit to parent."

"Fit to parent," Poppy growls, "Do they not understand that this is their kid?"

Webber shuffles, making the phone crackle. "Of course they do, but this isn't as simple as their kid going missing and being returned. She doesn't know you from Adam. She's been abandoned and she remembers it, that shit stays with you, she's got friends and a life there and from what I'm hearing a very close bond with some of her carers.

2 WEEKS LATER

The state can't just rip her away and put her with strangers, that's not how it works. This has to be handled delicately."

"We understand," I utter because as hard as it is to accept, I really do understand. "When can we meet her?"

"Soon as you call her social worker, his name's David Michaelson, he'll set you up with a meeting and talk you through everything else." Webber chuckles, a happy sound. "Don't stress guys, any judge worth their shit will see how much love you guys have for your kid, and I will personally speak for you. Ain't got nothing bad to say."

"Webber." I inhale and exhale. "Thank you."

"Shit, don't thank me. Not for this. Did my duty and failed you for eight years, still kicking myself over that missed email account."

"Naw," Kane snaps, "If you blame yourself for that I gotta blame myself for never finding Immy. Shit happens. We miss things. It's all workin' out."

"Hell yeah it is," Poppy cheers and her beaming smile shines on us all. "This is so exciting!"

"I'm gonna leave y'all to it," Webber states, "got a ton of other cases to work on. If you need anything, you call. Email should have hit your inbox by now."

I thought Kane moved fast before, but he snatches up my phone and looks for my email app before I can even think about getting to it.

Seeing him read that email and dial that number without hesitation tells me just how much Kane Jessop loves his kid. Part of me knows I couldn't blame him if he hated me for the rest of his life for what I kept from him, but a bigger part of me knows that Kane Jessop understands stupid decision making and has forgiven me despite the fact I haven't asked him for it yet.

"It's all gonna work out," Poppy insists, rubbing my back as I listen to the feint dial tone.

"It really is," I breathe.

"Hello?" a male voice questions and Kane breathes a sigh of relief.

"Is this David Michaelson?" Kane questions, his voice

2 WEEKS LATER

commanding and gruff and I pull the phone away from his ear so I can press the loudspeaker icon.

"It sure is, can I ask who is calling?" His voice fills the room just like Webber's did and my heart swells in my chest from the excitement and adrenaline.

"It's Kane Jessop, Webber sent us your details."

"Ah, yes! Connie's biological parents." He sounds so happy to hear from us. "I've been so excited for your call. It's not often these days that we get such a happy outcome."

"You sound so sure of that."

"Because you're her parents," he says around a laugh. "I'm not in the business of separating families or keeping them separated. I'm going to be the one to bring you all back together and that is exactly why I signed up for this job."

He sounds so confident. I'm glad he does, I don't feel it. This all feels way too good to be true.

"What do we need to do to meet her?"

"Nothin', I'm gonna come and assess your situations. With her bein' older and having the difficulties she has, I need to ensure that the people coming into her life, parents or not, have her best interests at heart."

"Of course," I agree because he's one hundred percent right.

"So I'll come and see y'all when you're available. We'll talk through what's gonna happen with Connie and where you want her to live, and what I think is best for her in terms of schooling and what needs to happen with y'all. But don't worry about any of that. I'm not a dictator, I'm not here to judge, I'm just here to guide you all to the right place so Connie can come home. That is the goal. That is, right now, my only goal."

Damn he can talk for America, but I do appreciate what he's saying.

"So if we set up a meeting and then after we've spoken we will introduce you to Connie on a supervised basis."

2 WEEKS LATER

"Does she know about us?" I ask, voice trembling. "Does she know I didn't give her away?"

"She does."

"And how did she take it."

He clears his throat and my hope starts to wither away. "She was... emotional. She doesn't quite believe it and nobody can really blame her for that. But she'll come around."

"You said she has difficulties and Webber said she has abandonment issues," Kane puts in, sounding guarded and wary. "What does that mean exactly?"

"It means that Connie struggles to form relationships with people. She was abandoned at a church with no reason as to why and unfortunately her adoptive parents were a little too transparent with her over that fact, and then she was abandoned again by them and she never understood why. She loved those parents like any kid would. She remembers being happy, she remembers baking and painting and going on trips to the park and museums. They didn't even say goodbye when they left her."

My heart breaks.

"It was my colleague who dealt with her case back then and it took her six months to get Connie to stop sitting in the hall, waiting for them to come back. It's a tragic case really. I wish things could have been different for her."

Kane's hands have balled into fists. "Don't ever tell me their names, Chief."

"Sometimes, in this line of work, *and I never said this*, but... I wish I could say their names." He laughs sadly. "It's gut wrenching and I know it must be hard to hear but kids are so resilient and so strong. Connie will start connecting with people, she'll learn to love again, and you guys will be such a beautiful family. What happened in her past will become just that. The past."

If she's anything like me she'll never be able to let it go.

A tear slips from my eye, I've been desperately holding onto it

2 WEEKS LATER

because I don't want my voice to shake while I talk. Kane hooks me around the shoulders and kisses my temple.

"Right, so when can I come see y'all? The sooner the better. I want complete honesty from both of you. Don't pretend like you've gotta be together or you've gotta live together. I'm here to help you figure all that out. You don't have to parent together you've just got to support each other and most importantly, always prioritize Connie. She cannot take another hit. She cannot be in another family that's going to break."

"We will do anything..." Kane bites out through gritted teeth. "*Anything* for that kid. Understand that. You'll have the whole picture of who me and Imogen are. Don't worry about that."

"Good." There's a pause as he seems to shuffle through something, maybe papers but I can't be sure as I'm only hearing it. "Right then. When can I come and see y'all?"

"Soon as you like?"

CONNIE – 8 YEARS OLD

I've been raised my entire life to respect my elders and always use my manners. Because manners don't cost nothing. I disagree, these old people always doing me wrong. Why should I use manners or be respectful? I'm not some little girly princess wanting a fairytale like all the other girls I share a room with. I had parents; they weren't nothing special. Which means I ain't nothing special. Which means I don't deserve nothing special.

The girls in my room all are waiting for it, that *something special*. Daydreaming about a happy home, refusing to believe they could be loved by the family who already failed them. I'm not that deluded, and I wish they wouldn't be either.

Deluded is my new word of the week.

"It's perfetic," I declare, folding my arms over my chest and wincing as Stacey pulls the brush through my hair.

"Pathetic," she corrects.

"I can't say that, Stacey, you know I ain't got enough teef!"

She laughs at my reflection in the mirror and twists three strands of my hair into a tight braid.

"Stop laughin' at me."

CONNIE – 8 YEARS OLD

"I'm laughing *with* you," she insists, laughing harder when I scowl.

"Those people still comin' today?" I ask with a lisp.

She raises a brow, the perfect pointed end lifts making her green eyes look bigger. "You mean your parents?"

I snort and roll my eyes.

"You be kind to them Connie. I'm warnin' you."

I roll my eyes again, this time with a sigh. "I'm never mean."

"We both know that's not true."

"Okay then I'm never mean on purpose."

She grins and shakes her head as her fingers wind a hair tie around the end of my braid. "We both definitely know that's not true."

"You're always bullyin' me."

At that she laughs and gives my hair a tug. "You're ready. Did you brush your teeth? Or what's left of them anyway."

"Yes ma'am."

"Good. Then let's go meet your parents, shall we?"

A girl from my room, her name is Melody, let's out a happy sound and insists, "You're so lucky, Connie."

Stacey taps me on the head and gives me a pointed look. "Don't you roll your eyes."

"Don't you tell me how to live my life," I retort and stand. "Melody, I ain't lucky. Give it a week or two and these people will never come back."

Melody's smile fades and she looks at Stacey for comfort. "She doesn't want them. Can I have them?"

"Oh sweetie," Stacey utters, and they hug it out.

I puff out my cheeks and glower at myself in the mirror. Thick brown hair, weird blue eyes, no front teeth so I can stick my tongue through them. All the girls my age lost their front teeth ages ago, Stacey tells me I'm just a late bloomer and there ain't nothing wrong with that. She doesn't see this face in the mirror every day.

"Just remember," Stacey utters after ushering Melody from the

CONNIE – 8 YEARS OLD

room. She places her hands on my shoulders and I frown at her nails. I don't like nail biting. It's a nasty habit. "It's not their fault that they didn't get to keep you. Just like it's not your fault. And they're your momma and daddy, they're gonna have loved you before they ever got to meet you. Let them have that. Let them be affectionate. Let them give you that love and then maybe one day, and hopefully soon, you'll trust them enough to love them back in return."

I don't say anything, I just nod and let her guide me out of the bedroom with her hands still on my shoulders.

It has been a month since that cop man and my social worker, David, both sat me down and told me about them. Feels a lot less.

I thought they'd have given up by now but I guess they've gotta see me first. When they see me and when they see I'm not lovable, they'll leave. That's what happened before... *twice*... and that's what will happen again. I ain't holding my breath.

"You ready?" Stacey asks, pulling up my grey leggings and pulling down my pink top. It has a unicorn on it that changes color depending which way you smooth the sequins. When I said to my teacher that this type of top was made by men as an excuse to touch the chests of little girls, I had to go see my therapist again but I thought I had a good point.

My therapist thought it was funny, so did Stacey. They both say I'm a very witty and switched on kid. I don't know what that means, so long as they don't think I'm deluded.

As we approach the door of the meeting lounge, a special room designed for moments like this, I can hear them whispering inside and my heart starts beating so hard in my chest. They're going to hate me. They're going to take one look at me and hate me. Or worse, they're going to love me like a new kitty and then get rid of me when they lose interest. That's why I'm here. That's also why we have the fuzzy cat that used to live three doors down the street.

I don't want to do this. I don't want to be here. This ain't fair. I don't want to go through this again.

I stop and Stacey hits my back and we both almost fall.

CONNIE – 8 YEARS OLD

"No," I say, pulling away but she grabs my arm. "No no no!"

"Connie," Stacey implores. "They drove all this way."

"Then they can drive all that way back!" I shout, pulling away but she grips me harder. I beat on her arm with my fist, breath coming out in pants. "LET GO OF ME!"

I kick her in the shin so hard she releases me and shouts the word caterpillar instead of a real swear. Then I bolt, letting my legs carry me to the front door but David appears and grabs me around the middle.

"Connie," he admonishes as I punch and kick at every part of him I can.

"I DON'T WANT TO!" I screech, tears burning my cheeks. "I DON'T! LET ME GO! YOU CAN'T MAKE ME! YOU CAN'T MAKE ME!"

"Let her go, Jesus H Christ," shouts the biggest man I ever saw. David drops me on the ground and I look up at the man with long hair and tattoos peeking over his white button up. "Forcing her ain't gonna help none!"

"Kane," the woman standing slightly behind him to his right whispers. She has really pretty, really kind eyes.

"I was just stopping her from bolting," David assures him, grabbing my arm again and helping me to my feet. "Connie, you good?"

I sniffle and dry my face on my arm. "Let go of me."

"She looks just like you," the woman whispers to the big man and he grins this weird grin that makes her grin. They're both crazy people.

I'm pretty sure I have the same eyes as him though. Does that mean I'll be giant too? Maybe then I can stomp on everyone and everything in my big boots like the ones he's wearing.

"That's going to bruise, you know that right?" Stacey tells me, showing me a red mark on her shin. "Not cool, Connie. You're too old to be throwing tantrums and hitting people."

"Says who?" I bite back.

She huffs, frustrated. "Apologize."

CONNIE – 8 YEARS OLD

"I'm sorry you're a baby."

"Connie..." David is also using *a tone*. "This ain't like you. Don't be spoiling your good behavior or you won't get your tablet this weekend."

My cheeks flame as they all stare at me. "I didn't do anything wrong."

"Yes you did," Stacey insists and bends to my level. I hate it when she does this, it always means she's about to explain something and try make me learn something I don't wanna learn. "You know you did and that's not nice. You really hurt me back there."

"You wouldn't let me go."

She presses her lips together, stands to full height and looks at the giant and his lady. "She's embarrassed, she gets stubborn when she's embarrassed."

"Sounds like somebody else I know," the lady utters, and I decide I like her voice and accent.

"Watch it," the man with the big arms and chest snaps but he's smiling at her. Why do they look at each other like that? It's all gooey eyed and weird.

My last parents didn't look at each other like that, they mostly just ignored each other from what I can remember.

"Why don't we go back into the room?" David suggests and I notice some of the girls sitting on the stairs watching the exchange.

"Connie is such a brat," Ellie, one of the older girls says with a roll of her eyes. I glare at her and stick out my tongue.

I am not a brat. I just don't like people very much.

"And you smell like feet!"

"Okay," David calls and steers me back the way we just came. "Let's carry this on in the meeting room. You can draw us a picture, Connie. Show off your mad skills."

"I don't much feel like drawing." I lift myself up into the chair at the end of the table and swing my legs, the toes of my shoes just skim the ground. I'm not short, these chairs are just real big.

CONNIE – 8 YEARS OLD

David slides a blank sketchpad my way and my favorite pack of crayons. I hate that they know what crayons I like to us.

"Immy can draw," the big man says, sitting in the seat two down. His lady, aka Immy, sits to my left between us. "She's real good. You got her talent?"

"I can't draw," I respond, pushing the pad away but secretly I really want to show them something I've done, and I really want to see what she can do.

She pulls the pad her way. "You like unicorns?"

"I like zombies."

"Me too," the big man growls. His voice is so rough and deep. I bet he's good at telling stories. Bet I could make him tell me one.

No, because spending time with people makes you like them and then love them. Like Stacey. I feel bad that I hurt her because I like her. She's nice to me most of the time. But when she changes her job she'll leave, so I don't love her, so I don't spend time with her. It's simple people math.

"Well I draw the best zombies," Immy says with a soft smile and I can see tears in her eyes. "How do we like them? The crazy virus kind, or the melting skin kind?"

"Guts everywhere," I tell her, feeling kind of into it now. "Guts and gore."

"Let's try and keep this child friendly," David prompts nervously but Immy either doesn't hear him, or she doesn't listen on purpose. The big guy winks at me when my eyes drift his way.

"I'm Kane by the way."

"I know," I respond.

"You keep lookin' at me like you want to say somethin'. Thought maybe you'd forgotten my name."

I chew on my lip and then let them part. "How'd you get so big? Because Stacey said if I eat my greens I'll get big and strong, but I don't wanna get *that* big. I think I might stop eatin' broccoli."

He chuckles and Immy laughs at her drawing.

"Nice try, kid. You've still got to eat your veg." Stacey snaps, winking at me from across the room. "David."

David looks her way with a happy sparkle in his eyes.

"I've got to sort the other girls. Do you need me here?"

He shakes his head at her and she mouths at me before leaving, "Be nice."

I scrunch my nose up at her.

"Getting arms like his and shoulders like his comes from lifting some really heavy stuff every day and eating right. You gotta work for a body like that, it doesn't just happen," Immy explains, looking at me with those soft eyes again. She slides the drawing my way and my jaw hits the desk with a clatter. It's a really good zombie, way better than anything I could ever draw. "You like it?"

"It's really cool."

"Want me to teach you how to draw like that?"

Excitement flutters through me like butterfly wings all over my skin but I jump and stomp on it in my head, making it disappear. "No. I don't want anything from you."

Her smile fades and I feel a bit bad, so I quickly look at David, "I want to go back to my room."

"Connie," he tries but I slam my hand down on the table.

"I want to go back to my room!"

"But—" He blows out a breath and glances at the strangers that are supposed to be my parents.

"Let her go," Kane insists. "We'll be here for an hour, if she decides she wants to come back down, that's cool. If she doesn't, that's also cool. After that hour we will come back tomorrow."

I don't wait for confirmation, I exit before anyone can change their mind.

IMMY

"I saw her get excited, she wanted to learn," Kane puts in and it makes me feel a little better as I stare at the door my daughter just exited through.

I rest my temple on his shoulder and smile sadly when he kisses my hair. "Do you think she hates us?"

"I think she's just overwhelmed."

David nods his agreement. "Give it time, she'll come around. She's stubborn but once she sees she can trust you, she'll open up and let you in."

"We ain't givin' up," Kane insists and I agree with every fiber of my being.

"Not a chance," I put in and tilt my head back. "She looks just like you, Kane. She's even got the same scowl you constantly wore as a child."

Chuckling, his eyes drift to the door and there's a sadness deep in them that only I know is there. "She's got your attitude."

"God help us all then," I murmur and David smiles at us softly. "Can we come back tomorrow?"

"Absolutely. So long as it doesn't interfere with her schoolwork

IMMY

and y'all don't try to take her beyond the boundaries of the property, you can come back as often as you like."

My eyes burn with tears because I know what that means, it means he trusts us and if he trusts us, that means we will eventually get her back.

"It might not be me tomorrow, but I'll update the other home appointed social worker on your progress."

"How did we do?" I ask him, chewing nervously on my lip.

"I think you both kept it together better than I ever would have in that situation. Without sounding patronizing, I'm proud of you both, not only for keeping to the plan, but also for never giving up. I wish all my cases had a happy ending like this." He zips up his jacket and stands and my heart warms in my chest at his words. Truthfully I wanted to break down and sob the moment I saw her, I wanted to grab her and pull her into my arms. I wanted to promise her the world and give her my soul to keep with her at all times but I couldn't. "Let me show you around the place so you know what sort of establishment she's living in."

"Shouldn't one of us stay here?" I ask, glancing at the door. "Just in case she comes back?"

"She ain't comin' back today," Kane says with a tender smile.

"I'm inclined to agree with him. That girl is stubborn as a mule. You're gonna have to work for it."

"Convinced this one she liked me when really she hated me." Kane tugs on my hair. "We got this."

"How goes the living situation?" David asks us both while holding open the door for us to go through.

Kane holds it and waits for him, ain't nobody holding a door open for Kane Jessop unless his arms are full of groceries or something heavy. "We're doin' like you said."

"I've put my store on the market," I say with a shrug. "Already got some interest. Will use what money I get from that to buy a place in Austin and open my own shop."

"For now she's commuting between me and Chicago but we want to make the move permanent."

"So y'all are giving your relationship a go then?"

"We ain't complicating things, ain't usin' labels," Kane answers and David nods. "She'll have a place in Austin regardless and I'll have my place in Faceless. So long as both are good for Connie does it matter our situation?"

"Not at all, this is a huge change for all of you, don't rush it, don't force it and what will be will be. When it comes to Connie coming to live with you, if you're still living separately we will figure it out. If you're living together, we will figure that out too."

I don't know what we would have done if we got a social worker that wasn't as kind and as understanding as David.

"But that's something y'all need to discuss too. Who will Connie live with full time if you're both separated? Joint custody is fine but if you're both in different places, one of them has to be the main one. She can't go to school in two places."

I look at Kane with concern but he winks at me knowingly and I feel instantly placated. We have a plan already; we've spoken about this tirelessly. There isn't a chance in hell we are separating now. Kane wouldn't let me leave him if I tried and he told me that in those exact words too.

We share a smile of excitement. The ball is finally rolling and soon enough we will have our daughter at home with us.

CONNIE

1 WEEK LATER

They have been coming every single day at random times, never when I'm in classes which isn't fair because I hate school. I honestly thought they'd have given up by now but they're like a rash. Still... even rashes don't last forever.

David, Stacey, and Tiana the other social worker all keep making me spend time with them even when I don't want to but secretly I kind of do.

Immy bought me a new sketchbook with my name in glitter on the front and some of these really cool crayons that I can smudge with my finger. She showed me how to use them and it was fun, too much fun. It reminded me of when my momma... the fake one... used to help me read stories at bedtime. She'd tickle me every time I'd read a word right. I loved her; I miss her.

I don't want to love Immy. I don't want to miss Immy.

"Do you like it?" she asked softly and I immediately started snapping the crayons and ripping up the book. I don't want gifts from strangers. I don't want gifts from anyone. Even though I do.

They need to leave.

Stacey grounded me from TV time and made me sit on time out to think about what I'd done.

I saw the look in Immy's eyes when I did what I did. She was sad and it's eating away at me. But I thought she'd hate me and leave and never come back. She still came back the next day, without a gift, but she still came back. So did Kane the giant.

The past two days I haven't let anybody force me to see them. I've been in trouble, but I don't care. This isn't fair. I should get a choice.

Today David has basically dragged me down to the room and forced me into the chair.

Immy's arms aren't covered today and she has tattoos all up one arm from her wrist to her shoulder. I love tattoos. The other girls think people with tattoos are scary. An old lady at Sunday school used to say people with tattoos have the devil in them.

I don't know why people get worked up about drawings. Once I drew myself stabbing my old History teacher through the belly with a sword longer than me and everybody freaked out. He was an old troll and I had to put a stop to his Tinnary! Or is it Tyranny? I forget.

I wasn't actually gonna stab him. Duh. Just like Immy probably doesn't have the devil in her because she has drawings on her arms.

"You like?" Immy asks, catching me staring at her arm. "This is what I do, you know? I put tattoos on people."

That's so cool.

"I don't care," I snap and look away. My hands ball into fists on the table.

"Why don't you tell us something you do care about," Kane puts in and I think back to how my friend Nelly said that he looks so scary. He doesn't scare me, not one bit. I'll kick him in the shin just like I did to Stacey.

"I don't care about anything," I reply haughtily.

"What about the movie theatre? You like the movies?" Immy questions. "David said we can probably start going out places together as soon as you stop being so difficult."

CONNIE

I glower at her and feel annoyed when her lips twitch. "I'm not difficult and I'm not going anywhere."

"You don't like the movies?"

"No," I lie. We went once for a school trip a year ago and it was the best thing ever.

"What do you like then?"

"Nuffin'."

They share a look and I wonder if I'm finally getting through to them that I'm not interested.

"Can I go now?" I ask them, scowling at the table.

"No," Kane states firmly and the lady shoots a look his way. Her head whipped around so fast. "You're gonna sit with us, kid. You don't gotta like it, but you gotta do it."

"Why?" I'm not liking this at all. Mostly because he said I won't like it and I really don't.

"Because we're your parents and this is how it's gonna be." His accent is so thick but I still understand what he's saying.

"No it isn't."

"Give us a chance, Connie, let us prove to you that we aren't going anywhere."

"No." My arms fold across my chest so tight my shoulders are pulling.

"We could have so much fun."

"I don't wanna have fun with you!" I yell, standing so suddenly my chair falls backwards.

"Why?" Immy pushes and I also want to kick her in the shin. "Tell us why."

I stare at them both still sitting there, hardly reacting to my anger. Why aren't they mad that I'm talking back? "Because I don't like you."

Hurt flickers in her hazel eyes and I feel guilt, but not enough to make me stop.

"And I know you don't like me too."

"That ain't true," Kane responds calmly. "We like you a lot."

His words make my eyes burn. I don't want them to say that. They don't need to. "Well then in a week you ain't gonna like me, or in two weeks you ain't gonna like me, and then you'll leave and I'll never see you again!"

"We won't leave you," Immy promises and reaches for my hand. "I'm your momma, I would never leave you."

"Yes you will," I cry, tears streaming down my face. "My last momma did!"

"My blood is in your veins. Her blood wasn't."

I point at the door. "Melody's momma's blood runs through her veins too and she left her and didn't come back! All these kids here, their mommas and their dads didn't come back for them. We're unlovable. All of us."

"Connie." Immy stands, tears making her cheeks shiny too. "Places like this are so tragic and I'm so sorry that all your friends don't have good mommies and daddies. But everyone's situation is different."

"I don't care!" I scream, backing away from the table towards the door. "I don't care! I don't care! I DON'T CARE!"

"Connie," Kane warns. "You ain't unlovable. Nobody is unlovable."

"You don't know anything about it!"

"Neither do you."

"Kane." Immy shakes her head at him and I take this moment of distraction to bolt from the room like a rabbit from danger.

I'm trembling, my entire body is shaking. I've never felt so many things at once.

The back door at the end of the kitchen opens with ease and I stumble out into the warm air. They let me go, knowing I can't get far because this place is a fortress. The only way out the back is through a metal gate and I don't have the key for it.

I run all the way to the end, my legs are burning, and I grab the metal bars and pull. Sometimes I come out here and pretend I can

CONNIE

bend them with my mind, or maybe fly over them, and then I run away to a mall and live in a candy store where nobody can bother me because I'll blast them all into space with my cool laser beams! I'd make the best super person ever.

IMMY

"I feel useless," I admit, looking at the man I love. "She's so fucking stubborn she's not giving us an inch. I don't know how to get through to her."

"The good thing about this is, that girl has the will of an iron rhino." David laughs gently at his own words. "Nobody will stop her from following her dreams once she realizes what they are."

"Something's gotta give. She hates us."

"She doesn't hate us," Kane replies with a heavy sigh. "She wants to hate us."

I walk to the window where I can see my daughter sitting at the far end of the small field, throwing stones at the metal bars that line the property. Apparently, she often goes there to think things through and usually comes back in a better mood.

"She doesn't like to open up," Stacey utters gently, also looking towards Connie. "Not even with me and I've been with her for two years now."

"That doesn't bring me hope," I admit, feeling my heart break even more.

"She won't open up because she knows eventually I'll leave. She knows as much as I love these kids that one day I might change jobs or maybe my bosses will assign me different kids. She's sharp as a whip. But when she knows you guys aren't leaving, she'll open up to you, I know it. That kid has the softest center and the biggest heart." Stacey places her hand on my shoulder but releases me when Kane sneaks up behind me and wraps his arms around my waist.

"We knew this would be a challenge," he says, his voice deep and gruff, a soothing velvet on my jagged nerves. "We've just gotta keep on. She'll crack."

"Will we damage her in the process?" I ask, terrified that our actions aren't going to make her inability to open up any better. "I'm scared of hurting or scarring her beyond what she already is."

"She's tough as nails," Kane reassures me. "That kid is not going to let anyone stand in her way or drag her down."

"We just need to somehow show her that we aren't going to do either, that we just want to love and support her."

Kane releases me and pushes a hand through his hair. "I'm gonna talk to her."

All eyes, including mine, fly his way.

"Alone."

David looks uneasy.

"Enough of this pussyfooting around her. She's gotta listen eventually, it needs to be now."

"What are you going to say to her?" David questions, trying to be a good protector of our child but I know Kane's brute energy frightens him.

"What I say to my kid is between me and my kid. But I ain't gonna threaten her or anythin' like that." Resolute, he cups my face with his hands. "Trust me?"

"With our kid? More than anyone."

He kisses me and looks across the field then around the room. "Save your objections. Your way isn't workin'."

David holds up his hands. "Wasn't gonna object."

IMMY

Kane dips his chin, looking so handsome and sexy and determined. Then he strides from the room and we all watch him conquer the length of the field with big steps, looking confident and willful. I keep my fingers crossed that Connie finally listens, just enough for her to let us in.

CONNIE

I hear his big feet before I feel him sit down beside me. I'm annoyed he is upsetting my moment but I don't run, not again. I don't want to give him the satisfaction of thinking I'm a brat. He called me that the other day, I heard him. Said I act like a brat and then Immy said, just like you then.

Instead I scowl ahead and scowl deeper when his eyes hit my face and his lips twitch. He thinks I'm funny and cute. He said that the other day too.

"Why you throwin' stones at open bars?" he questions, an amused lilt to his voice.

"Why do you care?"

He lifts a shoulder. "Guess I don't. Was just curious about what's goin' through your head. Can't be good things, not with you convincin' yourself that you're unlovable and your friends are unlovable. That's not a nice thing to say about yourself, it's especially not a nice thing to say about your friends."

"It's true. They've gotta stop gettin' their hopes up. I'm sick of hearing them sob when it doesn't work out right for them."

Kane pulls on the end of my braid.

"Ouch."

"You're a cynical little git ain't you."

"I don't know what that means."

"It means you don't trust nothin' or no one."

I think on it for a moment and file that word away as my new word of the week. "What's your point?"

He rests his hands over his bent knees and stares in the same direction I am. "You wanna know somethin' about us kid? You willin' to listen?"

"Do I gotta choice?"

He laughs and it kinda sounds like mine. I've been seeing a lot of things that remind me of myself in both of them since we met.

"When I was around your age, your momma in there was playin' with her brother when I beat his ass and stole his bike."

He said ass. *That's so cool.*

"That's mean."

"Absolutely. And for years after I shoved her around, called her names, bullied her so bad."

"Why?"

He shrugs. "I don't know, I can't explain it or excuse it, she just rubbed me the wrong way, bein' all prissy and lovin' God like she did with what looked like such a perfect family. I bet you know the type."

Don't I ever, I think but don't say.

"My momma was not a good lady, and just like you I got it in my head that I was just as unlovable as she said I was."

"She said that to you?"

He nods, his lips a flat line. "She said a lot of things to me that messed with my head before my daddy stepped in and took me away but the pain stayed, the betrayal stayed and I clung to it so tight I wore it like a second skin. I couldn't understand why my momma didn't love me but I thought it must have been somethin' I did so I kept on making people think that, kept on treatin' people like crap so that none of them would ever try."

I look up at him into his eyes that are as blue as mine. "What happened?"

"Exactly what I wanted. I had friends but not many, my daddy was fed up, my step-momma was fed up. I stopped gettin' invited to parties and everything I thought was true about myself came true. Nobody loved me, nobody wanted me. I was a burden and even though I brought it on myself I couldn't break outta that cycle."

"Oh."

"Yeah."

"So if you were so mean to my momma, how did you make me?"

He laughs like I'm hilarious and this time I don't mind it. "Well I wish I could tell you, kid. Your momma saw somethin' in me I was sure I had never shown her. She loved me regardless and hell if I didn't love her too. She completed my world, made the most unlovable boy in the United States, become the most loved. Ain't nothin' she wouldn't have done for me and ain't nothin' I wouldn't have done for her." He pulls on my braid like before trying to make me look into his eyes again. "So don't you be telling me you ain't loveable because I'm tellin' you right now, if that lady can love me for me... she certainly can love you for all that is you." He leans in. "Give me your eyes, little darlin'."

I do and I feel them burn with moisture.

"And hell if I don't love you just as much as she does too." He uses his thumb to catch my tears and rubs the moisture off the rough pad with his finger. "Love doesn't come with conditions, it just is. When you figure that out, you'll feel it just the same and we ain't goin' anywhere while you work on that."

"You love me?"

"As much as, if not more than I love your momma."

"You really love her," I comment quietly because I know he does, I can tell when he looks at her all gooey. It's so gross.

"Your momma is so easy to love."

"Easier than me?"

"Ain't nobody in this entire world who is easier to love than you," he' states and my lower lip trembles. "Behavin' the way you do ain't gonna make people stop loving you. It's just gonna make you miss out on stuff we all know you'll love. Like going to the movies for example with your giant dad here." He bangs on his chest like a gorilla which makes me almost fall back laughing. "Or going to Travis County Fair with your momma in there who *hates* all the big rides but it's funny watchin' her scream. You really wanna miss that?"

I shake my head because I really don't want to miss that. "You'd take me to the county fair."

"Little darlin', I'll take you anywhere you want to go that's not ridiculously dangerous. But you gotta give us a chance in return. Okay?"

Nodding, I wipe my eyes on my wrist. "Okay."

"Good, then let's go figure out your schedule."

Smiling now, no... *beaming*, I stand up as he does and place my hand in his when he offers it. It's so big and warm. He winks at me and we walk together, every two steps of mine make almost one of his.

When we reach the house, Immy is standing in the kitchen with a cup of something hot. I can see the steam rising out of the top.

"We good?" Immy asks, her eyes glancing between the two of us.

Kane smiles down at me. "We're good." He lets go of my hand after giving it a squeeze and lifts me up onto the counter which makes me giggle because I wasn't expecting it. "Let's start making plans, shall we? Before bolter here hops the fence and legs it to Mexico."

Grinning, I look at Immy who slides a pen and paper closer to me and writes in block letters at the top of the page, "DAYS OUT."

"What do you really want to do, that you never get to do?" Immy asks and my heart starts hammering in my chest.

"Anything?"

"Yep, if we can do it, we'll do it."

I chew on my lip and look around the room. I'm nervous. What if they say no? I don't want to feel stupid.

"Go on," Stacey mouths.

"I like Disney."

Immy writes Disney movies down.

"Anythin' else?"

"There's this cake place in the city," I admit, mouthwatering at the thought. "Where they do you like a spread of cupcakes to taste allll their flavors. Melody got to go for her birthday with her uncle. I really want to go."

"You want to go eat cake?" Immy asks, lips twitching.

I nod and sigh wistfully. "I love cake."

"Me too," Kane agrees and we bump fists. "Definitely put that on the list."

"I'm tryin' to watch my waistline," Immy jests as she scribbles it down. For somebody who is so good at art, her handwriting is like mine. Very messy.

"I didn't say *you* have to eat it."

She yanks on my braid like Kane did and smiles fondly at me. I never want her to look at me in any other way.

IMMY

2 MONTHS LATER

"You've gotta crank this and hold on real tight, okay?" West Jessop tells my eight-year-old daughter as he climbs onto the back of the quad she's about to drive. She's kitted out from helmet to booted toe, but my heart is still racing.

"They'll be fine," Kane whispers in my ear, kissing the shell. "Let him have this."

"I'm not about to stop them."

"You sure? You're holding onto that grill fork like you're ready to poke him with it."

I look at my white knuckles around the handle of the arm length tool and quickly hang it back on the grill.

One month ago Connie Felicia Jessop decided not only that we could give her a new middle name and surname, but that she was ready to come and live with us at Kane's home in Faceless. And though social services are still present in our lives and will be for the next six months or so, she's staying right where she is. And so am I.

We have decorated her room to suit her tastes which consists of dark purples and greens and a medley of other random dark shades of colors. Whatever floats her boat of course. She seems to love it and I just love having her here. I read to her every night if she lets me, sometimes it makes her sad and she opened up to me a week ago and said it reminds her of her first momma. So I said well if we keep doing it, maybe all our story time memories will erase the memories that bring her pain.

We're in a good routine. Every morning before school she goes with her daddy to the garage and helps him open up, because I have to leave to make the forty-five-minute drive to Austin where I've set up my tattoo shop. I don't mind it. We made the right choice in living arrangements. I miss Chicago but I feel like I'm at home here.

In Faceless, Connie has family, we have friends, the roads and streets are a lot safer than a busy city, the school is more intimate, and everybody knows everybody. Even though my experience growing up here wasn't the best, my memories of playing on these streets absolutely are.

We sold Mee-maw's house as planned, it went a lot quicker than expected but then small towns like this have so much charm for city families which is who we sold it to. I didn't give my momma a dime much to her dismay, I did however, slap an injunction on her ass to keep her away and then I put the money I was going to give to her in a trust fund for my baby whose life was stolen because of that bitch and her mother. My brother keeps trying to contact me too to reconnect and though we've had a brief conversation, I'm not interested in building bridges right now. I want to focus all my time and attention on the little girl I lost because of him.

I suppose I could say the three of them are responsible for what happened to me and I don't need to forgive any of them for any of it. It is not going to bring me any kind of peace. I find enough peace in hating them, thanking you kindly.

Marshall holds open a bun for me to slap a burger patty into. I'm so glad he's here. I didn't think he'd come due to him being worried he'll bump into his parents who are a sore subject for him for obvious reasons. I'm hoping if he does, they're over their bigotry and can love him for who he is and not based on who he loves.

What I keep drilling into Connie's head is that love is unconditional for a lot of people, but some, such as Marshall and her friends back in care, aren't as fortunate to have people in their lives that know how to love unconditionally. It doesn't come easy.

"Look, Immy!" Connie squeals as she rides past me, I only just hear her through her thick helmet and over the roar of the engine.

"She still ain't callin' you momma," Felicia utters as she approaches. She's been trying to get Connie to say it since the day she met her. I appreciate her efforts, especially since I don't want Connie to feel like I'm forcing her into anything. "I keep sayin' your momma this and your momma that but she still just ain't sayin' it back."

"She'll get there," Marshall offers and winks at me. "I don't think Immy minds too much. She's just happy to have her."

I nod because he's right. Being here with her day in day out is a dream I never thought would become a reality. The darkness that shadowed me for so long no longer seems to exist.

We are getting our happy ending. Sure, we've got to work for it. Especially with my depression that I still have to keep fighting back, and Connie's trust issues, and Kane's anger, oh and Connie's anger as proven when she kicked a classmate in her crotch the second day of school. But somehow, the three of us so far just keep each other grounded and happy and full of love. I couldn't ask for a better support group.

"Y'all keep having these cookouts I'm going to gain about fifty pounds," Poppy calls, waddling up the driveway with her pregnant belly that seems to have just popped out over the past couple of months.

She didn't tell us she was pregnant because she didn't want to steal our thunder with Connie. Which of course is ridiculous. She also didn't want to worry us because the guy she was seeing bailed when she told him she was pregnant, so she's moving back into town to be a single momma just like her momma did with her.

"There's my little devil bean," I say in jest and molest her stomach.

"No hello for the incubator carrying it?"

"Shhhh, your voice is too scratchy for the little devil's ears," I hiss, still groping my friend.

She laughs and wraps her arms around my shoulders. "Couldn't do this without you."

I hug her back, squishing her six-month along pregnant belly between us. "Duh. I'm its daddy now." Truth be told her being pregnant is such a welcome blessing.

Kane and me have had that conversation and though I'd love to experience motherhood by his side, it's just not something either of us are emotionally ready for right now, and Connie needs all of us, not some of us. When she's older and in a better place mentally we'll consider introducing another child to the world. Until then I'll be surrogate momma to Poppy's little boy and I'll love every second.

"Pretty sure it was sex that made you gain fifty pounds," Marshall jokes and she reaches around me to smack his arm.

"Seriously though, this is the third one in three weeks. Not that I'm complaining."

I lift a shoulder and lean into Kane who pulls me into his side. He always does that when I lean into him, he just seems to know I need his heat and energy in that moment. "It's the only way they can really see Connie and get her doing shit. We aren't allowed to introduce sleepovers at her grandparents or even unsupervised visits. It's strict and crazy but we're following the rules."

"Yeah, it's not worth the risk," Poppy agrees, smiling at West who almost falls off the back of the quad as Connie takes a turn in the field by the house just a bit too sharp.

"Losing your balance, old man?" I shout with my hands cupped around my mouth. He flips me the bird and points in the direction Connie needs to go.

She returns to us a minute later, sweaty under the helmet with a huge grin on her face. "That was awesome!"

"She's almost ready for a solo ride," West announces and Kane high fives Connie while I scowl at the two of them.

"Don't be tellin' her that," Felicia admonishes and yanks on his beard before I get the chance to.

I sit in the lounge chair when Kane takes over the food and I'm equal parts surprised and absolutely fucking elated when Connie comes and plonks herself on my lap, hair damp from the heat, cheeks rosy, arms freckled and covered in sun lotion. She leans back against my chest and I tickle her arm kind of like Kane does to me when I need to unwind.

"I guess because you and Kane were so young when you had me, that nobody else you know really has any kids," she says softly as she looks around us all.

I wrap my arms around her waist and lock them across her stomach. She's so dainty and tall. Just like I was at her age. "You miss havin' friends to play with?"

"Makes sense, what with her growing up in a place with a hundred other girls." Felicia clicks her fingers. "Tell you what, how about I call my friend Jamie and see if she'll bring her kids next time?"

"Okay."

They share a smile and Connie nudges her way to a comfier position.

"Are you happy?" I ask her, resting my chin on her head.

"Yeah. Just really warm."

I laugh a little. "Me too."

"Want me to get off your lap?"

"Nope. You can stay right here forever."

EPILOGUE

"Oh my God you are such a little brat but you are just *so cute!*" Our fourteen-year old daughter says to our two-year old son who just jumped on her lap and started scrubbing at her makeup with a wet wipe. His daddy told him to.

"Bryant," I admonish weakly because I don't mean it. Connie should not be wearing as much makeup as she is. I get that she's experimenting, but I didn't realize gothic clown was a *look*.

Kane chuckles and yanks me into his body as Connie drops Bryant on the soft rug and exits the room grumbling about how she's got to fix her face. He toddles along after her, adoring her like he always has and hopefully always will.

"Show me your panties," Kane whispers in my ear and pushes his hands into the back of my jeans to grip my rear. He bites my neck and kisses my lips until I'm breathless. "Think we've got time for a quickie in the restroom?"

"No," I answer, giggling as he holds me tighter and grinds against me harder. "You need to stop. Connie's date will be here soon."

Kane wouldn't agree to her going on a date until the boy's dad, Arnold, said he'd be supervising from a few rows back. Since Arnold and Kane are friends, Kane reluctantly put his trust in the man. Connie is just happy to be going out with a boy.

"I don't get it. I was not bothered about boys at her age," I whisper when my mind takes me back there.

Kane's eyes darken. "If I recall, at her age you were making out on the patch with *my* friend."

I giggle and sigh dreamily for added effect. "Oh yeah."

"Oh yeah? Why the fuck you sayin' *oh yeah* like that?"

Fluttering my lashes I place my hand on my chest. "Whatever do you mean?"

"Immy," he warns, his eyes sparking with that familiar jealousy I just love to put there. Which isn't hard to do. Especially when he sees the kind of men I tattoo. Though he never gives me hell for it, he just fucks me so hard my eyes spin.

"Oh come on, it was years ago and it was my first kiss."

He growls and yanks me back to him again. "You shouldn't be able to remember your first kiss that wasn't with me."

"Shut up you big baby," I remark, biting hard on his lower lip. "I didn't want Mallick, I just liked the attention."

Kane scoffs. "Oh you remember his name now too?"

I laugh so hard I can't breathe, that is until he backs me into the door and shoves his tongue into my mouth. We makeout for a while and then he pulls back and pushes my hand onto his dick.

"Gonna see Connie off, then I'm gonna put Bryant down for a nap and then I'm going to stick this in your mouth to get his name out of it."

"Oh my," I jest, sighing happily. "Oh that just sounds God awful, sir."

He pinches my rear just as the doorbell sounds, and Connie comes bounding down the stairs.

"Bye guys!" she tries to yell but Kane has vanished from my path and appeared in hers faster than The Flash.

"I don't think so," Kane grumbles and I hear the door swing open. "Oi! You! Kid!"

"Daaaaad," Connie hisses and I have to stifle my laugh.

"You ain't gonna come greet my daughter at the door, she ain't goin' on a date with you," Kane barks and I snatch up Bryant before he can squeeze between his daddy's legs and escape.

"I was just getting the flowers from the back seat, sir," the boy says with a nervous tone.

"Good man." Kane winks at Connie whose white cheeks are bright red.

"I hate you," she mouths at Kane who only grins bigger.

"I'm AJ, Arnold Junior, it's good to see you again, sir." The boy raises his chin, trying to look confident as he extends his hand to Kane who shakes it. Then he hands the flowers to Connie and stammers, "These... uh... are for... uh... you."

"Thank you," she murmurs, her cheeks even redder. I cannot control my grin. This boy has it bad for her. It's so sweet.

"We'll take those and put them in your pretty vase in your bedroom won't we Bryant?"

"Yessss," he says one of the only words he can say as he tries to grapple the flowers from my free hand.

"Well, you both have fun now," Kane says but his tone screams fake. "Be home for ten."

"I will make sure she is home by then, sir."

"You have such lovely manners, AJ," I say gently to help soften this moment.

"Thank you, ma'am."

Kane laughs at my expression and shuts the door after shoving Connie out of it. "Ma'am."

"When did I become a ma'am?"

Kane scoops both Bryant and me up in his big arms and Bryant grabs at his hair just because he likes to pull it. Bryant looks more like me than his dad, which is nice because Connie is Kane's double which obviously means she is stunningly gorgeous. She turns heads with her beauty. I'm hoping Bryant won't be a heart stopper like his daddy, I couldn't live with the stress.

Although Kane often tells me even though he hated me he always said I was the hottest girl in school. Ren confirmed that admission too. So maybe we'll be screwed either way.

"Babe?" Kane calls, snapping me out of my daydream. "Give me your eyes."

I do, looking deep into his ocean blues and he must see something in mine because his soften and he kisses me tenderly, like I'm made of glass.

"Hey Bryant, reckon your momma knows how much I love her?"

"Yessss," Bryant answers and my smile reaches my eyes.

"Bryant, reckon your daddy knows how much I love him back?"

"Yesss," Bryant answers again, while squirming to be put down. I do so and watch him run to the closed door in search of his sister.

Kane kisses me hard and fast and then we part. He grabs Bryant for his nap, I put the flowers into water in Connie's black, twisted vase. Even her vase is goth. Then I let Kane drag me into the bedroom and take every name of every man I've ever mentioned right out of my mouth with his cock. Kane Jessop now a family man, will always have a vicious taint to him that I'll never stop loving for as long as I live. I vowed it five years ago and I meant it.

THE END

HAVE YOU READ...

BROKEN
by A. E. Murphy (Excerpt)

"You shouldn't be working in your condition." I wince at the sound of his voice and turn to face him, two cups of coffee in my hands. "You look exhausted."

I stare at Nathan and then I look away. "Why are you here?" Please leave, you look too much like him.

I place the drinks on a tray and slide them towards my boss.

"I followed you," he states without hesitation. "I didn't realise your pregnancy was so far along." His familiar brown eyes flick to my protruding stomach.

"I didn't realise you cared," I say and it's supposed to sound snappy but my voice sounds dead and flat. Exactly how I feel inside.

Nathan leans on the counter, chewing his lip like his brother did. It makes my eyes burn. "Where are you staying?"

"Why are you here?" My life isn't his business. He didn't care about his brother so why should he care about me? Not to mention the fact he assaulted Caleb the last time we saw him. "You live hours away. What do you want?"

"I asked you a question." A muscle in his jaw jumps, his eyes narrowing with irritation.

"And I asked you three."

"If you don't want my help then fine. It's on you, not me."

My mouth drops open. "I never asked for your help and no, you're right. I don't want it!"

He shakes his head and stalks away. I don't realise all eyes are on me until the moment he leaves and I stop thinking about how much he looks like Caleb from behind.

"He's such an arsehole," I say to my boss, who frowns at the door where Nathan just exited. "I've met the guy once before and he just swans into town... what a bastard."

"Who is he?" My boss asks with raised brows.

"Caleb's older brother by two years."

"Maybe you should've accepted his offer."

I laugh once and stare at my boss incredulously. "He didn't offer to help. He just asked me where I was staying. And this was after he'd already walked away once."

"It sounded like he was offering to help then." He gives a small shrug. "But I only heard half of the conversation."

I relent. "He did, in a strange way, but... he's infuriating and mean."

"He's also the only option you have right now. Hear him out. See what he has to say. Not many people would care about their family members' woes and you're technically not family."

I want to slap him. I know I'm hormonal but he doesn't have a clue what I'm going through right now. He doesn't understand the complexity that is Caleb's childhood. He doesn't get it, so maybe he should just let me work, sign my cheques and stay the hell out of it.

Work goes slowly and I'm glad for this as my night is still uncertain.

When I'm done here, I have no idea what I'm supposed to be doing. I'll go to Sasha's for the night. I know she won't mind. I just don't like putting on people, but either way I need to stay somewhere.

I text her to let her know and, as suspected, she agrees.

What have you done to me, Caleb? Why am I doing this alone?

I'm thinking about it again. I need to stop thinking about him.

Every time that I do my body trembles, my hands especially shaking.

It's tough but I'll get through this. I have to for our baby's sake.

Is it wrong that I'm hoping for a boy? I want him to be a boy so I can look into his eyes every day and see his father smiling back at me.

What kind of a life can I give him now, though? I have nothing to offer him.

Deep breaths, Gwen, deep breaths.

After half an hour of driving aimlessly, I fill up the tank and head to Sasha's. As I'm taking the turn towards campus, I notice a large black car following me. It's definitely him. Christ this is becoming irritating.

"What does he want now?" I say out loud and pull over when he flashes his lights twice.

His body moves with ease and grace as he climbs out of his vehicle and strolls towards me. After a few attempts, I finally manage to stand by the door of my own vehicle. I still have to tip my head back to look at him. Much like I did with... no I won't go there. I focus on the brisk chill in the air instead.

"Problem?" I ask, trying not to sound as exasperated as I feel.

"You shouldn't be getting in and out of a car that low," he remarks and already I want to hit him.

"Well it's not like I have another option is it?"

He frowns. "Follow me. We need to talk."

"I don't have anything to say to you." I try to get back in the car, but his hand closes around my arm and effortlessly tugs me away. "What?"

"Please?" He grits out and I can see just that one little word takes a whole lot of effort for him to say.

"Fine," I relent. It's not like my day can get any worse. "What's this about?"

"Follow me and you'll find out." He places his hand on my back and the other under my arm to support me as I sit. I'm not sure whether to be irritated that he touched me, or relieved that my arse didn't hit the car seat as hard as it usually does.

I wait for him to drive ahead before following directly behind him. He leads me quite a distance; I'm lucky I stopped for petrol.

We finally pull into a swanky hotel set on the edge of town, one I've never even been inside before. It's not my thing. I like simple and basic beauty, not elegance and fine china.

After parking beside him, he climbs out and this time helps me up and out of my vehicle. I didn't realise how hard it was until he started assisting me. He's right, the car is low.

"Come," he orders and leads me inside with his hand gripping my arm. I'm nervous as to what he wants. Does he want to help me or is this some kind of ruse? Is it a way for his family to ensure that they get the child I'll be birthing soon? The thought makes me nauseous.

I almost want to turn around and run.

When we enter, we go straight to the desk. The woman takes a look at me and my stomach before training her eyes on Nathan. There's no small amount of admiration and lust there, that's for sure.

Ewww.

"Send up some tea and something to eat that's safe for pregnant women."

Seriously? I give him a look, but he ignores it and propels me towards the elevator.

It's awkward, quiet and uncomfortable as we ascend. I find myself wanting to rock on my heels or whistle just to disturb the silence.

As soon as the doors open he takes my arm again and leads me through the patterned beige hallway. I huff, sick of being led around in silence. Again he ignores me.

Once inside his fabulous room, he takes my coat and hangs it by the door before leading me to a large and expensive looking couch. It's black, pure black, with silver scatter cushions. It looks amazing. "Sit."

I guess I'll sit then.

He doesn't. He shrugs off his jacket and hangs it by mine, undoes his buttoned shirt sleeves and rolls them up to his elbows. Is he planning on delivering the baby? This thought almost makes me smile. Not quite but nearly.

"Okay." He rubs his hands together, drawing my attention to the black leather gloves that cover them, and sits on the coffee table only four feet away from me. He's wearing gloves again. Was he wearing them earlier? I can't recall. "You have nowhere to live. I have space."

"Come again?"

"I think it's appropriate that at this point in time you stay with me. I live only a few hours away in a very nice and quiet village only an hour's drive from London. Just until you get back on your feet. I think you'll find my home to be of good taste," he says calmly and I can't help but note that he talks weird.

"W... what?"

He sighs. "You do speak English, correct?"

"Correct."

"Then listen to what I'm saying."

"I am listening, I just don't get it."

He pinches the bridge of his nose. "I'm missing work to be here right now. I don't appreciate your blatant lack of respect."

Scoff. "I don't know you well enough to respect you and so far you've been nothing but rude to me. Not to mention the fact the last time I saw you with Caleb, your fist was connecting with his cheek. Forgive me for not wanting to be all smiles to such an arsehole at such a difficult period of my life."

His glare is open and cold. "I understand you're hormonal, but I never want to hear such language. It's improper for a female to curse."

"Fuck you," I murmur, feeling even more irate.

"You're carrying my brother's child." His hands fist between his open knees, his cold brown eyes staring into mine.

ACKNOWLEDGMENTS

To Jami Kehr, thank you for your endless notes, your fast reading, and your love of this book that matched my own. Without you I don't think I would have finished this one, especially not this soon.

My sister Siobhan, a hero in my eyes.

To my amazing ARCy Beasts who read and reviewed my last release, Dance or Die. Thank you so much, your generosity and support of my words is so very humbling.

Abby Johnson Capps, Adriana Noriega, Amanda Anderson, Andrea Morgan, Beth Butts, Charlotte Austin, Clare Harrison, Diane Norwood, BJ Steele, Heather Packer, Jami Kehr, Jessica Covey-Wannamaker, Laura Marrero, Laura Petersen, Lauren Ackerman, Magdalena Korczyńska, Miz Biheiv, Nicki Nicole Michelle, Shannon Garner, Tania Emma Shrimpton, Tania Renteria, Victoria Full, Molly Dowers, Booksaholic, Krystal Uppole, Samantha Farrell, La Sra De Galvez, Kristy Gilliland Odom, Gizel N. Alvarez.

While I'm writing this acknowledgement, it is 13/04/2020, we are in the fourth week of the lockdown in the UK during the horrific pandemic that has struck the globe. We all know it as Covid-19. At the moment so many people are dying every single day. It is devastating. So, I want to say how grateful I am to our key workers, our drivers, shelf stockers, cashiers, nurses, doctors, etc. who are all still risking their lives for our country. Without you our world would not keep on keeping on.

I hope the next time I'm writing my acknowledgements Covid-19 is a thing of the past.

Stay safe and healthy guys. Keep washing your hands, even without a virus. Hygiene is everything.

ABOUT THE AUTHOR

A. E. Murphy is the queen of sarcasm and satire, she likes long walks in the park, as much as ice cubes like to chill in a roasting oven. She's effortlessly independent and so good at adulting it's unfair on the rest of the world. She only napped twice today and has only avoided the dishes for three days before making the child slaves do them this morning. Winning! Her favourite hobby is writing, her worst hobby is reading through that writing. Also, she has three cats that carry toys to the top of the stairs and drop them down so they can chase them. They do this repeatedly in the middle of the night. Who cares if she has work the next morning? Not the cats, that's for sure. And if it's not the cats doing the waking, it's the toddler crawling into bed with her and pulling individual hairs from her scalp with pudgy little fingers for comfort.

This is likely why she's in a constant state of grump unless there's chocolate and coffee. P.S. Please leave feedback, if not on the book then on this ridiculous bio she wrote herself. It's the least you can do seeing as she'll forever talk in the third person now. Alex loves her readers. Alex says thank you. Alex smiles.

Contact

Website
aemurphyauthor.com

Twitter
twitter.com/A_E_Murphy

Facebook
www.facebook.com/a.e.murphy.author
www.facebook.com/XelaKnight

Email
a.e.murphy@hotmail.com

ALSO BY THE AUTHOR

Standalone Novels

Masked Definitions

HIS FATHER

STEPDORK

NAKED OR DEAD

DANCE OR DIE

Becoming His Mistress

VICIOUS

Seas of Seduction

Seizing Rain

Freeing Calder

The Little Bits Series

A Little Bit of Crazy

A Little Bit of Us

A Little Bit of Trouble

A Little Bit of Truth

A Little Bit of Guilt

The Distraction Trilogy

Distraction

Destruction

Distinction

The Broken Trilogy

Broken

Connected

Forever

A Broken Story

Disconnected (Dillan)

Sweet Demands Trilogy

Lockhart

Lockdown

Unlocked

Colouring Books

NAKED OR DEAD colouring book edition

Laurie's Life Lessons a colouring book novella (Becoming His Mistress Spin-off)

Audiobooks

NAKED OR DEAD

HIS FATHER

BECOMING HIS MISTRESS

Printed in Great Britain
by Amazon

57675462R00228